ENDER'S
SHADOW

TOR BOOKS BY ORSON SCOTT CARD

The Folk of the Fringe
Future on Fire (editor)
Future on Ice (editor)
Lovelock (with Kathryn Kidd)
Pastwatch: The Redemption of Christopher Columbus
Saints
Songmaster
The Worthing Saga
Wyrms

THE TALES OF ALVIN MAKER
Seventh Son
Red Prophet
Prentice Alvin
Alvin Journeyman
Heartfire

ENDER
Ender's Game
Speaker for the Dead
Xenocide
Children of the Mind
Ender's Shadow

HOMECOMING
The Memory of Earth
The Call of Earth
The Ships of Earth
Earthfall
Earthborn

SHORT FICTION
Maps in a Mirror: The Short Fiction of Orson Scott Card (hardcover)
Maps in a Mirror, Volume 1: The Changed Man (paperback)
Maps in a Mirror, Volume 2: Flux (paperback)
Maps in a Mirror, Volume 3: Cruel Miracles (paperback)
Maps in a Mirror, Volume 4: Monkey Sonatas (paperback)

ENDER'S SHADOW

Orson Scott Card

TOR®

A TOM DOHERTY ASSOCIATES BOOK
NEW YORK

Car

This is a work of fiction. All the characters and events
portrayed in this novel are either fictitious
or are used fictitiously.

ENDER'S SHADOW

Edited by Beth Meacham

A Tor Book
Published by Tom Doherty Associates, LLC
175 Fifth Avenue
New York, NY 10010

www.tor.com

Tor® is a registered trademark of Tom Doherty Associates, LLC

ISBN 0-312-86860-X
ISBN 0-312-87297-6 (ltd. ed.)

First Edition: September 1999

Printed in the United States of America

0 9 8 7 6 5 4 3 2 1

TO DICK AND HAZIE BROWN
IN WHOSE HOME NO ONE IS HUNGRY
AND IN WHOSE HEARTS
NO ONE IS A STRANGER

CONTENTS

ENDER'S SHADOW

FOREWORD

This book is, strictly speaking, not a sequel, because it begins about where *Ender's Game* begins, and also ends, very nearly, at the same place. In fact, it is another telling of the same tale, with many of the same characters and settings, only from the perspective of another character. It's hard to know what to call it. A companion novel? A parallel novel? Perhaps a "parallax," if I can move that scientific term into literature.

Ideally, this novel should work as well for readers who have never read *Ender's Game* as for those who have read it several times. Because it is not a sequel, there is nothing you need to know from the novel *Ender's Game* that is not contained here. And yet, if I have achieved my literary goal, these two books complement and fulfill each other. Whichever one you read first, the other novel should still work on its own merits.

For many years, I have gratefully watched as *Ender's Game* has grown in popularity, especially among school-age readers. Though it was never intended as a young-adult novel, it has been embraced by many in that age group and by many teachers who find ways to use the book in their classrooms.

I have never found it surprising that the existing sequels—*Speaker for the Dead, Xenocide,* and *Children of the Mind*—never appealed as strongly to those younger readers. The obvious reason is that *Ender's Game* is centered around a child, while the sequels are about adults; perhaps more important, *Ender's Game* is, at least on the surface, a heroic, adventurous novel, while the sequels are a completely different kind of fiction, slower paced, more contemplative and idea-centered, and dealing with themes of less immediate import to younger readers.

Recently, however, I have come to realize that the 3,000-year gap between *Ender's Game* and its sequels leaves plenty of room for other sequels that are more closely tied to the original. In fact, in one sense *Ender's Game* has no sequels, for the other three books make one continuous story in themselves, while *Ender's Game* stands alone.

For a brief time I flirted seriously with the idea of opening up the *Ender's Game* universe to other writers, and went so far as to invite a writer whose work I greatly admire, Neal Shusterman, to consider working with me to create novels about Ender Wiggin's companions in Battle School. As we talked, it became clear that the most obvious character to begin with would be Bean, the child-soldier whom Ender treated as he had been treated by his adult teachers.

And then something else happened. The more we talked, the more jealous I became that Neal might be the one to write such a book, and not me. It finally dawned on me that, far from being finished with writing about "kids in space," as I cynically described the project, I actually had more to say, having actually learned something in the intervening dozen years since *Ender's Game* first appeared in 1985. And so, while still hoping that Neal and I can work together on something, I deftly swiped the project back.

I soon found that it's harder than it looks, to tell the same story twice, but differently. I was hindered by the fact that even though the viewpoint characters were different, the author was the same, with the same core beliefs about the world. I was helped by the fact that in the intervening years, I have learned a few things, and was able to bring different concerns and a deeper understanding to the project. Both books come from the same mind, but not the same; they draw on the same memories of childhood, but from a different perspective. For the reader, the parallax is created by Ender and Bean, standing a little ways apart as they move through the same events. For the writer, the parallax was created by a dozen years in which my older children grew up, and younger ones were born, and the world changed around me, and I learned a few things about human nature and about art that I had not known before.

Now you hold this book in your hands. Whether the literary experiment succeeds for you is entirely up to you to judge. For me it was worth dipping again into the same well, for the water was greatly changed this time, and if it has not been turned exactly into wine, at least it has a different flavor because of the different vessel that it was carried in, and I hope that you will enjoy it as much, or even more.

—Greensboro, North Carolina, January 1999

Part One

URCHIN

1

POKE

"You think you've found somebody, so suddenly my program gets the ax?"

"It's not about this kid that Graff found. It's about the low quality of what you've been finding."

"We knew it was long odds. But the kids I'm working with are actually fighting a war just to stay alive."

"Your kids are so malnourished that they suffer serious mental degradation before you even begin testing them. Most of them haven't formed any normal human bonds, they're so messed up they can't get through a day without finding something they can steal, break, or disrupt."

"They also represent possibility, as all children do."

"That's just the kind of sentimentality that discredits your whole project in the eyes of the I.F."

Poke kept her eyes open all the time. The younger children were supposed to be on watch, too, and sometimes they could be quite observant, but they just didn't notice all the things they needed to notice, and that meant that Poke could only depend on herself to see danger.

There was plenty of danger to watch for. The cops, for instance. They didn't show up often, but when they did, they seemed especially bent on clearing the streets of children. They would flail about them with their magnetic whips, landing cruel stinging blows on even the smallest children, haranguing them as vermin, thieves, pestilence, a plague on the fair city of

Rotterdam. It was Poke's job to notice when a disturbance in the distance suggested that the cops might be running a sweep. Then she would give the alarm whistle and the little ones would rush to their hiding places till the danger was past.

But the cops didn't come by that often. The real danger was much more immediate—big kids. Poke, at age nine, was the matriarch of her little crew (not that any of them knew for sure that she was a girl), but that cut no ice with the eleven- and twelve- and thirteen-year-old boys and girls who bullied their way around the streets. The adult-size beggars and thieves and whores of the street paid no attention to the little kids except to kick them out of the way. But the older children, who were among the kicked, turned around and preyed on the younger ones. Any time Poke's crew found something to eat—especially if they located a dependable source of garbage or an easy mark for a coin or a bit of food—they had to watch jealously and hide their winnings, for the bullies liked nothing better than to take away whatever scraps of food the little ones might have. Stealing from younger children was much safer than stealing from shops or passersby. And they enjoyed it, Poke could see that. They liked how the little kids cowered and obeyed and whimpered and gave them whatever they demanded.

So when the scrawny little two-year-old took up a perch on a garbage can across the street, Poke, being observant, saw him at once. The kid was on the edge of starvation. No, the kid was starving. Thin arms and legs, joints that looked ridiculously oversized, a distended belly. And if hunger didn't kill him soon, the onset of autumn would, because his clothing was thin and there wasn't much of it even at that.

Normally she wouldn't have paid him more than passing attention. But this one had eyes. He was still looking around with intelligence. None of that stupor of the walking dead, no longer searching for food or even caring to find a comfortable place to lie while breathing their last taste of the stinking air of Rotterdam. After all, death would not be such a change for them. Everyone knew that Rotterdam was, if not the capital, then the main seaport of Hell. The only difference between Rotterdam and death was that with Rotterdam, the damnation wasn't eternal.

This little boy—what was he doing? Not looking for food. He wasn't eyeing the pedestrians. Which was just as well—there was no chance that anyone would leave anything for a child that small. Anything he might get would be taken away by any other child, so why should he bother? If he wanted to survive, he should be following older scavengers and licking food wrappers behind them, getting the last sheen of sugar or dusting of flour clinging to the packaging, whatever the first comer hadn't licked off.

There was nothing for this child out here on the street, not unless he got taken in by a crew, and Poke wouldn't have him. He'd be nothing but a drain, and her kids were already having a hard enough time without adding another useless mouth.

He's going to ask, she thought. He's going to whine and beg. But that only works on the rich people. I've got my crew to think of. He's not one of them, so I don't care about him. Even if he is small. He's nothing to me.

A couple of twelve-year-old hookers who didn't usually work this strip rounded a corner, heading toward Poke's base. She gave a low whistle. The kids immediately drifted apart, staying on the street but trying not to look like a crew.

It didn't help. The hookers knew already that Poke was a crew boss, and sure enough, they caught her by the arms and slammed her against a wall and demanded their "permission" fee. Poke knew better than to claim she had nothing to share—she always tried to keep a reserve in order to placate hungry bullies. These hookers, Poke could see why they were hungry. They didn't look like what the pedophiles wanted, when they came cruising through. They were too gaunt, too old-looking. So until they grew bodies and started attracting the slightly-less-perverted trade, they had to resort to scavenging. It made Poke's blood boil, to have them steal from her and her crew, but it was smarter to pay them off. If they beat her up, she couldn't look out for her crew now, could she? So she took them to one of her stashes and came up with a little bakery bag that still had half a pastry in it.

It was stale, since she'd been holding it for a couple of days for just such an occasion, but the two hookers grabbed it, tore open the bag, and one of them bit off more than half before offering the remainder to her friend. Or rather, her former friend, for of such predatory acts are feuds born. The two of them started fighting, screaming at each other, slapping, raking at each other with clawed hands. Poke watched closely, hoping that they'd drop the remaining fragment of pastry, but no such luck. It went into the mouth of the same girl who had already eaten the first bite—and it was that first girl who won the fight too, sending the other one running for refuge.

Poke turned around, and there was the little boy right behind her. She nearly tripped over him. Angry as she was at having had to give up food to those street-whores, she gave him a knee and knocked him to the ground. "Don't stand behind people if you don't want to land on your butt," she snarled.

He simply got up and looked at her, expectant, demanding.

"No, you little bastard, you're not getting nothing from me," said Poke. "I'm not taking one bean out of the mouths of my crew, you aren't *worth* a bean."

Her crew was starting to reassemble, now that the bullies had passed.

"Why you give your food to them?" said the boy. "You need that food."

"Oh, excuse me!" said Poke. She raised her voice, so her crew could hear her. "I guess you ought to be the crew boss here, is that it? You being so big, you got no trouble keeping the food."

"Not me," said the boy. "I'm not worth a bean, remember?"

"Yeah, I remember. Maybe *you* ought to remember and shut up."

Her crew laughed.

But the little boy didn't. "You got to get your own bully," he said.

"I don't *get* bullies, I get rid of them," Poke answered. She didn't like the way he kept talking, standing up to her. In a minute she was going to have to hurt him.

"You give food to bullies every day. Give that to *one* bully and get him to keep the others away from you."

"You think I never thought of that, stupid?" she said. "Only once he's bought, how I keep him? He won't fight for us."

"If he won't, then kill him," said the boy.

That made Poke mad, the stupid impossibility of it, the power of the idea that she knew she could never lay hands on. She gave him a knee again, and this time kicked him when he went down. "Maybe I start by killing you."

"I'm not worth a bean, remember?" said the boy. "You kill one bully, get another to fight for you, he want your food, he scared of you too."

She didn't know what to say to such a preposterous idea.

"They eating you up," said the boy. "Eating you up. So you got to kill one. Get him down, everybody as small as me. Stones crack any size head."

"You make me sick," she said.

"'Cause you didn't think of it," he said.

He was flirting with death, talking to her that way. If she injured him at all, he'd be finished, he must know that.

But then, he had death living with him inside his flimsy little shirt already. Hard to see how it would matter if death came any closer.

Poke looked around at her crew. She couldn't read their faces.

"I don't need no baby telling me to kill what we can't kill."

"Little kid come up behind him, you shove, he fall over," said the boy. "Already got you some big stones, bricks. Hit him in the head. When you see brains you done."

"He no good to me dead," she said. "I want my own bully, he keep us safe, I don't want no dead one."

The boy grinned. "So now you like my idea," he said.

"Can't trust no bully," she answered.

"He watch out for you at the charity kitchen," said the boy. "You get in at the kitchen." He kept looking her in the eye, but he was talking for the others to hear. "He get you *all* in at the kitchen."

"Little kid get into the kitchen, the big kids, they beat him," said Sergeant. He was eight, and mostly acted like he thought he was Poke's second-in-command, though truth was she didn't have a second.

"You get you a bully, he make them go away."

"How he stop two bullies? Three bullies?" asked Sergeant.

"Like I said," the boy answered. "You push him down, he not so big. You get your rocks. You be ready. Ben't you a soldier? Don't they call you Sergeant?"

"Stop talking to him, Sarge," said Poke. "I don't know why any of us is talking to some two-year-old."

"I'm four," said the boy.

"What your name?" asked Poke.

"Nobody ever said no name for me," he said.

"You mean you so stupid you can't remember your own name?"

"Nobody ever said no name," he said again. Still he looked her in the eye, lying there on the ground, the crew around him.

"Ain't worth a bean," she said.

"Am so," he said.

"Yeah," said Sergeant. "One damn bean."

"So now you got a name," said Poke. "You go back and sit on that garbage can, I think about what you said."

"I need something to eat," said Bean.

"If I get me a bully, if what you said works, then maybe I give you something."

"I need something now," said Bean.

She knew it was true.

She reached into her pocket and took out six peanuts she had been saving. He sat up and took just one from her hand, put it in his mouth and slowly chewed.

"Take them all," she said impatiently.

He held out his little hand. It was weak. He couldn't make a fist. "Can't hold them all," he said. "Don't hold so good."

Damn. She was wasting perfectly good peanuts on a kid who was going to die anyway.

But she was going to try his idea. It was audacious, but it was the first plan she'd ever heard that offered any hope of making things better, of changing something about their miserable life without her having to put on girl clothes and going into business. And since it was his idea, the crew had to see that she treated him fair. That's how you stay crew boss, they always see you be fair.

So she kept holding her hand out while he ate all six peanuts, one at a time.

After he swallowed the last one, he looked her in the eye for another long moment, and then said, "You better be ready to kill him."

"I want him alive."

"Be ready to kill him if he ain't the right one." With that, Bean toddled back across the street to his garbage can and laboriously climbed on top again to watch.

"You ain't no four years old!" Sergeant shouted over to him.

"I'm four but I'm just little," he shouted back.

Poke hushed Sergeant up and they went looking for stones and bricks and cinderblocks. If they were going to have a little war, they'd best be armed.

Bean didn't like his new name, but it was a name, and having a name meant that somebody else knew who he was and needed something to call him, and that was a good thing. So were the six peanuts. His mouth hardly knew what to do with them. Chewing hurt.

So did watching as Poke screwed up the plan he gave her. Bean didn't choose her because she was the smartest crew boss in Rotterdam. Quite the opposite. Her crew barely survived because her judgment wasn't that good. And she was too compassionate. Didn't have the brains to make sure she got enough food herself to look well fed, so while her own crew knew she was nice and liked her, to strangers she didn't look prosperous. Didn't look good at her job.

But if she really *was* good at her job, she would never have listened to him. He never would have got close. Or if she did listen, and did like his idea, she would have got rid of him. That's the way it worked on the street. Nice kids died. Poke was almost too nice to stay alive. That's what Bean was counting on. But that's what he now feared.

All this time he invested in watching people while his body ate itself up, it would be wasted if she couldn't bring it off. Not that Bean hadn't wasted a lot of time himself. At first when he watched the way kids did things on the street, the way they were stealing from each other, at each other's throats, in each other's pockets, selling every part of themselves that they could sell, he saw how things could be better if somebody had any brains, but he didn't trust his own insight. He was sure there must be something else that he just didn't get. He struggled to learn more—of everything. To learn to read so he'd know what the signs said on trucks and stores and wagons and bins. To learn enough Dutch and enough I.F. Common to understand everything that was said around him. It didn't help that hunger constantly distracted him. He probably could have found more to eat if he hadn't spent so much time studying the people. But finally he realized: He already understood it. He had understood it from the start. There was no secret that Bean just didn't get yet because he was only little. The reason all these kids handled everything so stupidly was because they were stupid.

They were stupid and he was smart. So why was he starving to death while these kids were still alive? That was when he decided to act. That was when he picked Poke as his crew boss. And now he sat on a garbage can watching her blow it.

She chose the wrong bully, that's the first thing she did. She needed a guy who made it on size alone, intimidating people. She needed somebody big and dumb, brutal but controllable. Instead, she thinks she needs somebody *small*. No, stupid! Stupid! Bean wanted to scream at her as she saw her target coming, a bully who called himself Achilles after the comics hero. He was little and mean and smart and quick, but he had a gimp leg. So she thought she could take him down more easily. Stupid! The idea isn't just to take him down—you can take *anybody* down the first time because they won't expect it. You need somebody who will *stay* down.

But he said nothing. Couldn't get her mad at him. See what happens. See what Achilles is like when he's beat. She'll see—it won't work and she'll have to kill him and hide the body and try again with another bully before word gets out that there's a crew of little kids taking down bullies.

So up comes Achilles, swaggering—or maybe that was just the rolling gait that his bent leg forced on him—and Poke makes an exaggerated show of cowering and trying to get away. Bad job, thought Bean. Achilles gets it already. Something's wrong. You were supposed to act like you normally do! Stupid! So Achilles looks around a lot more. Wary. She tells him she's got something stashed—that part's normal—and she leads him into the trap in the alley. But look, he's holding back. Being careful. It isn't going to work.

But it does work, because of the gimp leg. Achilles can see the trap being sprung but he can't get away, a couple of little kids pile into the backs of his legs while Poke and Sergeant push him from the front and down he goes. Then there's a couple of bricks hitting his body and his bad leg and they're thrown hard—the little kids get it, they do their job, even if Poke is stupid—and yeah, that's good, Achilles *is* scared, he thinks he's going to die.

Bean was off his perch by now. Down the alley, watching, closer. Hard to see past the crowd. He pushes his way in, and the little kids—who are all bigger than he is—recognize him, they know he earned a view of this, they let him in. He stands right at Achilles' head. Poke stands above him, holding a big cinderblock, and she's talking.

"You get us into the food line at the shelter."

"Sure, right, I will, I promise."

Don't believe him. Look at his eyes, checking for weakness.

"You get more food this way, too, Achilles. You get my crew. We get enough to eat, we have more strength, we bring more to you. You need a crew. The other bullies shove you out of the way—we've seen them!—but with us, you don't got to take no shit. See how we do it? An army, that's what we are."

OK, now he was getting it. It *was* a good idea, and he wasn't stupid, so it made sense to him.

"If this is so smart, Poke, how come you didn't do this before now?"

She had nothing to say to that. Instead, she glanced at Bean.

Just a momentary glance, but Achilles saw it. And Bean knew what he was thinking. It was so obvious.

"Kill him," said Bean.

"Don't be stupid," said Poke. "He's in."

"That's right," said Achilles. "I'm in. It's a good idea."

"Kill him," said Bean. "If you don't kill him now, he's going to kill *you*."

"You let this little walking turd get away with talking shit like this?" said Achilles.

"It's your life or his," said Bean. "Kill him and take the next guy."

"The next guy won't have my bad leg," said Achilles. "The next guy won't think he needs you. I know I do. I'm in. I'm the one you want. It makes sense.''

Maybe Bean's warning made her more cautious. She didn't cave in quite yet. ''You won't decide later that you're embarrassed to have a bunch of little kids in your crew?''

''It's *your* crew, not mine,'' said Achilles.

Liar, thought Bean. Don't you see that he's lying to you?

''What this is to me,'' said Achilles, ''this is my family. These are my kid brothers and sisters. I got to look after my family, don't I?''

Bean saw at once that Achilles had won. Powerful bully, and he had called these kids his sisters, his brothers. Bean could see the hunger in their eyes. Not the regular hunger, for food, but the real hunger, the deep hunger, for family, for love, for belonging. They got a little of that by being in Poke's crew. But Achilles was promising more. He had just beaten Poke's best offer. Now it was too late to kill him.

Too late, but for a moment it looked as if Poke was so stupid she was going to go ahead and kill him after all. She raised the cinderblock higher, to crash it down.

''No,'' said Bean. ''You can't. He's family now.''

She lowered the cinderblock to her waist. Slowly she turned to look at Bean. ''You get the hell out of here,'' she said. ''You no part of my crew. You get *nothing* here.''

''No,'' said Achilles. ''You better go ahead and kill me, you plan to treat him that way.''

Oh, that sounded brave. But Bean knew Achilles wasn't brave. Just smart. He had already won. It meant nothing that he was lying there on the ground and Poke still had the cinderblock. It was his crew now. Poke was finished. It would be a while before anybody but Bean and Achilles understood that, but the test of authority was here and now, and Achilles was going to win it.

''This little kid,'' said Achilles, ''he may not be part of your crew, but he's part of my family. You don't go telling my brother to get lost.''

Poke hesitated. A moment. A moment longer.

Long enough.

Achilles sat up. He rubbed his bruises, he checked out his contusions. He looked in joking admiration to the little kids who had bricked him. ''Damn, you bad!'' They laughed—nervously, at first. Would he hurt them because they hurt him? ''Don't worry,'' he said. ''You showed me what you can do. We have to do this to more than a couple of bullies, you'll see. I had to know you could do it right. Good job. What's your name?''

One by one he learned their names. Learned them and remembered them, or when he missed one he'd make a big deal about it, apologize, visibly work at remembering. Fifteen minutes later, they loved him.

If he could do this, thought Bean, if he's this good at making people love him, why didn't he do it before?

Because these fools always look up for power. People above you, they never want to share power with you. Why you look to them? They give you nothing. People below you, you give them hope, you give them respect, *they* give you power, cause they don't think they have any, so they don't mind giving it up.

Achilles got to his feet, a little shaky, his bad leg more sore than usual. Everybody stood back, gave him some space. He could leave now, if he wanted. Get away, never come back. Or go get some more bullies, come back and punish the crew. But he stood there, then smiled, reached into his pocket, took out the most incredible thing. A bunch of raisins. A whole handful of them. They looked at his hand as if it bore the mark of a nail in the palm.

"Little brothers and sisters first," he said. "Littlest first." He looked at Bean. "You."

"Not him!" said the next littlest. "We don't even know him."

"Bean was the one wanted us to *kill* you," said another.

"Bean," said Achilles. "Bean, you were just looking out for my family, weren't you?"

"Yes," said Bean.

"You want a raisin?"

Bean nodded.

"You first. You the one brought us all together, OK?"

Either Achilles would kill him or he wouldn't. At this moment, all that mattered was the raisin. Bean took it. Put it in his mouth. Did not even bite down on it. Just let his saliva soak it, bringing out the flavor of it.

"You know," said Achilles, "no matter how long you hold it in your mouth, it never turns back into a grape."

"What's a grape?"

Achilles laughed at him, still not chewing. Then he gave out raisins to the other kids. Poke had never shared out so many raisins, because she had never had so many to share. But the little kids wouldn't understand that. They'd think, Poke gave us garbage, and Achilles gave us raisins. That's because they were stupid.

2

KITCHEN

"I know you've already looked through this area, and you're probably almost done with Rotterdam, but something's been happening lately, since you visited, that . . . oh, I don't know if it's really anything, I shouldn't have called."

"Tell me, I'm listening."

"There's always been fighting in the line. We try to stop them, but we only have a few volunteers, and they're needed to keep order inside the dining room, that and serve the food. So we know that a lot of kids who should get a turn can't even get in the line, because they're pushed out. And if we do manage to stop the bullies and let one of the little ones in, then they get beaten up afterward. We never see them again. It's ugly."

"Survival of the fittest."

"Of the cruelest. Civilization is supposed to be the opposite of that."

"*You're* civilized. They're not."

"Anyway, it's changed. All of a sudden. Just in the past few days. I don't know why. But I just—you said that anything unusual— and whoever's behind it—I mean, can civilization suddenly evolve all over again, in the middle of a jungle of children?"

"That's the only place it ever evolves. I'm through in Delft. There was nothing for us here. I already have enough blue plates."

Bean kept to the background during the weeks that followed. He had nothing to offer now—they already had his best idea. And he knew that gratitude wouldn't last long. He wasn't big and he didn't eat much, but if he was constantly underfoot, annoying people and chattering at them, it would soon become not only fun but popular to deny him food in hopes that he'd die or go away.

Even so, he often felt Achilles' eyes on him. He noticed this without fear. If Achilles killed him, so be it. He had been a few days from death anyway. It would just mean his plan didn't work so well after all, but since it was his only plan, it didn't matter if it turned out not to have been good. If Achilles remembered how Bean urged Poke to kill him—and of course he did remember—and if Achilles was planning how and when he would die, there was nothing Bean could do to prevent it.

Sucking up wouldn't help. That would just look like weakness, and Bean had seen for a long time how bullies—and Achilles was still a bully at heart—thrived on the terror of other children, how they treated people even worse when they showed their weakness. Nor would offering more clever ideas, first because Bean didn't have any, and second because Achilles would think it was an affront to his authority. And the other kids would resent it if Bean kept acting like he thought he was the only one with a brain. They already resented him for having thought of this plan that had changed their lives.

For the change was immediate. The very first morning, Achilles had Sergeant go stand in the line at Helga's Kitchen on Aert Van Nes Straat, because, he said, as long as we're going to get the crap beaten out of us anyway, we might as well try for the best free food in Rotterdam in case we get to eat before we die. He talked like that, but he had made them practice their moves till the last light of day the night before, so they worked together better and they didn't give themselves away so soon, the way they did when they were going after him. The practice gave them confidence. Achilles kept saying, "They'll expect this," and "They'll try that," and because he was a bully himself, they trusted him in a way they had never trusted Poke.

Poke, being stupid, kept trying to act as if she was in charge, as if she had only delegated their training to Achilles. Bean admired the way that Achilles did not argue with her, and did not change his plans or instructions in any way because of what she said. If she urged him to do what he was already doing, he'd keep doing it. There was no show of defiance. No struggle for power. Achilles acted as if he had already won, and because the other kids followed him, he had.

The line formed in front of Helga's early, and Achilles watched carefully as bullies who arrived later inserted themselves in line in a kind of hierarchy—the bullies knew which ones got pride of place. Bean tried to understand the principle Achilles used to pick which bully Sergeant should pick a fight with. It wasn't the weakest, but that was smart, since beating the weakest bully would only set them up for more fights every day. Nor was it the strongest. As Sergeant walked across the street, Bean tried to see what it was about the target bully that made Achilles pick him. And then Bean realized—this was the strongest bully who had no friends with him.

The target was big and he looked mean, so beating him would look like an important victory. But he talked to no one, greeted no one. He was out of his territory, and several of the other bullies were casting resentful glances at him, sizing him up. There might have been a fight here today even if Achilles hadn't picked this soup line, this stranger.

Sergeant was cool as you please, slipping into place directly in front of the target. For a moment, the target just stood there looking at him, as if he couldn't believe what he was seeing. Surely this little kid would realize his deadly mistake and run away. But Sergeant didn't even act as if he noticed the target was there.

"Hey!" said the target. He shoved Sergeant hard, and from the angle of the push, Sergeant should have been propelled away from the line. But, as Achilles had told him, he planted a foot right away and launched himself forward, hitting the bully in front of the target in line, even though that was not the direction in which the target had pushed him.

The bully in front turned around and snarled at Sergeant, who pleaded, "He pushed me."

"He hit you himself," said the target.

"Do I look that stupid?" said Sergeant.

The bully-in-front sized up the target. A stranger. Tough, but not un-beatable. "Watch yourself, skinny boy."

That was a dire insult among bullies, since it implied incompetence and weakness.

"Watch your own self."

During this exchange, Achilles led a picked group of younger kids toward Sergeant, who was risking life and limb by staying right up between the two bullies. Just before reaching them, two of the younger kids darted through the line to the other side, taking up posts against the wall just beyond the target's range of vision. Then Achilles started screaming.

"What the hell do you think you're doing, you turd-stained piece of toilet paper! I send my boy to hold my place in line and you *shove* him? You *shove* him into my *friend* here?"

Of course they weren't friends at all—Achilles was the lowest-status bully in this part of Rotterdam and he always took his place as the last of the bullies in line. But the target didn't know that, and he wouldn't have time to find out. For by the time the target was turned to face Achilles, the boys behind him were already leaping against his calves. There was no waiting for the usual exchange of shoves and brags before the fight began. Achilles began it and ended it with brutal swiftness. He pushed hard just as the younger boys hit, and the target hit the cobbled street hard. He lay there dazed, blinking. But already two other little kids were handing big loose cobblestones to Achilles, who smashed them down, one, two, on the target's chest. Bean could hear the ribs as they popped like twigs.

Achilles pulled him by his shirt and flopped him right back down on the street. He groaned, struggled to move, groaned again, lay still.

The others in line had backed away from the fight. This was a violation of protocol. When bullies fought each other, they took it into the alleys, and they didn't try for serious injury, they fought until supremacy was clear and it was over. This was a new thing, using cobblestones, breaking bones. It scared them, not because Achilles was so fearsome to look at, but because he had done the forbidden thing, and he had done it right out in the open.

At once Achilles signaled Poke to bring the rest of the crew and fill in the gap in the line. Meanwhile, Achilles strutted up and down the line, ranting at the top of his voice. "You can disrespect me, I don't care, I'm just a cripple, I'm just a guy with a gimp leg! But don't you go shoving my family! Don't you go shoving one of my children out of line! You hear me? Because if you do that some truck's going to come down this street and knock you down and break your bones, just like happened to this little pinprick, and next time maybe your head's going to be what breaks till your brains fall out on the street. You got to watch out for speeding trucks like the one that knocked down this fart-for-brains right here in front of my soup kitchen!"

There it was, the challenge. *My* kitchen. And Achilles didn't hold back, didn't show a spark of timidity about it. He kept the rant going, limping up and down the line, staring each bully in the face, daring him to argue. Shadowing his movements on the other side of the line were the two younger boys who had helped take down the stranger, and Sergeant strutted at Achilles' side, looking happy and smug. They reeked of confidence, while the other bullies kept glancing over their shoulders to see what those leg-grabbers behind them were doing.

And it wasn't just talk and brag, either. When one of the bullies started looking belligerent, Achilles went right up into his face. However, as he had planned beforehand, he didn't actually go after the belligerent one—he was ready for trouble, asking for it. Instead, the boys launched themselves at the bully directly after him in line. Just as they leapt, Achilles turned and shoved the new target, screaming, "What do you think is so damn funny!" He had another cobblestone in his hands at once, standing over the fallen one, but he did not strike. "Go to the end of the line, you moron! You're lucky I'm letting you eat in my kitchen!"

It completely deflated the belligerent one, for the bully Achilles knocked down and obviously could have smashed was the one next *lower* in status. So the belligerent one hadn't been threatened or harmed, and yet Achilles had scored a victory right in his face and he hadn't been a part of it.

The door to the soup kitchen opened. At once Achilles was with the woman who opened it, smiling, greeting her like an old friend. "Thank you for feeding us today," he said. "I'm eating last today. Thank you for bringing in my friends. Thank you for feeding my family."

The woman at the door knew how the street worked. She knew Achilles, too, and that something very strange was going on here. Achilles always ate last of the bigger boys, and rather shamefacedly. But his new patronizing attitude hardly had time to get annoying before the first of Poke's crew came to the door. "My family," Achilles announced proudly, passing each of the little kids into the hall. "You take good care of my children."

Even Poke he called his child. If she noticed the humiliation of it, though, she didn't show it. All she cared about was the miracle of getting into the soup kitchen. The plan had worked.

And whether she thought of it as her plan or Bean's didn't matter to Bean in the least, at least not till he had the first soup in his mouth. He drank it as slowly as he could, but it was still gone so fast that he could hardly believe it. Was this all? And how had he managed to spill so much of the precious stuff on his shirt?

Quickly he stuffed his bread inside his clothing and headed for the door. Stashing the bread and leaving, that was Achilles' idea and it was a good one. Some of the bullies inside the kitchen were bound to plan retribution. The sight of little kids eating would be galling to them. They'd get used to it soon enough, Achilles promised, but this first day it was important that all the little kids get out while the bullies were still eating.

When Bean got to the door, the line was still coming in, and Achilles stood by the door, chatting with the woman about the tragic accident there in the line. Paramedics must have been summoned to carry the injured boy away—he was no longer groaning in the street. "It could have been one of the little kids," he said. "We need a policeman out here to watch the traffic. That driver would never have been so careless if there was a cop here."

The woman agreed. "It could have been awful. They said half his ribs were broken and his lung was punctured." She looked mournful, her hands fretting.

"This line forms up when it's still dark. It's dangerous. Can't we have a light out here? I've got my children to think about," said Achilles. "Don't you want my little kids to be safe? Or am I the only one who cares about them?"

The woman murmured something about money and how the soup kitchen didn't have much of a budget.

Poke was counting children at the door while Sergeant ushered them out into the street.

Bean, seeing that Achilles was trying to get the adults to protect them in line, decided the time was right for him to be useful. Because this woman was compassionate and Bean was by far the smallest child, he knew he had the most power over her. He came up to her, tugged on her woollen skirt. "Thank you for watching over us," he said. "It's the first time I ever got into a real kitchen. Papa Achilles told us that *you* would keep us safe so we little ones could eat here every day."

"Oh, you poor thing! Oh, look at you." Tears streamed down the woman's face. "Oh, oh, you poor darling." She embraced him.

Achilles looked on, beaming. "I got to watch out for them," he said quietly. "I got to keep them safe."

Then he led his family—it was no longer in any sense Poke's crew—away from Helga's kitchen, all marching in a line. Till they rounded the corner of a building and then they ran like hell, joining hands and putting as much distance between them and Helga's kitchen as they could. For the rest of the day they were going to have to lie low. In twos and threes the bullies would be looking for them.

But they *could* lie low, because they didn't need to forage for food today. The soup already gave them more calories than they normally got, and they had the bread.

Of course, the first tax on that bread belonged to Achilles, who had eaten no soup. Each child reverently offered his bread to their new papa, and he took a bite from each one and slowly chewed it and swallowed it before reaching for the next offered bread. It was quite a lengthy ritual. Achilles took a mouthful of every piece of bread except two: Poke's and Bean's.

"Thanks," said Poke.

She was so stupid, she thought it was a gesture of respect. Bean knew better. By not eating their bread, Achilles was putting them outside the family. We are dead, thought Bean.

That's why Bean hung back, why he held his tongue and remained unobtrusive during the next few weeks. That was also why he endeavored never to be alone. Always he was within arm's reach of one of the other kids.

But he didn't linger near Poke. That was a picture he didn't want to get locked in anyone's memory, him tagging along with Poke.

From the second morning, Helga's soup kitchen had an adult outside watching, and a new light fixture on the third day. By the end of a week the adult guardian was a cop. Even so, Achilles never brought his group out of hiding until the adult was there, and then he would march the whole family right to the front of the line, and loudly thank the bully in first position for helping him look out for his children by saving them a place in line.

It was hard on all of them, though, seeing how the bullies looked at them. They had to be on their best behavior while the doorkeeper was watching, but murder was on their minds.

And it didn't get better; the bullies didn't "get used to it," despite Achilles' bland assurances that they would. So even though Bean was determined to be unobtrusive, he knew that something had to be done to turn the bullies away from their hatred, and Achilles, who thought the war was over and victory achieved, wasn't going to do it.

So as Bean took his place in line one morning, he deliberately hung back to be last of the family. Usually Poke brought up the rear—it was her way of trying to pretend that she was somehow involved in ushering the little ones in. But this time Bean deliberately got in place behind her, with the hate-filled stare of the bully who should have had first position burning on his head.

Right at the door, where the woman was standing with Achilles, both of them looking proud of his family, Bean turned to face the bully behind him and asked, in his loudest voice, "Where's *your* children? How come you don't bring *your* children to the kitchen?"

The bully would have snarled something vicious, but the woman at the door was watching with raised eyebrows. "You look after little children, too?" she asked. It was obvious she was delighted about the idea and wanted the answer to be yes. And stupid as this bully was, he knew that it was good to please adults who gave out food. So he said, "Of course I do."

"Well, you can bring them, you know. Just like Papa Achilles here. We're always glad to see the little children."

Again Bean piped up. "They let people with little children come inside *first!*"

"You know, that's such a good idea," said the woman. "I think we'll make that a rule. Now, let's move along, we're holding up the hungry children."

Bean did not even glance at Achilles as he went inside.

Later, after breakfast, as they were performing the ritual of giving bread to Achilles, Bean made it a point to offer his bread yet again, though there was danger in reminding everyone that Achilles never took a share from him. Today, though, he had to see how Achilles regarded him, for being so bold and intrusive.

"If they all bring little kids, they'll run out of soup faster," said Achilles coldly. His eyes said nothing at all—but that, too, was a message.

"If they all become papas," said Bean, "they won't be trying to kill us."

At that, Achilles' eyes came to life a little. He reached down and took the bread from Bean's hand. He bit down on the crust, tore away a huge piece of it. More than half. He jammed it into his mouth and chewed it slowly, then handed the remnant of the bread back to Bean.

It left Bean hungry that day, but it was worth it. It didn't mean that Achilles wasn't going to kill him someday, but at least he wasn't separating him from the rest of the family anymore. And that remnant of bread was far more food than he used to get in a day. Or a week, for that matter.

He was filling out. Muscles grew in his arms and legs again. He didn't get exhausted just crossing a street. He could keep up easily now, when the others jogged along. They all had more energy. They were healthy, compared to street urchins who didn't have a papa. Everyone could see it. The other bullies would have no trouble recruiting families of their own.

Sister Carlotta was a recruiter for the International Fleet's training program for children. It had caused a lot of criticism in her order, and finally she won the right to do it by pointedly mentioning the Earth Defense Treaty, which was a veiled threat. If she reported the order for obstructing her work on behalf of the I.F., the order could lose its tax-exempt and draft-exempt status. She knew, however, that when the war ended and the treaty expired, she would no doubt be a nun in search of a home, for there would be no place for her among the Sisters of St. Nicholas.

But her mission in life, she knew, was to care for little children, and the way she saw it, if the Buggers won the next round of the war, all the little children of the Earth would die. Surely God did not mean that to happen—but in her judgment, at least, God did not want his servants to sit around waiting for God to work miracles to save them. He wanted his servants to labor as best they could to bring about righteousness. So it was her business, as a Sister of St. Nicholas, to use her training in child development in order to serve the war effort. As long as the I.F. thought it worthwhile to recruit extraordinarily gifted children to train them for command roles in the battles to come, then she would help them by finding the children that would otherwise be overlooked. They would never pay anyone to do something as fruitless as scouring the filthy streets of every overcrowded city in the world, searching among the malnourished savage children who begged and stole and starved there; for the chance of finding a child with the intelligence and ability and character to make a go of it in Battle School was remote.

To God, however, all things were possible. Did he not say that the weak would be made strong, and the strong weak? Was Jesus not born to a humble carpenter and his bride in the country province of Galilee? The brilliance of children born to privilege and bounty, or even to bare sufficiency, would hardly show forth the miraculous power of God. And it was the miracle she was searching for. God had made humankind in his own image, male and female he created them. No Buggers from another planet were going to blow down what God had created.

Over the years, though, her enthusiasm, if not her faith, had flagged a little. Not one child had done better than a marginal success on the tests. Those children were indeed taken from the streets and trained, but it wasn't Battle School. They weren't on the course that might lead them to save the world. So she began to think that her real work was a different kind of miracle—giving the children hope, finding even a few to be lifted out of the morass, to be given special attention by the local authorities. She made it a point to indicate the most promising children, and then follow up on them with email to the authorities. Some of her early successes had already graduated from college; they said they owed their lives to Sister Carlotta, but she knew they owed their lives to God.

Then came the call from Helga Braun in Rotterdam, telling her of certain changes in the children who came to her charity kitchen. Civilization, she had called it. The children, all by themselves, were becoming civilized.

Sister Carlotta came at once, to see a thing which sounded like a miracle. And indeed, when she beheld it with her own eyes, she could hardly believe it. The line for breakfast was now flooded with little children. Instead of the bigger ones shoving them out of the way or intimidating them into not even bothering to try, they were shepherding them, protecting them, making sure each got his share. Helga had panicked at first, fearful that she would run out of food—but she found that when potential benefactors saw how these children were acting, donations increased. There was always plenty now—not to mention an increase in volunteers helping.

"I was at the point of despair," she told Sister Carlotta. "On the day when they told me that a truck had hit one of the boys and broken his ribs. Of course that was a lie, but there he lay, right in the line. They didn't even try to conceal him from me. I was going to give up. I was going to leave the children to God and move in with my oldest boy in Frankfurt, where the government is not required by treaty to admit every refugee from any part of the globe."

"I'm glad you didn't," said Sister Carlotta. "You can't leave them to God, when God has left them to us."

"Well, that's the funny thing. Perhaps that fight in the line woke up these children to the horror of the life they were living, for that very day one of the big boys—but the weakest of them, with a bad leg, they call him Achilles—well, I suppose *I* gave him that name years ago, because Achilles had a weak heel, you know—Achilles, anyway—he showed up in the line with a group of little children. He as much as asked me for protection, warning me that what happened to that poor boy with the broken ribs—he was the one I call Ulysses, because he wanders from kitchen to kitchen—he's still in hospital, his ribs were completely smashed in, can you believe the brutality?—Achilles, anyway, he warned me that the same thing might happen to his little ones, so I made the special effort, I came early to watch over the line, and badgered the police to finally give me a man, off-duty volunteers at first, on part pay, but now regulars—you'd think I would have been watching over the line all along, but don't you see? It didn't make any difference because they didn't do their intimidation in the line, they did it where I couldn't see, so no matter how I watched over them, it was only the bigger, meaner boys who ended up in the line, and yes, I know they're God's children too and I fed them and tried to preach the gospel to them as they ate, but I was losing heart, they were so heartless themselves, so devoid of compassion, but Achilles, anyway, he had taken on a whole group of them, including the littlest child I ever saw on the streets, it just broke my heart, they call him Bean, so *small*, he looked to be two years old, though I've learned since that he thinks he's four, and he *talks* like he's ten at least, very precocious, I suppose that's why he lived long enough to get under Achilles' protection, but he was skin and bone, people say that when somebody's skinny, but in the case of this little Bean, it was true, I didn't know how he had muscles enough to walk, to *stand,* his arms and legs were as thin as an ant—oh, isn't that awful? To compare him to the Buggers? Or I should say, the Formics, since they're saying now that *Buggers* is a bad word in English, even though I.F. Common is *not* English, even though it began that way, don't you think?"

"So, Helga, you're telling me it began with this Achilles."

"Do call me Hazie. We're friends now, aren't we?" She gripped Sister Carlotta's hand. "You must meet this boy. Courage! Vision! Test him, Sister Carlotta. He is a leader of men! He is a civilizer!"

Sister Carlotta did not point out that civilizers often didn't make good soldiers. It was enough that the boy was interesting, and she had missed him the first time around. It was a reminder to her that she must be thorough.

In the dark of early morning, Sister Carlotta arrived at the door where the line had already formed. Helga beckoned to her, then pointed ostentatiously at a rather good-looking young man surrounded by smaller children. Only when she got closer and saw him take a couple of steps did she realize just how bad his right leg was. She tried to diagnose the condition. Was it an early case of rickets? A clubfoot, left uncorrected? A break that healed wrong?

It hardly mattered. Battle School would not take him with such an injury.

Then she saw the adoration in the eyes of the children, the way they called him Papa and looked to him for approval. Few adult men were good fathers. This boy of—what, eleven? twelve?—had already learned to be an extraordinarily good father. Protector, provider, king, god to his little ones. Even as ye do it unto the least of these, ye have done it unto me. Christ had a special place deep in his heart for this boy Achilles. So she *would* test him, and maybe the leg could be corrected; or, failing that, she could surely find a place for him in some good school in one of the cities of the Netherlands—pardon, the International Territory—that was not completely overwhelmed by the desperate poverty of refugees.

He refused.

"I can't leave my children," he said.

"But surely one of the others can look after them."

A girl who dressed as a boy spoke up. "I can!"

But it was obvious she could not—she was too small herself. Achilles was right. His children depended on him, and to leave them would be irresponsible. The reason she was here was because he was civilized; civilized men do not leave their children.

"Then I will come to you," she said. "After you eat, take me where you spend your days, and let me teach you all in a little school. Only for a few days, but that would be good, wouldn't it?"

It *would* be good. It had been a long time since Sister Carlotta had actually taught a group of children. And never had she been given such a class as this. Just when her work had begun to seem futile even to her, God gave her such a chance. It might even be a miracle. Wasn't it the business of Christ to make the lame walk? If Achilles did well on the tests, then surely God would let the leg also be fixed, would let it be within the reach of medicine.

"School's good," said Achilles. "None of these little ones can read."

Sister Carlotta knew, of course, that if Achilles could read, he certainly couldn't do it well.

But for some reason, perhaps some almost unnoticeable movement, when Achilles said that none of the little ones could read, the smallest of them all, the one called Bean, caught her eye. She looked at him, into eyes with sparks in them like distant campfires in the darkest night, and she knew that *he* knew how to read. She knew, without knowing how, that it was not Achilles at all, that it was this little one that God had brought her here to find.

She shook off the feeling. It was Achilles who was the civilizer, doing the work of Christ. It was the leader that the I.F. would want, not the weakest and smallest of the disciples.

━━━━━

Bean stayed as quiet as possible during the school sessions, never speaking up and never giving an answer even when Sister Carlotta tried to insist. He knew that it wouldn't be good for him to let anyone know that he could already read and do numbers, nor that he could understand every language spoken in the street, picking up new languages the way other children picked up stones. Whatever Sister Carlotta was doing, whatever gifts she had to bestow, if it ever seemed to the other children that Bean was trying to show them up, trying to get ahead of them, he knew that he would not be back for another day of school. And even though she mostly taught things he already knew how to do, in her conversation there were many hints of a wider world, of great knowledge and wisdom. No adult had ever taken the time to speak to them like this, and he luxuriated in the sound of high language well spoken. When she taught it was in I.F. Common, of course, that being the language of the street, but since many of the children had also learned Dutch and some were even native Dutch speakers, she would often explain hard points in that language. When she was frustrated though, and muttered under her breath, that was in Spanish, the language of the merchants of Jonker Frans Straat, and he tried to piece together the meanings of new words from her muttering. Her knowledge was a banquet, and if he remained quiet enough, he would be able to stay and feast.

School had only been going for a week, however, when he made a mistake. She passed out papers to them, and they had writing on them. Bean read his paper at once. It was a "Pre-Test" and the instructions said to circle the right answers to each question. So he began circling answers and was halfway down the page when he realized that the entire group had fallen silent.

They were all looking at him, because Sister Carlotta was looking at him.

"What are you doing, Bean?" she asked. "I haven't even told you what to do yet. Please give me your paper."

Stupid, inattentive, careless—if you die for this, Bean, you deserve it.

He handed her the paper.

She looked at it, then looked back at him very closely. "Finish it," she said.

He took the paper back from her hand. His pencil hovered over the page. He pretended to be struggling with the answer.

"You did the first fifteen in about a minute and a half," said Sister Carlotta. "Please don't expect me to believe that you're suddenly having a hard time with the next question." Her voice was dry and sarcastic.

"I can't do it," he said. "I was just playing anyway."

"Don't lie to me," said Carlotta. "Do the rest."

He gave up and did them all. It didn't take long. They were easy. He handed her the paper.

She glanced over it and said nothing. "I hope the rest of you will wait until I finish the instructions and read you the questions. If you try to guess at what the hard words are, you'll get all the answers wrong."

Then she proceeded to read each question and all the possible answers out loud. Only then could the other children set their marks on the papers.

Sister Carlotta didn't say another thing to call attention to Bean after that, but the damage was done. As soon as school was over, Sergeant came over to Bean. "So you can read," he said.

Bean shrugged.

"You been lying to us," said Sergeant.

"Never said I couldn't."

"Showed us all up. How come *you* didn't teach us?"

Because I was trying to survive, Bean said silently. Because I didn't want to remind Achilles that I was the smart one who thought up the original plan that got him this family. If he remembers that, he'll also remember who it was who told Poke to kill him.

The only answer he actually gave was a shrug.

"Don't like it when somebody holds out on us."

Sergeant nudged him with a foot.

Bean did not have to be given a map. He got up and jogged away from the group. School was out for him. Maybe breakfast, too. He'd have to wait till morning to find that out.

He spent the afternoon alone on the streets. He had to be careful. As the smallest and least important of Achilles' family, he might be overlooked. But it was more likely that those who hated Achilles would have taken special notice of Bean as one of the most memorable. They might take it into their heads that killing Bean or beating him to paste and leaving him would make a dandy warning to Achilles that he was still resented, even though life was better for everybody.

Bean knew there were plenty of bullies who felt that way. Especially the ones who weren't able to maintain a family, because they kept being too mean with the little children. The little ones learned quickly that when a papa got too nasty, they could punish him by leaving him alone at breakfast and attaching themselves to some other family. They would eat before him. They would have someone else's protection from him. He would eat last. If they ran out of food, he would get nothing, and Helga wouldn't even mind, because *he* wasn't a papa, *he* wasn't watching out for little ones. So those bullies, those marginal ones, they hated the way things worked these days, and they didn't forget that it was Achilles who had changed it all. Nor could they go to some other kitchen—the word had spread among the adults who gave out food, and now all the kitchens had a rule that groups with little children got to be first in line. If you couldn't hold on to a family, you could get pretty hungry. And nobody looked up to you.

Still, Bean couldn't resist trying to get close enough to some of the other families to hear their talk. Find out how the other groups worked.

The answer was easy to learn: They didn't work all that well. Achilles really was a good leader. That sharing of bread—none of the other groups did that. But there was a lot of punishing, the bully smacking kids who didn't do what he wanted. Taking their bread away from them because they didn't do something, or didn't do it quickly enough.

Poke had chosen right, after all. By dumb luck, or maybe she wasn't all that stupid. Because she had picked, not just the weakest bully, the easiest to beat, but also the smartest, the one who understood how to win and hold the loyalty of others. All Achilles had ever needed was the chance.

Except that Achilles still didn't share her bread, and now she was beginning to realize that this was a bad thing, not a good one. Bean could see it in her face when she watched the others do the ritual of sharing with Achilles. Because he got soup now—Helga brought it to him at the door—he took much smaller pieces, and instead of biting them off he tore them and ate them with a smile. Poke never got that smile from him. Achilles was never going to forgive her, and Bean could see that she was beginning to feel the pain of that. For she loved Achilles now, too, the way the other children did, and the way he kept her apart from the others was a kind of cruelty.

Maybe that's enough for him, thought Bean. Maybe that's his whole vengeance.

Bean happened to be curled up behind a newsstand when several bullies began a conversation near him. "He's full of brag about how Achilles is going to pay for what he did."

"Oh, right, Ulysses is going to punish him, right."

"Well, maybe not directly."

"Achilles and his stupid family will just take him apart. And this time they won't aim for his chest. He said so, didn't he? Break open his head and put his brains on the street, that's what Achilles'll do."

"He's still just a cripple."

"Achilles gets away with everything. Give it up."

"I'm hoping Ulysses does it. Kills him, flat out. And then none of us take in any of his bastards. You got that? Nobody takes them in. Let them all die. Put them all in the river."

The talk went on that way until the boys drifted away from the newsstand.

Then Bean got up and went in search of Achilles.

3

PAYBACK

"I think I have someone for you."

"You've thought that before."

"He's a born leader. But he does not meet your physical specifications."

"Then you'll pardon me if I don't waste time on him."

"If he passes your exacting intellectual and personality requirements, it is quite possible that for a minuscule portion of the brass button or toilet paper budget of the I.F., his physical limitations might be repaired."

"I never knew nuns could be sarcastic."

"I can't reach you with a ruler. Sarcasm is my last resort."

"Let me see the tests."

"I'll let you see the boy. And while we're at it, I'll let you see another."

"Also physically limited?"

"Small. Young. But so was the Wiggin boy, I hear. And this one—somehow on the streets he taught himself to read."

"Ah, Sister Carlotta, you help me fill the empty hours of my life."

"Keeping you out of mischief is how I serve God."

Bean went straight to Achilles with what he heard. It was too dangerous, to have Ulysses out of the hospital and word going around that he meant to get even for his humiliation.

"I thought that was all behind us," said Poke sadly. "The fighting I mean."

"Ulysses has been in bed for all this time," said Achilles. "Even if he knows about the changes, he hasn't had time to get how it works yet."

"So we stick together," said Sergeant. "Keep you safe."

"It might be safer for all," said Achilles, "if I disappear for a few days. To keep *you* safe."

"Then how will we get in to eat?" asked one of the younger ones. "They'll never let us in without you."

"Follow Poke," said Achilles. "Helga at the door will let you in just the same."

"What if Ulysses gets you?" asked one of the young ones. He rubbed the tears out of his eyes, lest he be shamed.

"Then I'll be dead," said Achilles. "I don't think he'll be content to put me in the hospital."

The child broke down crying, which set another to wailing, and soon it was a choir of boo-hoos, with Achilles shaking his head and laughing. "I'm not going to die. You'll be safe if I'm out of the way, and I'll come back after Ulysses has time to cool down and get used to the system."

Bean watched and listened in silence. He didn't think Achilles was handling it right, but he had given the warning and his responsibility was over. For Achilles to go into hiding was begging for trouble—it would be taken as a sign of weakness.

Achilles slipped away that night to go somewhere that he couldn't tell them so that nobody could accidentally let it slip. Bean toyed with the idea of following him to see what he really did, but realized he would be more useful with the main group. After all, Poke would be their leader now, and Poke was only an ordinary leader. In other words, stupid. She needed Bean, even if she didn't know it.

That night Bean tried to keep watch, for what he did not know. At last he did sleep, and dreamed of school, only it wasn't the sidewalk or alley school with Sister Carlotta, it was a real school, with tables and chairs. But in the dream Bean couldn't sit at a desk. Instead he hovered in the air over it, and when he wanted to he flew anywhere in the room. Up to the ceiling. Into a crevice in the wall, into a secret dark place, flying upward and upward as it got warmer and warmer and . . .

He woke in darkness. A cold breeze stirred. He needed to pee. He also wanted to fly. Having the dream end almost made him cry out with the pain of it. He couldn't remember ever dreaming of flying before. Why did he have to be little, with these stubby legs to carry him from place to place?

When he was flying he could look down at everyone and see the tops of their silly heads. He could pee or poop on them like a bird. He wouldn't have to be afraid of them because if they got mad he could fly away and they could never catch him.

Of course, if I *could* fly, everyone else could fly too and I'd still be the smallest and slowest and they'd poop and pee on me anyway.

There was no going back to sleep. Bean could feel that in himself. He was too frightened, and he didn't know why. He got up and went into the alley to pee.

Poke was already there. She looked up and saw him.

"Leave me alone for a minute," she said.

"No," he said.

"Don't give me any crap, little boy," she said.

"I know you squat to pee," he said, "and I'm not looking anyway."

Glaring, she waited until he turned his back to urinate against the wall. "I guess if you were going to tell about me you already would have," she said.

"They all know you're a girl, Poke. When you're not there, Papa Achilles talks about you as 'she' and 'her.' "

"He's not my papa."

"So I figured," said Bean. He waited, facing the wall.

"You can turn around now." She was up and fastening her pants again.

"I'm scared of something, Poke," said Bean.

"What?"

"I don't know."

"You don't know what you're scared of?

"That's why it's so scary."

She gave a soft, sharp laugh. "Bean, all that means is that you're four years old. Little kids see shapes in the night. Or they don't see shapes. Either way they're scared."

"Not me," said Bean. "When I'm scared, it's because something's wrong."

"Ulysses is looking to hurt Achilles, that's what."

"That wouldn't make you sad, would it?"

She glared at him. "We're eating better than ever. Everybody's happy. It was your plan. And I never cared about being the boss."

"But you hate him," said Bean.

She hesitated. "It feels like he's always laughing at me."

"How do *you* know what little kids are scared of?"

"Cause I used to be one," said Poke. "And I remember."

"Ulysses isn't going to hurt Achilles," said Bean.

"I know that," said Poke.

"Because you're planning to find Achilles and protect him."

"I'm planning to stay right here and watch out for the children."

"Or else maybe you're planning to find Ulysses first and kill him."

"How? He's bigger than me. By a lot."

"You didn't come out here to pee," said Bean. "Or else your bladder's the size of a gumball."

"You *listened?*"

Bean shrugged. "You wouldn't let me watch."

"You think too much, but you don't know enough to make sense of what's going on."

"I think Achilles was lying to us about what he's going to do," said Bean, "and I think you're lying to me right now."

"Get used to it," said Poke. "The world is full of liars."

"Ulysses doesn't care who he kills," said Bean. "He'd be just as happy to kill you as Achilles."

Poke shook her head impatiently. "Ulysses is nothing. He isn't going to hurt anybody. He's all brag."

"So why are you up?" asked Bean.

Poke shrugged.

"*You're* going to try to kill Achilles, aren't you," said Bean. "And make it look like Ulysses did it."

She rolled her eyes. "Did you drink a big glass of stupid juice tonight?"

"I'm smart enough to know you're lying!"

"Go back to sleep," she said. "Go back to the other children."

He regarded her for a while, and then obeyed.

Or rather, seemed to obey. He went back into the crawl space where they slept these days, but immediately crept out the back way and clambered up crates, drums, low walls, high walls, and finally got up onto a low-hanging roof. He walked to the edge in time to see Poke slip out of the alley into the street. She *was* going somewhere. To meet someone.

Bean slid down a pipe onto a rainbarrel, and scurried along Korte Hoog Straat after her. He tried to be quiet, but she wasn't trying, and there were other noises of the city, so she never heard his footfalls. He clung to the shadows of walls, but didn't dodge around too much. It was pretty straight-forward, following her—she only turned twice. Headed for the river. Meeting someone.

Bean had two guesses. It was either Ulysses or Achilles. Who else did

she know, that wasn't already asleep in the nest? But then, why meet either
of them? To plead with Ulysses for Achilles' life? To heroically offer herself in his place? Or to try to persuade Achilles to come back and face
down Ulysses instead of hiding? No, these were all things that Bean might
have thought of doing—but Poke didn't think that far ahead.

Poke stopped in the middle of an open space on the dock at Scheep-
makershaven and looked around. Then she saw what she was looking for.
Bean strained to see. Someone waiting in a deep shadow. Bean climbed up
on a big packing crate, trying to get a better view. He heard the two
voices—both children—but he couldn't make out what they were saying.
Whoever it was, he was taller than Poke. But that could be either Achilles
or Ulysses.

The boy wrapped his arms around Poke and kissed her.

This was really weird. Bean had seen grownups do that plenty of times,
but what would kids do it for? Poke was nine years old. Of course there
were whores that age, but everybody knew that the johns who bought them
were perverts.

Bean had to get closer, to hear what they were saying. He dropped
down the back of the packing crate and slowly walked into the shadow of
a kiosk. They, as if to oblige him, turned to face him; in the deep shadow
he was invisible, at least if he kept still. He couldn't see them any better
than they could see him, but he could hear snatches of their conversation
now.

"You promised," Poke was saying. The guy mumbled in return.

A boat passing on the river scanned a spotlight across the riverside and
showed the face of the boy Poke was with. It was Achilles.

Bean didn't want to see any more. To think he had once believed
Achilles would someday kill Poke. This thing between girls and boys was
something he just didn't get. In the midst of hate, this happens. Just when
Bean was beginning to make sense of the world.

He slipped away and ran up Posthoornstraat.

But he did not head back to their nest in the crawlspace, not yet. For
even though he had all the answers, his heart was still jumping; something
is wrong, it was saying to him, something is wrong.

And then he remembered that Poke wasn't the only one hiding something from him. Achilles had also been lying. Hiding something. Some plan.
Was it just this meeting with Poke? Then why all this business about hiding
from Ulysses? To take Poke as his girl, he didn't have to hide to do that.
He could do that right out in the open. Some bullies did that, the older

ones. They usually didn't take nine-year-olds, though. Was that what Achilles was hiding?

"You promised," Poke said to Achilles there on the dock.

What did Achilles promise? That was why Poke came to him—to pay him for his promise. But what could Achilles be promising her that he wasn't already giving her as part of his family? Achilles didn't have anything.

So he must have been promising *not* to do something. Not to kill her? Then that would be too stupid even for Poke, to go off alone with Achilles.

Not to kill *me,* thought Bean. That's the promise. Not to kill *me.*

Only I'm not the one in danger, or not the most danger. I might have said to kill him, but Poke was the one who knocked him down, who stood over him. That picture must still be in Achilles' mind, all the time he must remember it, must dream about it, him lying on the ground, a nine-year-old girl standing over him with a cinderblock, threatening to kill him. A cripple like him, somehow he had made it into the ranks of the bullies. So he was tough—but always mocked by the boys with two good legs, the lowest-status bully. And the lowest moment of his life had to be then, when a nine-year-old girl knocked him down and a bunch of little kids stood over him.

Poke, he blames you most. You're the one he has to smash in order to wipe out the agony of that memory.

Now it was clear. Everything Achilles had said today was a lie. He wasn't hiding from Ulysses. He would face Ulysses down—probably still would, tomorrow. But when he faced Ulysses, Achilles would have a much bigger grievance. You killed Poke! He would scream the accusation. Ulysses would look so stupid and weak, denying it after all the bragging he'd done about how he'd get even. He might even admit to killing her, just for the brag of it. And then Achilles would strike at Ulysses and nobody would blame him for killing the boy. It wouldn't be mere self-defense, it would be defense of his family.

Achilles was just too damn smart. And patient. Waiting to kill Poke until there was somebody else who could be blamed for it.

Bean ran back to warn her. As fast as his little legs would move, the longest strides he could take. He ran forever.

There was nobody there on the dock where Poke had met Achilles.

Bean looked around helplessly. He thought of calling out, but that would be stupid. Just because it was Poke that Achilles hated most didn't mean that he had forgiven Bean, even if he did let Bean give him bread.

Or maybe I've gone crazy over nothing. He was hugging her, wasn't he? She came willingly, didn't she? There are things between boys and girls that I just don't understand. Achilles is a provider, a protector, not a murderer. It's *my* mind that works that way, *my* mind that thinks of killing someone who is helpless, just because he might pose a danger later. Achilles is the good one. I'm the bad one, the criminal.

Achilles is the one who knows how to love. I'm the one who doesn't.

Bean walked to the edge of the dock and looked across the channel. The water was covered with a low-flowing mist. On the far bank, the lights of Boompjes Straat twinkled like Sinterklaas Day. The waves lapped like tiny kisses against the pilings.

He looked down into the river at his feet. Something was bobbing in the water, bumped up against the wharf.

Bean looked at it for a while, uncomprehending. But then he understood that he had known all along what it was, he just didn't want to believe it. It was Poke. She was dead. It was just as Bean had feared. Everybody on the street would believe that Ulysses was guilty of the murder, even if nothing could be proved. Bean had been right about everything. Whatever it was that passed between boys and girls, it didn't have the power to block hatred, vengeance for humiliation.

And as Bean stood there, looking down into the water, he realized: I either have to tell what happened, right now, this minute, to everybody, or I have to decide never to tell anybody, because if Achilles gets any hint that I saw what I saw tonight, he'll kill me and not give it a second thought. Achilles would simply say: Ulysses strikes again. Then he can pretend to be avenging two deaths, not one, when he kills Ulysses.

No, all Bean could do was keep silence. Pretend that he hadn't seen Poke's body floating in the river, her upturned face clearly recognizable in the moonlight.

She was stupid. Stupid not to see through Achilles' plans, stupid to trust him in any way, stupid not to listen to me. As stupid as I was, to walk away instead of calling out a warning, maybe saving her life by giving her a witness that Achilles could not hope to catch and therefore could not silence.

She was the reason Bean was alive. She was the one who gave him a name. She was the one who listened to his plan. And now she had died for it, and he could have saved her. Sure, he told her at the start to kill Achilles, but in the end she had been right to choose him—he was the only one of the bullies who could have figured it all out and brought it off with such style. But Bean had also been right. Achilles was a champion liar, and when he decided that Poke would die, he began building up the lies that would surround the murder—lies that would get Poke off by herself where he could kill her without witnesses; lies to alibi himself in the eyes of the younger kids.

I trusted him, thought Bean. I knew what he was from the start, and yet I trusted him.

Aw, Poke, you poor, stupid, kind, decent girl. You saved me and I let you down.

It's not *just* my fault. *She's* the one who went off alone with him.

Alone with him, trying to save my life? What a mistake, Poke, to think of anyone but yourself!

Am I going to die from her mistakes, too?

No. I'll die from my own damn mistakes.

Not tonight, though. Achilles had not set any plan in motion to get Bean off by himself. But from now on, when he lay awake at night, unable to drift off, he would think about how Achilles was just waiting. Biding his time. Till the day when Bean, too, would find himself in the river.

Sister Carlotta tried to be sensitive to the pain these children were suffering, so soon after one of their own was strangled and thrown in the river. But Poke's death was all the more reason to push forward on the testing. Achilles had not been found yet—with this Ulysses boy having already struck once, it was unlikely that Achilles would come out of hiding for some time. So Sister Carlotta had no choice but to proceed with Bean.

At first the boy was distracted, and did poorly. Sister Carlotta could not understand how he could fail even the elementary parts of the test, when he was so bright he had taught himself to read on the street. It had to be the death of Poke. So she interrupted the test and talked to him about death, about how Poke was caught up in spirit into the presence of God and the saints, who would care for her and make her happier than she had ever been in life. He did not seem interested. If anything, he did worse as they began the next phase of the test.

Well, if compassion didn't work, sternness might.

"Don't you understand what this test is for, Bean?" she asked.

"No," he said. The tone of his voice added the unmistakable idea "and I don't care."

"All you know about is the life of the street. But the streets of Rotterdam are only a part of a great city, and Rotterdam is only one city in a world of thousands of such cities. The whole human race, Bean, that's what this test is about. Because the Formics—''

''The Buggers,'' said Bean. Like most street urchins, he sneered at euphemism.

''They will be back, scouring the Earth, killing every living soul. This test is to see if you are one of the children who will be taken to Battle School and trained to be a commander of the forces that will try to stop them. This test is about saving the world, Bean.''

For the first time since the test began, Bean turned his full attention to her. ''Where is Battle School?''

''In an orbiting platform in space,'' she said. ''If you do well enough on this test, you get to be a spaceman!''

There was no childlike eagerness in his face. Only hard calculation.

''I've been doing real bad so far, haven't I,'' he said.

''The test results so far show that you're too stupid to walk and breathe at the same time.''

''Can I start over?''

''I have another version of the tests, yes,'' said Sister Carlotta.

''Do it.''

As she brought out the alternate set, she smiled at him, tried to relax him again. ''So you want to be a spaceman, is that it? Or is it the idea of being part of the International Fleet?''

He ignored her.

This time through the test, he finished everything, even though the tests were designed not to be finished in the allotted time. His scores were not perfect, but they were close. So close that nobody would believe the results.

So she gave him yet another battery of tests, this one designed for older children—the standard tests, in fact, that six-year-olds took when being considered for Battle School at the normal age. He did not do as well on these; there were too many experiences he had not had yet, to be able to understand the content of some of the questions. But he still did remarkably well. Better than any student she had ever tested.

And to think she had thought it was Achilles who had the real potential. This little one, this infant, really—he was astonishing. No one would believe she had found him on the streets, living at the starvation level.

A suspicion crept into her mind, and when the second test ended and she recorded the scores and set them aside, she leaned back in her chair and smiled at bleary-eyed little Bean and asked him, ''Whose idea was it, this family thing that the street children have come up with?''

"Achilles' idea," said Bean.

Sister Carlotta waited.

"His idea to call it a family, anyway," said Bean.

She still waited. Pride would bring more to the surface, if she gave him time.

"But having a bully protect the little ones, that was my plan," said Bean. "I told it to Poke and she thought about it and decided to try it and she only made one mistake."

"What mistake was that?"

"She chose the wrong bully to protect us."

"You mean because he couldn't protect her from Ulysses?"

Bean laughed bitterly as tears slid down his cheeks.

"Ulysses is off somewhere bragging about what he's going to do."

Sister Carlotta knew but did not want to know. "Do you know who killed her, then?"

"I told her to kill him. I told her he was the wrong one. I saw it in his face, lying there on the ground, that he would never forgive her. But he's cold. He waited so long. But he never took bread from her. That should have told her. She shouldn't have gone off alone with him." He began crying in earnest now. "I think she was protecting *me*. Because I told her to kill him that first day. I think she was trying to get him not to kill me."

Sister Carlotta tried to keep emotion out of her voice. "Do you believe you might be in danger from Achilles?"

"I am now that I told you," he said. And then, after a moment's thought. "I was already. He doesn't forgive. He pays back, always."

"You realize that this isn't the way Achilles seems to me, or to Hazie. Helga, that is. To us, he seems—civilized."

Bean looked at her like she was crazy. "Isn't that what it *means* to be civilized? That you can *wait* to get what you want?"

"You want to get out of Rotterdam and go to Battle School so you can get away from Achilles."

Bean nodded.

"What about the other children. Do you think they're in danger from him?"

"No," said Bean. "He's their papa."

"But not yours. Even though he took bread from you."

"He hugged her and kissed her," said Bean. "I saw them on the dock, and she let him kiss her and then she said something about how he promised, and so I left, but then I realized and I ran back and it couldn't have been long, just running for maybe six blocks, and she was dead with her eye stabbed out, floating in the water, bumping up against the dock. He can kiss you and kill you, if he hates you enough.''

Sister Carlotta drummed her fingers on the desk. ''What a quandary.''

''What's a quandary?''

''I was going to test Achilles, too. I think he could get into Battle School.''

Bean's whole body tightened. ''Then don't send me. Him or me.''

''Do you really think . . .'' Her voice trailed off. ''You think he'd try to kill you there?''

''*Try?*'' His voice was scornful. ''Achilles doesn't just *try.*''

Sister Carlotta knew that the trait Bean was speaking of, that ruthless determination, was one of the things that they looked for in Battle School. It might make Achilles more attractive to them than Bean. And they could channel such murderous violence up there. Put it to good use.

But civilizing the bullies of the street had not been Achilles' idea. It had been Bean who thought of it. Incredible, for a child so young to conceive of it and bring it about. This child was the prize, not the one who lived for cold vengeance. But one thing was certain. It would be wrong of her to take them both. Though she could certainly take the other one and get him into a school here on Earth, get him off the street. Surely Achilles would become truly civilized then, where the desperation of the street no longer drove children to do such hideous things to each other.

Then she realized what nonsense she had been thinking. It wasn't the desperation of the street that drove Achilles to murder Poke. It was pride. It was Cain, who thought that being shamed was reason enough to take his brother's life. It was Judas, who did not shrink to kiss before killing. What was she thinking, to treat evil as if it were a mere mechanical product of deprivation? All the children of the street suffered fear and hunger, helplessness and desperation. But they didn't all become cold-blooded, calculating murderers.

If, that is, Bean was right.

But she had no doubt that Bean was telling her the truth. If Bean was lying, she would give up on herself as a judge of children's character. Now that she thought about it, Achilles was slick. A flatterer. Everything he said was calculated to impress. But Bean said little, and spoke plainly when he did speak. And he was young, and his fear and grief here in this room were real.

Of course, he also had urged that a child be killed.

But only because he posed a danger to others. It wasn't pride.

How can I judge? Isn't Christ supposed to be the judge of quick and dead? Why is this in my hands, when I am not fit to do it?

"Would you like to stay here, Bean, while I transmit your test results to the people who make the decisions about Battle School? You'll be safe here."

He looked down at his hands, nodded, then laid his head on his arms and sobbed.

Achilles came back to the nest that morning. "I couldn't stay away," he said. "Too much could go wrong." He took them to breakfast, just like always. But Poke and Bean weren't there.

Then Sergeant did his rounds, listening here and there, talking to other kids, talking to an adult here and there, finding out what was happening, anything that might be useful. It was along the Wijnhaven dock that he heard some of the longshoremen talking about the body found in the river that morning. A little girl. Sergeant found out where her body was being held till the authorities arrived. He didn't shy away, he walked right up to the body under a tarpaulin, and without asking permission from any of the others standing there, he pulled it back and looked at her.

"What are you doing, boy!"

"Her name is Poke," he said.

"You know her? Do you know who might have killed her?"

"A boy named Ulysses, that's who killed her," said Sergeant. Then he dropped the tarp and his rounds were over. Achilles had to know that his fears had been justified, that Ulysses was taking out anybody he could from the family.

"We've got no choice but to kill him," said Sergeant.

"There's been enough bloodshed," said Achilles. "But I'm afraid you're right."

Some of the younger children were crying. One of them explained, "Poke fed me when I was going to die."

"Shut up," said Sergeant. "We're eating better now than we ever did when Poke was boss."

Achilles put a hand on Sergeant's arm, to still him. "Poke did the best a crew boss could do. And she's the one who got me into the family. So in a way, anything I get for you, she got for you."

Everyone nodded solemnly at that.

A kid asked, "You think Ulysses got Bean, too?"

"Big loss if he did," said Sergeant.

"Any loss to my family is a big loss," said Achilles. "But there'll be no more. Ulysses will either leave the city, now, or he's dead. Put the word out, Sergeant. Let it be known on the street that the challenge stands. Ulysses doesn't eat in any kitchen in town, until he faces me. That's what he decided for himself, when he chose to put a knife in Poke's eye."

Sergeant saluted him and took off at a run. The picture of businesslike obedience.

Except that as he ran, he, too, was crying. For he had not told anyone how Poke died, how her eye was a bloody wound. Maybe Achilles knew some other way, maybe he had already heard but didn't mention it till Sergeant came back with the news. Maybe maybe. Sergeant knew the truth. Ulysses didn't raise his hand against anybody. Achilles did it. Just as Bean warned in the beginning. Achilles would never forgive Poke for beating him. He killed her now because Ulysses would get blamed for it. And then sat there talking about how good she was and how they should all be grateful to her and everything Achilles got for them, it was really Poke who got it.

So Bean was right all along. About everything. Achilles might be a good papa to the family, but he was also a killer, and he never forgives.

Poke knew that, though. Bean warned her, and she knew it, but she chose Achilles for their papa anyway. Chose him and then died for it. She was like Jesus that Helga preached about in her kitchen while they ate. She died for her people. And Achilles, he was like God. He made people pay for their sins no matter what they did.

The important thing is, stay on the good side of God. That's what Helga teaches, isn't it? Stay right with God.

I'll stay right with Achilles. I'll honor my papa, that's for sure, so I can stay alive until I'm old enough to go out on my own.

As for Bean, well, he was smart, but not smart enough to stay alive, and if you're not smart enough to stay alive, then you're better off dead.

By the time Sergeant got to his first corner to spread the word about Achilles' ban on Ulysses from any kitchen in town, he was through crying. Grief was done. This was about survival now. Even though Sergeant knew Ulysses hadn't killed anybody, he meant to, and it was still important for the family's safety that he die. Poke's death provided a good excuse to demand that the rest of the papas stand back and let Achilles deal with him. When it was all over, Achilles would be the leader among all the papas of Rotterdam. And Sergeant would stand beside him, knowing the secret of his vengeance and telling no one, because that's how Sergeant, that's how the family, that's how all the urchins of Rotterdam would survive.

4

MEMORIES

"I was mistaken about the first one. He tests well, but his character is not well suited to Battle School."

"I don't see that on the tests you've shown me."

"He's very sharp. He gives the right answers, but they aren't true."

"And what test did you use to determine this?"

"He committed murder."

"Well, that is a drawback. And the other one? What am I supposed to do with so young a child? A fish this small I would generally throw back into the stream."

"Teach him. Feed him. He'll grow."

"He doesn't even have a name."

"Yes he does."

"Bean? That isn't a name, it's a joke."

"It won't be when he's done with it."

"Keep him until he's five. Make of him what you can and show me your results then."

"I have other children to find."

"No, Sister Carlotta, you don't. In all your years of searching, this one is the best you've found. And there isn't time to find another. Bring this one up to snuff, and all your work will be worth it, as far as the I.F. is concerned."

"You frighten me, when you say there isn't time."

"I don't see why. Christians have been expecting the imminent end of the world for millennia."

"But it keeps not ending."
"So far, so good."

At first all Bean cared about was the food. There was enough of it. He ate everything they put before him. He ate until he was full—that most miraculous of words, which till now had had no meaning for him. He ate until he was stuffed. He ate until he was sick. He ate so often that he had bowel movements every day, sometimes twice a day. He laughed about it to Sister Carlotta. "All I do is eat and poop!" he said.

"Like any beast of the forest," said the nun. "It's time for you to begin to earn that food."

She was already teaching him, of course, daily lessons in reading and arithmetic, bringing him "up to level," though what level she had in mind, she never specified. She also gave him time to draw, and there were sessions where she had him sit there and try to remember every detail about his earliest memories. The clean place in particular fascinated her. But there were limits to memory. He was very small then, and had very little language. Everything was a mystery. He did remember climbing over the railing around his bed and falling to the floor. He didn't walk well at the time. Crawling was easier, but he liked walking because that's what the big people did. He clung to objects and leaned on walls and made good progress on two feet, only crawling when he had to cross an open space.

"You must have been eight or nine months old," Sister Carlotta said. "Most people don't remember that far back."

"I remember that everybody was upset. That's why I climbed out of bed. All the children were in trouble."

"All the children?"

"The little ones like me. And the bigger ones. Some of the grownups came in and looked at us and cried."

"Why?"

"Bad things, that's all. I knew it was a bad thing coming and I knew it would happen to all of us who were in the beds. So I climbed out. I wasn't the first. I don't know what happened to the others. I heard the grownups yelling and getting all upset when they found the empty beds. I hid from them. They didn't find me. Maybe they found the others, maybe they didn't. All I know is when I came out all the beds were empty and the room was very dark except a lighted sign that said *exit*."

"You could read then?" She sounded skeptical.

"When I *could* read, I remembered that those were the letters on the sign,'' said Bean. ''They were the only letters I saw back then. Of course I remembered them.''

''So you were alone and the beds were empty and the room was dark.''

''They came back. I heard them talking. I didn't understand most of the words. I hid again. And this time when I came out, even the beds were gone. Instead, there were desks and cabinets. An office. And no, I didn't know what an office was then, either, but now I do know what an office is and I remember that's what the rooms had all become. Offices. People came in during the day and worked there, only a few at first but my hiding place turned out not to be so good, when people were working there. And I was hungry.''

''Where did you hide?''

''Come on, you know. Don't you?''

''If I knew, I wouldn't ask.''

''You saw the way I acted when you showed me the toilet.''

''You hid inside the toilet?''

''The tank on the back. It was hard to get the lid up. And it wasn't comfortable in there. I didn't know what it was for. But people started using it and the water rose and fell and the pieces moved and it scared me. And like I said, I was hungry. Plenty to drink, except that I peed in it myself. My diaper was so waterlogged it fell off my butt. I was naked.''

''Bean, do you understand what you're telling me? That you were doing all this before you were a year old?''

''You're the one who said how old I was,'' said Bean. ''I didn't know about ages then. You told me to remember. The more I tell you, the more comes back to me. But if you don't believe me . . .''

''I just . . . I do believe you. But who were the other children? What was the place where you lived, that clean place? Who were those grown-ups? Why did they take away the other children? Something illegal was going on, that's certain.''

''Whatever,'' said Bean. ''I was just glad to get out of the toilet.''

''But you were naked, you said. And you left the place?''

''No, I got found. I came out of the toilet and a grownup found me.''

''What happened?''

''He took me home. That's how I got clothing. I called them clothings then.''

''You were talking.''

''Some.''

''And this grownup took you home and bought you clothing.''

''I think he was a janitor. I know more about jobs now and I think that's what he was. It was night when he worked, and he didn't wear a uniform like a guard.''

''What happened?''

''That's when I first found out about legal and illegal. It wasn't legal for him to have a child. I heard him yelling at this woman about me and most of it I didn't understand, but at the end I knew he had lost and she had won, and he started talking to me about how I had to go away, and so I went.''

''He just turned you loose in the streets?''

''No, I left. I think now he was going to have to give me to somebody else, and it sounded scary, so I left before he could do it. But I wasn't naked or hungry anymore. He was nice. After I left I bet he didn't have any more trouble.''

''And that's when you started living on the streets.''

''Sort of. A couple of places I found, they fed me. But every time, other kids, big ones, would see that I was getting fed and they'd come shouting and begging and the people would stop feeding me or the bigger kids would shove me out of the way or take the food right out of my hands. I was scared. One time a big kid got so mad at me for eating that he put a stick down my throat and made me throw up what I just ate, right on the street. He even tried to eat it but he couldn't, it made him try to throw up, too. That was the scariest time. I hided all the time after that. Hid. All the time.''

''And starved.''

''And watched,'' said Bean. ''I ate some. Now and then. I didn't die.''

''No, you didn't.''

''I saw plenty who did. Lots of dead children. Big ones and little ones. I kept wondering how many of them were from the clean place.''

''Did you recognize any of them?''

''No. Nobody looked like they ever lived in the clean place. Everybody looked hungry.''

''Bean, thank you for telling me all this.''

''You asked.''

''Do you realize that there is no way you could have survived for three years as an infant?''

''I guess that means I'm dead.''

''I just . . . I'm saying that God must have been watching over you.''

''Yeah. Well, sure. So why didn't he watch over all those dead kids?''

''He took them to his heart and loved them.''

''So then he *didn't* love me?''

"No, he loved you too, he—"

"Cause if he was watching so careful, he could have given me something to eat now and then."

"He brought me to you. He has some great purpose in mind for you, Bean. You may not know what it is, but God didn't keep you alive so miraculously for no reason."

Bean was tired of talking about this. She looked so happy when she talked about God, but he hadn't figured it out yet, what God even was. It was like, she wanted to give God credit for every good thing, but when it was bad, then she either didn't mention God or had some reason why it was a good thing after all. As far as Bean could see, though, the dead kids would rather have been alive, just with more food. If God loved them so much, and he could do whatever he wanted, then why wasn't there more food for these kids? And if God just wanted them dead, why didn't he let them die sooner or not even be born at all, so they didn't have to go to so much trouble and get all excited about trying to be alive when he was just going to take them to his heart. None of it made any sense to Bean, and the more Sister Carlotta explained it, the less he understood it. Because if there was somebody in charge, then he ought to be fair, and if he wasn't fair, then why should Sister Carlotta be so happy that he was in charge?

But when he tried to say things like that to her, she got really upset and talked even more about God and used words he didn't know and it was better just to let her say what she wanted and not argue.

It was the reading that fascinated him. And the numbers. He loved that. Having paper and pencil so he could actually write things, that was really good.

And maps. She didn't teach him maps at first, but there were some on the walls and the shapes of them fascinated him. He would go up to them and read the little words written on them and one day he saw the name of the river and realized that the blue was rivers and even bigger blue areas were places with even more water than the river, and then he realized that some of the other words were the same names that had been written on the street signs and so he figured out that somehow this thing was a picture of Rotterdam, and then it all made sense. Rotterdam the way it would look to a bird, if the buildings were all invisible and the streets were all empty. He found where the nest was, and where Poke had died, and all kinds of other places.

When Sister Carlotta found out that he understood the map, she got very excited. She showed him maps where Rotterdam was just a little patch of lines, and one where it was just a dot, and one where it was too small even to be seen, but she knew where it *would* be. Bean had never realized the world was so big. Or that there were so many people.

But Sister Carlotta kept coming back to the Rotterdam map, trying to get him to remember where things from his earliest memories were. Nothing looked the same, though, on the map, so it wasn't easy, and it took a long time for him to figure out where some of the places were where people had fed him. He showed these to Sister Carlotta, and she made a mark right on the map, showing each place. And after a while he realized—all those places were grouped in one area, but kind of strung out, as if they marked a path from where he found Poke leading back through time to . . .

To the clean place.

Only that was too hard. He had been too scared, coming out of the clean place with the janitor. He didn't know where it was. And the truth was, as Sister Carlotta herself said, the janitor might have lived anywhere compared to the clean place. So all she was going to find by following Bean's path backward was maybe the janitor's flat, or at least where he lived three years ago. And even then, what would the janitor know?

He would know where the clean place was, that's what he'd know. And now Bean understood: It was very important to Sister Carlotta to find out where Bean came from.

To find out who he really was.

Only . . . he already knew who he really was. He tried to say this to her. "I'm right here. This is who I really am. I'm not pretending."

"I know that," she said, laughing, and she hugged him, which was all right. It felt good. Back when she first started doing it, he didn't know what to do with his hands. She had to show him how to hug her back. He had seen some little kids—the ones with mamas or papas—doing that but he always thought they were holding on tight so they wouldn't drop off onto the street and get lost. He didn't know that you did it just because it felt good. Sister Carlotta's body had hard places and squishy places and it was very strange to hug her. He thought of Poke and Achilles hugging and kissing, but he didn't want to kiss Sister Carlotta and after he got used to what hugging was, he didn't really want to do that either. He let her hug him. But he didn't ever think of hugging her himself. It just didn't come into his mind.

He knew that sometimes she hugged him instead of explaining things to him, and he didn't like that. She didn't want to tell him why it mattered that she find the clean place, so she hugged him and said, "Oh, you dear thing,'' or ''Oh, you poor boy.'' But that only meant that it was even more important than she was saying, and she thought he was too stupid or ignorant to understand if she tried to explain.

He kept trying to remember more and more, if he could, only now he didn't tell her everything because she didn't tell *him* everything and fair was fair. He would find the clean room himself. Without her. And then tell her if he decided it would be good for him to have her know. Because what if she found the wrong answer? Would she put him back on the street? Would she keep him from going to school in the sky? Because that's what she promised at first, only after the tests she said he did very well only he would *not* go in the sky until he was five and maybe not even then because it was not entirely her decision and that's when he knew that she didn't have the power to keep her own promises. So if she found out the wrong thing about him, she might not be able to keep *any* of her promises. Not even the one about keeping him safe from Achilles. That's why he had to find out on his own.

He studied the map. He pictured things in his mind. He talked to himself as he was falling asleep, talked and thought and remembered, trying to get the janitor's face back into his mind, and the room he lived in, and the stairs outside where the mean lady stood to scream at him.

And one day, when he thought he had remembered enough, Bean went to the toilet—he liked the toilets, he liked to make them flush even though it scared him to see things disappear like that—and instead of coming back to Sister Carlotta's teaching place, he went the other way down the corridor and went right out the door onto the street and no one tried to stop him.

That's when he realized his mistake, though. He had been so busy trying to remember the janitor's place that it never occurred to him that he had no idea where *this* place was on the map. And it wasn't in a part of town that he knew. In fact, it hardly seemed like the same world. Instead of the street being full of people walking and pushing carts and riding bikes or skating to get from one place to another, the streets were almost empty, and there were cars parked everywhere. Not a single store, either. All houses and offices, or houses made into offices with little signs out front. The only building that was different was the very one he had just come out of. It was blocky and square and bigger than the others, but it had no sign out in front of it at all.

He knew where he was going, but he didn't know how to get there from here. And Sister Carlotta would start looking for him soon.

His first thought was to hide, but then he remembered that she knew all about his story of hiding in the clean place, so she would also think of hiding and she would look for him in a hiding place close to the big building.

So he ran. It surprised him how strong he was now. It felt like he could run as fast as a bird flying, and he didn't get tired, he could run forever. All the way to the corner and around it onto another street.

Then down another street, and another, until he would have been lost except he started out lost and when you start out completely lost, it's hard to get loster. As he walked and trotted and jogged and ran up and down streets and alleys, he realized that all he had to do was find a canal or a stream and it would lead him to the river or to a place that he recognized. So the first bridge that went over water, he saw which way the water flowed and chose streets that would keep him close. It wasn't as if he knew where he was yet, but at least he was following a plan.

It worked. He came to the river and walked along it until he recognized, off in the distance and partly around a bend in the river, Maasboulevard, which led to the place where Poke was killed.

The bend in the river—he knew it from the map. He knew where all of Sister Carlotta's marks had been. He knew that he had to go through the place where he used to live on the streets in order to get past them and closer to the area where the janitor might have lived. And that wouldn't be easy, because he would be known there, and Sister Carlotta might even have the cops looking for him and *they* would look there because that's where all the street urchins were and they would expect him to become a street urchin again.

What they were forgetting was that Bean wasn't hungry anymore. And since he wasn't hungry, he wasn't in a hurry.

He walked the long way around. Far from the river, far from the busy part of town where the urchins were. Whenever the streets started looking crowded he would widen his circle and stay away from the busy places. He took the rest of that day and most of the next making such a wide circle that for a while he was not in Rotterdam anymore at all, and he saw some of the countryside, just like the pictures—farmland and the roads built up higher than the land around them. Sister Carlotta had explained to him once that most of the farmland was lower than the level of the sea, and great dikes were the only thing keeping the sea from rushing back onto the land and covering it. But Bean knew that he would never get close to any of the big dikes. Not by walking, anyway.

He drifted back into town now, into the Schiebroek district, and late in the afternoon of the second day he recognized the name of Rindijk Straat and soon found a cross street whose name he knew, Erasmus Singel, and then it was easy to get to the earliest place he could remember, the back door of a restaurant where he had been fed when he was still a baby and didn't talk right and grownups rushed to feed him and help him instead of kicking him out of the way.

He stood there in the dusk. Nothing had changed. He could almost picture the woman with the little bowl of food, holding it out to him and waving a spoon in her hand and saying something in a language he didn't understand. Now he could read the sign above the restaurant and realized that it was Armenian and that's probably what the woman had been speaking.

Which way had he walked to come here? He had smelled the food when he was walking along . . . here? He walked a little way up, a little way down the street, turning and turning to reorient himself.

"What are you doing here, fatso?"

It was two kids, maybe eight years old. Belligerent but not bullies. Probably part of a crew. No, part of a family, now that Achilles had changed everything. If the changes had spread to this part of town.

"I'm supposed to meet my papa here," said Bean.

"And who's your papa?"

Bean wasn't sure whether they took the word "papa" to mean his father or the papa of his "family." He took the chance, though, of saying "Achilles."

They scoffed at the idea. "He's way down by the river, why would he meet a fatso like you clear up here?"

But their derision was not important—what mattered was that Achilles' reputation had spread this far through the city.

"I don't have to explain his business to you," said Bean. "And all the kids in Achilles' family are fat like me. That's how well we eat."

"Are they all short like you?"

"I used to be taller, but I asked too many questions," said Bean, pushing past them and walking across Rozenlaan toward the area where the janitor's flat seemed likeliest to be.

They didn't follow him. Such was the magic of Achilles' name—or perhaps it was just Bean's utter confidence, paying them no notice as if he had nothing to fear from them.

Nothing looked familiar. He kept turning around and checking to see if he recognized things when looking in the direction he might have been going after leaving the janitor's flat. It didn't help. He wandered until it was dark, and kept wandering even then.

Until, quite by chance, he found himself standing at the foot of a street lamp, trying to read a sign, when a set of initials carved on the pole caught his attention. P♡DVM, it said. He had no idea what it meant; he had never thought of it during all his attempts to remember; but he knew that he had seen it before. And not just once. He had seen it several times. The janitor's flat was very close.

He turned slowly, scanning the area, and there it was: A small apartment building with both an inside and an outside stairway.

The janitor lived on the top floor. Ground floor, first floor, second floor, third. Bean went to the mailboxes and tried to read the names, but they were set too high on the wall and the names were all faded, and some of the tags were missing entirely.

Not that he ever knew the janitor's name, truth to tell. There was no reason to think he would have recognized it even if he had been able to read it on the mailbox.

The outside stairway did not go all the way up to the top floor. It must have been built for a doctor's office on the first floor. And because it was dark, the door at the top of the stairs was locked.

There was nothing to do but wait. Either he would wait all night and get into the building through one entrance or another in the morning, or someone would come back in the night and Bean would slip through a door behind him.

He fell asleep and woke up, slept and woke again. He worried that a policeman would see him and shove him away, so when he woke the second time he abandoned all pretense of being on watch and crept under the stairs and curled up there for the night.

He was awakened by drunken laughter. It was still dark, and beginning to rain just a little—not enough to start dripping off the stairs, though, so Bean was dry. He stuck his head out to see who was laughing. It was a man and a woman, both merry with alcohol, the man furtively pawing and poking and pinching, the woman fending him off with halfhearted slaps. "Can't you wait?" she said.

"No," he said.

"You're just going to fall asleep without doing anything," she said.

"Not this time," he said. Then he threw up.

She looked disgusted and walked on without him. He staggered after her. "I feel better now," he said. "It'll be better."

"The price just went up," she said coldly. "And you brush your teeth first."

"Course I brush my teeth."

They were right at the front of the building now. Bean was waiting to slip in after them.

Then he realized that he didn't have to wait. The man *was* the janitor from all those years before.

Bean stepped out of the shadows. "Thanks for bringing him home," he said to the woman.

They both looked at him in surprise.

"Who are you?" asked the janitor.

Bean looked at the woman and rolled his eyes. "He's not *that* drunk, I hope," said Bean. To the janitor he said, "Mama will not be happy to see you come home like this again."

"Mama!" said the janitor. "Who the hell are you talking about?"

The woman gave the janitor a shove. He was so off balance that he lurched against the wall, then slid down it to land on his buttocks on the sidewalk. "I should have known," she said. "You bring me home to your *wife?*"

"I'm not married," said the janitor. "This kid isn't mine."

"I'm sure you're telling the truth on both points," said the woman. "But you better let him help you up the stairs anyway. Mama's waiting." She started to walk away.

"What about my forty gilders?" he asked plaintively, knowing the answer even as he asked.

She made an obscene gesture and walked on into the night.

"You little bastard," said the janitor.

"I had to talk to you alone," said Bean.

"Who the hell are you? Who's your mama?"

"That's what I'm here to find out," said Bean. "I'm the baby you found and brought home. Three years ago."

The man looked at him in stupefaction.

Suddenly a light went on, then another. Bean and the janitor were bathed in overlapping flashlight beams. Four policemen converged on them.

"Don't bother running, kid," said a cop. "Nor you, Mr. Fun Time."

Bean recognized Sister Carlotta's voice. "They aren't criminals," she said. "I just need to talk to them. Up in his apartment."

"You followed me?" Bean asked her.

"I knew you were searching for him," she said. "I didn't want to interfere until you found him. Just in case you think you were really smart, young man, we intercepted four street thugs and two known sex offenders who were after you."

Bean rolled his eyes. "You think I've forgotten how to deal with them?"

Sister Carlotta shrugged. "I didn't want this to be the first time you ever made a mistake in your life." She did have a sarcastic streak.

"So as I told you, there was nothing to learn from this Pablo de Noches. He's an immigrant who lives to pay for prostitutes. Just another of the worthless people who have gravitated here ever since the Netherlands became international territory."

Sister Carlotta had sat patiently, waiting for the inspector to wind down his I-told-you-so speech. But when he spoke of a man's worthlessness, she could not let the remark go unchallenged. "He took in that baby," she said. "And fed the child and cared for him."

The inspector waved off the objection. "We needed one more street urchin? Because that's all that people like this ever produce."

"You didn't learn *nothing* from him," Sister Carlotta said. "You learned the location where the boy was found."

"And the people renting the building during that time are untraceable. A company name that never existed. Nothing to go on. No way to track them down."

"But that nothing *is* something," said Sister Carlotta. "I tell you that these people had many children in this place, which they closed down in a hurry, with all the children but one taken away. You tell me that the company was a false name and can't be traced. So now, in your experience, doesn't that tell you a great deal about what was going on in that building?"

The inspector shrugged. "Of course. It was obviously an organ farm."

Tears came to Sister Carlotta's eyes. "And that is the only possibility?"

"A lot of defective babies are born to rich families," said the inspector. "There is an illegal market in infant and toddler organs. We close down the organ farms whenever we find out where they are. Perhaps we were getting close to this organ farm and they got wind of it and closed up shop. But there is no paper in the department on any organ farm that we actually found at that time. So perhaps they closed down for another reason. Still, nothing."

Patiently, Sister Carlotta ignored his inability to realize how valuable this information was. "Where do the babies come from?"

The inspector looked at her blankly. As if he thought she was asking him to explain the facts of life.

"The organ farm," she said. "Where do they get the babies?"

The inspector shrugged. "Late-term abortions, usually. Some arrangement with the clinics, a kickback. That sort of thing."

"And that's the only source?"

"Well, I don't know. Kidnappings? I don't think that could be much of a factor, there aren't *that* many babies leaking through the security systems in the hospitals. People selling babies? It's been heard of, yes. Poor refugees arrive with eight children, and then a few years later they have only six, and they cry about the ones who died but who can prove anything? But nothing you can trace."

"The reason I'm asking," said Sister Carlotta, "is that this child is unusual. *Extremely* unusual."

"Three arms?" asked the inspector.

"Brilliant. Precocious. He escaped from this place before he was a year old. Before he could walk."

The inspector thought about that for a few moments. "He *crawled* away?"

"He hid in a toilet tank."

"He got the lid up before he was a year old?"

"He said it was hard to lift."

"No, it was probably cheap plastic, not porcelain. You know how these institutional plumbing fixtures are."

"You can see, though, why I want to know about the child's parentage. Some miraculous combination of parents."

The inspector shrugged. "Some children are born smart."

"But there is a hereditary component in this, inspector. A child like this must have . . . remarkable parents. Parents likely to be prominent because of the brilliance of their own minds."

"Maybe. Maybe not," said the inspector. "I mean, some of these refugees, they might be brilliant, but they're caught up in desperate times. To save the other children, maybe they sell a baby. That's even a *smart* thing to do. It doesn't rule out refugees as the parents of this brilliant boy you have."

"I suppose that's possible," said Sister Carlotta.

"It's the most information you'll ever have. Because this Pablo de Noches, he knows nothing. He barely could tell me the name of the town he came from in Spain."

"He was drunk when he was questioned," said Sister Carlotta.

"We'll question him again when he's sober," said the inspector. "We'll let you know if we learn anything more. In the meantime, though, you'll have to make do with what I've already told you, because there isn't anything more.''

''I know all I need to know for now,'' said Sister Carlotta. ''Enough to know that this child truly is a miracle, raised up by God for some great purpose.''

''I'm not Catholic,'' said the inspector.

''God loves you all the same,'' said Sister Carlotta cheerfully.

Part Two

LAUNCHY

5

READY OR NOT

"Why are you giving me a five-year-old street urchin to tend?"

"You've seen the scores."

"Am I supposed to take those seriously?"

"Since the whole Battle School program is based on the reliability of our juvenile testing program, yes, I think you should take his scores seriously. I did a little research. No child has ever done better. Not even your star pupil."

"It's not the validity of the tests that I doubt. It's the tester."

"Sister Carlotta is a nun. You'll never find a more honest person."

"Honest people have been known to deceive themselves. To want so desperately, after all these years of searching, to find one—just one—child whose value will be worth all that work."

"And she's found him."

"Look at the *way* she found him. Her first report touts this Achilles child, and this—this Bean, this Legume—he's just an afterthought. Then Achilles is gone, not another mention of him—did he die? Wasn't she trying to get a leg operation for him?—and it's Haricot Vert who is now her candidate."

" 'Bean' is the name he calls himself. Rather as your Andrew Wiggin calls himself 'Ender.' "

"He's not *my* Andrew Wiggin."

"And Bean is not Sister Carlotta's child, either. If she were inclined to fudge the scores or administer tests unfairly, she would have pushed other students into the program long before now, and we'd already know how unreliable she was. She has never done that. She washes out her most hopeful children herself, then finds some place for them on Earth or in a non-command program. I think you're merely annoyed because you've already decided to focus all your attention and energy on the Wiggin boy, and you don't want any distraction."

"When did I lie down on your couch?"

"If my analysis is wrong, do forgive me."

"Of course I'll give this little one a chance. Even if I don't for one second believe these scores."

"Not just a chance. Advance him. Test him. Challenge him. Don't let him languish."

"You underestimate our program. We advance and test and challenge all our students."

"But some are more equal than others."

"Some take better advantage of the program than others."

"I'll look forward to telling Sister Carlotta about your enthusiasm."

Sister Carlotta shed tears when she told Bean that it was time for him to leave. Bean shed none.

"I understand that you're afraid, Bean, but don't be," she said. "You'll be safe there, and there's so much to learn. The way you drink down knowledge, you'll be very happy there in no time. So you won't really miss me at all."

Bean blinked. What sign had he given that made her think he was afraid? Or that he would miss her?

He felt none of those things. When he first met her, he might have been prepared to feel something for her. She was kind. She fed him. She was keeping him safe, giving him a life.

But then he found Pablo the janitor, and there was Sister Carlotta, stopping Bean from talking to the man who had saved him long before she did. Nor would she tell him anything that Pablo had said, or anything she had learned about the clean place.

From that moment, trust was gone. Bean knew that whatever Sister Carlotta was doing, it wasn't for him. She was using him. He didn't know what for. It might even be something he would have chosen to do himself.

But she wasn't telling him the truth. She had secrets from him. The way Achilles kept secrets.

So during the months that she was his teacher, he had grown more and more distant from her. Everything she taught, he learned—and much that she didn't teach as well. He took every test she gave him, and did well; but he showed her nothing he had learned that she hadn't taught him.

Of course life with Sister Carlotta was better than life on the street— he had no intention of going back. But he did not trust her. He was on guard all the time. He was as careful as he had ever been back in Achilles' family. Those brief days at the beginning, when he wept in front of her, when he let go of himself and spoke freely—that had been a mistake that he would not repeat. Life was better, but he wasn't safe, and this wasn't home.

Her tears were real enough, he knew. She really did love him, and would really miss him when he left. After all, he had been a perfect child, compliant, quick, obedient. To her, that meant he was "good." To him, it was only a way of keeping his access to food and learning. He wasn't stupid.

Why did she assume he was afraid? Because she was afraid *for* him. Therefore there might indeed be something to fear. He would be careful.

And why did she assume that he would miss her? Because she would miss him, and she could not imagine that what she was feeling, he might not feel as well. She had created an imaginary version of him. Like the games of Let's Pretend that she tried to play with him a couple of times. Harking back to her own childhood, no doubt, growing up in a house where there was always enough food. Bean didn't have to pretend things in order to exercise his imagination when he was on the street. Instead he had to imagine his plans for how to get food, for how to insinuate himself into a crew, for how to survive when he knew he seemed useless to everyone. He had to imagine how and when Achilles would decide to act against him for having advocated that Poke kill him. He had to imagine danger around every corner, a bully ready to seize every scrap of food. Oh, he had plenty of imagination. But he had no interest at all in playing Let's Pretend.

That was *her* game. She played it all the time. Let's pretend that Bean is a good little boy. Let's pretend that Bean is the son that this nun can never have for real. Let's pretend that when Bean leaves, he'll cry—that he's not crying now because he's too afraid of this new school, this journey into space, to let his emotions show. Let's pretend that Bean loves me.

And when he understood this, he made a decision: It will do no harm to me if she believes all this. And she wants very much to believe it. So why not give it to her? After all, Poke let me stay with the crew even though she didn't need me, because it would do no harm. It's the kind of thing Poke would do.

So Bean slid off his chair, walked around the table to Sister Carlotta, and put his arms as far around her as they would reach. She gathered him up onto her lap and held him tight, her tears flowing into his hair. He hoped her nose wasn't running. But he clung to her as long as she clung to him, letting go only when she let go of him. It was what she wanted from him, the only payment that she had ever asked of him. For all the meals, the lessons, the books, the language, for his future, he owed her no less than to join her in this game of Let's Pretend.

Then the moment passed. He slid off her lap. She dabbed at her eyes. Then she rose, took his hand, and led him out to the waiting soldiers, to the waiting car.

As he approached the car, the uniformed men loomed over him. It was not the grey uniform of the I.T. police, those kickers of children, those wielders of sticks. Rather it was the sky blue of the International Fleet that they wore, a cleaner look, and the people who gathered around to watch showed no fear, but rather admiration. This was the uniform of distant power, of safety for humanity, the uniform on which all hope depended. This was the service he was about to join.

But he was so small, and as they looked down at him he *was* afraid after all, and clung more tightly to Sister Carlotta's hand. Was he going to become one of them? Was he going to be a man in such a uniform, with such admiration directed at him? Then why was he afraid?

I'm afraid, Bean thought, because I don't see how I can ever be so tall.

One of the soldiers bent down to him, to lift him into the car. Bean glared up at him, defying him to dare such a thing. "I can do it," he said.

The soldier nodded slightly, and stood upright again. Bean hooked his leg up onto the running board of the car and hoisted himself in. It was high off the ground, and the seat he held to was slick and offered scant purchase to his hands. But he made it, and positioned himself in the middle of the back seat, the only position where he could see between the front seats and have some idea of where the car would be going.

One of the soldiers got into the driver's seat. Bean expected the other to get into the back seat beside Bean, and anticipated an argument about whether Bean could sit in the middle or not. Instead, he got into the front on the other side. Bean was alone in back.

He looked out the side window at Sister Carlotta. She was still dabbing at her eyes with a handkerchief. She gave him a little wave. He waved back. She sobbed a little. The car glided forward along the magnetic track in the road. Soon they were outside the city, gliding through the countryside at a hundred and fifty kilometers an hour. Ahead was the Amsterdam airport, one of only three in Europe that could launch one of the shuttles that could fly into orbit. Bean was through with Rotterdam. For the time being, at least, he was through with Earth.

Since Bean had never flown on an airplane, he did not understand how different the shuttle was, though that seemed to be all that the other boys could talk about at first. I thought it would be bigger. Doesn't it take off straight up? That was the old shuttle, stupid. There aren't any tray tables! That's cause in null-G you can't set anything down anyway, bonehead.

To Bean, the sky was the sky, and all he'd ever cared about was whether it was going to rain or snow or blow or burn. Going up into space did not seem any more strange to him than going up to the clouds.

What fascinated him were the other children. Boys, most of them, and all older than him. Definitely all larger. Some of them looked at him oddly, and behind him he heard one whisper, "Is he a kid or a doll?" But snide remarks about his size and his age were nothing new to him. In fact, what surprised him was that there was only the one remark, and it was whispered.

The kids themselves fascinated him. They were all so fat, so soft. Their bodies were like pillows, their cheeks full, their hair thick, their clothes well fitted. Bean knew, of course, that he had more fat on him now than at any time since he left the clean place, but he didn't see himself, he only saw them, and couldn't help comparing them to the kids on the street. Sergeant could take any of them apart. Achilles could . . . well, no use thinking about Achilles.

Bean tried to imagine them lining up outside a charity kitchen. Or scrounging for candy wrappers to lick. What a joke. They had never missed a meal in their lives. Bean wanted to punch them all so hard in the stomach that they would puke up everything they ate that day. Let them feel some pain there in their gut, that gnawing hunger. And then let them feel it again the next day, and the next hour, morning and night, waking and sleeping, the constant weakness fluttering just inside your throat, the faintness behind your eyes, the headache, the dizziness, the swelling of your joints, the distension of your belly, the thinning of your muscles until you barely have strength to stand. These children had never looked death in the face and then chosen to live anyway. They were confident. They were unwary.

These children are no match for me.

And, with just as much certainty: I will never catch up to them. They'll always be bigger, stronger, quicker, healthier. Happier. They talked to each other boastfully, spoke wistfully of home, mocked the children who had failed to qualify to come with them, pretended to have inside knowledge about how things really were in Battle School. Bean said nothing. Just listened, watched them maneuver, some of them determined to assert their place in the hierarchy, others quieter because they knew their place would be lower down; a handful relaxed, unworried, because they had never had to worry about the pecking order, having been always at the top of it. A part of Bean wanted to engage in the contest and win it, clawing his way to the top of the hill. Another part of him disdained the whole group of them. What would it mean, really, to be top dog in this mangy pack?

Then he glanced down at his small hands, and at the hands of the boy sitting next to him.

I really do look like a doll compared to the rest of them.

Some of the kids were complaining about how hungry they were. There was a strict rule against eating for twenty-four hours before the shuttle flight, and most of these kids had never gone so long without eating. For Bean, twenty-four hours without food was barely noticeable. In his crew, you didn't worry about hunger until the second week.

The shuttle took off, just like any airplane, though it had a long, long runway to get it up to speed, it was so heavy. Bean was surprised at the motion of the plane, the way it charged forward yet seemed to hold still, the way it rocked a little and sometimes bumped, as if it were rolling over irregularities in an invisible road.

When they got up to a high altitude, they rendezvoused with two fuel planes, in order to take on the rest of the rocket fuel needed to achieve escape velocity. The plane could never have lifted off the ground with that much fuel on board.

During the refueling, a man emerged from the control cabin and stood at the front of the rows of seats. His sky blue uniform was crisp and perfect, and his smile looked every bit as starched and pressed and unstainable as his clothes.

"My dear darling little children," he said. "Some of you apparently can't read yet. Your seat harnesses are to remain in place throughout the entire flight. Why are so many of them unfastened? Are you going somewhere?"

Lots of little clicks answered him like scattered applause.

"And let me also warn you that no matter how annoying or enticing some other child might be, keep your hands to yourself. You should keep in mind that the children around you scored every bit as high as you did on every test you took, and some of them scored higher.''

Bean thought: That's impossible. Somebody here had to have the highest score.

A boy across the aisle apparently had the same thought. "Right," he said sarcastically.

"I was making a point, but I'm willing to digress," said the man. "Please, share with us the thought that so enthralled you that you could not contain it silently within you."

The boy knew he had made a mistake, but decided to tough it out. "Somebody here has the highest score."

The man continued looking at him, as if inviting him to continue.

Inviting him to dig himself a deeper grave, thought Bean.

"I mean, you said that everybody scored as high as everybody else, and some scored higher, and that's just obviously not true."

The man waited some more.

"That's all I had to say."

"Feel better?" said the man.

The boy sullenly kept his silence.

Without disturbing his perfect smile, the man's tone changed, and instead of bright sarcasm, there was now a sharp whiff of menace. "I asked you a question, boy."

"No, I don't feel better."

"What's your name?" asked the man.

"Nero."

A couple of children who knew a little bit about history laughed at the name. Bean knew about the emperor Nero. He did not laugh, however. He knew that a child named Bean was wise not to laugh at other kids' names. Besides, a name like that could be a real burden to bear. It said something about the boy's strength or at least his defiance that he didn't give some nickname.

Or maybe Nero *was* his nickname.

"Just . . . Nero?" asked the man.

"Nero Boulanger."

"French? Or just hungry?"

Bean did not get the joke. Was Boulanger a name that had something to do with food?

"Algerian."

"Nero, you are an example to all the children on this shuttle. Because most of them are so foolish, they think it is better to keep their stupidest thoughts to themselves. You, however, understand the profound truth that you must reveal your stupidity openly. To hold your stupidity inside you is to embrace it, to cling to it, to protect it. But when you expose your stupidity, you give yourself the chance to have it caught, corrected, and replaced with wisdom. Be brave, all of you, like Nero Boulanger, and when you have a thought of such surpassing ignorance that you think it's actually smart, make sure to make some noise, to let your mental limitations squeak out some whimpering fart of a thought, so that you have a chance to learn.''

Nero grumbled something.

''Listen—another flatulence, but this time even less articulate than before. Tell us, Nero. Speak up. You are teaching us all by the example of your courage, however half-assed it might be.''

A couple of students laughed.

''And listen—your fart has drawn out other farts, from people equally stupid, for they think they are somehow superior to you, and that they could not just as easily have been chosen to be examples of superior intellect.''

There would be no more laughter.

Bean felt a kind of dread, for he knew that somehow, this verbal sparring, or rather this one-sided verbal assault, this torture, this public exposure, was going to find some twisted path that led to him. He did not know how he sensed this, for the uniformed man had not so much as glanced at Bean, and Bean had made no sound, had done nothing to call attention to himself. Yet he knew that he, not Nero, would end up receiving the cruelest thrust from this man's dagger.

Then Bean realized why he was sure it would turn against him. This had turned into a nasty little argument about whether someone had higher test scores than anyone else on the shuttle. And Bean had assumed, for no reason whatsoever, that he was the child with the highest scores.

Now that he had seen his own belief, he knew it was absurd. These children were all older and had grown up with far more advantages. He had had only Sister Carlotta as a teacher—Sister Carlotta and, of course, the street, though few of the things he learned *there* had shown up on the tests. There was no way that Bean had the highest score.

Yet he still knew, with absolute certainty, that this discussion was full of danger for him.

''I told you to speak up, Nero. I'm waiting.''

''I still don't see how anything I said was stupid,'' said Nero.

''First, it was stupid because I have all the authority here, and you have none, so I have the power to make your life miserable, and you have no power to protect yourself. So how much intelligence does it take just to keep your mouth shut and avoid calling attention to yourself? What could be a more obvious decision to make when confronted with such a lopsided distribution of power?''

Nero withered in his seat.

"Second, you seemed to be listening to me, not to find out useful information, but to try to catch me in a logical fallacy. This tells us all that you are used to being smarter than your teachers, and that you listen to them in order to catch them making mistakes and prove how smart you are to the other students. This is such a pointless, stupid way of listening to teachers that it is clear you are going to waste months of our time before you finally catch on that the only transaction that matters is a transfer of useful information from adults who possess it to children who do not, and that catching mistakes is a criminal misuse of time.''

Bean silently disagreed. The criminal misuse of time was *pointing out* the mistakes. Catching them—noticing them—that was essential. If you did not in your own mind distinguish between useful and erroneous information, then you were not *learning* at all, you were merely replacing ignorance with false belief, which was no improvement.

The part of the man's statement that was true, however, was about the uselessness of speaking up. If I know that the teacher is wrong, and say nothing, then I remain the only one who knows, and that gives me an advantage over those who believe the teacher.

"Third,'' said the man, "my statement only seems to be self-contradictory and impossible because you did not think beneath the surface of the situation. In fact it is not necessarily true that one person has the highest scores of everyone on this shuttle. That's because there were many tests, physical, mental, social, and psychological, and many ways to define 'highest' as well, since there are many ways to be physically or socially or psychologically fit for command. Children who tested highest on stamina may not have tested highest on strength; children who tested highest on memory may not have tested highest on anticipatory analysis. Children with remarkable social skills might be weaker in delay of gratification. Are you beginning to grasp the shallowness of your thinking that led you to your stupid and useless conclusion?''

Nero nodded.

"Let us hear the sound of your flatulence again, Nero. Be just as loud in acknowledging your errors as you were in making them.''

"I was wrong.''

There was not a boy on that shuttle who would not have avowed a preference for death to being in Nero's place at that moment. And yet Bean felt a kind of envy as well, though he did not understand why he would envy the victim of such torture.

"And yet," said the man, "you happen to be less wrong on this particular shuttle flight than you would have been in any other shuttle filled with launchies heading for Battle School. And do you know why?"

He did not choose to speak.

"Does anyone know why? Can anyone guess? I am inviting speculation."

No one accepted the invitation.

"Then let me choose a volunteer. There is a child here named— improbable as it might sound—'Bean.' Would that child please speak?"

Here it comes, thought Bean. He was filled with dread; but he was also filled with excitement, because this was what he wanted, though he did not know why. Look at me. Talk to me, you with the power, you with the authority.

"I'm here, sir," said Bean.

The man made a show of looking and looking, unable to see where Bean was. Of course it was a sham—he knew exactly where Bean was sitting before he ever spoke. "I can't see where your voice came from. Would you raise a hand?"

Bean immediately raised his hand. He realized, to his shame, that his hand did not even reach to the top of the high-backed seat.

"I still can't see you," said the man, though of course he could. "I give you permission to unstrap and stand on your seat."

Bean immediately complied, peeling off the harness and bounding to his feet. He was barely taller than the back of the seat in front of him.

"Ah, there you are," said the man. "Bean, would you be so kind as to speculate about why, in this shuttle, Nero comes closer to being correct than on any other?"

"Maybe somebody here scored highest on a lot of tests."

"Not just a lot of tests, Bean. All the tests of intellect. All the psychological tests. All the tests pertinent to command. Every one of them. Higher than anyone else on this shuttle."

"So I *was* right," said the newly defiant Nero.

"No you were not," said the man. "Because that remarkable child, the one who scored highest on all the tests related to command, happens to have scored the very lowest on the physical tests. And do you know why?"

No one answered.

"Bean, as long as you're standing, can you speculate about why this one child might have scored lowest on the physical tests?"

Bean knew how he had been set up. And he refused to try to hide from the obvious answer. He would say it, even though the question was designed to make the others detest him for answering it. After all, they would detest him anyway, no matter who said the answer.

"Maybe he scored lowest on the physical tests because he's very, very small."

Groans from many boys showed their disgust at his answer. At the arrogance and vanity that it suggested. But the man in uniform only nodded gravely.

"As should be expected from a boy of such remarkable ability, you are exactly correct. Only this boy's unusually small stature prevented Nero from being correct about there being one child with higher scores than everybody else." He turned to Nero. "So close to not being a complete fool," he said. "And yet . . . even if you had been right, it would only have been by accident. A broken clock is right two times a day. Sit down now, Bean, and put on your harness. The refueling is over and we're about to boost."

Bean sat down. He could feel the hostility of the other children. There was nothing he could do about that right now, and he wasn't sure that it was a disadvantage, anyway. What mattered was the much more puzzling question: Why did the man set him up like that? If the point was to get the kids competing with each other, they could have passed around a list with everyone's scores on all the tests, so they all could see where they stood. Instead, Bean had been singled out. He was already the smallest, and knew from experience that he was therefore a target for every mean-spirited impulse in a bully's heart. So why did they draw this big circle around him and all these arrows pointing at him, practically demanding that he be the main target of everyone's fear and hate?

Draw your targets, aim your darts. I'm going to do well enough in this school that someday I'll be the one with the authority, and then it won't matter who likes *me*. What will matter is who *I* like.

"As you may remember," said the man, "before the first fart from the mouthhole of Nero Bakerboy here, I was starting to make a point. I was telling you that even though some child here may seem like a prime target for your pathetic need to assert supremacy in a situation where you are unsure of being recognized for the hero that you want people to think you are, you must control yourself, and refrain from poking or pinching, jabbing or hitting, or even making snidely provocative remarks or sniggering like warthogs just because you think somebody is an easy target. And the reason why you should refrain from doing this is because you don't know who in this group is going to end up being *your* commander in the future, the admiral when you're a mere captain. And if you think for one moment that they will forget how you treated them now, today, then you really are a fool. If they're good commanders, they'll use you effectively in combat no matter how they despise you. But they don't have to be helpful to you in advancing your career. They don't have to nurture you and bring you along. They don't have to be kind and forgiving. Just think about that. The people you see around you will someday be giving you orders that will decide whether you live or die. I'd suggest you work on earning their respect, not trying to put them down so you can show off like some schoolyard punk.''

The man turned his icy smile on Bean one more time.

''And I'll bet that Bean, here, is already planning to be the admiral who gives you all orders someday. He's even planning how he'll order *me* to stand solitary watch on some asteroid observatory till my bones melt from osteoporosis and I ooze around the station like an amoeba.''

Bean hadn't given a moment's thought to some future contest between him and this particular officer. He had no desire for vengeance. He wasn't Achilles. Achilles was stupid. And this officer was stupid for thinking that Bean would think that way. No doubt, however, the man thought Bean would be grateful because he had just warned the others not to pick on him. But Bean had been picked on by tougher bastards than these could possibly be; this officer's ''protection'' was not needed, and it made the gulf between Bean and the other children wider than before. If Bean could have lost a couple of tussles, he would have been humanized, accepted perhaps. But now there would be no tussles. No easy way to build bridges.

That was the reason for the annoyance that the man apparently saw on Bean's face. ''I've got a word for you, Bean. I don't care what you do to me. Because there's only one enemy that matters. The Buggers. And if you can grow up to be the admiral who can give us victory over the Buggers and keep Earth safe for humanity, then make me eat my own guts, ass-first, and I'll still say, Thank you, sir. The Buggers are the enemy. Not Nero. Not Bean. Not even me. So keep your hands off each other.''

He grinned again, mirthlessly.

''Besides, the last time somebody tried picking on another kid, he ended up flying through the shuttle in null-G and got his arm broken. It's one of the laws of strategy. Until you know that you're tougher than the enemy, you maneuver, you don't commit to battle. Consider that your first lesson in Battle School.''

First lesson? No wonder they used this guy to tend children on the shuttle flights instead of having him teach. If you followed *that* little piece of wisdom, you'd be paralyzed against a vigorous enemy. Sometimes you *have* to commit to a fight even when you're weak. You don't *wait* till you *know* you're tougher. You *make* yourself tougher by whatever means you can, and then you strike by surprise, you sneak up, you backstab, you blindside, you cheat, you lie, you do whatever it takes to make sure that you come out on top.

This guy might be real tough as the only adult on a shuttle full of kids, but if he were a kid on the streets of Rotterdam, he'd ''maneuver'' himself into starvation in a month. If he wasn't killed before that just for talking like he thought his piss was perfume.

The man turned to head back to the control cabin.

Bean called out to him.

''What's your name?''

The man turned and fixed him with a withering stare. ''Already drafting the orders to have my balls ground to powder, Bean?''

Bean didn't answer. Just looked him in the eye.

''I'm Captain Dimak. Anything else you want to know?''

Might as well find out now as later. ''Do you teach at Battle School?''

''Yes,'' he said. ''Coming down to pick up shuttle-loads of little boys and girls is how we get Earthside leave. Just as with you, my being on this shuttle means my vacation is over.''

The refueling planes peeled away and rose above them. No, it was their own craft that was sinking. And the tail was sinking lower than the nose of the shuttle.

Metal covers came down over the windows. It felt like they were falling faster, faster . . . until, with a bone-shaking roar, the rockets fired and the shuttle began to rise again, higher, faster, faster, until Bean felt like he was going to be pushed right through the back of his chair. It seemed to go on forever, unchanging.

Then . . . silence.

Silence, and then a wave of panic. They were falling again, but this time there was no downward direction, just nausea and fear.

Bean closed his eyes. It didn't help. He opened them again, tried to reorient himself. No direction provided equilibrium. But he had schooled himself on the street not to succumb to nausea—a lot of the food he had to eat had already gone a little bad, and he couldn't afford to throw it up. So he went into his anti-nausea routine—deep breaths, distracting himself by concentrating on wiggling his toes. And, after a surprisingly short time, he was used to the null-G. As long as he didn't expect any direction to be down, he was fine.

The other kids didn't have his routine, or perhaps they were more susceptible to the sudden, relentless loss of balance. Now the reason for the prohibition against eating before the launch became clear. There was plenty of retching going on, but with nothing to throw up, there was no mess, no smell.

Dimak came back into the shuttle cabin, this time standing on the ceiling. Very cute, thought Bean. Another lecture began, this time about how to get rid of planetside assumptions about directions and gravity. Could these kids possibly be so stupid they needed to be told such obvious stuff?

Bean occupied the time of the lecture by seeing how much pressure it took to move himself around within his loosely-fitting harness. Everybody else was big enough that the harnesses fit snugly and prevented movement. Bean alone had room for a little maneuvering. He made the most of it. By the time they arrived at Battle School, he was determined to have at least a little skill at movement in null-G. He figured that in space, his survival might someday depend on knowing just how much force it would take to move his body, and then how much force it would take to stop. Knowing it in his mind wasn't half so important as knowing it with his body. Analyzing things was fine, but good reflexes could save your life.

6

ENDER'S SHADOW

"Normally your reports on a launch group are brief. A few troublemakers, an incident report, or—best of all—nothing."

"You're free to disregard any portion of my report, sir."

"Sir? My, but aren't we the prickly martinet today."

"What part of my report did you think was excessive?"

"I think this report is a love song."

"I realize that it might seem like sucking up, to use with every launch the technique you used with Ender Wiggin—"

"You use it with *every* launch?"

"As you noticed yourself, sir, it has interesting results. It causes an immediate sorting out."

"A sorting out into categories that might not otherwise exist. Nevertheless, I accept the compliment implied by your action. But seven pages about Bean—really, did you actually learn that much from a response that was primarily silent compliance?"

"That is just my point, sir. It was not compliance at all. It was—I was performing the experiment, but it felt as though his were the big eye looking down the microscope, and I were the specimen on the slide."

"So he unnerved you."

"He would unnerve anyone. He's cold, sir. And yet—"

"And yet hot. Yes, I read your report. Every scintillating page of it."

"Yes sir."

"I think you know that it is considered good advice for us *not* to get crushes on our students."

"Sir?"

"In this case, however, I am delighted that you are so interested in Bean. Because, you see, I am not. I already have the boy I think gives us our best chance. Yet there is considerable pressure, because of Bean's damnable faked-up test scores, to give him special attention. Very well, he shall have it. And you shall give it to him."

"But sir . . ."

"Perhaps you are unable to distinguish an order from an invitation."

"I'm only concerned that . . . I think he already has a low opinion of me."

"Good. Then he'll underestimate you. Unless you think his low opinion might be correct."

"Compared to him, sir, we might all be a little dim."

"Close attention is your assignment. Try not to worship him."

All that Bean had on his mind was survival, that first day in Battle School. No one would help him—that had been made clear by Dimak's little charade in the shuttle. They were setting him up to be surrounded by . . . what? Rivals at best, enemies at worst. So it was the street again. Well, that was fine. Bean had survived on the street. And would have kept on surviving, even if Sister Carlotta hadn't found him. Even Pablo—Bean might have made it even without Pablo the janitor finding him in the toilet of the clean place.

So he watched. He listened. Everything the others learned, he had to learn just as well, maybe better. And on top of that, he had to learn what the others were oblivious to—the workings of the group, the systems of the Battle School. How teachers got on with each other. Where the power was. Who was afraid of whom. Every group had its bosses, its suckups, its rebels, its sheep. Every group had its strong bonds and its weak ones, friendships and hypocrisies. Lies within lies within lies. And Bean had to find them all, as quickly as possible, in order to learn the spaces in which he could survive.

They were taken to their barracks, given beds, lockers, little portable desks that were much more sophisticated than the one he had used when studying with Sister Carlotta. Some of the kids immediately began to play with them, trying to program them or exploring the games built into them, but Bean had no interest in that. The computer system of Battle School was not a person; mastering it might be helpful in the long run, but for today it was irrelevant. What Bean needed to find out was all outside the launchy barracks.

Which is where, soon enough, they went. They arrived in the "morning" according to space time—which, to the annoyance of many in Europe and Asia, meant Florida time, since the earliest stations had been controlled from there. For the kids, having launched from Europe, it was late afternoon, and that meant they would have a serious time-lag problem. Dimak explained that the cure for this was to get vigorous physical exercise and then take a short nap—no more than three hours—in the early afternoon, following which they would again have plenty of physical exercise so they could fall asleep that night at the regular bedtime for students.

They piled out to form a line in the corridor. "Green Brown Green," said Dimak, and showed them how those lines on the corridor walls would always lead them back to their barracks. Bean found himself jostled out of line several times, and ended up right at the back. He didn't care—mere jostling drew no blood and left no bruise, and last in line was the best place from which to observe.

Other kids passed them in the corridor, sometimes individuals, sometimes pairs or trios, most with brightly-colored uniforms in many different designs. Once they passed an entire group dressed alike and wearing helmets and carrying extravagant sidearms, jogging along with an intensity of purpose that Bean found intriguing. They're a crew, he thought. And they're heading off for a fight.

They weren't too intense to notice the new kids walking along the corridor, looking up at them in awe. Immediately there were catcalls. "Launchies!" "Fresh meat!" "Who make cocó in the hall and don't clean it up!" "They even smell stupid!" But it was all harmless banter, older kids asserting their supremacy. It meant nothing more than that. No real hostility. In fact it was almost affectionate. They remembered being launchies themselves.

Some of the launchies ahead of Bean in line were resentful and called back some vague, pathetic insults, which only caused more hooting and derision from the older kids. Bean had seen older, bigger kids who hated younger ones because they were competition for food, and drove them away, not caring if they caused the little ones to die. He had felt real blows, meant to hurt. He had seen cruelty, exploitation, molestation, murder. These other kids didn't know love when they saw it.

What Bean wanted to know was how that crew was organized, who led it, how he was chosen, what the crew was *for*. The fact that they had their own uniform meant that it had official status. So that meant that the adults were ultimately in control—the opposite of the way crews were organized in Rotterdam, where adults tried to break them up, where newspapers wrote about them as criminal conspiracies instead of pathetic little leagues for survival.

That, really, was the key. Everything the children did here was shaped by adults. In Rotterdam, the adults were either hostile, unconcerned, or, like Helga with her charity kitchen, ultimately powerless. So the children could shape their own society without interference. Everything was based on survival—on getting enough food without getting killed or injured or sick. Here, there were cooks and doctors, clothing and beds. Power wasn't about access to food—it was about getting the approval of adults.

That's what those uniforms meant. Adults chose them, and children wore them because adults somehow made it worth their while.

So the key to everything was understanding the teachers.

All this passed through Bean's mind, not so much verbally as with a clear and almost instantaneous understanding that within that crew there was no power at all, compared to the power of the teachers, before the uniformed catcallers reached him. When they saw Bean, so much smaller than any of the other kids, they broke out laughing, hooting, howling. "That one isn't big enough to be a turd!" "I can't believe he can *walk!*" "Did'ums wose um's mama?" "Is it even *human?*"

Bean tuned them out immediately. But he could feel the enjoyment of the kids ahead of him in line. They had been humiliated in the shuttle; now it was Bean's turn to be mocked. They loved it. And so did Bean—because it meant that he was seen as less of a rival. By diminishing him, the passing soldiers had made him just that much safer from . . .

From what? What was the *danger* here?

For there would be danger. That he knew. There was always danger. And since the teachers had all the power, the danger would come from them. But Dimak had started things out by turning the other kids against him. So the children themselves were the weapons of choice. Bean had to get to know the other kids, not because they themselves were going to be his problem, but because their weaknesses, their desires could be used against him by the teachers. And, to protect himself, Bean would have to work to undercut their hold on the other children. The only safety here was to subvert the teachers' influence. And yet that was the greatest danger—if he was caught doing it.

They palmed in on a wall-mounted pad, then slid down a pole—the first time Bean had ever done it with a smooth shaft. In Rotterdam, all his sliding had been on rainspouts, signposts, and lightpoles. They ended up in a section of Battle School with higher gravity. Bean did not realize how light they must have been on the barracks level until he felt how heavy he was down in the gym.

"This is just a little heavier than Earth normal gravity," said Dimak. "You have to spend at least a half-hour a day here, or your bones start to dissolve. And you have to spend the time exercising, so you keep at peak endurance. And that's the key—endurance exercise, not bulking up. You're too small for your bodies to endure that kind of training, and it fights you here. Stamina, that's what we want."

The words meant almost nothing to the kids, but soon the trainer had made it clear. Lots of running on treadmills, riding on cycles, stair-stepping, pushups, situps, chinups, backups, but no weights. Some weight equipment was there, but it was all for the use of teachers. "Your heartrate is monitored from the moment you enter here," said the trainer. "If you don't have your heartrate elevated within five minutes of arrival and you don't keep it elevated for the next twenty-five minutes, it goes on your record *and* I see it on my control board here."

"I get a report on it too," said Dimak. "And you go on the pig list for everyone to see you've been lazy."

Pig list. So that's the tool they used—shaming them in front of the others. Stupid. As if Bean cared.

It was the monitoring board that Bean was interested in. How could they possibly monitor their heartrates and know what they were doing, automatically, from the moment they arrived? He almost asked the question, until he realized the only possible answer: The uniform. It was in the clothing. Some system of sensors. It probably told them a lot more than heartrate. For one thing, they could certainly track every kid wherever he was in the station, all the time. There must be hundreds and hundreds of kids here, and there would be computers reporting the whereabouts, the heartrates, and who could guess what other information about them. Was there a room somewhere with teachers watching every step they took?

Or maybe it wasn't the clothes. After all, they had to palm in before coming down here, presumably to identify themselves. So maybe there were special sensors in this room.

Time to find out. Bean raised his hand. "Sir," he said.

"Yes?" The trainer did a doubletake on seeing Bean's size, and a smile played around the corners of his mouth. He glanced at Dimak. Dimak did not crack a smile or show any understanding of what the trainer was thinking.

"Is the heartrate monitor in our clothing? If we take off any part of our clothes while we're exercising, does it—"

"You are not authorized to be out of uniform in the gym," said the trainer. "The room is kept cold on purpose so that you will not need to remove clothing. You will be monitored at all times."

Not really an answer, but it told him what he needed to know. The monitoring depended on the clothes. Maybe there was an identifier in the clothing and by palming in, they told the gym sensors which kid was wearing which set of clothing. That would make sense.

So clothing was probably anonymous from the time you put on a clean set until you palmed in somewhere. That was important—it meant that it might be possible to be untagged without being naked. Naked, Bean figured, would probably be conspicuous around here.

They all exercised and the trainer told them which of them were not up to the right heartrate and which of them were pushing too hard and would fatigue themselves too soon. Bean quickly got an idea of the level he had to work at, and then forgot about it. He'd remember by reflex, now that he knew.

It was mealtime, then. They were alone in the mess hall—as fresh arrivals, they were on a separate schedule that day. The food was good and there was a lot of it. Bean was stunned when some of the kids looked at their portion and complained about how little there was. It was a feast! Bean couldn't finish it. The whiners were informed by the cooks that the quantities were all adapted to their individual dietary needs—each kid's portion size came up on a computer display when he palmed in upon entering the mess hall.

So you don't eat without your palm on a pad. Important to know.

Bean soon found out that his size was going to get official attention. When he brought his half-finished tray to the disposal unit, an electronic chiming sound brought the on-duty nutritionist to speak to him. "It's your first day, so we aren't going to be rigid about it. But your portions are scientifically calibrated to meet your dietary needs, and in the future you will finish every bit of what you are served."

Bean looked at him without a word. He had already made his decision. If his exercise program made him hungrier, then he'd eat more. But if they were expecting him to gorge himself, they could forget it. It would be a simple enough matter to dump excess food onto the trays of the whiners.

They'd be happy with it, and Bean would eat only as much as his body wanted. He remembered hunger very well, but he had lived with Sister Carlotta for many months, and he knew to trust his own appetite. For a while he had let her goad him into eating more than he actually was hungry for. The result had been a sense of loginess, a harder time sleeping and a harder time staying awake. He went back to eating only as much as his body wanted, letting his hunger be his guide, and it kept him sharp and quick. That was the only nutritionist he trusted. Let the whiners get sluggish.

Dimak stood after several of them had finished eating. "When you're through, go back to the barracks. If you think you can find it. If you have any doubt, wait for me and I'll bring the last group back myself."

The corridors were empty when Bean went out into the corridor. The other kids palmed the wall and their green-brown-green strip turned on. Bean watched them go. One of them turned back. "Aren't you coming?" Bean said nothing. There was nothing to say. He was obviously standing still. It was a stupid question. The kid turned around and jogged on down the corridor toward the barracks.

Bean went the other way. No stripes on the wall. He knew that there was no better time to explore than now. If he was caught out of the area he was supposed to be in, they'd believe him if he claimed to have got lost.

The corridor sloped up both behind him and in front of him. To his eyes it looked like he was always going uphill, and when he looked back, it was uphill to go back the way he had come. Strange. But Dimak had already explained that the station was a huge wheel, spinning in space so that centrifugal force would replace gravity. That meant the main corridor on each level was a big circle, so you'd always come back to where you started, and "down" was always toward the outside of the circle. Bean made the mental adjustment. It was dizzying at first, to picture himself on his side as he walked along, but then he mentally changed the orientation so that he imagined the station as a wheel on a cart, with him at the bottom of it no matter how much it turned. That put the people above him upside down, but he didn't care. Wherever he was was the bottom, and that way down stayed down and up stayed up.

The launchies were on the mess hall level, but the older kids must not be, because after the mess halls and the kitchens, there were only classrooms and unmarked doors with palmpads high enough that they were clearly not meant for children to enter. Other kids could probably reach those pads, but not even by jumping could Bean hope to palm one. It didn't matter. They wouldn't respond to any child's handprint, except to bring some adult to find out what the kid thought he was doing, trying to enter a room where he had no business.

By long habit—or was it instinct?—Bean regarded such barriers as only temporary blocks. He knew how to climb over walls in Rotterdam, how to get up on roofs. Short as he was, he still found ways to get wherever he needed to go. Those doors would not stop him if he decided he needed to get beyond them. He had no idea right now how he'd do it, but he had no doubt that he would find a way. So he wasn't annoyed. He simply tucked the information away, waiting until he thought of some way to use it.

Every few meters there was a pole for downward passage or a ladder-way for going up. To get down the pole to the gym, he had had to palm a pad. But there seemed to be no pad on most of these. Which made sense. Most poles and ladderways would merely let you pass between floors—no, they called them decks; this was the International Fleet and so everything pretended to be a ship—while only one pole led down to the gym, to which they needed to control access so that it didn't get overcrowded with people coming when they weren't scheduled. As soon as he had made sense of it, Bean didn't have to think of it anymore. He scrambled up a ladder.

The next floor up had to be the barracks level for the older kids. Doors were more widely spaced, and each door had an insignia on it. Using the colors of some uniform—no doubt based on their stripe colors, though he doubted the older kids ever had to palm the wall to find their way around—there was also the silhouette of an animal. Some of them he didn't recognize, but he recognized a couple of birds, some cats, a dog, a lion. Whatever was in use symbolically on signs in Rotterdam. No pigeon. No fly. Only noble animals, or animals noted for courage. The dog silhouette looked like some kind of hunting animal, very thin around the hips. Not a mongrel.

So this is where the crews meet, and they have animal symbols, which means they probably call themselves by animal names. Cat Crew. Or maybe Lion Crew. And probably not Crew. Bean would soon learn what they called themselves. He closed his eyes and tried to remember the colors and insignia on the crew that passed and mocked him in the corridor earlier. He could see the shape in his mind, but didn't see it on any of the doors he passed. It didn't matter—not worth traveling the whole corridor in search of it, when that would only increase his risk of getting caught.

Up again. More barracks, more classrooms. How many kids in a barracks? This place was bigger than he thought.

A soft chime sounded. Immediately, several doors opened and kids began to pour out into the corridor. A changeover time.

At first Bean felt more secure among the big kids, because he thought he could get lost in the crowd, the way he always did in Rotterdam. But that habit was useless here. This wasn't a random crowd of people on their own errands. These might be kids but they were military. They knew where everybody was supposed to be, and Bean, in his launchy uniform, was way out of place. Almost at once a couple of older kids stopped him.

"You don't belong on this deck," said one. At once several others stopped to look at Bean as if he were an object washed into the street by a storm.

"Look at the size of this one."

"Poor kid gots to sniff everybody's butt, neh?"

"Eh!"

"You're out of area, launchy."

Bean said nothing, just looked at each one as he spoke. Or she.

"What are your colors?" asked a girl.

Bean said nothing. Best excuse would be that he didn't remember, so he couldn't very well name them now.

"He's so small he could walk between my legs without touching my—"

"Oh, shut up, Dink, that's what you said when Ender—"

"Yeah, Ender, right."

"You don't think this is the kid they—"

"Was Ender *this* small when he arrived?"

"—been saying, he another Ender?"

"Right, like this one's going to shoot to the top of the standings."

"It wasn't Ender's fault that Bonzo wouldn't let him fire his weapon."

"But it's a fluke, that's all I'm saying—"

"This the one they talking about? One like Ender? Top scores?"

"Just get him down to the launchy level."

"Come with me," said the girl, taking him firmly by the hand.

Bean came along meekly.

"My name is Petra Arkanian," she said.

Bean said nothing.

"Come on, you may be little and you may be scared, but they don't let you in here if you're deaf or stupid."

Bean shrugged.

"Tell me your name before I break your stubby little fingers."

"Bean," he said.

"That's not a name, that's a lousy meal."

He said nothing.

"You don't fool me," she said. "This mute thing, it's just a cover. You came up here on purpose."

He kept his silence but it stabbed at him, that she had figured him out so easily.

"Kids for this school, they're chosen because they're smart and they've got initiative. So of course you wanted to explore. The thing is, they expect it. They probably know you're doing it. So there's no point in hiding it. What are they going to do, give you some big bad piggy points?"

So that's what the older kids thought about the pig list.

"This stubborn silence thing, it'll just piss people off. I'd forget about it if I were you. Maybe it worked with Mommy and Daddy, but it just makes you look stubborn and ridiculous because anything that matters, you're going to tell anyway, so why not just talk?"

"OK," said Bean.

Now that he was complying, she didn't crow about it. The lecture worked, so the lecture was over. "Colors?" she asked.

"Green brown green."

"Those launchy colors sound like something you'd find in a dirty toilet, don't you think?"

So she was just another one of the stupid kids who thought it was cute to make fun of launchies.

"It's like they designed everything to get the older kids to make fun of the younger ones."

Or maybe she wasn't. Maybe she was just talking. She was a talker. There weren't a lot of talkers on the streets. Not among the kids, anyway. Plenty of them among the drunks.

"The system around here is screwed. It's like they want us to act like little kids. Not that that's going to bother *you*. Hell, you're already doing some dumb lost-little-kid act."

"Not now," he said.

"Just remember this. No matter what you do, the teachers know about it and they already have some stupid theory about what this means about your personality or whatever. They *always* find a way to use it against you, if they want to, so you might as well not try. No doubt it's already in your report that you took this little jaunt when you were supposed to be having beddy-bye time and that probably tells them that you 'respond to insecurity by seeking to be alone while exploring the limits of your new environment.' " She used a fancy voice for the last part.

And maybe she had more voices to show off to him, but he wasn't going to stick around to find out. Apparently she was a take-charge person and didn't have anybody to take charge of until he came along. He wasn't interested in becoming her project. It was all right being Sister Carlotta's project because she could get him out of the street and into Battle School. But what did this Petra Arkanian have to offer him?

He slid down a pole, stopped in front of the first opening, pushed out into the corridor, ran to the next ladderway, and scooted up two decks before emerging into another corridor and running full out. She was probably right in what she said, but one thing was certain—he was not going to have her hold his hand all the way back to green-brown-green. The last thing he needed, if he was going to hold his own in this place, was to show up with some older kid holding his hand.

Bean was four decks above the mess level where he was supposed to be right now. There were kids moving through here, but nowhere near as many as the deck below. Most of the doors were unmarked, but a few stood open, including one wide arch that opened into a game room.

Bean had seen computer games in some of the bars in Rotterdam, but only from a distance, through the doors and between the legs of men and women going in and out in their endless search for oblivion. He had never seen a child playing a computer game, except on the vids in store windows. Here it was real, with only a few players catching quick games between classes so that each game's sounds stood out. A few kids playing solo games, and then four of them playing a four-sided space game with a holographic display. Bean stood back far enough not to intrude in their sightlines and watched them play. Each of them controlled a squadron of four tiny ships, with the goal of either wiping out all the other fleets or capturing—but not destroying—each player's slow-moving mothership. He learned the rules and the terminology by listening to the four boys chatter as they played.

The game ended by attrition, not by any cleverness—the last boy simply happened to be the least stupid in his use of his ships. Bean watched as they reset the game. No one put in a coin. The games here were free.

Bean watched another game. It was just as quick as the first, as each boy committed his ships clumsily, forgetting about whichever one was not actively engaged. It was as if they thought of their force as one active ship and three reserves.

Maybe the controls didn't allow anything different. Bean moved closer. No, it was possible to set the course for one, flip to control another ship, and another, then return to the first ship to change its course at any time.

How did these boys get into Battle School if this was all they could think of? Bean had never played a computer game before, but he saw at once that any competent player could quickly win if this was the best competition available.

"Hey, dwarf, want to play?"

One of them had noticed him. Of course the others did, too.

"Yes," said Bean.

"Well Bugger that," said the one who invited him. "Who do you think you are, Ender Wiggin?"

They laughed and then all four of them walked away from the game, heading for their next class. The room was empty. Class time.

Ender Wiggin. The kids in the corridor talked about him, too. Something about Bean made these kids think of Ender Wiggin. Sometimes with admiration, sometimes with resentment. This Ender must have beaten some older kids at a computer game or something. And he was at the top of the standings, that's what somebody said. Standings in what?

The kids in the same uniform, running like one crew, heading for a fight—that was the central fact of life here. There was one core game that everyone played. They lived in barracks according to what team they were on. Every kid's standings were reported so everybody else knew them. And whatever the game was, the adults ran it.

So this was the shape of life here. And this Ender Wiggin, whoever he was, he was at the top of it all, he led the standings.

Bean reminded people of him.

That made him a little proud, yes, but it also annoyed him. It was safer not to be noticed. But because this other small kid had done brilliantly, everybody who saw Bean thought of Ender and that made Bean memorable. That would limit his freedom considerably. There was no way to disappear here, as he had been able to disappear in crowds in Rotterdam.

Well, who cared? He couldn't be hurt now, not really. No matter what happened, as long as he was here at Battle School he would never be hungry. He'd always have shelter. He had made it to heaven. All he had to do was the minimum required to not get sent home early. So who cared if people noticed him or not? It made no difference. Let them worry about their standings. Bean had already won the battle for survival, and after that, no other competition mattered.

But even as he had that thought, he knew it wasn't true. Because he did care. It wasn't enough just to survive. It never had been. Deeper than his need for food had been his hunger for order, for finding out how things worked, getting a grasp on the world around him. When he was starving, of course he used what he learned in order to get himself into Poke's crew and get her crew enough food that there would be enough to trickle some down to him at the bottom of the pecking order. But even when Achilles had turned them into his family and they had something to eat every day, Bean hadn't stopped being alert, trying to understand the changes, the dynamics in the group. Even with Sister Carlotta, he had spent a lot of effort trying to understand why and how she had the power to do for him what she was doing, and the basis on which she had chosen him. He had to know. He had to have the picture of everything in his mind.

Here, too. He could have gone back to the barracks and napped. Instead, he risked getting in trouble just to find out things that no doubt he would have learned in the ordinary course of events.

Why did I come up here? What was I looking for?

The key. The world was full of locked doors, and he had to get his hands on every key.

He stood still and listened. The room was nearly silent. But there was white noise, background rumble and hiss that made it so sounds didn't carry throughout the entire station.

With his eyes closed, he located the source of the faint rushing sound. Eyes open, he then walked to where the vent was. An out-flowing vent with slightly warmer air making a very slight breeze. The rushing sound was not the hiss of air here at the vent, but rather a much louder, more distant sound of the machinery that pumped air throughout the Battle School.

Sister Carlotta had told him that in space, there was no air, so wherever people lived, they had to keep their ships and stations closed tight, holding in every bit of air. And they also had to keep changing the air, because the oxygen, she said, got used up and had to be replenished. That's what this air system was about. It must go everywhere through the ship.

Bean sat before the vent screen, feeling around the edges. There were no visible screws or nails holding it on. He got his fingernails under the rim and carefully slid his fingers around it, prying it out a little, then a little more. His fingers now fit under the edges. He pulled straight forward. The vent came free, and Bean toppled over backward.

Only for a moment. He set aside the screen and tried to see into the vent. The vent duct was only about fifteen centimeters deep from front to back. The top was solid, but the bottom was open, leading down into the duct system.

Bean sized up the vent opening just the way he had, years before, stood on the seat of a toilet and studied the inside of the toilet tank, deciding whether he could fit in it. And the conclusion was the same—it would be cramped, it would be painful, but he could do it.

He reached an arm inside and down. He couldn't feel the bottom. But with arms as short as his, that didn't mean much. There was no way to tell by looking which way the duct went when it got down to the floor level. Bean could imagine a duct leading under the floor, but that felt wrong to him. Sister Carlotta had said that every scrap of material used to build the station had to be hauled up from Earth or the manufacturing plants on the moon. They wouldn't have big gaps between the decks and the ceilings below because that would be wasted space into which precious air would have to be pumped without anyone breathing it. No, the ductwork would be in the outside walls. It was probably no more than fifteen centimeters deep anywhere.

He closed his eyes and imagined an air system. Machinery making a warm wind blow through the narrow ducts, flowing into every room, carrying fresh breathable air everywhere.

No, that wouldn't work. There had to be a place where the air was getting sucked in and drawn back. And if the air blew in at the outside walls, then the intake would be . . . in the corridors.

Bean got up and ran to the door of the game room. Sure enough, the corridor's ceiling was at least twenty centimeters lower than the ceiling inside the room. But no vents. Just light fixtures.

He stepped back into the room and looked up. All along the top of the wall that bordered on the corridor there was a narrow vent that looked more decorative than practical. The opening was about three centimeters. Not even Bean could fit through the intake system.

He ran back to the open vent and took off his shoes. No reason to get hung up because his feet were so much bigger than they needed to be.

He faced the vent and swung his feet down into the opening. Then he wriggled until his legs were entirely down the hole and his buttocks rested on the rim of the vent. His feet still hadn't found bottom. Not a good sign. What if the vent dropped straight down into the machinery?

He wriggled back out, then went in the other way. It was harder and more painful, but now his arms were more usable, giving him a good grip on the floor as he slid chest-deep into the hole.

His feet touched bottom.

Using his toes, he probed. Yes, the ductwork ran to the left and the right, along the outside wall of the room. And the opening was tall enough that he could slide down into it, then wriggle—always on his side—along from room to room.

That was all he needed to know at present. He gave a little jump so his arms reached farther out onto the floor, meaning to use friction to let him pull himself up. Instead, he just slid back down into the vent.

Oh, this was excellent. Someone would come looking for him, eventually, or he'd be found by the next batch of kids who came in to play games, but he did not want to be found like this. More to the point, the ductwork would only give him an alternate route through the station if he could climb out of the vents. He had a mental image of somebody opening a vent and seeing his skull looking out at them, his dead body completely dried up in the warm wind of the air ducts where he starved to death or died of thirst trying to get out of the vents.

As long as he was just standing there, though, he might as well find out if he could cover the vent opening from the inside.

He reached over and, with difficulty, got a finger on the screen and was able to pull it toward him. Once he got a hand solidly on it, it wasn't hard at all to get it over the opening. He could even pull it in, tightly enough that it probably wouldn't be noticeably different to casual observers on the other side. With the vent closed, though, he had to keep his head turned to one side. There wasn't room enough for him to turn it. So once he got in the duct system, his head would either stay turned to the left or to the right. Great.

He pushed the vent back out, but carefully, so that it didn't fall to the floor. Now it was time to climb out in earnest.

After a couple more failures, he finally realized that the screen was exactly the tool he needed. Laying it down on the floor in front of the vent, he hooked his fingers under the far end. Pulling back on the screen provided him with the leverage to lift his body far enough to get his chest over the rim of the vent opening. It hurt, to hang the weight of his body on such a sharp edge, but now he could get up on his elbows and then on his hands, lifting his whole body up through the opening and back into the room.

He thought carefully through the sequence of muscles he had used and then thought about the equipment in the gym. Yes, he could strengthen those muscles.

He put the vent screen back into place. Then he pulled up his shirt and looked at the red marks on his skin where the rim of the vent opening had scraped him mercilessly. There was some blood. Interesting. How would he explain it, if anyone asked? He'd have to see if he could reinjure the same spot by climbing around on the bunks later.

He jogged out of the game room and down the corridor to the nearest pole, then dropped to the mess hall level. All the way, he wondered why he had felt such urgency about getting into the ducts. Whenever he got like that in the past, doing some task without knowing why it even mattered, it had turned out that there was a danger that he had sensed but that hadn't yet risen to his conscious mind. What was the danger here?

Then he realized—in Rotterdam, out on the street, he had always made sure he knew a back way out of everything, an alternate path to get from one place to another. If he was running from someone, he never dodged into a cul-de-sac to hide unless he knew another way out. In truth, he never really *hid* at all—he evaded pursuit by keeping on the move, always. No matter how awful the danger following him might be, he could not hold still. It felt terrible to be cornered. It hurt.

It hurt and was wet and cold and he was hungry and there wasn't enough air to breathe and people walked by and if they just lifted the lid they would find him and he had no way to run if they did that, he just had to sit there waiting for them to pass without noticing him. If they used the toilet and flushed it, the equipment wouldn't work right because the whole weight of his body was pressing down on the float. A lot of the water had spilled out of the tank when he climbed in. They'd notice something was wrong and they'd find him.

It was the worst experience of his life, and he couldn't stand the idea of ever hiding like that again. It wasn't the small space that bothered him, or that it was wet, or that he was hungry or alone. It was the fact that the only way out was into the arms of his pursuers.

Now that he understood that about himself, he could relax. He hadn't found the ductwork because he sensed some danger that hadn't yet risen to his conscious mind. He found the ductwork because he remembered how bad it felt to hide in the toilet tank as a toddler. So whatever danger there might be, he hadn't sensed it yet. It was just a childhood memory coming to the surface. Sister Carlotta had told him that a lot of human behavior was really acting out our responses to dangers long past. It hadn't sounded sensible to Bean at the time, but he didn't argue, and now he could see that she was right.

And how could he know there would never be a time when that narrow, dangerous highway through the ductwork might not be exactly the route he needed to save his life?

He never did palm the wall to light up green-brown-green. He knew exactly where his barracks was. How could he not? He had been there before, and knew every step between the barracks and every other place he had visited in the station.

And when he got there, Dimak had not yet returned with the slow eaters. His whole exploration hadn't taken more than twenty minutes, including his conversation with Petra and watching two quick computer games during the class break.

He awkwardly hoisted himself up from the lower bunk, dangling for a while from his chest on the rim of the second bunk. Long enough that it hurt in pretty much the same spot he had injured climbing out of the vent. "What are you doing?" asked one of the launchies near him.

Since the truth wouldn't be understood, he answered truthfully. "Injuring my chest," he said.

"I'm trying to sleep," said the other boy. "You're supposed to sleep, too."

"Naptime," said another boy. "I feel like I'm some stupid four-year-old."

Bean wondered vaguely what these boys' lives had been like, when taking a nap made them think of being four years old.

Sister Carlotta stood beside Pablo de Noches, looking at the toilet tank. "Old-fashioned kind," said Pablo. "Norteamericano. Very popular for a while back when the Netherlands first became international."

She lifted the lid on the toilet tank. Very light. Plastic.

As they came out of the lavatory, the office manager who had been showing them around looked at her curiously. "There's not any kind of danger from using the toilets, is there?" she asked.

"No," said Sister Carlotta. "I just had to see it, that's all. It's Fleet business. I'd appreciate it if you didn't talk about our visit here."

Of course, that almost guaranteed that she would talk about nothing else. But Sister Carlotta counted on it sounding like nothing more than strange gossip.

Whoever had run an organ farm in this building would not want to be discovered, and there was a lot of money in such evil businesses. That was how the devil rewarded his friends—lots of money, up to the moment he betrayed them and left them to face the agony of hell alone.

Outside the building, she spoke again to Pablo. "He really hid in there?"

"He was very tiny," said Pablo de Noches. "He was crawling when I found him, but he was soaking wet up to his shoulder on one side, and his chest. I thought he peed himself, but he said no. Then he showed me the toilet. And he was red here, here, where he pressed against the mechanism."

"He was talking," she said.

"Not a lot. A few words. So *tiny*. I could not believe a child so small could talk."

"How long was he in there?"

Pablo shrugged. "Shriveled up skin like old lady. All over. Cold. I was thinking, he will die. Not warm water like a swimming pool. Cold. He shivered all night."

"I can't understand why he *didn't* die," said Sister Carlotta.

Pablo smiled. "No hay nada que Dios no puede hacer."

"True," she answered. "But that doesn't mean we can't figure out *how* God works his miracles. Or why."

Pablo shrugged. "God does what he does. I do my work and live, the best man I can be."

She squeezed his arm. "You took in a lost child and saved him from people who meant to kill him. God saw you do that and he loves you."

Pablo said nothing, but Sister Carlotta could guess what he was thinking—how many sins, exactly, were washed away by that good act, and would it be enough to keep him out of hell?

"Good deeds do not wash away sins," said Sister Carlotta. "Solo el redentor puede limpiar su alma."

Pablo shrugged. Theology was not his skill.

"You don't do good deeds for yourself," said Sister Carlotta. "You do them because God is in you, and for those moments you are his hands and his feet, his eyes and his lips."

"I thought God was the baby. Jesus say, if you do it to this little one, you do it to me."

Sister Carlotta laughed. "God will sort out all the fine points in his own due time. It is enough that we try to serve him."

"He was so small," said Pablo. "But God was in him."

She bade him good-bye as he got out of the taxi in front of his apartment building.

Why did I have to see that toilet with my own eyes? My work with Bean is done. He left on the shuttle yesterday. Why can't I leave the matter alone?

Because he should have been dead, that's why. And after starving on the streets for all those years, even if he lived he was so malnourished he should have suffered serious mental damage. He should have been permanently retarded.

That was why she could not abandon the question of Bean's origin. Because maybe he *was* damaged. Maybe he *is* retarded. Maybe he started out so smart that he could lose half his intellect and still be the miraculous boy he is.

She thought of how St. Matthew kept saying that all the things that happened in Jesus' childhood, his mother treasured them in her heart. Bean is not Jesus, and I am not the Holy Mother. But he is a boy, and I have loved him as my son. What he did, no child of that age could do.

No child of less than a year, not yet walking by himself, could have such clear understanding of his danger that he would know to do the things that Bean did. Children that age often climbed out of their cribs, but they did not hide in a toilet tank for hours and then come out alive and ask for help. I can call it a miracle all I want, but I have to understand it. They use the dregs of the Earth in those organ farms. Bean has such extraordinary gifts that he could only have come from extraordinary parents.

And yet for all her research during the months that Bean lived with her, she had never found a single kidnapping that could possibly have been Bean. No abducted child. Not even an accident from which someone might have taken a surviving infant whose body was therefore never found. That wasn't proof—not every baby that disappeared left a trace of his life in the newspapers, and not every newspaper was archived and available for a search on the nets. But Bean had to be the child of parents so brilliant that the world took note of them—didn't he? Could a mind like his come from ordinary parents? Was that the miracle from which all other miracles flowed?

No matter how much Sister Carlotta tried to believe it, she could not. Bean was not what he seemed to be. He was in Battle School now, and there was a good chance he would end up someday as the commander of a great fleet. But what did anyone know about him? Was it possible that he was not a natural human being at all? That his extraordinary intelligence had been given him, not by God, but by someone or something else?

There was the question: If not God, then who could make such a child?

Sister Carlotta buried her face in her hands. Where did such thoughts come from? After all these years of searching, why did she have to keep doubting the one great success she had?

We have seen the beast of Revelation, she said silently. The Bugger, the Formic monster bringing destruction to the Earth, just as prophesied. We have seen the beast, and long ago Mazer Rackham and the human fleet, on the brink of defeat, slew that great dragon. But it will come again, and St. John the Revelator said that when it did, there would be a prophet who came with him.

No, no. Bean is good, a good-hearted boy. He is not any kind of devil, not the servant of the beast, just a boy of great gifts that God may have raised up to bless this world in the hour of its greatest peril. I know him as a mother knows her child. I am not wrong.

Yet when she got back to her room, she set her computer to work, searching now for something new. For reports from or about scientists who had been working, at least five years ago, on projects involving alterations in human DNA.

And while the search program was querying all the great indexes on the nets and sorting their replies into useful categories, Sister Carlotta went to the neat little pile of folded clothing waiting to be washed. She would not wash it after all. She put it in a plastic bag along with Bean's sheets and pillowcase, and sealed the bag. Bean had worn this clothing, slept on this bedding. His skin was in it, small bits of it. A few hairs. Maybe enough DNA for a serious analysis.

He was a miracle, yes, but she would find out just what the dimensions of this miracle might be. For her ministry had not been to save the children of the cruel streets of the cities of the world. Her ministry had been to help save the one species made in the image of God. That was still her ministry. And if there was something wrong with the child she had taken into her heart as a beloved son, she would find out about it, and give warning.

7

EXPLORATION

"So this launch group was slow getting back to their barracks."

"There is a twenty-one-minute discrepancy."

"Is that a lot? I didn't even know this sort of thing was tracked."

"For safety. And to have an idea, in the event of emergency, where everyone is. Tracking the uniforms that departed from the mess hall and the uniforms that entered the barracks, we come up with an aggregate of twenty-one minutes. That could be twenty-one children loitering for exactly one minute, or one child for twenty-one minutes."

"That's very helpful. Am I supposed to ask them?"

"No! They aren't supposed to know that we track them by their uniforms. It isn't good for them to know how much we know about them."

"And how little."

"Little?"

"If it was one student, it wouldn't be good for him to know that our tracking methods don't tell us who it was."

"Ah. Good point. And . . . actually, I came to you because I believe that it *was* one student only."

"Even though your data aren't clear?"

"Because of the arrival pattern. Spaced out in groups of two or three, a few solos. Just the way they left the mess hall. A little bit of clumping—three solos become a threesome, two twos arrive as four—but if there had been some kind of major distraction in the corridor, it would have caused major coalescing, a much larger group arriving at once after the disturbance ended."

"So. One student with twenty-one minutes unaccounted for."

"I thought you should at least be aware."

"What would he do with twenty-one minutes?"

"You know who it was?"

"I will, soon enough. Are the toilets tracked? Are we sure it wasn't somebody so nervous he went in to throw up his lunch?"

"Toilet entry and exit patterns were normal. In and out."

"Yes, I'll find out who it was. And keep watching the data for this launch group."

"So I was right to bring this to your attention?"

"Did you have any doubt of it?"

Bean slept lightly, listening, as he always did, waking twice that he remembered. He didn't get up, just lay there listening to the breathing of the others. Both times, there was a little whispering somewhere in the room. Always children's voices, no urgency about them, but the sound was enough to rouse Bean and kindle his attention, just for a moment till he was sure there was no danger.

He woke the third time when Dimak entered the room. Even before sitting up, Bean knew that's who it was, from the weight of his step, the sureness of his movement, the press of authority. Bean's eyes were open before Dimak spoke; he was on all fours, ready to move in any direction, before Dimak finished his first sentence.

"Naptime is over, boys and girls, time for work."

It was not about Bean. If Dimak knew what Bean had done after lunch and before their nap, he gave no sign. No immediate danger.

Bean sat on his bunk as Dimak instructed them in the use of their lockers and desks. Palm the wall beside the locker and it opens. Then turn on the desk and enter your name and a password.

Bean immediately palmed his own locker with his right hand, but did not palm the desk. Instead, he checked on Dimak—busy helping another student near the door—then scrambled to the unoccupied third bunk above his own and palmed *that* locker with his left hand. There was a desk inside that one, too. Quickly he turned on his own desk and typed in his name and a password. Bean. Achilles. Then he pulled out the other desk and turned it on. Name? Poke. Password? Carlotta.

He slipped the second desk back into the locker and closed the door, then tossed his first desk down onto his own bunk and slipped down after it. He did not look around to see if anyone noticed him. If they did, they'd say something soon enough; visibly checking around would merely call attention to him and make people suspect him who would not otherwise have noticed what he did.

Of course the adults would know what he had done. In fact, Dimak was certainly noticing already, when one child complained that his locker wouldn't open. So the station computer knew how many students there were and stopped opening lockers when the right total had been opened. But Dimak did not turn and demand to know who had opened two lockers. Instead, he pressed his own palm against the last student's locker. It popped open. He closed it again, and now it responded to the student's palm.

So they were going to let him have his second locker, his second desk, his second identity. No doubt they would watch him with special interest to see what he did with it. He would have to make a point of fiddling with it now and then, clumsily, so they'd think they knew what he wanted a second identity for. Maybe some kind of prank. Or to write down secret thoughts. That would be fun—Sister Carlotta was always prying after his secret thoughts, and no doubt these teachers would, too. Whatever he wrote, they'd eat it up.

Therefore they wouldn't be looking for his truly private work, which he would perform on his own desk. Or, if it was risky, on the desk of one of the boys across from him, both of whose passwords he had carefully noticed and memorized. Dimak was lecturing them about protecting their desks at all times, but it was inevitable that kids would be careless, and desks would be left lying around.

For now, though, Bean would do nothing riskier than what he had already done. The teachers had their own reasons for letting him do it. What mattered is that they not know his own.

After all, he didn't know himself. It was like the vent—if he thought of something that might get him some advantage later, he did it.

Dimak went on talking about how to submit homework, the directory of teachers' names, and the fantasy game that was on every desk. "You are not to spend study time playing the game," he said. "But when your studies are done, you are permitted a few minutes to explore."

Bean understood at once. The teachers *wanted* the students to play the game, and knew that the best way to encourage it was to put strict limits on it . . . and then not enforce them. A game—Sister Carlotta had used games to try to analyze Bean from time to time. So Bean always turned them into the same game: Try to figure out what Sister Carlotta is trying to learn from the way I play this game.

In this case, though, Bean figured that anything he did with the game would tell them things that he didn't want them to know about him. So he would not play at all, unless they compelled him. And maybe not even then. It was one thing to joust with Sister Carlotta; here, they no doubt had real experts, and Bean was not going to give them a chance to learn more about him than he knew himself.

Dimak took them on the tour, showing them most of what Bean had already seen. The other kids went ape over the game room. Bean did not so much as glance at the vent into which he had climbed, though he did make it a point to fiddle with the game he had watched the bigger boys play, figuring out how the controls worked and verifying that his tactics could, in fact, be carried out.

They did a workout in the gym, in which Bean immediately began working on the exercises that he thought he'd need—one-armed pushups and pullups being the most important, though they had to get a stool for him to stand on in order to reach the lowest chinning bar. No problem. Soon enough he'd be able to jump to reach it. With all the food they were giving him, he could build up strength quickly.

And they seemed grimly determined to pack food into him at an astonishing rate. After the gym they showered, and then it was suppertime. Bean wasn't even hungry yet, and they piled enough food onto his tray to feed his whole crew back in Rotterdam. Bean immediately headed for a couple of the kids who had whined about their small portions and, without even asking permission, scraped his excess onto their trays. When one of them tried to talk to him about it, Bean just put his finger to his lips. In answer, the boy grinned. Bean still ended up with more food than he wanted, but when he turned in his tray, it was scraped clean. The nutritionist would be happy. It remained to be seen if the janitors would report the food Bean left on the floor.

Free time. Bean headed back to the game room, hoping that tonight he'd actually see the famous Ender Wiggin. If he was there, he would no doubt be the center of a group of admirers. But at the center of the groups he saw were only the ordinary prestige-hungry clique-formers who thought they were leaders and so would follow their group anywhere in order to maintain that delusion. No way could any of them be Ender Wiggin. And Bean was not about to ask.

Instead, he tried his hand at several games. Each time, though, the moment he lost for the first time, other kids would push him out of the way. It was an interesting set of social rules. The students knew that even the shortest, greenest launchy was entitled to his turn—but the moment a turn ended, so did the protection of the rule. And they were rougher in shoving him than they needed to be, so the message was clear—you shouldn't have been using that game and making me wait. Just like the food lines at the charity kitchens in Rotterdam—except that absolutely nothing that mattered was at stake.

That was interesting, to find that it wasn't hunger that caused children to become bullies on the street. The bulliness was already in the child, and whatever the stakes were, they would find a way to act as they needed to act. If it was about food, then the children who lost would die; if it was about games, though, the bullies did not hesitate to be just as intrusive and send the same message. Do what I want, or pay for it.

Intelligence and education, which all these children had, apparently didn't make any important difference in human nature. Not that Bean had really thought they would.

Nor did the low stakes make any difference in Bean's response to the bullies. He simply complied without complaint and took note of who the bullies were. Not that he had any intention of punishing them or of avoiding them, either. He would simply remember who acted as a bully and take that into account when he was in a situation where that information might be important.

No point in getting emotional about anything. Being emotional didn't help with survival. What mattered was to learn everything, analyze the situation, choose a course of action, and then move boldly. Know, think, choose, do. There was no place in that list for "feel." Not that Bean didn't have feelings. He simply refused to think about them or dwell on them or let them influence his decisions, when anything important was at stake.

"He's even smaller than Ender was."

Again, again. Bean was so tired of hearing that.

"Don't talk about that hijo de puta to me, bicho."

Bean perked up. Ender had an enemy. Bean was wondering when he'd spot one, for someone who was first in the standings *had* to have provoked something besides admiration. Who said it? Bean drifted nearer to the group the conversation had come from. The same voice came up again. Again. And then he knew: That one was the boy who had called Ender an hijo de puta.

He had the silhouette of some kind of lizard on his uniform. And a single triangle on his sleeve. None of the boys around him had the triangle. All were focused on him. Captain of the team?

Bean needed more information. He tugged on the sleeve of a boy standing near him.

"What," said the boy, annoyed.

"Who's that boy there?" asked Bean. "The team captain with the lizard."

"It's a salamander, pinhead. Salamander *army*. And he's the *commander*."

Teams are called armies. Commander is the triangle rank. "What's his name?"

"Bonzo Madrid. And he's an even bigger asshole than you." The boy shrugged himself away from Bean.

So Bonzo Madrid was bold enough to declare his hatred for Ender Wiggin, but a kid who was not in Bonzo's army had contempt for *him* in turn and wasn't afraid to say so to a stranger. Good to know. The only enemy Ender had, so far, was contemptible.

But . . . contemptible as Bonzo might be, he *was* a commander. Which meant it was possible to become a commander without being the kind of boy that everybody respected. So what was their standard of judgment, in assigning command in this war game that shaped the life of Battle School?

More to the point, how do I get a command?

That was the first moment that Bean realized that he even had such a goal. Here in Battle School, he had arrived with the highest scores in his launch group—but he was the smallest and youngest and had been isolated even further by the deliberate actions of his teacher, making him a target of resentment. Somehow, in the midst of all this, Bean had made the decision that this would not be like Rotterdam. He was not going to live on the fringes, inserting himself only when it was absolutely essential for his own survival. As rapidly as possible, he was going to put himself in place to command an army.

Achilles had ruled because he was brutal, because he was willing to kill. That would always trump intelligence, when the intelligent one was physically smaller and had no strong allies. But here, the bullies only shoved and spoke rudely. The adults controlled things tightly and so brutality would not prevail, not in the assignment of command. Intelligence, then, had a chance to win out. Eventually, Bean might not have to live under the control of stupid people.

If this was what Bean wanted—and why not try for it, as long as some more important goal didn't come along first?—then he had to learn how the teachers made their decisions about command. Was it solely based on performance in classes? Bean doubted it. The International Fleet had to have smarter people than that running this school. The fact that they had that fantasy game on every desk suggested that they were looking at personality as well. Character. In the end, Bean suspected, character mattered more than intelligence. In Bean's litany of survival—know, think, choose, do—intelligence only mattered in the first three, and was the decisive factor only in the second one. The teachers knew that.

Maybe I *should* play the game, thought Bean.

Then: Not yet. Let's see what happens when I don't play.

At the same time he came to another conclusion he did not even know he had been concerned about. He would talk to Bonzo Madrid.

Bonzo was in the middle of a computer game, and he was obviously the kind of person who thought of anything unexpected as an affront to his dignity. That meant that for Bean to accomplish what he wanted, he could not approach Bonzo in a cringing way, like the suckups who surrounded him as he played, commending him even for his stupid mistakes in gameplay.

Instead, Bean pushed close enough to see when Bonzo's onscreen character died—again. "Señor Madrid, puedo hablar convozco?" The Spanish came to mind easily enough—he had listened to Pablo de Noches talk to fellow immigrants in Rotterdam who visited his apartment, and on the telephone to family members back in Valencia. And using Bonzo's native language had the desired effect. He didn't ignore Bean. He turned and glared at him.

"What do you want, bichinho?" Brazilian slang was common in Battle School, and Bonzo apparently felt no need to assert the purity of his Spanish.

Bean looked him in the eye, even though he was about twice Bean's height, and said, "People keep saying that I remind them of Ender Wiggin, and you're the only person around here who doesn't seem to worship him. I want to know the truth."

The way the other kids fell silent told Bean that he had judged aright—it was dangerous to ask Bonzo about Ender Wiggin. Dangerous, but that's why Bean had phrased his request so carefully.

"Damn right I don't worship the farteating insubordinate traitor, but why should I tell *you* about him?"

"Because you won't lie to me," said Bean, though he actually thought it was obvious Bonzo would probably lie outrageously in order to make himself look like the hero of what was obviously a story of his own humiliation at Ender's hands. "And if people are going to keep comparing me to the guy, I've got to know what he really is. I don't want to get iced because I do it all wrong here. You don't owe me nothing, but when you're small like me, you gots to have somebody who can tell you the stuff you gots to know to survive." Bean wasn't quite sure of the slang here yet, but what he knew, he used.

One of the other kids chimed in, as if Bean had written him a script and he was right on cue. "Get lost, launchy, Bonzo Madrid doesn't have time to change diapers."

Bean rounded on him and said fiercely, "I can't ask the teachers, they don't tell the truth. If Bonzo don't talk to me who I ask then? *You?* You don't know zits from zeroes."

It was pure Sergeant, that spiel, and it worked. Everybody laughed at the kid who had tried to brush him off, and Bonzo joined in, then put a hand on Bean's shoulder. "I'll tell you what I know, kid, it's about time somebody wanted to hear the truth about that walking rectum." To the kid that Bean had just fronted, Bonzo said, "Maybe you better finish my game, it's the only way you'll ever get to play at that level."

Bean could hardly believe a commander would say such a pointlessly offensive thing to one of his own subordinates. But the boy swallowed his anger and grinned and nodded and said, "That's right, Bonzo," and turned to the game, as instructed. A real suckup.

By chance Bonzo led him to stand right in front of the wall vent where Bean had been stuck only a few hours before. Bean gave it no more than a glance.

"Let me tell you about Ender. He's all about beating the other guy. Not just winning—he has to beat the other guy into the ground or he isn't happy. No rules for him. You give him a plain order, and he acts like he's going to obey it, but if he sees a way to make himself look good and all he has to do is disobey the order, well, all I can say is, I pity whoever has him in his army."

"He used to be Salamander?"

Bonzo's face reddened. "He wore a uniform with our colors, his name was on my roster, but he was *never* Salamander. The minute I saw him, I knew he was trouble. That cocky look on his face, like he thinks the whole Battle School was made just to give him a place to strut. I wasn't having it. I put in to transfer him the second he showed up and I refused to let him practice with us, I knew he'd learn our whole system and then take it to some other army and use what he learned from me to stick it to my army as fast as he could. I'm not stupid!''

In Bean's experience, that was a sentence never uttered except to prove its own inaccuracy.

"So he didn't follow orders."

"It's more than that. He goes crying like a baby to the teachers about how I don't let him practice, even though they *know* I've put in to transfer him out, but he whines and they let him go in to the battleroom during freetime and practice alone. Only he starts getting kids from his launch group and then kids from other armies, and they go in there as if he was their commander, doing what he tells them. That really pissed off a lot of us. And the teachers always give that little suckup whatever he wants, so when we commanders *demanded* that they bar our soldiers from practicing with him, they just said, 'Freetime is *free*,' but everything is part of the game, sabe? Everything, so they're letting him cheat, and every lousy soldier and sneaky little bastard goes to Ender for those freetime practices so every army's system is compromised, sabe? You plan your strategy for a game and you never know if your plans aren't being told to a soldier in the enemy army the second they come out of your mouth, sabe?''

Sabe sabe sabe. Bean wanted to shout back at him, Sí, yo *sé*, but you couldn't show impatience with Bonzo. Besides, this was all fascinating. Bean was getting a pretty good picture of how this army game shaped the life of Battle School. It gave the teachers a chance to see not only how the kids handled command, but also how they responded to incompetent commanders like Bonzo. Apparently, he had decided to make Ender the goat of his army, only Ender refused to take it. This Ender Wiggin was the kind of kid who got it that the teachers ran everything and used them by getting that practice room. He didn't ask them to get Bonzo to stop picking on him, he asked them for an alternate way to train himself. Smart. The teachers had to love that, and Bonzo couldn't do a thing about it.

Or could he?

"What did you do about it?''

"It's what we're going to do. I'm about fed up. If the teachers won't stop it, somebody else will have to, neh?'' Bonzo grinned wickedly. "So I'd stay out of Ender Wiggin's freetime practice if I were you."

"Is he really number one in the standings?''

"Number one is piss," said Bonzo. "He's dead last in loyalty. There's not a commander who wants him in his army.''

"Thanks," said Bean. "Only now it kind of pisses me off that people say I'm like him."

"Just because you're small. They made him a soldier when he was still way too young. Don't let them do that to you, and you'll be OK, sabe?"

"Ahora sé," said Bean. He gave Bonzo his biggest grin.

Bonzo smiled back and clapped him on his shoulder. "You'll do OK. When you get big enough, if I haven't graduated yet, maybe you'll be in Salamander."

If they leave you in command of an army for another day, it's just so that the other students can learn how to make the best of taking orders from a higher-ranking idiot. "I'm not going to be a soldier for a *long* time," said Bean.

"Work hard," said Bonzo. "It pays off." He clapped him on the shoulder yet again, then walked off with a big grin on his face. Proud of having helped a little kid. Glad to have convinced somebody of his own twisted version of dealing with Ender Wiggin, who was obviously smarter farting than Bonzo was talking.

And there was a threat of violence against the kids who practiced with Ender Wiggin in freetime. That was good to know. Bean would have to decide now what to do with that information. Get the warning to Ender? Warn the teachers? Say nothing? Be there to watch?

Freetime ended. The game room cleared out as everyone headed to their barracks for the time officially dedicated to independent study. Quiet time, in other words. For most of the kids in Bean's launch group, though, there was nothing to study—they hadn't had any classes yet. So for tonight, study meant playing the fantasy game on their desks and bantering with each other to assert position. Everybody's desk popped up with the suggestion that they could write letters home to their families. Some of the kids chose to do that. And, no doubt, they all assumed that's what Bean was doing.

But he was not. He signed on to his first desk as Poke and discovered that, as he suspected, it didn't matter which desk he used, it was the name and password that determined everything. He would never have to pull that second desk out of its locker. Using the Poke identity, he wrote a journal entry. This was not unexpected—"diary" was one of the options on the desk.

What should he be? A whiner? "Everybody pushed me out of the way in the game room just because I'm little, it isn't fair!" A baby? "I miss Sister Carlotta so so so much, I wish I could be in my own room back in Rotter-

dam.'' Ambitious? "I'll get the best scores on everything, they'll see."
In the end, he decided on something a little more subtle.

What would Achilles do if he were me? Of course he's not little,
but with his bad leg it's almost the same thing. Achilles always knew
how to wait and not show them anything. That's what I've got to
do, too. Just wait and see what pops up. Nobody's going to want
to be my friend at first. But after a while, they'll get used to me and
we'll start sorting ourselves out in the classes. The first ones who'll
let me get close will be the weaker ones, but that's not a problem.
You build your crew based on loyalty first, that's what Achilles did,
build loyalty and train them to obey. You work with what you have,
and go from there.

Let them stew on *that*. Let them think he was trying to turn Battle School
into the street life that he knew. They'd believe it. And in the meantime, he'd
have time to learn as much as he could about how Battle School actually
worked, and come up with a strategy that actually fit the situation.

Dimak came in one last time before lights out. "Your desk keep working after lights out," he said, "but if you use it when you're supposed to
be sleeping, we'll know about it and we'll know what you're doing. So it
better be important, or you go on the pig list."

Most of the kids put their desks away; a couple of them defiantly kept
them out. Bean didn't care either way. He had other things to think about.
Plenty of time for the desk tomorrow, or the next day.

He lay in the near-darkness—apparently the babies here had to have a
little light so they could find their way to the toilet without tripping—and
listened to the sounds around him, learning what they meant. A few whis-
pers, a few shushes. The breathing of boys and girls as, one by one, they
fell asleep. A few even had light child-snores. But under those human
sounds, the windsound from the air system, and random clicking and distant
voices, sounds of the flexing of a station rotating into and out of sunlight,
the sound of adults working through the night.

This place was so expensive. Huge, to hold thousands of kids and
teachers and staff and crew. As expensive as a ship of the fleet, surely. And
all of it just to train little children. The adults may keep the kids wrapped
up in a game, but it was serious business to *them*. This program of training
children for war wasn't just some wacko educational theory gone mad,
though Sister Carlotta was probably right when she said that a lot of people

thought it was. The I.F. wouldn't maintain it at this level if it weren't expected to give serious results. So these kids snoring and soughing and whispering their way into the darkness, they really mattered.

They expect results from me. It's not just a party up here, where you come for the food and then do what you want. They really do want to make commanders out of us. And since Battle School has been going for a while, they probably have proof that it works—kids who already graduated and went on to compile a decent service record. That's what I've got to keep in mind. Whatever the system is here, it works.

A different sound. Not regular breathing. Jagged little breaths. An occasional gasp. And then . . . a sob.

Crying. Some boy was crying himself to sleep.

In the nest, Bean had heard some of the kids cry in their sleep, or as they neared sleep. Crying because they were hungry or injured or sick or cold. But what did these kids have to cry about here?

Another set of soft sobs joined the first.

They're homesick, Bean realized. They've never been away from mommy and daddy before, and it's getting to them.

Bean just didn't get it. He didn't feel that way about anybody. You just live in the place you're in, you don't worry about where you used to be or where you wish you were, *here* is where you are and here's where you've got to find a way to survive and lying in bed boo-hooing doesn't help much with *that*.

No problem, though. Their weakness just puts me farther ahead. One less rival on my road to becoming a commander.

Is that how Ender Wiggin thought about things? Bean recalled everything he had learned about Ender so far. The kid was resourceful. He didn't openly fight with Bonzo, but he didn't put up with his stupid decisions, either. It was fascinating to Bean, because on the street the one rule he knew for sure was, you don't stick your neck out unless your throat's about to be slit anyway. If you have a stupid crew boss, you don't tell him he's stupid, you don't show him he's stupid, you just go along and keep your head down. That's how kids survived.

When he had to, Bean had taken a bold risk. Got himself onto Poke's crew that way. But that was about food. That was about not dying. Why did Ender take such a risk when there was nothing at stake but his standing in the war game?

Maybe Ender knew something Bean didn't know. Maybe there was some reason why the game was more important than it seemed.

Or maybe Ender was one of those kids who just couldn't stand to lose, ever. The kind of kid who's for the team only as long as the team is taking him where he wants to go, and if it isn't, then it's every man for himself. That's what Bonzo thought. But Bonzo was stupid.

Once again, Bean was reminded that there were things he didn't understand. Ender wasn't doing every man for himself. He didn't practice alone. He opened his free time practice to other kids. Launchies, too, not just kids who could do things for him. Was it possible he did that just because it was a decent thing to do?

The way Poke had offered herself to Achilles in order to save Bean's life?

No, Bean didn't *know* that's what she did, he didn't *know* that's why she died.

But the possibility was there. And in his heart, he believed it. That was the thing he had always despised about her. She acted tough but she was soft at heart. And yet . . . that softness was what saved his life. And try as he might, he couldn't get himself to take the too-bad-for-her attitude that prevailed on the street. She listened to me when I talked to her, she did a hard thing that risked her own life on the chance that it would lead to a better life for all her crew. Then she offered me a place at her table and, in the end, she put herself between me and danger. Why?

What was this great secret? Did Ender know it? How did he learn it? Why couldn't Bean figure it out for himself? Try as he might, though, he couldn't understand Poke. He couldn't understand Sister Carlotta, either. Couldn't understand the arms she held him with, the tears she shed over him. Didn't they understand that no matter how much they loved him, he was still a separate person, and doing good for him didn't improve *their* lives in any way?

If Ender Wiggin has this weakness, then I will not be anything like him. I am not going to sacrifice myself for anybody. And the beginning of that is that I refuse to lie in my bed and cry for Poke floating there in the water with her throat slit, or boo-hoo because Sister Carlotta isn't asleep in the next room.

He wiped his eyes, rolled over, and willed his body to relax and go to sleep. Moments later, he was dozing in that light, easy-to-rouse sleep. Long before morning his pillow would be dry.

He dreamed, as human beings always dream—random firings of memory and imagination that the unconscious mind tries to put together into coherent stories. Bean rarely paid attention to his own dreams, rarely even remembered that he dreamed at all. But this morning he awoke with a clear image in his mind.

Ants, swarming from a crack in the sideway. Little black ants. And larger red ants, doing battle with them, destroying them. All of them scurrying. None of them looking up to see the human shoe coming down to stamp the life out of them.

When the shoe came back up, what was crushed under it was not ant bodies at all. They were the bodies of children, the urchins from the streets of Rotterdam. All of Achilles' family. Bean himself—he recognized his own face, rising above his flattened body, peering around for one last glimpse at the world before death.

Above him loomed the shoe that killed him. But now it was worn on the end of a bugger's leg, and the bugger laughed and laughed.

Bean remembered the laughing bugger when he awoke, and remembered the sight of all those children crushed flat, of his own body mashed like gum under a shoe. The meaning was obvious: While we children play at war, the buggers are coming to crush us. We must look above the level of our private struggles and keep in mind the greater enemy.

Except that Bean rejected that interpretation of his own dream the moment he thought of it. Dreams have no meaning at all, he reminded himself. And even if they do mean something, it's a meaning that reveals what I feel, what I fear, not some deep abiding truth. So the buggers are coming. So they might crush us all like ants under their feet. What's that to me? My business right now is to keep Bean alive, to advance myself to a position where I might be useful in the war against the buggers. There's nothing I can do to stop them right now.

Here's the lesson Bean took from his own dream: Don't be one of the scurrying, struggling ants.

Be the shoe.

Sister Carlotta had reached a dead end in her search of the nets. Plenty of information on human genetics studies, but nothing like what she was looking for.

So she sat there, doodling with a nuisance game on her desk while trying to think of what to do next and wondering why she was bothering to look into Bean's beginnings at all, when the secure message arrived from the I.F. Since the message would erase itself a minute after arrival, to be re-sent every minute until it was read by the recipient, she opened it at once and keyed in her first and second passwords.

FROM: Col.Graff@BattleSchool.IF
TO: Ss.Carlotta@SpecAsn.RemCon.IF
RE: Achilles

Please report all info on ''Achilles'' as known to
subject.

As usual, a message so cryptic that it didn't actually have to be encrypted, though of course it had been. This was a secure message, wasn't it? So why not just use the kid's name. "Please report on 'Achilles' as known to *Bean*."

Somehow Bean had given them the name Achilles, and under circumstances such that they didn't want to ask him directly to explain. So it had to be in something he had written. A letter to her? She felt a little thrill of hope and then scoffed at her own feelings. She knew perfectly well that mail from the kids in Battle School was almost never passed along, and besides, the chance of Bean actually writing to her was remote. But they had the name somehow, and wanted to know from her what it meant.

The trouble is, she didn't want to give him that information without knowing what it would mean for Bean.

So she prepared an equally cryptic reply:

Will reply by secure conference only.

Of course this would infuriate Graff, but that was just a perk. Graff was so used to having power far beyond his rank that it would be good for him to have a reminder that all obedience was voluntary and ultimately depended on the free choice of the person receiving the orders. And she *would* obey, in the end. She just wanted to make sure Bean was not going to suffer from the information. If they knew he had been so closely involved with both the perpetrator and the victim of a murder, they might drop him from the program. And even if she was sure it would be all right to talk about it, she might be able to get a quid pro quo.

It took another hour before the secure conference was set up, and when Graff's head appeared in the display above her computer, he was not happy. "What game are you playing today, Sister Carlotta?"

"You've been putting on weight, Colonel Graff. That's not healthy."

"Achilles," he said.

"Man with a bad heel," she said. "Killed Hector and dragged his body around the gates of Troy. Also had a thing for a captive girl named Bris-eis.''

"You know that's not the context."

"I know more than that. I know you must have got the name from something Bean wrote, because the name is not pronounced uh-KILL-eez, it's pronounced ah-SHEEL. French.''

"Someone local there."

"Dutch is the native language here, though Fleet Common has just about driven it out as anything but a curiosity."

"Sister Carlotta, I don't appreciate your wasting the expense of this conference."

"And I'm not going to talk about it until I know why you need to know."

Graff took a few deep breaths. She wondered if his mother taught him to count to ten, or if, perhaps, he had learned to bite his tongue from dealing with nuns in Catholic school.

"We are trying to make sense of something Bean wrote."

"Let me see it and I'll help you as I can."

"He's not your responsibility anymore, Sister Carlotta," said Graff.

"Then why are you asking me about him? He's your responsibility, yes? So I can get back to work, yes?"

Graff sighed and did something with his hands, out of sight in the display. Moments later the text of Bean's diary entry appeared on her display below and in front of Graff's face. She read it, smiling slightly.

"Well?" asked Graff.

"He's doing a number on you, Colonel."

"What do you mean?"

"He knows you're going to read it. He's misleading you."

"You *know* this?"

"Achilles might indeed be providing him with an example, but not a good one. Achilles once betrayed someone that Bean valued highly."

"Don't be vague, Sister Carlotta."

"I wasn't vague. I told you precisely what I wanted you to know. Just as Bean told you what he wanted you to hear. I can promise you that his diary entries will only make sense to you if you recognize that he is writing these things for you, with the intent to deceive."

"Why, because he didn't keep a diary down there?"

"Because his memory is perfect," said Sister Carlotta. "He would never, never commit his real thoughts to a readable form. He keeps his own counsel. Always. You will never find a document written by him that is not meant to be read.''

"Would it make a difference if he was writing it under another identity? Which he thinks we don't know about?''

"But you *do* know about it, and so he *knows* you will know about it, so the other identity is there only to confuse you, and it's working.''

"I forgot, you think this kid is smarter than God.''

"I'm not worried that you don't accept my evaluation. The better you know him, the more you'll realize that I'm right. You'll even come to believe those test scores.''

"What will it take to get you to help me with this?'' asked Graff.

"Try telling me the truth about what this information will mean to Bean.''

"He's got his primary teacher worried. He disappeared for twenty-one minutes on the way back from lunch—we have a witness who talked to him on a deck where he had no business, and that still doesn't account for that last seventeen minutes of his absence. He doesn't play with his desk—''

"You think setting up false identities and writing phony diary entries isn't playing?''

"There's a diagnostic/therapeutic game that all the children play—he hasn't even signed on yet.''

"He'll know that the game is psychological, and he won't play it until he knows what it will cost him.''

"Did you teach him that attitude of default hostility?''

"No, I learned it from him.''

"Tell me straight. Based on this diary entry, it looks as though he plans to set up his own crew here, as if this were the street. We need to know about this Achilles so we'll know what he actually has in mind.''

"He plans no such thing,'' said Sister Carlotta.

"You say it so forcefully, but without giving me a single reason to trust your conclusion.''

"You called *me,* remember?''

"That's not enough, Sister Carlotta. Your opinions on this boy are suspect.''

"He would never emulate Achilles. He would never write his true plans where you could find them. He does not build crews, he joins them and uses them and moves on without a backward glance.''

"So investigating this Achilles won't give us a clue about Bean's future behavior?''

"Bean prides himself on not holding grudges. He thinks they're counterproductive. But at some level, I believe he wrote about Achilles specifically because you would read what he wrote and would want to know more about Achilles, and if you investigated him you would discover a very bad thing that Achilles did."

"To Bean?"

"To a friend of his."

"So he *is* capable of having friendships?"

"The girl who saved his life here on the street."

"And what's *her* name?"

"Poke. But don't bother looking for her. She's dead."

Graff thought about that a moment. "Is that the bad thing Achilles did?"

"Bean has reason to believe so, though I don't think it would be evidence enough to convict in court. And as I said, all these things may be unconscious. I don't think Bean would knowingly try to get even with Achilles, or anybody else, for that matter, but he might hope you'd do it for him."

"You're still holding back, but I have no choice but to trust your judgment, do I?"

"I promise you that Achilles is a dead end."

"And if you think of a reason why it might not be so dead after all?"

"I want your program to succeed, Colonel Graff, even more than I want Bean to succeed. My priorities are not skewed by the fact that I do care about the child. I really have told you everything now. But I hope you'll help me also."

"Information isn't traded in the I.F., Sister Carlotta. It flows from those who have it to those who need it."

"Let me tell you what I want, and you decide if I need it."

"Well?"

"I want to know of any illegal or top secret projects involving the alteration of the human genome in the past ten years."

Graff looked off into the distance. "It's too soon for you to be off on a new project, isn't it. So this is the same old project. This is about Bean."

"He came from somewhere."

"You mean his mind came from somewhere."

"I mean the whole package. I think you're going to end up relying on this boy, betting all our lives on him, and I think you need to know what's going on in his genes. It's a poor second to knowing what's happening in his mind, but that, I suspect, will always be out of reach for you."

"You sent him up here, and then you tell me something like this. Don't you realize that you have just guaranteed that I will never let him move to the top of our selection pool?"

"You say that now, when you've only had him for a day," said Sister Carlotta. "He'll grow on you."

"He damn well better not shrink or he'd get sucked away by the air system."

"Tut-tut, Colonel Graff."

"Sorry, Sister," he answered.

"Give me a high enough clearance and I'll do the search myself."

"No," he said. "But I'll get summaries sent to you."

She knew that they would give her only as much information as they thought she should have. But when he tried to fob her off with useless drivel, she'd deal with that problem, too. Just as she would try to get to Achilles before the I.F. found him. Get him away from the streets and into a school. Under another name. Because if the I.F. found him, in all likelihood they would test him—or find her scores on him. If they tested him, they would fix his foot and bring him up to Battle School. And she had promised Bean that he would never have to face Achilles again.

8

GOOD STUDENT

"He doesn't play the fantasy game at *all?*"

"He has never so much as chosen a figure, let alone come through the portal."

"It's not possible that he hasn't discovered it."

"He reset the preferences on his desk so that the invitation no longer pops up."

"From which you conclude . . ."

"He knows it isn't a game. He doesn't want us analyzing the workings of his mind."

"And yet he wants us to advance him."

"I don't know that. He buries himself in his studies. For three months he's been getting perfect scores on every test. But he only reads the lesson material once. His study is on other subjects of his own choosing."

"Such as?"

"Vauban."

"Seventeenth-century ortifications? What is he *thinking?*"

"You see the problem?"

"How does he get along with the other children?"

"I think the classic description is 'loner.' He is polite. He volunteers nothing. He asks only what he's interested in. The kids in his launch group think he's strange. They know he scores better than them on everything, but they don't hate him. They treat him like a force of nature. No friends, but no enemies."

"That's important, that they don't hate him. They should, if he stays aloof like that."

"I think it's a skill he learned on the street—to turn away anger. He never gets angry himself. Maybe that's why the teasing about his size stopped."

"Nothing that you're telling me suggests that he has command potential."

"If you think he's trying to show command potential and failing at it, then you're right."

"So . . . what do you *think* he's doing?"

"Analyzing *us*."

"Gathering information without giving any. Do you really think he's that sophisticated?"

"He stayed alive on the street."

"I think it's time for you to probe a little."

"And let him know that his reticence bothers us?"

"If he's as clever as you think, he already knows."

Bean didn't mind being dirty. He had gone years without bathing, after all. A few days didn't bother him. And if other people minded, they kept their opinions to themselves. Let them add it to the gossip about him. Smaller and younger than Ender! Perfect scores on every test! Stinks like a pig!

That shower time was precious. That's when he could sign on to his desk as one of the boys bunking near him—while they were showering. They were naked, wearing only towels to the shower, so their uniforms weren't tracking them. During that time Bean could sign on and explore the system without letting the teachers know that he was learning the tricks of the system. It tipped his hand, just a little, when he altered the preferences so he didn't have to face that stupid invitation to play their mind game every time he changed tasks on his desk. But that wasn't a very difficult hack, and he decided they wouldn't be particularly alarmed that he'd figured it out.

So far, Bean had found only a few really useful things, but he felt as though he was on the verge of breaking through more important walls. He knew that there was a virtual system that the students were meant to hack through. He had heard the legends about how Ender (of course) had hacked the system on his first day and signed on as God, but he knew that while

Ender might have been unusually quick about it, he wasn't doing anything that wasn't expected of bright, ambitious students.

Bean's first achievement was to find the way the teachers' system tracked student computer activity. By avoiding the actions that were automatically reported to the teachers, he was able to create a private file area that they wouldn't see unless they were deliberately looking for it. Then, whenever he found something interesting while signed on as someone else, he would remember the location, then go and download the information into his secure area and work on it at his leisure—while his desk reported that he was reading works from the library. He actually read those works, of course, but far more quickly than his desk reported.

With all that preparation, Bean expected to make real progress. But far too quickly he ran into the firewalls—information the system had to have but wouldn't yield. He found several workarounds. For instance, he couldn't find any maps of the whole station, only of the student-accessible areas, and those were always diagrammatic and cute, deliberately out of scale. But he did find a series of emergency maps in a program that would automatically display them on the walls of the corridors in the event of a pressure-loss emergency, showing the nearest safety locks. These maps *were* to scale, and by combining them into a single map in his secure area, he was able to create a schema of the whole station. Nothing was labeled except the locks, of course, but he learned of the existence of a parallel system of corridors on either side of the student area. The station must be not one but three parallel wheels, cross-linked at many points. That's where the teachers and staff lived, where the life support was located, the communications with the Fleet. The bad news was that they had separate air-circulation systems. The ductwork in one would not lead him to either of the others. Which meant that while he could probably spy on anything going on in the student wheel, the other wheels were out of reach.

Even within the student wheel, however, there were plenty of secret places to explore. The students had access to four decks, plus the gym below A-Deck and the battleroom above D-Deck. There were actually nine decks, however, two below A-Deck and three above D. Those spaces had to be used for something. And if they thought it was worth hiding it from the students, Bean figured it was worth exploring.

And he would have to start exploring soon. His exercise was making him stronger, and he was staying lean by not overeating—it was unbelievable how much food they tried to force on him, and they kept increasing his portions, probably because the previous servings hadn't caused him to gain as much weight as they wanted him to gain. But what he could not control was the increase in his height. The ducts would be impassable for him before too long—if they weren't already. Yet using the air system to get him access to the hidden decks was not something he could do during showers. It would mean losing sleep. So he kept putting it off—one day wouldn't make that much difference.

Until the morning when Dimak came into the barracks first thing in the morning and announced that everyone was to change his password immediately, with his back turned to the rest of the room, and was to tell no one what the new password was. "Never type it in where anyone can see," he said.

"Somebody's been using other people's passwords?" asked a kid, his tone suggesting that he thought this an appalling idea. Such dishonor! Bean wanted to laugh.

"It's required of all I.F. personnel, so you might as well develop the habit now," said Dimak. "Anyone found using the same password for more than a week will go on the pig list."

But Bean could only assume that they had caught on to what he was doing. That meant they had probably looked back into his probing for the past months and knew pretty much what he had found out. He signed on and purged his secure file area, on the chance that they hadn't actually found it yet. Everything he really needed there, he had already memorized. He would never rely on the desk again for anything his memory could hold.

Stripping and wrapping his towel around him, Bean headed for the showers with the others. But Dimak stopped him at the door.

"Let's talk," he said.

"What about my shower?" asked Bean.

"Suddenly you care about cleanliness?" asked Dimak.

So Bean expected to be chewed out for stealing passwords. Instead, Dimak sat beside him on a lower bunk near the door and asked him far more general questions. "How are you getting on here?"

"Fine."

"I know your test scores are good, but I'm concerned that you aren't making many friends among the other kids."

"I've got a lot of friends."

"You mean you know a lot of people's names and don't quarrel with anybody."

Bean shrugged. He didn't like this line of questioning any better than he would have liked an inquiry into his computer use.

"Bean, the system here was designed for a reason. There are a lot of factors that go into our decisions concerning a student's ability to command. The classwork is an important part of that. But so is leadership."

"Everybody here is just full of leadership ability, right?"

Dimak laughed. "Well, that's true, you can't all be leaders at once."

"I'm about as big as a three-year-old," said Bean. "I don't think a lot of kids are eager to start saluting me."

"But you could be building networks of friendship. The other kids are. You don't."

"I guess I don't have what it takes to be a commander."

Dimak raised an eyebrow. "Are you suggesting you *want* to be iced?"

"Do my test scores look like I'm trying to fail?"

"What *do* you want?" asked Dimak. "You don't play the games the other kids play. Your exercise program is weird, even though you know the regular program is designed to strengthen you for the battleroom. Does that mean you don't intend to play that game, either? Because if that's your plan, you really *will* get iced. That's our primary means of assessing command ability. That's why the whole life of the school is centered around the armies."

"I'll do fine in the battleroom," said Bean.

"If you think you can do it without preparation, you're mistaken. A quick mind is no replacement for a strong, agile body. You have no idea how physically demanding the battleroom can be."

"I'll join the regular workouts, sir."

Dimak leaned back and closed his eyes with a small sigh. "My, but you're compliant, aren't you, Bean."

"I try to be, sir."

"That is such complete bullshit," said Dimak.

"Sir?" Here it comes, thought Bean.

"If you devoted the energy to making friends that you devote to hiding things from the teachers, you'd be the most beloved kid in the school."

"That would be Ender Wiggin, sir."

"And don't think we haven't picked up on the way you obsess about Wiggin."

"Obsess?" Bean hadn't asked about him after that first day. Never joined in discussions about the standings. Never visited the battleroom during Ender's practice sessions.

Oh. What an obvious mistake. Stupid.

"You're the only launchy who has completely avoided so much as seeing Ender Wiggin. You track his schedule so thoroughly that you are never in the same room with him. That takes real effort.''

"I'm a launchy, sir. He's in an army.''

"Don't play dumb, Bean. It's not convincing and it wastes my time.''

Tell a useless and obvious truth, that was the rule. "Everyone compares me to Ender all the time 'cause I came here so young and small. I wanted to make my own way.''

"I'll accept that for now because there's a limit to how deeply I want to wade into your bullshit,'' said Dimak.

But in saying what he'd said about Ender, Bean wondered if it might not be true. Why shouldn't I have such a normal emotion as jealousy? I'm not a machine. So he was a little offended that Dimak seemed to assume that something more subtle had to be going on. That Bean was lying no matter what he said.

"Tell me,'' said Dimak, "why you refuse to play the fantasy game.''

"It looks boring and stupid,'' said Bean. That was certainly true.

"Not good enough,'' said Dimak. "For one thing, it *isn't* boring and stupid to any other kid in Battle School. In fact, the game adapts itself to your interests.''

I have no doubt of *that,* thought Bean. "It's all pretending,'' said Bean. "None of it's real.''

"Stop hiding for one second, can't you?'' snapped Dimak. "You know perfectly well that we use the game to analyze personality, and that's why you refuse to play.''

"Sounds like you've analyzed my personality anyway,'' said Bean.

"You just don't let up, do you?''

Bean said nothing. There was nothing to say.

"I've been looking at your reading list,'' said Dimak. "Vauban?''

"Yes?''

"Fortification engineering from the time of Louis the Fourteenth?''

Bean nodded. He thought back to Vauban and how his strategies had adapted to fit Louis's ever-more-straitened finances. Defense in depth had given way to a thin line of defenses; building new fortresses had largely been abandoned, while razing redundant or poorly placed ones continued. Poverty triumphing over strategy. He started to talk about this, but Dimak cut him off.

"Come on, Bean. Why are you studying a subject that has nothing to do with war in space?''

Bean didn't really have an answer. He had been working through the history of strategy from Xenophon and Alexander to Caesar and Machiavelli. Vauban came in sequence. There was no plan—mostly his readings were a cover for his clandestine computer work. But now that Dimak was asking him, what *did* seventeenth-century fortifications have to do with war in space?

"I'm not the one who put Vauban in the library."

"We have the full set of military writings that are found in every library in the fleet. Nothing more significant than that."

Bean shrugged.

"You spent two hours on Vauban."

"So what? I spent as long on Frederick the Great, and I don't think we're doing field drills, either, or bayoneting anyone who breaks ranks during a march into fire."

"You didn't actually read Vauban, did you," said Dimak. "So I want to know what you *were* doing."

"I *was* reading Vauban."

"You think we don't know how fast you read?"

"And *thinking* about Vauban?"

"All right then, what were you thinking?"

"Like you said. About how it applies to war in space." Buy some time here. What *does* Vauban have to do with war in space?

"I'm waiting," said Dimak. "Give me the insights that occupied you for two hours just yesterday."

"Well of course fortifications are impossible in space," said Bean. "In the traditional sense, that is. But there are things you can do. Like his mini-fortresses, where you leave a sallying force outside the main fortification. You can station squads of ships to intercept raiders. And there are barriers you can put up. Mines. Fields of flotsam to cause collisions with fast-moving ships, holing them. That sort of thing."

Dimak nodded, but said nothing.

Bean was beginning to warm to the discussion. "The real problem is that unlike Vauban, we have only one strong point worth defending—Earth. And the enemy is not limited to a primary direction of approach. He could come from anywhere. From anywhere all at once. So we run into the classic problem of defense, cubed. The farther out you deploy your defenses, the more of them you have to have, and if your resources are limited, you soon have more fortifications than you can man. What good are bases on moons Jupiter or Saturn or Neptune, when the enemy doesn't even have to come in on the plane of the ecliptic? He can bypass all our fortifications. The way Nimitz and MacArthur used two-dimensional island-hopping against the defense in depth of the Japanese in World War II. Only our enemy can work in three dimensions. Therefore we cannot possibly maintain defense in depth. Our only defense is early detection and a single massed force.''

Dimak nodded slowly. His face showed no expression. "Go on."

Go on? That wasn't enough to explain two hours of reading? "Well, so I thought that even that was a recipe for disaster, because the enemy is free to divide his forces. So even if we intercept and defeat ninety-nine of a hundred attacking squadrons, he only has to get one squadron through to cause terrible devastation on Earth. We saw how much territory a single ship could scour when they first showed up and started burning over China. Get ten ships to Earth for a single day—and if they spread us out enough, they'd have a lot more than a day!—and they could wipe out most of our main population centers. All our eggs are in that one basket.''

"And all this you got from Vauban,'' said Dimak.

Finally. That was apparently enough to satisfy him. "From thinking about Vauban, and how much harder our defensive problem is.''

"So,'' said Dimak, "what's your solution?''

Solution? What did Dimak think Bean was? I'm thinking about how to get control of the situation here in Battle School, not how to save the world! "I don't think there is a solution,'' said Bean, buying time again. But then, having said it, he began to believe it. "There's no point in trying to defend Earth at all. In fact, unless they have some defensive device we don't know about, like some way of putting an invisible shield around a planet or something, the enemy is just as vulnerable. So the only strategy that makes any sense at all is an all-out attack. To send our fleet against *their* home world and destroy it.''

"What if our fleets pass in the night?'' asked Dimak. "We destroy each other's worlds and all we have left are ships?''

"No,'' said Bean, his mind racing. "Not if we sent out a fleet immediately after the Second Bugger War. After Mazer Rackham's strike force defeated them, it would take time for word of their defeat to come back to them. So we build a fleet as quickly as possible and launch it against their home world immediately. That way the news of their defeat reaches them at the same time as our devastating counterattack.''

Dimak closed his eyes. "Now you tell us.''

"No,'' said Bean, as it dawned on him that he was right about everything. "That fleet was already sent. Before anybody on this station was born, that fleet was launched.''

"Interesting theory,'' said Dimak. "Of course you're wrong on every point.''

"No I'm not," said Bean. He knew he wasn't wrong, because Dimak's air of calm was not holding. Sweat was standing out on his forehead. Bean had hit on something really important here, and Dimak knew it.

"I mean your theory is right, about the difficulty of defense in space. But hard as it is, we still have to do it, and that's why you're here. As to some fleet we supposedly launched—the Second Bugger War exhausted humanity's resources, Bean. It's taken us this long to get a reasonable-sized fleet again. And to get better weaponry for the next battle. If you learned anything from Vauban, you should have learned that you can't build more than your people have resources to support. Besides which, you're assuming we know where the enemy's home world is. But your analysis is good insofar as you've identified the magnitude of the problem we face."

Dimak got up from the bunk. "It's nice to know that your study time isn't completely wasted on breaking into the computer system," he said.

With that parting shot, he left the barracks.

Bean got up and walked back to his own bunk, where he got dressed. No time for a shower now, and it didn't matter anyway. Because he knew that he had struck a nerve in what he said to Dimak. The Second Bugger War hadn't exhausted humanity's resources, Bean was sure of that. The problems of defending a planet were so obvious that the I.F. couldn't possibly have missed them, especially not in the aftermath of a nearly-lost war. They knew they had to attack. They built the fleet. They launched it. It was gone. It was inconceivable that they had done anything else.

So what was all this nonsense with the Battle School for? Was Dimak right, that Battle School was simply about building up the defensive fleet around Earth to counter any enemy assault that might have passed our invasion fleet on the way?

If that were true, there would be no reason to conceal it. No reason to lie. In fact, all the propaganda on Earth was devoted to telling people how vital it was to prepare for the next Bugger invasion. So Dimak had done nothing more than repeat the story that the I.F. had been telling everybody on Earth for three generations. Yet Dimak was sweating like a fish. Which suggested that the story wasn't true.

The defensive fleet around Earth was already fully manned, that was the problem. The normal process of recruitment would have been enough. Defensive war didn't take brilliance, just alertness. Early detection, cautious interception, protection of an adequate reserve. Success depended, not on the quality of command, but on the quantity of available ships and the quality of the weaponry. There was no reason for Battle School—Battle

School only made sense in the context of an offensive war, a war where maneuver, strategy, and tactics would play an important role. But the offensive fleet was already gone. For all Bean knew, the battle had already been fought years ago and the I.F. was just waiting for news about whether we had won or lost. It all depended on how many lightyears away the Bugger home planet was.

For all we know, thought Bean, the war is already over, the I.F. knows that we won, and they simply haven't told anybody.

And the reason for that was obvious. The only thing that had ended war on Earth and bound together all of humanity was a common cause—defeating the Buggers. As soon as it was known that the Bugger threat was eliminated, all the pent-up hostilities would be released. Whether it was the Muslim world against the West, or long-restrained Russian imperialism and paranoia against the Atlantic alliance, or Indian adventurism, or . . . or all of them at once. Chaos. The resources of the International Fleet would be co-opted by mutinying commanders from one faction or another. Conceivably it could mean the destruction of Earth—without any help from the Formics at all.

That's what the I.F. was trying to prevent. The terrible cannibalistic war that would follow. Just as Rome tore itself apart in civil war after the final elimination of Carthage—only far worse, because the weapons were more terrible and the hatreds far deeper, national and religious hatreds rather than the mere personal rivalries among leading citizens of Rome.

The I.F. was determined to prevent it.

In that context, Battle School made perfect sense. For many years, almost every child on Earth had been tested, and those with any potential brilliance in military command were taken out of their homeland and put into space. The best of the Battle School graduates, or at least those most loyal to the I.F., might very well be used to command armies when the I.F. finally announced the end of the war and struck preemptively to eliminate national armies and unify the world, finally and permanently, under one government. But the main purpose of the Battle School was to get these kids off Earth so that they could not become commanders of the armies of any one nation or faction.

After all, the invasion of France by the major European powers after the French Revolution led to the desperate French government discovering and promoting Napoleon, even though in the end he seized the reins of power instead of just defending the nation. The I.F. was determined that there would be no Napoleons on Earth to lead the resistance. All the potential Napoleons were here, wearing silly uniforms and battling each other for supremacy in a stupid game. It was all pig lists. By taking us, they have tamed the world.

"If you don't get dressed, you'll be late for class," said Nikolai, the boy who slept on the bottommost bunk directly across from Bean.

"Thanks," said Bean. He shed his dry towel and hurriedly pulled on his uniform.

"Sorry I had to tell them about your using my password," said Nikolai. Bean was dumfounded.

"I mean, I didn't *know* it was you, but they started asking me what I was looking for in the emergency map system, and since I didn't know what they were talking about, it wasn't hard to guess that somebody was signing on as me, and there you are, in the perfect place to see my desk whenever I sign on, and . . . I mean, you're really smart. But it's not like I set out to tell on you."

"That's fine," said Bean. "Not a problem."

"But, I mean, what *did* you find out? From the maps?"

Until this moment, Bean would have blown off the question—and the boy. Nothing much, I was just curious, that's what he would have said. But now his whole world had changed. Now it mattered that he have connections with the other boys, not so he could show his leadership ability to the teachers, but so that when war did break out on Earth, and when the I.F.'s little plan failed, as it was bound to do, he would know who his allies and enemies were among the commanders of the various national and factional armies.

For the I.F.'s plan *would* fail. It was a miracle it hadn't failed already. It depended too heavily on millions of soldiers and commanders being more loyal to the I.F. than to their homeland. It would not happen. The I.F. itself would break up into factions, inevitably.

But the plotters no doubt were aware of that danger. They would have kept the number of plotters as small as possible—perhaps only the triumvirate of Hegemon, Strategos, and Polemarch and maybe a few people here at Battle School. Because this station was the heart of the plan. Here was where every single gifted commander for two generations had been studied intimately. There were records on every one of them—who was most talented, most valuable. What their weaknesses were, both in character and in command. Who their friends were. What their loyalties were. Which of them, therefore, should be approached to command the I.F.'s forces in the intrahuman wars to come, and which should be stripped of command and held incommunicado until hostilities were over.

No wonder they were worried about Bean's lack of participation in their little mind game. It made him an unknown quantity. It made him dangerous.

Now it was even more dangerous for Bean to play than ever. Not playing might make them suspicious and fearful—but in whatever move they planned against him, at least they wouldn't know anything about him. While if he did play, then they might be less suspicious—but if they did move against him, they would do it knowing whatever information the game gave to them. And Bean was not at all confident of his ability to outplay the game. Even if he tried to give them misleading results, that strategy in itself might tell them more about him than he wanted them to know.

And there was another possibility, too. He might be completely wrong. There might be key information that he did not have. Maybe no fleet had been launched. Maybe they hadn't defeated the Buggers at their home world. Maybe there really was a desperate effort to build a defensive fleet. Maybe maybe maybe.

Bean had to get more information in order to have some hope that his analysis was correct and that his choices would be valid.

And Bean's isolation had to end.

"Nikolai," said Bean, "you wouldn't believe what I found out from those maps. Did you know there are nine decks, not just four?"

"Nine?"

"And that's just in this wheel. There are two other wheels they never tell us about."

"But the pictures of the station show only the one wheel."

"Those pictures were all taken when there *was* only one wheel. But in the plans, there are three. Parallel to each other, turning together."

Nikolai looked thoughtful. "But that's just the plans. Maybe they never built those other wheels."

"Then why would they still have maps for them in the emergency system?"

Nikolai laughed. "My father always said, bureaucrats never throw anything away."

Of course. Why hadn't he thought of that? The emergency map system was no doubt programmed before the first wheel was ever brought into service. So all those maps would already be in the system, even if the other wheels were never built, even if two-thirds of the maps would never have a corridor wall to be displayed on. No one would bother to go into the system and clean them out.

"I never thought of that," said Bean. He knew, given his reputation for brilliance, that he could pay Nikolai no higher compliment. As indeed the reaction of the other kids in nearby bunks showed. No one had ever had such a conversation with Bean before. No one had ever thought of something that Bean hadn't obviously thought of first. Nikolai was blushing with pride.

"But the nine decks, that makes sense," said Nikolai.

"Wish I knew what was on them," said Bean.

"Life support," said the girl named Corn Moon. "They got to be making oxygen somewhere here. That takes a lot of plants."

More kids joined in. "And staff. All we ever see are teachers and nutritionists."

"And maybe they *did* build the other wheels. We don't *know* they didn't."

The speculation ran rampant through the group. And at the center of it all: Bean.

Bean and his new friend, Nikolai.

"Come on," said Nikolai, "we'll be late for math."

Part Three

SCHOLAR

9

GARDEN OF SOFIA

"So he found out how many decks there are. What can he possibly do with that information?"

"Yes, that's the exact question. What was he planning, that he felt it necessary to find that out? Nobody else even looked for that, in the whole history of this school."

"You think he's plotting revolution?"

"All we know about this kid is that he survived on the streets of Rotterdam. It's a hellish place, from what I hear. The kids are vicious. They make *Lord of the Flies* look like *Pollyanna*."

"When did you read *Pollyanna*?"

"It was a book?"

"How can he plot a revolution? He doesn't have any friends."

"I never said anything about revolution, that's *your* theory."

"I don't have a theory. I don't understand this kid. I never even wanted him up here. I think we should just send him home."

"No."

"No *sir*, I'm sure you meant to say."

"After three months in Battle School, he figured out that defensive war makes no sense and that we must have launched a fleet against the Bugger home worlds right after the end of the last war."

"He knows *that*? And you come telling me he knows how many *decks* there are?"

"He doesn't *know* it. He guessed. I told him he was wrong."

"I'm sure he believed you."

"I'm sure he's in doubt."

"This is all the more reason to send him back to Earth. Or out to some distant base somewhere. Do you realize the nightmare if there's a breach of security on this?"

"Everything depends on how he uses the information."

"Only we don't know anything about him, so we have no way of knowing how he'll use it."

"Sister Carlotta—"

"Do you *hate* me? That woman is even more inscrutable than your little dwarf."

"A mind like Bean's is not to be thrown away just because we fear there might be a security breach."

"Nor is security to be thrown away for the sake of one really smart kid."

"Aren't we smart enough to create new layers of deception for him? Let him find out something that he'll think is the truth. All we have to do is come up with a lie that we think he'll believe."

Sister Carlotta sat in the terrace garden, across the tiny table from the wizened old exile.

"I'm just an old Russian scientist living out the last years of his life on the shores of the Black Sea." Anton took a long drag on his cigarette and blew it out over the railing, adding it to the pollution flowing from Sofia out over the water.

"I'm not here with any law enforcement authority," said Sister Carlotta.

"You have something much more dangerous to me. You are from the Fleet."

"You're in no danger."

"That's true, but only because I'm not going to tell you anything."

"Thank you for your candor."

"You value candor, but I don't think you would appreciate it if I told you the thoughts your body arouses in the mind of this old Russian."

"Trying to shock nuns is not much sport. There is no trophy."

"So you take nunnitude seriously."

Sister Carlotta sighed. "You think I came here because I know something about you and you don't want me to find out more. But I came here because of what I can't find out about you."

"Which is?"

"Anything. Because I was researching a particular matter for the I.F., they gave me a summary of articles on the topic of research into altering the human genome."

"And my name came up?"

"On the contrary, your name was never mentioned."

"How quickly they forget."

"But when I read the few papers available from the people they did mention—always early work, before the I.F. security machine clamped down on them—I noticed a trend. Your name was always cited in their footnotes. Cited constantly. And yet not a word of yours could be found. Not even abstracts of papers. Apparently you have never published."

"And yet they quote me. Almost miraculous, isn't it? You people do collect miracles, don't you? To make saints?"

"No beatification until after you're dead, sorry."

"I have only one lung left as it is," said Anton. "So I don't have that long to wait, as long as I keep smoking."

"You could stop."

"With only one lung, it takes twice as many cigarettes to get the same nicotine. Therefore I have had to increase my smoking, not cut down. This should be obvious, but then, you do not think like a scientist, you think like a woman of faith. You think like an obedient person. When you find out something is bad, you don't do it."

"Your research was into genetic limitations on human intelligence."

"Was it?"

"Because it's in that area that you are always cited. Of course, these papers were never *about* that exact subject, or they too would have been classified. But the titles of the articles mentioned in the footnotes—the ones you never wrote, since you never published anything—are all tied to that area."

"It is so easy in a career to find oneself in a rut."

"So I want to ask you a hypothetical question."

"My favorite kind. Next to rhetorical ones. I can nap equally well through either kind."

"Suppose someone were to break the law and attempt to alter the human genome, specifically to enhance intelligence."

"Then someone would be in serious danger of being caught and punished."

"Suppose that, using the best available research, he found certain genes that he could alter in an embryo that would enhance the intelligence of the person when he was born."

"Embryo! Are you testing me? Such changes can only happen in the egg. A single cell."

"And suppose a child was born with these alterations in place. The child was born and he grew up enough for his great intelligence to be noticed."

"I assume you are not speaking of your own child."

"I'm speaking of no child at all. A hypothetical child. How would someone recognize that this child had been genetically altered? Without actually examining the genes."

Anton shrugged. "What does it matter if you examine the genes? They will be normal."

"Even though you altered them?"

"It is such a little change. Hypothetically speaking."

"Within the normal range of variation?"

"It is two switches, one that you turn on, one that you turn off. The gene is already there, you see."

"What gene?"

"Savants were the key, for me. Autistic, usually. Dysfunctional. They have extraordinary mental powers. Lightning-fast calculations. Phenomenal memories. But they are inept, even retarded in other areas. Square roots of twelve-digit numbers in seconds, but incapable of conducting a simple purchase in a store. How can they be so brilliant, and so stupid?"

"That gene?"

"No, it was another, but it showed me what was possible. The human brain could be far smarter than it is. But is there a, how you say, bargain?"

"Trade-off."

"A terrible bargain. To have this great intellect, you have to give up everything else. That's how the brains of autistic savants accomplish such feats. They do one thing, and the rest is a distraction, an annoyance, beyond the reach of any conceivable interest. Their attention truly is undivided."

"So all hyperintelligent people would be retarded in some other way."

"That is what we all assumed, because that is what we saw. The exceptions seemed to be only mild savants, who were thus able to spare some concentration on ordinary life. Then I thought . . . but I can't tell you what I thought, because I have been served with an order of inhibition."

He smiled helplessly. Sister Carlotta's heart fell. When someone was a proven security risk, they implanted in his brain a device that caused any kind of anxiety to launch a feedback loop, leading to a panic attack. Such people were then given periodic sensitization to make sure that they felt a great deal of anxiety when they contemplated talking about the forbidden subject. Viewed one way, it was a monstrous intrusion on a person's life; but if it was compared to the common practice of imprisoning or killing people who could not be trusted with a vital secret, an order of intervention could look downright humane.

That explained, of course, why Anton was amused by everything. He had to be. If he allowed himself to become agitated or angry—any strong negative emotion, really—then he would have a panic attack even without talking about forbidden subjects. Sister Carlotta had read an article once in which the wife of a man equipped with such a device said that their life together had never been happier, because now he took everything so calmly, with good humor. "The children love him now, instead of dreading his time at home." She said that, according to the article, only hours before he threw himself from a cliff. Life was better, apparently, for everyone but him.

And now she had met a man whose very memories had been rendered inaccessible.

"What a shame," said Sister Carlotta.

"But stay. My life here is a lonely one. You're a sister of mercy, aren't you? Have mercy on a lonely old man, and walk with me."

She wanted to say no, to leave at once. At that moment, however, he leaned back in his chair and began to breathe deeply, regularly, with his eyes closed, as he hummed a little tune to himself.

A ritual of calming. So . . . at the very moment of inviting her to walk with him, he had felt some kind of anxiety that triggered the device. That meant there was something important about his invitation.

"Of course I'll walk with you," she said. "Though technically my order is relatively unconcerned with mercy to individuals. We are far more pretentious than that. Our business is trying to save the world."

He chuckled. "One person at a time would be too slow, is that it?"

"We make our lives of service to the larger causes of humanity. The Savior already died for sin. We work on trying to clean up the consequences of sin on other people."

"An interesting religious quest," said Anton. "I wonder whether my old line of research would have been considered a service to humanity, or just another mess that someone like you would have to clean up."

"I wonder that myself," said Sister Carlotta.

"We will never know." They strolled out of the garden into the alley behind the house, and then to a street, and across it, and onto a path that led through an untended park.

"The trees here are very old," Sister Carlotta observed.

"How old are *you,* Carlotta?"

"Objectively or subjectively?"

"Stick to the Gregorian calendar, please, as most recently revised."

"That switch away from the Julian system still sticks in the Russian craw, does it?"

"It forced us for more than seven decades to commemorate an October Revolution that actually occurred in November."

"You are much too young to remember when there were Communists in Russia."

"On the contrary, I am old enough now to have all the memories of my people locked within my head. I remember things that happened long before I was born. I remember things that never happened at all. I live in memory."

"Is that a pleasant place to dwell?"

"Pleasant?" He shrugged. "I laugh at all of it because I must. Because it is so sweetly sad—all the tragedies, and yet nothing is learned."

"Because human nature never changes," she said.

"I have imagined," he said, "how God might have done better, when he made man—in his own image, I believe."

"Male and female created he them. Making his image anatomically vague, one must suppose."

He laughed and clapped her rather too forcefully on the back. "I didn't know you could laugh about such things! I am pleasantly surprised!"

"I'm glad I could bring cheer into your bleak existence."

"And then you sink the barb into the flesh." They reached an overlook that had rather less of a view of the sea than Anton's own terrace. "It is not a bleak existence, Carlotta. For I can celebrate God's great compromise in making human beings as we are."

"Compromise?"

"Our bodies could live forever, you know. We don't have to wear out. Our cells are all alive; they can maintain and repair themselves, or be replaced by fresh ones. There are even mechanisms to keep replenishing our bones. Menopause need not stop a woman from bearing children. Our brains need not decay, shedding memories or failing to absorb new ones. But God made us with death inside."

"You are beginning to sound serious about God."

"God made us with death inside, and also with intelligence. We have our seventy years or so—perhaps ninety, with care—in the mountains of Georgia, a hundred and thirty is not unheard of, though I personally believe they are all liars. They would claim to be immortal if they thought they could get away with it. We could live forever, if we were willing to be stupid the whole time.''

"Surely you're not saying that God had to choose between long life and intelligence for human beings!''

"It's there in your own Bible, Carlotta. Two trees—knowledge and life. You eat of the tree of knowledge, and you will surely die. You eat of the tree of life, and you remain a child in the garden forever, undying.''

"You speak in theological terms, and yet I thought you were an unbeliever.''

"Theology is a joke to me. Amusing! I laugh at it. I can tell amusing stories about theology, to jest with believers. You see? It pleases me and keeps me calm.''

At last she understood. How clearly did he have to spell it out? He was telling her the information she asked about, but doing it in code, in a way that fooled not only any eavesdroppers—and there might well be listeners to every word they said—but even his own mind. It was all a jest; therefore he could tell her the truth, as long as he did it in this form.

"Then I don't mind hearing your wild humorous forays into theology.''

"Genesis tells of men who lived to be more than nine hundred years old. What it does not tell you is how very stupid these men all were.''

Sister Carlotta laughed aloud.

"That's why God had to destroy humanity with his little flood,'' Anton went on. "Get rid of those stupid people and replace them with quicker ones. Quick quick quick, their minds moved, their metabolism. Rushing onward into the grave.''

"From Methuselah at nearly a millennium of life to Moses with his hundred and twenty years, and now to us. But our lives are getting longer.''

"I rest my case.''

"Are we stupider now?''

"So stupid that we would rather have long life for our children than see them become too much like God, knowing . . . good and evil . . . knowing . . . everything.'' He clutched at his chest, gasping. "Ah, God! God in heaven!'' He sank to his knees. His breath was shallow and rapid now. His eyes rolled back in his head. He fell over.

Apparently he hadn't been able to maintain his self-deception. His body finally caught on to how he had managed to tell his secret to this woman by speaking it in the language of religion.

She rolled him onto his back. Now that he had fainted, his panic attack was subsiding. Not that fainting was trivial in a man of Anton's age. But he would not need any heroism to bring him back, not this time. He would wake up calm.

Where were the people who were supposed to be monitoring him? Where were the spies who were listening in to their conversation?

Pounding feet on the grass, on the leaves.

"A bit slow, weren't you?" she said without looking up.

"Sorry, we didn't expect anything." The man was youngish, but not terribly bright-looking. The implant was supposed to keep him from spilling his tale; it was not necessary for his guards to be clever.

"I think he'll be all right."

"What were you talking about?"

"Religion," she said, knowing that her account would probably be checked against a recording. "He was criticizing God for mis-making human beings. He claimed to be joking, but I think that a man of his age is never really joking when he talks about God, do you?"

"Fear of death gets in them," said the young man sagely—or at least as sagely as he could manage.

"Do you think he accidentally triggered this panic attack by agitating his own anxiety about death?" If she asked it as a question, it wasn't actually a lie, was it?

"I don't know. He's coming around."

"Well, I certainly don't want to cause him any more anxiety about religious matters. When he wakes up, tell him how grateful I am for our conversation. Assure him that he has clarified for me one of the great questions about God's purpose."

"Yes, I'll tell him," said the young man earnestly.

Of course he would garble the message hopelessly.

Sister Carlotta bent over and kissed Anton's cold, sweaty forehead. Then she rose to her feet and walked away.

So that was the secret. The genome that allowed a human being to have extraordinary intelligence acted by speeding up many bodily processes. The mind worked faster. The child developed faster. Bean was indeed the product of an experiment in unlocking the savant gene. He had been given the fruit of the tree of knowledge. But there was a price. He would not be able to taste of the tree of life. Whatever he did with his life, he would have to do it young, because he would not live to be old.

Anton had not done the experiment. He had not played God, bringing forth human beings who would live in an explosion of intelligence, sudden fireworks instead of single, long-burning candles. But he had found a key

God had hidden in the human genome. Someone else, some follower, some insatiably curious soul, some would-be visionary longing to take human beings to the next stage of evolution or some other such mad, arrogant cause—this someone had taken the bold step of turning that key, opening that door, putting the killing, brilliant fruit into the hand of Eve. And because of that act—that serpentine, slithering crime—it was Bean who had been expelled from the garden. Bean who would now, surely, die—but die like a god, knowing good and evil.

10

SNEAKY

"I can't help you. You didn't give me the information I asked for."

"We gave you the damned summaries."

"You gave me nothing and you know it. And now you come to me asking me to evaluate Bean for you—but you do not tell me why, you give me no context. You expect an answer but you deprive me of the means of providing it."

"Frustrating, isn't it?"

"Not for me. I simply won't give you any answer."

"Then Bean is out of the program."

"If your mind is made up, no answer of mine will change you, especially because you have made certain my answer will be unreliable."

"You know more than you've told me, and I must have it."

"How marvelous. You have achieved perfect empathy with me, for that is the exact statement I have repeatedly made to you."

"An eye for an eye? How Christian of you."

"Unbelievers always want *other* people to act like Christians."

"Perhaps you haven't heard, but there's a war on."

"Again, I could have said the same thing to you. There's a war on, yet you fence me around with foolish secrecy. Since there is no evidence of the Formic enemy spying on us, this secrecy is not about the war. It's about the Triumvirate maintaining their power over humanity. And I am not remotely interested in that."

"You're wrong. That information is secret in order to prevent some terrible experiments from being performed."

"Only a fool closes the door when the wolf is already inside the barn."

"Do you have proof that Bean is the result of a genetic experiment?"

"How can I prove it, when you have cut me off from all evidence? Besides, what matters is not *whether* he has altered genes, but what those genetic changes, if he has them, might lead him to do. Your tests were all designed to allow you to predict the behavior of normal human beings. They may not apply to Bean."

"If he's that unpredictable, then we can't rely on him. He's out."

"What if he's the only one who can win the war? Do you drop him from the program then?"

Bean didn't want to have much food in his body, not tonight, so he gave away almost all his food and turned in a clean tray long before anyone else was done. Let the nutritionist be suspicious—he had to have time alone in the barracks.

The engineers had always located the intake at the top of the wall over the door into the corridor. Therefore the air must flow into the room from the opposite end, where the extra bunks were unoccupied. Since he had not been able to see a vent just glancing around that end of the room, it had to be located under one of the lower bunks. He couldn't search for it when others would see him, because no one could be allowed to know that he was interested in the vents. Now, alone, he dropped to the floor and in moments was jimmying at the vent cover. It came off readily. He tried putting it back on, listening carefully for the level of noise that operation caused. Too much. The vent screen would have to stay off. He laid it on the floor beside the opening, but out of the way so he wouldn't accidentally bump into it in the darkness. Then, to be sure, he took it completely out from under that bunk and slid it under the one directly across.

Done. He then resumed his normal activities.

Until night. Until the breathing of the others told him that most, if not all, were asleep.

Bean slept naked, as many of the boys did—his uniform would not give him away. They were told to wear their towels when going to and from the toilet in the night, so Bean assumed that it, too, could be tracked.

So as Bean slid down from his bunk, he pulled his towel from its hook on the bunk frame and wrapped it around himself as he trotted to the door of the barracks.

Nothing unusual. Toilet trips were allowed, if not encouraged, after lights out, and Bean had made it a point to make several such runs during his time in Battle School. No pattern was being violated. And it was a good idea to make his first excursion with an empty bladder.

When he came back, if anyone was awake all they saw was a kid in a towel heading back to his bunk.

But he walked past his bunk and quietly sank down and slid under the last bunk, where the uncovered vent awaited him. His towel remained on the floor under the bunk, so that if anyone woke enough to notice that Bean's bunk was empty, they would see that his towel was missing and assume he had gone to the toilet.

It was no less painful this time, sliding into the vent, but once inside, Bean found that his exercise had paid off. He was able to slide down at an angle, always moving slowly enough to make no noise and to avoid snagging his skin on any protruding metal. He wanted no injuries he'd have to explain.

In the utter darkness of the air duct, he had to keep his mental map of the station constantly in mind. The faint nightlight of each barracks cast only enough light into the air ducts to allow him to make out the location of each vent. But what mattered was not the location of the other barracks on this level. Bean had to get either up or down to a deck where teachers lived and worked. Judging from the amount of time it took Dimak to get to their barracks the rare times that a quarrel demanded his attention, Bean assumed that his quarters were on another deck. And because Dimak always arrived breathing a little heavily, Bean also assumed it was a deck below their own level, not above—Dimak had to climb a ladder, not slide down a pole, to reach them.

Nevertheless, Bean had no intention of going down first. He had to see whether he could successfully climb to a higher deck before getting himself potentially trapped on a lower one.

So when he finally—after passing three barracks—came to a vertical shaft, he did not climb down. Instead, he probed the walls to see how much larger it was than the horizontals. It was much wider—Bean could not reach all the way across it. But it was only slightly deeper, front to back. That was good. As long as Bean didn't work too hard and sweat too much, friction between his skin and the front and back walls of the duct would allow him to inch his way upward. And in the vertical duct, he could face forward, giving his neck a much-needed respite from being perpetually turned to one side.

Downward was almost harder than upward, because once he started sliding it was harder to stop. He was also aware that the lower he went, the heavier he would become. And he had to keep checking the wall beside him, looking for another side duct.

But he didn't have to find it by probing, after all. He could see the side duct, because there was light in both directions. The teachers didn't have the same lights-out rules as the students, and their quarters were smaller, so that vents came more frequently, spilling more light into the duct.

In the first room, a teacher was awake and working at his desk. The trouble was that Bean, peering out of a vent screen near the floor, could not see a thing he was typing.

It would be that way in all the rooms. The floor vents would not work for him. He had to get into the air-intake system.

Back to the vertical duct. The wind was coming from above, and so that was where he had to go if he was to cross over from one system to another. His only hope was that the duct system would have an access door before he reached the fans, and that he would be able to find it in the dark.

Heading always into the wind, and finding himself noticeably lighter after climbing past seven decks, he finally reached a wider area with a small light strip. The fans were much louder, but he still wasn't near enough to see them. It didn't matter. He would be out of this wind.

The access door was clearly marked. It also might be wired to sound an alarm if it was opened. But he doubted it. That was the kind of thing that was done in Rotterdam to guard against burglars. Burglary wasn't a serious problem on space stations. This door would only have been alarmed if all doors in the station were fitted with alarms. He'd find out soon enough.

He opened the door, slipped out into a faintly lighted space, closed the door behind him.

The structure of the station was visible here, the beams, the sections of metal plating. There were no solid surfaces. The room was also noticeably colder, and not just because he was out of the hot wind. Cold hard space was on the other side of those curved plates. The furnaces might be located here, but the insulation was very good, and they had not bothered to pump much of that hot air into this space, relying instead on seepage to heat it. Bean hadn't been this cold since Rotterdam . . . but compared to wearing thin clothing in the winter streets with the wind off the North Sea, this was still almost balmy. It annoyed Bean that he had become so pampered here that he even cared about such a slight chill. And yet he couldn't keep himself from shivering a couple of times. Even in Rotterdam, he hadn't been naked.

Following the ductwork, he climbed up the workmen's ladderways to the furnaces and then found the air-intake ducts and followed them back down. It was easy to find an access door and enter the main vertical duct.

Because the air in the intake system did not have to be under positive pressure, the ducts did not have to be so narrow. Also, this was the part of the system where dirt had to be caught and removed, so it was more important to maintain access; by the time air got past the furnaces, it was already as clean as it was ever going to get. So instead of shinnying up and down narrow shafts, Bean scrambled easily down a ladder, and in the low light still had no trouble reading the signs telling which deck each side opening led to.

The side passages weren't really ducts at all. Instead, they consisted of the entire space between the ceiling of one corridor and the floor of the one above. All the wiring was here, and the water pipes—hot, cold, sewer. And besides the strips of dim worklights, the space was frequently lighted by the vents on both sides of the space—those same narrow strips of vent openings that Bean had seen from the floor below on his first excursion.

Now he could see easily down into each teacher's quarters. He crept along, making as little noise as possible—a skill he had perfected prowling through Rotterdam. He quickly found what he was looking for—a teacher who was awake, but not working at his desk. The man was not well known to Bean, because he supervised an older group of launchies and did not teach any of the classes Bean was taking. He was heading for a shower. That meant he would come back to the room and, perhaps, would sign in again, allowing Bean to have a chance at getting both his log-in name and his password.

No doubt the teachers changed passwords often, so whatever he got wouldn't last long. Moreover, it was always possible that attempting to use a teacher's password on a student desk might set off some kind of alarm. But Bean doubted it. The whole security system was designed to shut students out, to monitor student behavior. The teachers would not be so closely watched. They frequently worked on their desks at odd hours, and they also frequently signed on to student desks during the day to call on their more powerful tools to help solve a student's problem or give a student more personalized computer resources. Bean was reasonably sure that the risk of discovery was outweighed by the benefits of snagging a teacher's identity.

While he waited, he heard voices a few rooms up. He wasn't quite close enough to make out the words. Did he dare risk missing the bather's return?

Moments later he was looking down into the quarters of . . . Dimak himself. Interesting. He was talking to a man whose holographic image appeared in the air over his desk. Colonel Graff, Bean realized. The commandant of Battle School.

"My strategy was simple enough," Graff was saying. "I gave in and got her access to the stuff she wanted. She was right, I can't get good answers from her unless I let her see the data she's asking for."

"So did she give you any answers?"

"No, too soon. But she gave me a very good question."

"Which is?"

"Whether the boy is actually human."

"Oh, come on. Does she think he's a Bugger larva in a human suit?"

"Nothing to do with the Buggers. Genetically enhanced. It would explain a lot."

"But still human, then."

"Isn't that debatable? The difference between humans and chimpanzees is genetically slight. Between humans and neanderthals it had to be minute. How much difference would it take for him to be a different species?"

"Philosophically interesting, but in practical terms—"

"In practical terms, we don't know what this kid will do. There's no data on his species. He's a primate, which suggests certain regularities, but we can't assume anything about his motivations that—"

"Sir, with all due respect, he's still a kid. He's a human being. He's not some alien—"

"That's precisely what we've got to find out before we determine how much we can rely on him. And that's why you are to watch him even more carefully. If you can't get him into the mind game, then find some other way to figure out what makes him tick. Because we can't use him until we know just how much we can rely on him."

Interesting that they openly call it the mind game among themselves, thought Bean.

Then he realized what they were saying. "Can't get him into the mind game." As far as Bean knew, he was the only kid who didn't play the fantasy game. They were talking about him. New species. Genetically altered. Bean felt his heart pounding in his chest. What am I? Not just smart, but . . . different.

"What about the breach of security?" Dimak asked.

"That's the other thing. You've got to figure out what he knows. Or at least how likely he is to spill it to any other kids. That's the greatest danger right now. Is the possibility of this kid being the commander we need great enough to balance the risk of breaching security and collapsing the program? I thought with Ender we had an all-or-nothing long-odds bet, but this one makes Ender look like a sure thing.''

''I didn't think of you as a gambler, sir.''

''I'm not. But sometimes you're forced into the game.''

''I'm on it, sir.''

''Encrypt everything you send me on him. No names. No discussions with other teachers beyond the normal. Contain this.''

''Of course.''

''If the only way we can beat the Buggers is to replace ourselves with a new species, Dimak, then have we really saved humanity?''

''One kid is not replacement of a species,'' said Dimak.

''Foot in the door. Camel's nose in the tent. Give them an inch.''

''*Them*, sir?''

''Yes, I'm paranoid and xenophobic. That's how I got this job. Cultivate those virtues and you, too, might rise to my lofty station.''

Dimak laughed. Graff didn't. His head disappeared from the display.

Bean had the discipline to remember that he was waiting to get a password. He crept back to the bather's room.

Still not back.

What breach of security were they talking about? It must have been recent, for them to be discussing it with such urgency. That meant it had to be Bean's conversation with Dimak about what was really going on with the Battle School. And yet his guess that the battle had already happened could not be it, or Dimak and Graff would not be talking about how he might be the only way they could beat the Buggers. If the Buggers were still unbeaten, the breach of security had to be something else.

It could still be that his earlier guess was partly right, and Battle School existed as much to strip the Earth of good commanders as to beat the Buggers. Graff and Dimak's fear might be that Bean would let other kids in on the secret. For some of them, at least, it might rekindle their loyalty to the nation or ethnic group or ideology of their parents.

And since Bean had definitely been planning to probe the loyalties of other students over the next months and years, he now would have to be doubly cautious not to let his pattern of conversation attract the attention of the teachers. All he needed to know was which of the best and brightest kids had the strongest home loyalties. Of course, for that Bean would need to figure out just how loyalty worked, so he would have some idea of how to weaken it or strengthen it, how to exploit it or turn it.

But just because this first guess of Bean's could explain their words didn't mean it was right. And just because the final Bugger war had not yet been fought didn't mean his initial guess was completely wrong. They might, for instance, have launched a fleet against the Bugger home world years ago, but were still preparing commanders to fight off an invasion fleet now approaching Earth. In that case, the security breach Graff and Dimak feared was that Bean would frighten others by letting them know how urgent and dire the situation of humanity was.

The irony was that of all the children Bean had ever known, none could keep a secret as well as he did. Not even Achilles, for in refusing his share of Poke's bread, he had tipped his hand.

Bean could keep a secret, but he also knew that sometimes you had to give some hint of what you knew in order to get more information. That was what had prompted Bean's conversation with Dimak. It was dangerous, but in the long run, if he could keep them from removing him from the school entirely in order to silence him—not to mention keeping them from killing him—he had learned more important information than he had given them. In the end, the only things they could learn from him were about himself. And what he learned from them was about everything else—a much larger pool of knowledge.

Himself. That was their puzzle—who he was. Silly to be concerned about whether he was human. What else *could* he be? He had never seen any child show any desire or emotion that he himself had not felt. The only difference was that Bean was stronger, and did not let his fleeting needs and passions control his actions. Did that make him alien? He was human— only better.

The teacher came back into the room. He hung up his damp towel, but even before he dressed he sat back down and logged on. Bean watched his fingers move over the keys. It was so quick. A blur of keystrokes. He would have to replay the memory in his mind many times to make sure. But at least he had seen it; nothing obstructed his view.

Bean crawled back toward the vertical intake shaft. The evening's expedition had already taken as long as he dared—he needed his sleep, and every minute away increased the risk of chance discovery.

In fact, he had been very lucky on this first foray through the ducts. To happen to hear Dimak and Graff conversing about him, to happen to watch a teacher who conveniently gave him a clear view of his log-in. For a moment it crossed Bean's mind that they might know he was in the air system, might even have staged all this for him, to see what he'd do. It might be just one more experiment.

No. It wasn't just luck that this teacher showed him the log-in. Bean had chosen to watch him because he was going to shower, because his desk was sitting on the table in such a way that Bean had a reasonable chance of seeing the log-in. It was an intelligent choice on Bean's part. He had gone with the best odds, and it paid off.

As for Dimak and Graff, it might have been chance that he overheard them talking, but it was his own choice to move closer at once in order to hear. And, come to think of it, he had chosen to go exploring in the ducts because of precisely the same event that had prompted Graff and Dimak to be so concerned. Nor was it a surprise that their conversation happened after lights-out for the children—that's when things would have quieted down, and, with duties done, there would be time for a conversation without Graff calling Dimak in for a special meeting, which might arouse questions in the minds of the other teachers. Not luck, really—Bean had made his own luck. He saw the log-in and overheard the conversation because he had made that quick decision to get into the intake system and acted on it at once.

He had always made his own luck.

Maybe that was something that went along with whatever genetic alteration Graff had found out about.

She, they had said. *She* had raised the question of whether Bean was genetically human. Some woman who was searching for information, and Graff had given in, was letting her have access to facts that had been hidden from her. That meant that he would receive more answers from this woman as she began to use that new data. More answers about Bean's origins.

Could it be Sister Carlotta who had doubted Bean's humanity?

Sister Carlotta, who wept when he left her and went into space? Sister Carlotta, who loved him as a mother loves her child? How could *she* doubt him?

If they wanted to find some inhuman human, some alien in a human suit, they ought to take a good long look at a nun who embraces a child as her own, and then goes around casting doubt about whether he's a real boy. The opposite of Pinocchio's fairy. She touches a real boy and turns him into something awful and fearful.

It could not have been Sister Carlotta they were talking about. Just another woman. His guess that it might be her was simply wrong, just like his guess that the final battle with the Buggers had already happened. That's why Bean never fully trusted his own guesses. He acted on them, but always kept himself open to the possibility that his interpretations might be wrong.

Besides, *his* problem was not figuring out whether he really was human or not. Whatever he was, he was himself and must act in such a way as to not only stay alive but also get as much control over his own future as possible. The only danger to him was that *they* were concerned about the issue of his possible genetic alteration. Bean's task was therefore to appear so normal that their fears on that score would be dispelled.

But how could he pretend to be normal? He hadn't been brought here because he was normal, he was brought here because he was extraordinary. For that matter, so were all the other kids. And the school put so much strain on them that some became downright odd. Like Bonzo Madrid, with his loud vendetta against Ender Wiggin. So in fact, Bean shouldn't appear normal, he should appear weird in the expected ways.

Impossible to fake that. He didn't know yet what signs the teachers were looking for in the behavior of the children here. He could find ten things to do, and do them, never guessing that there were ninety things he hadn't noticed.

No, what he had to do was not to *act* in predictable ways, but to *become* what they hoped their perfect commander would be.

When he got back to his barracks, climbed back up to his bunk, and checked the time on his desk, he found that he had done it all in less than an hour. He put away his desk and lay there replaying in his mind the image in his memory of the teacher's fingers, logging in. When he was reasonably certain of what the log-in and password were, he allowed himself to drift toward sleep.

Only then, as he was beginning to doze, did he realize what his perfect camouflage would be, quelling their fears and bringing him both safety and advancement.

He had to become Ender Wiggin.

11

DADDY

"Sir. I asked for a private interview."

"Dimak is here because your breach of security affects his work."

"Breach of security! This is why you reassign me?"

"There is a child who used your log-in to the master teacher system. He found the log-in record files and rewrote them to give himself an identity."

"Sir, I have faithfully adhered to all regulations. I never sign on in front of the students."

"Everyone *says* they never sign on, but then it turns out they do."

"Excuse me, sir, but Uphanad does not. He's always on the others when he catches them doing it. Actually, he's kind of anal about it. Drives us all crazy."

"You can check my log-in records. I never sign on during teaching hours. In fact, I never sign on outside my quarters."

"Then how could this child possibly get in using your log-in?"

"My desk sits on my table, like so. If I may use your desk to demonstrate."

"Of course."

"I sit like so. I keep my back to the door so no one can even see in. I never sign on in any other position."

"Well it's not like there's a window he can peek through!"

"Yes there is, sir."

"Dimak?"

"There *is* a window, sir. Look. The vent."

"Are you seriously suggesting that he could—"

"He *is* the smallest child who ever—"

"It was that little *Bean* child who got my log-in?"

"Excellent, Dimak, you've managed to let his name slip out, haven't you."

"I'm sorry, sir."

"Ah. Another security breach. Will you send Dimak home with me?"

"I'm not sending anybody home."

"Sir, I must point out that Bean's intrusion into the master teacher system is an excellent opportunity."

"To have a student romping through the student data files?"

"To study Bean. We don't have him in the fantasy game, but now we have the game *he* chooses to play. We watch where he goes in the system, what he does with this power he has created for himself."

"But the damage he can do is—"

"He won't do any damage, sir. He won't do anything to give himself away. This kid is too street-smart. It's information he wants. He'll look, not touch."

"So you've got him analyzed already, is that it? You know what he's doing at all times?"

"I know that if there's a story we really want him to believe, he has to discover it himself. He has to *steal* it from us. So I think this little security breach is the perfect way to heal a much more important one."

"What I'm wondering is, if he's been crawling through the ducts, what *else* has he heard?"

"If we close off the duct system, he'll know he was caught, and then he won't trust what we set up for him to find."

"So I have to permit a child to crawl around through the ductwork and—"

"He can't do it much longer. He's growing, and the ducts are extremely shallow."

"That's not much comfort right now. And, unfortunately, we'll still have to kill Uphanad for knowing too much."

"Please assure me that you're joking."

"Yes, I'm joking. You'll have him as a student soon enough, Captain Uphanad. Watch him very carefully. Speak of him only with me. He's unpredictable and dangerous. "

"Dangerous. Little Bean."

"He cleaned *your* clock, didn't he?"

"Yours too, sir, begging your pardon."

Bean worked his way through every student at Battle School, reading the records of a half dozen or so per day. Their original scores, he found, were the least interesting thing about them. Everyone here had such high scores on all the tests given back on Earth that the differences were almost trivial. Bean's own scores were the highest, and the gap between him and the next highest, Ender Wiggin, was wide—as wide as the gap between Ender and the next child after him. But it was all relative. The difference between Ender and Bean amounted to half of a percentage point; most of the children clustered between 97 and 98 percent.

Of course, Bean knew what they could not know, that for him getting the highest possible score on the tests had been easy. He could have done more, he could have done better, but he had reached the boundary of what the test could discover. The gap between him and Ender was much wider than they supposed.

And yet . . . in reading the records, Bean came to see that the scores were merely a guide to a child's potential. The teachers talked most about things like cleverness, insight, intuition; the ability to develop rapport, to outguess an opponent; the courage to act boldly, the caution to make certain before committing, the wisdom to know which course was the appropriate one. And in considering this, Bean realized that he was not necessarily any better at *these* things than the other students.

Ender Wiggin really did know things that Bean did not know. Bean might have thought to do as Wiggin did, arranging extra practices to make up for being with a commander who wouldn't train him. Bean even might have tried to bring in a few other students to train with him, since many things could not be done alone. But Wiggin had taken all comers, no matter how difficult it became to practice with so many in the battleroom, and according to the teachers' notes, he spent more time now training others than in working on his own technique. Of course, that was partly because he was no longer in Bonzo Madrid's army, so he got to take part in the regular practices. But he still kept working with the other kids, especially the eager launchies who wanted a head start before they were promoted into a regular army. Why?

Is he doing what I'm doing, studying the other students to prepare for a later war on Earth? Is he building some kind of network that reaches out into all the armies? Is he somehow mistraining them, so he can take advantage of their mistakes later?

From what Bean heard about Wiggin from the kids in his launch group who attended those practices, he came to realize that it was something else entirely. Wiggin seemed really to care about the other kids doing their best. Did he need so badly for them to like him? Because it was working, if that's what he was trying for. They worshiped him.

But there had to be more to it than some hunger for love. Bean couldn't get a handle on it.

He found that the teachers' observations, while helpful, didn't really help him get inside Wiggin's head. For one thing, they kept the psychological observations from the mind game somewhere else that Bean didn't have access to. For another, the teachers couldn't really get into Wiggin's mind because they simply didn't think at his level.

Bean did.

But Bean's project wasn't to analyze Wiggin out of scientific curiosity, or to compete with him, or even to understand him. It was to make himself into the kind of child that the teachers would trust, would rely on. Would regard as fully human. For that project, Wiggin was his teacher because Wiggin had already done what Bean needed to do.

And Wiggin had done it without being perfect. Without being, as far as Bean could tell, completely sane. Not that anyone was. But Wiggin's willingness to give up hours every day to training kids who could do nothing for him—the more Bean thought about it, the less sense it made. Wiggin was not building a network of supporters. Unlike Bean, he didn't have a perfect memory, so Bean was quite sure Wiggin was not compiling a mental dossier on every other kid in Battle School. The kids he worked with were not the best, and were often the most fearful and dependent of the launchies and of the losers in the regular armies. They came to him because they thought being in the same room with the soldier who was leading in the standings might bring some luck to them. But why did Wiggin keep giving his time to *them?*

Why did Poke die for me?

That was the same question. Bean knew it. He found several books about ethics in the library and called them up on his desk to read. He soon discovered that the only theories that explained altruism were bogus. The stupidest was the old sociobiological explanation of uncles dying for nephews—there were no blood ties in armies now, and people often died for strangers. Community theory was fine as far as it went—it explained why communities all honored sacrificial heroes in their stories and rituals, but it still didn't explain the heroes themselves.

For that was what Bean saw in Wiggin. This was the hero at his root.

Wiggin really does not care as much about himself as he does about these other kids who aren't worth five minutes of his time.

And yet this may be the very trait that makes everyone focus on him. Maybe this is why in all those stories Sister Carlotta told him, Jesus always had a crowd around him.

Maybe this is why I'm so afraid of Wiggin. Because *he's* the alien, not me. He's the unintelligible one, the unpredictable one. He's the one who doesn't do things for sensible, predictable reasons. I'm going to survive, and once you know that, there's nothing more to know about me. Him, though, he could do anything.

The more he studied Wiggin, the more mysteries Bean uncovered. The more he determined to act like Wiggin until, at some point, he came to see the world as Wiggin saw it.

But even as he tracked Wiggin—still from a distance—what Bean could not let himself do was what the younger kids did, what Wiggin's disciples did. He could not call him Ender. Calling him by his last name kept him at a distance. A microscope's distance, anyway.

What did Wiggin study when he read on his own? Not the books of military history and strategy that Bean had blown through in a rush and was now rereading methodically, applying everything to both space combat and modern warfare on Earth. Wiggin did his share of reading, too, but when he went into the library he was just as likely to look at combat vids, and the ones he watched most often were of Bugger ships. Those and the clips of Mazer Rackham's strike force in the heroic battle that broke the back of the Second Invasion.

Bean watched them too, though not over and over again—once he saw them, he remembered them perfectly and could replay them in his mind, with enough detail that he could notice things later that he hadn't realized at first. Was Wiggin seeing something new each time he went back to these vids? Or was he looking for something that he hadn't yet found?

Is he trying to understand the way the Buggers think? Why doesn't he realize that the library here simply doesn't have enough of the vids to make it useful? It's all propaganda stuff here. They withheld all the terrible scenes of dead guys, of fighting and killing hand to hand when ships were breached and boarded. They didn't have vids of defeats, where the Buggers blew the human ships out of the sky. All they had here was ships moving around in space, a few minutes of preparation for combat.

War in space? So exciting in the made-up stories, so boring in reality. Occasionally something would light up, mostly it was just dark.

And, of course, the obligatory moment of Mazer Rackham's victory.

What could Wiggin possibly hope to learn?

Bean learned more from the omissions than from what he actually saw. For instance, there was not one picture of Mazer Rackham anywhere in the library. That was odd. The Triumvirates' faces were everywhere, as were those of other commanders and political leaders. Why not Rackham? Had he died in the moment of victory? Or was he, perhaps, a fictitious figure, a deliberately-created legend, so that there could be a name to peg the victory to? But if that were the case, they'd have created a face for him—it was too easy to do that. Was he deformed?

Was he really, really small?

If I grow up to be the commander of the human fleet that defeats the Buggers, will they hide my picture, too, because someone so tiny can never be seen as a hero?

Who cares? I don't want to be a hero.

That's Wiggin's gig.

Nikolai, the boy across from him. Bright enough to make some guesses Bean hadn't made first. Confident enough not to get angry when he caught Bean intruding on him. Bean was so hopeful when he came at last to Nikolai's file.

The teacher evaluation was negative. "A place-holder." Cruel—but was it true?

Bean realized: I have been putting too much trust in the teachers' evaluations. Do I have any real evidence that they're right? Or do I believe in their evaluations because I am rated so highly? Have I let them flatter me into complacency?

What if all their evaluations were hopelessly wrong?

I had no teacher files on the streets of Rotterdam. I actually knew the children. Poke—I made my own judgment of her, and I was almost right, just a few surprises here and there. Sergeant—no surprises at all. Achilles— yes, I knew him.

So why have I stayed apart from the other students? Because they isolated me at first, and because I decided that the teachers had the power. But now I see that I was only partly right. The teachers have the power here and now, but someday I will not be in Battle School, and what does it matter then what the teachers think of me? I can learn all the military theory and history that I want, and it will do me no good if they never entrust me with command. And I will never be placed in charge of an army or a fleet unless they have reason to believe that other men would follow me.

Not men today, but boys, most of them, a few girls. Not men, but they *will* be men. How do they choose their leaders? How do I make them follow one who is so small, so resented?

What did Wiggin do?

Bean asked Nikolai which of the kids in their launch group practiced with Wiggin.

"Only a few. And they on the fringes, neh? Suckups and brags."

"But who are they?"

"You trying to get in with Wiggin?"

"Just want to find out about him."

"What you want to know?"

The questions bothered Bean. He didn't like talking so much about what he was doing. But he didn't sense any malice in Nikolai. He just wanted to know.

"History. He the best, neh? How he get that way?" Bean wondered if he sounded quite natural with the soldier slang. He hadn't used it that much. The music of it, he still wasn't quite there.

"You find out, you tell me." He rolled his eyes in self-derision.

"I'll tell you," said Bean.

"I got a chance to be best like Ender?" Nikolai laughed. "*You* got a chance, the way you learn."

"Wiggin's snot ain't honey," said Bean.

"What does that mean?"

"He human like anybody. I find out, I tell you, OK?"

Bean wondered why Nikolai already despaired about his own chances of being one of the best. Could it be that the teachers' negative evaluation was right after all? Or had they unconsciously let him see their disdain for him, and he believed them?

From the boys Nikolai had pointed out—the brags and suckups, which wasn't an inaccurate evaluation as far as it went—Bean learned what he wanted to know. The names of Wiggin's closest friends.

Shen. Alai. Petra—her again! But Shen the longest.

Bean found him in the library during study time. The only reason to go there was for the vids—all the books could be read from the desks. Shen wasn't watching vids, though. He had his desk with him, and he was playing the fantasy game.

Bean sat down beside him to watch. A lion-headed man in chain mail stood before a giant, who seemed to be offering him a choice of drinks— the sound was shaped so that Bean couldn't hear it from beside the desk, though Shen seemed to be responding; he typed in a few words. His lion-man figure drank one of the substances and promptly died.

Shen muttered something and shoved the desk away.

"That the Giant's Drink?" said Bean. "I heard about that."

"You've never played it?" said Shen. "You can't win it. I *thought.*"

"I heard. Didn't sound fun."

"*Sound* fun? You haven't tried it? It's not like it's hard to find."

Bean shrugged, trying to fake the mannerisms he'd seen other boys use. Shen looked amused. Because Bean did the cool-guy shrug wrong? Or because it looked cute to have somebody so small do it?

"Come on, you don't play the fantasy game?"

"What you said," Bean prompted him. "You *thought* nobody ever won it."

"I saw a guy in a place I'd never seen. I asked him where it was, and he said, 'Other side of the Giant's Drink.' "

"He tell you how to get there?"

"I didn't ask."

"Why not?"

Shen grinned, looked away.

"It be Wiggin, neh?" asked Bean.

The grin faded. "I didn't say that."

"I know you're his friend, that's why I came here."

"What is this? You spying on him? You from Bonzo?"

This was not going well. Bean hadn't realized how protective Wiggin's friends might be. "I'm from me. Look, nothing bad, OK? I just—look, I just want to know about—you know him from the start, right? They say you been his friend from launchy days."

"So what?"

"Look, he got friends, right? Like you. Even though he always does better in class, always the best on everything, right? But they don't hate him."

"Plenty bichão hate him."

"I got to make some friends, man." Bean knew that he shouldn't try to sound pitiful. Instead, he should sound like a pitiful kid who was trying really hard *not* to sound pitiful. So he ended his maudlin little plea with a laugh. As if he was trying to make it sound like a joke.

"You're pretty short," said Shen.

"Not on the planet I'm from," said Bean.

For the first time, Shen let a genuine smile come to his face. "The planet of the pygmies."

"Them boys too big for me."

"Look, I know what you're saying," said Shen. "I had this funny walk. Some of the kids were ragging me. Ender stopped them."

"How?"

"Ragged them more."

"I never heard he got a mouth."

"No, he didn't say nada. Did it on the desk. Sent a message from God."

Oh, yeah. Bean had heard about that. "He did that for you?"

"They were making fun of my butt. I had a big butt. Before workouts, you know? Back then. So he make fun of them for looking at my butt. But he signs it God."

"So they didn't know it was him."

"Oh, they knew. Right away. But he didn't *say* anything. Out loud."

"That's how you got to be friends? He the protector of the little guys?" Like Achilles . . .

"*Little* guys?" said Shen. "He was the smallest in our launch group. Not like you, but way small. Younger, see."

"He was youngest, but he became your protector?"

"No. Not like that. No, he kept it from going on, that's all. He went to the group—it was Bernard, he was getting together the biggest guys, the tough guys—"

"The bullies."

"Yeah, I guess. Only Ender, he goes to Bernard's number one, his best friend. Alai. He gets Alai to be his friend, too."

"So he stole away Bernard's support?"

"No, man. No, it's not like that. He made friends with Alai, and then got Alai to help him make friends with Bernard."

"Bernard . . . he's the one, Ender broke his arm in the shuttle."

"That's right. And I think, really, Bernard never forgave him, but he saw how things were."

"How were things?"

"Ender's *good,* man. You just—he doesn't hate anybody. If you're a good person, you're going to like him. You want him to like you. If he likes you, then you're OK, see? But if you're scum, he just makes you mad. Just knowing he exists, see? So Ender, he tries to wake up the good part of you.''

"How do you wake up 'good parts'?''

"I don't know, man. You think I know? It just . . . you know Ender long enough, he just makes you want him to be proud of you. That sounds so . . . sounds like I'm a baby, neh?''

Bean shook his head. What it sounded like to him was devotion. Bean hadn't really understood this. Friends were friends, he thought. Like Sergeant and Poke used to be, before Achilles. But it was never love. When Achilles came, they loved him, but it was more like worship, like . . . a god, he got them bread, they gave bread back to him. Like . . . well, like what he called himself. Papa. Was it the same thing? Was Ender Achilles all over again?

"You're smart, kid,'' said Shen. "I was there, neh? Only I never once thought, How did Ender *do* it? How can I do the same, be like him? It's like that was Ender, he's great, but it's nothing *I* could do. Maybe I should have tried. I just wanted to be . . . *with* him.''

"Cause you're good, too,'' said Bean.

Shen rolled his eyes. "I guess that's what I was saying, wasn't it? Implying, anyway. Guess that makes me a brag, neh?''

"Big old brag,'' said Bean, grinning.

"He's just . . . he makes you want to . . . I'd die for him. That sounds like hero talk, neh? But it's true. I'd die for him. I'd kill for him.''

"You'd fight for him.''

Shen got it at once. "That's right. He's a born commander.''

"Alai fight for him too?''

"A lot of us.''

"But some not, yes?''

"Like I said, the bad ones, they hate him, he makes them crazy.''

"So the whole world divides up—good people love Wiggin, bad people hate Wiggin.''

Shen's face went suspicious again. "I don't know why I told you all that merda. You too smart to believe any of it.''

"I do believe it,'' said Bean. "Don't be mad at me.'' He'd learned that one a long time ago. Little kid says, Don't be mad at me, they feel a little silly.

"I'm not mad,'' said Shen. "I just thought you were making fun of me.''

"I wanted to know how Wiggin makes friends."

"If I knew that, if I really understood that, I'd have more friends than I do, kid. But I got Ender as my friend, and all his friends are my friends too, and I'm their friend, so . . . it's like a family."

A family. Papa. Achilles again.

That old dread returned. That night after Poke died. Seeing her body in the water. Then Achilles in the morning. How he acted. Was that Wiggin? Papa until he got his chance?

Achilles was evil, and Ender was good. Yet they both created a family. Both had people who loved them, who would die for them. Protector, papa, provider, mama. Only parent to a crowd of orphans. We're all street kids up here in Battle School, too. We might not be hungry, but we're all still wishing for a family.

Except me. Last thing I need. Some papa smiling at me, waiting with a knife.

Better to *be* the papa than to have one.

How can I do that? Get somebody to love me the way Shen loves Wiggin?

No chance. I'm too little. Too cute. I got nothing they want. All I can do is protect myself, work the system. Ender's got plenty to teach those that have some hope of doing what he's done. But me, I have to learn my own way.

Even as he made the decision, though, he knew he wasn't done with Wiggin. Whatever Wiggin had, whatever Wiggin knew, Bean *would* learn it.

And so passed the weeks, the months. Bean did all his regular classwork. He attended the regular battleroom classes with Dimak teaching them how to move and shoot, the basic skills. On his own he completed all the enrichment courses you could take at your own desk, certifying in everything. He studied military history, philosophy, strategy. He read ethics, religion, biology. He kept track of every student in the school, from the newly arrived launchies to the students about to graduate. When he saw them in the halls, he knew more about them than they knew about themselves. He knew their nation of origin. He knew how much they missed their families and how important their native country or ethnic or religious group was to them. He knew how valuable they might be to a nationalist or idealist resistance movement.

And he kept reading everything Wiggin read, watching everything Wiggin watched. Hearing about Wiggin from the other kids. Watching Wiggin's standings on the boards. Meeting more of Wiggin's friends, hearing them talk about him. Bean listened to all the things Wiggin was quoted as saying and tried to fit them into some coherent philosophy, some worldview, some attitude, some plan.

And he found out something interesting. Despite Wiggin's altruism, despite his willingness to sacrifice, not one of his friends ever said that Wiggin came and talked over his problems. They all went to Wiggin, but who did Wiggin go to? He had no more *real* friends than Bean did. Wiggin kept his own counsel, just like Bean.

Soon Bean found himself being advanced out of classes whose work he had already mastered and being plunged into classwork with older and older groups, who looked at him with annoyance at first, but later simply with awe, as he raced past them and was promoted again before they were half done. Had Wiggin been pushed through his classwork at an accelerated rate? Yes, but not quite as fast. Was that because Bean was better? Or because the deadline was getting closer?

For the sense of urgency in teacher evaluations was getting greater. The ordinary students—as if any child here were ordinary—were getting briefer and briefer notations. They weren't being ignored, exactly. But the best were being identified and lifted out.

The *seeming* best. For Bean began to realize that the teachers' evaluations were often colored by which students they liked the best. The teachers pretended to be dispassionate, impartial, but in fact they got sucked in by the more charismatic children, just as the other students did. If a kid was likable, they gave him better comments on leadership, even if he was really just glib and athletic and needed to surround himself with a team. As often as not, they tagged the very students who would be the least effective commanders, while ignoring the ones who, to Bean, showed real promise. It was frustrating to watch them make such obvious mistakes. Here they had Wiggin right before their eyes—Wiggin, who was the real thing—and they still went on misreading everybody else. Getting all excited about some of these energetic, self-confident, ambitious kids even though they weren't actually producing excellent work.

Wasn't this whole school set up in order to find and train the best possible commanders? The Earthside testing did pretty well—there were no real dolts among the students. But the system had overlooked one crucial factor: How were the teachers chosen?

They were career military, all of them. Proven officers with real ability. But in the military you don't get trusted positions just because of your ability. You also have to attract the notice of superior officers. You have to be liked. You have to fit in with the system. You have to look like what the officers above you think that officers should look like. You have to think in ways that they are comfortable with.

The result was that you ended up with a command structure that was top-heavy with guys who looked good in uniform and talked right and did well enough not to embarrass themselves, while the really good ones quietly did all the serious work and bailed out their superiors and got blamed for errors they had advised against until they eventually got out.

That was the military. These teachers were all the kind of people who thrived in that environment. And they were selecting their favorite students based on precisely that same screwed-up sense of priorities.

No wonder a kid like Dink Meeker saw through it and refused to play. He was one of the few kids who was both likable *and* talented. His likability made them try to make him commander of his own army; his talent let him understand why they were doing it and turn them down because he couldn't believe in such a stupid system. And other kids, like Petra Arkanian, who had obnoxious personalities but could handle strategy and tactics in their sleep, who had the confidence to lead others into war, to trust their own decisions and act on them—they didn't care about trying to be one of the guys, and so they got overlooked, every flaw became magnified, every strength belittled.

So Bean began constructing his own anti-army. Kids who weren't getting picked out by the teachers, but were the real talents, the ones with heart and mind, not just face and chat. He began to imagine who among them should be officers, leading their own toons under the command of . . .

Of Ender Wiggin, of course. Bean could not imagine anyone else in that position. Wiggin would know how to use them.

And Bean knew just where he should be. Close to Wiggin. A toon leader, but the most trusted of them. Wiggin's righthand man. So when Wiggin was about to make a mistake, Bean could point out to him the error he was making. And so that Bean could be close enough to maybe understand why Wiggin was human and he himself was not.

Sister Carlotta used her new security clearance like a scalpel, most of the time, slicing her way into the information establishment, picking up answers here and new questions there, talking to people who never guessed what her project was, why she knew so much about their top-secret work, and quietly putting it all together in her own mind, in memos to Colonel Graff.

But sometimes she wielded her top security clearance like a meat-ax, using it to get past prison wardens and security officers, who saw her un-

believable level of need-to-know and then, when they checked to make sure
her documents weren't a stupid forgery, were screamed at by officers so
high-ranked that it made them want to treat Sister Carlotta like God.

That's how, at last, she came face to face with Bean's father. Or at
least the closest thing to a father that he had.

"I want to talk to you about your installation in Rotterdam."

He looked at her sourly. "I already reported on everything. That's why
I'm not dead, though I wonder if I made the right choice."

"They told me you were quite the whiner," said Sister Carlotta, utterly
devoid of compassion. "I didn't expect it to surface so quickly."

"Go to hell." He turned his back on her.

As if that meant anything. "Dr. Volescu, the records show that you
had twenty-three babies in your organ farm in Rotterdam."

He said nothing.

"But of course that's a lie."

Silence.

"And, oddly enough, I know that the lie is not your idea. Because I
know that your installation was not an organ farm indeed, and that the
reason you aren't dead is because you agreed to plead guilty to running an
organ farm in exchange for never discussing what you were *really* doing
there."

He slowly turned around again. Enough that he could look up and see
her with a sidelong glance. "Let me see that clearance you tried to show
me before."

She showed it to him again. He studied it.

"What do you know?" he asked.

"I know your real crime was continuing a research project after it was
closed down. Because you had these fertilized eggs that had been meticu-
lously altered. You had turned Anton's key. You wanted them to be born.
You wanted to see who they would become."

"If you know all that, why have you come to me? Everything I knew
is in the documents you must have read."

"Not at all," said Sister Carlotta. "I don't care about confessions. I
don't care about logistics. I want to know about the babies."

"They're all dead," he said. "We killed them when we knew we were
about to be discovered." He looked at her with bitter defiance. "Yes, in-
fanticide. Twenty-three murders. But since the government couldn't admit
that such children had ever existed, I was never charged with the crimes.
God judges me, though. God will press the charges. Is that why you're
here? Is that who gave you your clearance?"

You make jokes about this? "All I want to know is what you learned about them."

"I learned nothing, there was no time, they were still babies."

"You had them for almost a year. They developed. All the work done since Anton found his key was theoretical. *You* watched the babies grow."

A slow smile crept across his face. "This is like those Nazi medical crimes all over again. You deplore what I did, but you still want to know the results of my research."

"You monitored their growth. Their health. Their intellectual development."

"We were about to start the tracking of intellectual development. The project wasn't funded, of course, so it's not as if we could provide much more than a clean warm room and basic bodily needs."

"Their bodies, then. Their motor skills."

"Small," he said. "They are born small, they grow slowly. Undersized and underweight, all of them."

"But very bright?"

"Crawling very young. Making pre-speech sounds far earlier than normal. That's all we knew. I didn't see them often myself. I couldn't afford the risk of detection."

"So what was your prognosis?"

"Prognosis?"

"How did you see their future?"

"Dead. That's everyone's future. What are you talking about?"

"If they hadn't been slaughtered, Dr. Volescu, what would have happened?"

"They would have kept on growing, of course."

"And later?"

"There *is* no later. They keep on growing."

She thought for a moment, trying to process the information.

"That's right, Sister. You're getting it. They grow slowly, but they never stop. That's what Anton's key does. Unlocks the mind because the brain never stops growing. But neither does anything else. The cranium keeps expanding—it's never fully closed. The arms and legs, longer and longer."

"So when they reach adult height . . ."

"There is no adult height. There's just height at time of death. You can't keep growing like that forever. There's a reason why evolution builds a stop-clock into the growth control of long-lived bodies. You can't keep growing without some organ giving out, eventually. Usually the heart."

The implications filled Sister Carlotta with dread. "And the rate of this growth? In the children, I mean? How long until they are at normal height for their age?"

"My guess was that they'd catch up twice," said Volescu. "Once just before puberty, and then the normal kids would leap ahead for a while, but slow and steady wins the race, n'est-ce pas? By twenty, they would be giants. And then they'd die, almost certainly before age twenty-five. Do you have any idea how huge they would be? So my killing them, you see— it was a mercy."

"I doubt any of them would have chosen to miss out on even the mere twenty years you took from them."

"They never knew what happened to them. I'm not a monster. We drugged them all. They died in their sleep and then the bodies were incinerated."

"What about puberty? Would they ever mature sexually?"

"That's the part we'll never know, isn't it?"

Sister Carlotta got up to go.

"He lived, didn't he?" asked Volescu.

"Who?"

"The one we lost. The one whose body wasn't with the others. I counted only twenty-two going into the fire."

"When you worship Moloch, Dr. Volescu, you get no answers but the ones your chosen god provides."

"Tell me what he's like." His eyes were so hungry.

"You know it was a boy?"

"They were all boys," said Volescu.

"What, did you discard the girls?"

"How do you think I got the genes I worked with? I implanted my own altered DNA into denucleated eggs."

"God help us, they were all your own twins?"

"I'm not the monster you think I am," said Volescu. "I brought the frozen embryos to life because I had to know what they would become. Killing them was my greatest sorrow."

"And yet you did it—to save yourself."

"I was afraid. And the thought came to me: They're only copies. It isn't murder to discard the copies."

"Their souls and lives were their own."

"Do you think the government would have let them live? Do you really think they would have survived? Any of them?"

"You don't deserve to have a son," said Sister Carlotta.

"But I have one, don't I?" He laughed. "While you, Miss Carlotta, perpetual bride of the invisible God, how many do *you* have?"

"They may have been copies, Volescu, but even dead they're worth more than the original."

He continued laughing as she walked down the corridor away from him, but it sounded forced. She knew his laughter was a mask for grief. But it wasn't the grief of compassion, or even of remorse. It was the grief of a damned soul.

Bean. God be thanked, she thought, that you do not know your father, and never will. You're nothing like him. You're far more human.

In the back of her mind, though, she had one nagging doubt. Was she sure Bean had more compassion, more humanity? Or was Bean as cold of heart as this man? As incapable of empathy? Was he all mind?

Then she thought of him growing and growing, from this too-tiny child to a giant whose body could no longer sustain life. This was the legacy your father gave you. This was Anton's key. She thought of David's cry, when he learned of the death of his son. Absalom! Oh Absalom! Would God I could die for thee, Absalom, my son!

But he was not dead yet, was he? Volescu might have been lying, might simply be wrong. There might be some way to prevent it. And even if there was not, there were still many years ahead of Bean. And how he lived those years still mattered.

God raises up the children that he needs, and makes men and women of them, and then takes them from this world at his good pleasure. To him all of life is but a moment. All that matters is what that moment was used for. And Bean *would* use it well. She was sure of that.

Or at least she hoped it with such fervor that it felt like certainty.

12

ROSTER

"If Wiggin's the one, then let's get him to Eros."

"He's not ready for Command School yet. It's premature."

"Then we have to go with one of the alternates."

"That's your decision."

"*Our* decision! What do we have to go on but what you tell us?"

"I've told you about those older boys, too. You have the same data I have."

"Do we have all of it?"

"Do you *want* all of it?"

"Do we have the data on all the children with scores and evaluations at such a high level?"

"No."

"Why not?"

"Some of them are disqualified for various reasons."

"Disqualified by whom?"

"By me."

"On what grounds?"

"One of them is borderline insane, for instance. We're trying to find some structure in which his abilities will be useful. But he could not possibly bear the weight of complete command."

"That's one."

"Another is undergoing surgery to correct a physical defect."

"Is it a defect that limits his ability to command?"

"It limits his ability to be trained to command."

"But it's being fixed."

"He's about to have his third operation. If it works, he might amount to something. But, as you say, there won't be time."

"How many more children have you concealed from us?"

"I have *concealed* none of them. If you mean how many have I simply not referred to you as potential commanders, the answer is *all* of them. Except the ones whose names you already have."

"Let me be blunt. We hear rumors about a very young one."

"They're all young."

"We hear rumors about a child who makes the Wiggin boy look slow."

"They all have their different strengths."

"There are those who want you relieved of your command."

"If I'm not to be allowed to select and train these kids properly, I'd prefer to be relieved, sir. Consider this a request."

"So it was a stupid threat. Advance them all as quickly as you can. Just keep in mind that they need a certain amount of time in Command School, too. It does us no good to give them all your training if they don't have time to get ours."

Dimak met Graff in the battleroom control center. Graff conducted all his secure meetings here, until they could be sure Bean had grown enough that he couldn't get through the ducts. The battlerooms had their own separate air systems.

Graff had an essay on his desk display. "Have you read this? 'Problems in Campaigning Between Solar Systems Separated by Lightyears.'"

"It's been circulating pretty widely among the faculty."

"But it isn't signed," said Graff. "You don't happen to know who wrote it, do you?"

"No, sir. Did you write it?"

"I'm no scholar, Dimak, you know that. In fact, this was written by a student."

"At Command School?"

"A student here."

At that moment Dimak understood why he had been called in. "Bean."

"Six years old. The paper reads like a work of scholarship!"

"I should have guessed. He picks up the voice of the strategists he's been reading. Or their translators. Though I don't know what will happen now that he's he's been reading Frederick and Bulow in the original—French and German. He inhales languages and breathes them back out.''

''What did you think of this paper?''

''You already know it's killing me to keep key information from this boy. If he can write *this* with what he knows, what would happen if we told him everything? Colonel Graff, why can't we promote him right out of Battle School, set him loose as a theorist, and then watch what he spits out?''

''Our job isn't to find theorists here. It's too late for theory anyway.''

''I just think . . . look, a kid so small, who'd follow him? He's being wasted here. But when he writes, nobody knows how little he is. Nobody knows how young he is.''

''I see your point, but we're not going to breach security, period.''

''Isn't he already a grave security risk?''

''The mouse who scutters through the ducts?''

''No. I think he's grown too big for that. He doesn't do those side-arm pushups anymore. I thought the security risk came from the fact that he guessed that an offensive fleet had been launched generations ago, so why were we still training children for command?''

''From analysis of his papers, from his activities when he signs on as a teacher, we think he's got a theory and it's wonderfully wrong. But he believes his false theory *only* because he doesn't know about the ansible. Do you understand? Because that's the main thing we'd have to tell him about, isn't it?''

''Of course.''

''So you see, that's the one thing we can't tell him.''

''What is his theory?''

''That we're assembling children here in preparation for a war between nations, or between nations and the I.F. A landside war, back on Earth.''

''Why would we take the kids into space to prepare for a war on Earth?''

''Think just a minute and you'll get it.''

''Because . . . because when we've licked the Formics, there probably *will* be a little landside conflict. And all the talented commanders—the I.F. would already have them.''

''You see? We can't have this kid publishing, not even within the I.F. Not everybody has given up loyalty to groups on Earth.''

''So why did you call me in?''

''Because I *do* want to use him. We aren't running the war here, but we *are* running a school. Did you read his paper about the ineffectiveness of using officers as teachers?''

"Yes. I felt slapped.''

"This time he's mostly wrong, because he has no way of knowing how nontraditional our recruitment of faculty has always been. But he may also be a little bit right. Because our system of testing for officer potential was designed to produce candidates with the traits identified in the most highly regarded officers in the Second Invasion.''

"Hi-ho.''

"You see? Some of the highly regarded were officers who performed well in battle, but the war was too short to weed out the deadwood. The officers they tested included just the kind of people he criticized in his paper. So . . .''

"So he had the wrong reason, but the right result.''

"Absolutely. It gives us little pricks like Bonzo Madrid. You've known officers like him, haven't you? So why should we be surprised that our tests give him command of an army even though he has no idea what to do with it. All the vanity and all the stupidity of Custer or Hooker or—hell, pick your own vain incompetent, it's the most common kind of general officer.''

"May I quote you?''

"I'll deny it. The thing is, Bean has been studying the dossiers of all the other students. We think he's evaluating them for loyalty to their native identity group, and also for their excellence as commanders.''

"By *his* standards of excellence.''

"We need to get Ender the command of an army. We're under a lot of pressure to get our leading candidates into Command School. But if we bust one of the current commanders in order to make a place for Ender, it'll cause too much resentment.''

"So you have to give him a new army.''

"Dragon.''

"There are still kids here who remember the last Dragon Army.''

"Right. I like that. The jinx.''

"I see. You want to give Ender a running start.''

"It gets worse.''

"I thought it would.''

"We also aren't going to give him any soldiers that aren't already on their commanders' transfer list.''

"The dregs? What are you *doing* to this kid?''

"If we choose them, by our ordinary standards, then yes, the dregs. But we aren't going to choose Ender's army."

"Bean?"

"Our tests are worthless on this, right? Some of those dregs are the very best students, according to Bean, right? And he's been studying the launchies. So give him an assignment. Tell him to solve a hypothetical problem. Construct an army only out of launchies. Maybe the soldiers on the transfer lists, too."

"I don't think there's any way to do that without telling him that we're on to his fake teacher log-in."

"So tell him."

"Then he won't believe anything he found while searching."

"He didn't find anything," said Graff. "We didn't have to plant anything fake for him to find, because he had his false theory. See? So whether he thinks we planted stuff or not, he'll stay deceived and we're still secure."

"You seem to be counting on your understanding of his psychology."

"Sister Carlotta assures me that he differs from ordinary human DNA in only one small area."

"So now he's human again?"

"I've got to make decisions based on *something,* Dimak!"

"So the jury's still out on the human thing?"

"Get me a roster of the hypothetical army Bean would pick, so we can give it to Ender."

"He'll put himself in it, you know."

"He damn well better, or he's not as smart as we've been thinking."

"What about Ender? Is he ready?"

"Anderson thinks he is." Graff sighed. "To Bean, it's still just a game, because none of the weight has fallen on him yet. But Ender . . . I think he knows, deep down, where this is going to lead. I think he feels it already."

"Sir, just because you're feeling the weight doesn't mean he is."

Graff laughed. "You cut straight to the heart of things, don't you!"

"Bean's hungry for it, sir. If Ender isn't, then why not put the burden where it's wanted?"

"If Bean's hungry for it, it proves he's still too young. Besides, the hungry ones always have something to prove. Look at Napoleon. Look at Hitler. Bold at first, yes, but then *still* bold later on, when they need to cautious, to pull back. Patton. Caesar. Alexander. Always overreaching, never quite putting the finish on it. No, it's Ender, not Bean. Ender doesn't want to do it, so he won't have anything to prove."

"Are you sure you're not just picking the kind of commander you'd want to serve under?"

"That's precisely what I'm doing," said Graff. "Can you think of a better standard?"

"The thing is, you can't pass the buck on this one, can you? Can't say how it was the tests, you just followed the tests. The scores. Whatever."

"Can't run this like a machine."

"That's why you don't want Bean, isn't it? Because he was *made,* like a machine."

"I don't analyze myself. I analyze *them.*"

"So if we win, who really won the war? The commander you picked? Or you, for picking him?"

"The Triumvirate, for trusting me. After their fashion. But if we lose . . ."

"Well *then* it's definitely you."

"We're *all* dead then. What will they do? Kill me first? Or leave me till last so I can contemplate the consequences of my error?"

"Ender, though. I mean if he's the one. *He* won't say it's you. He'll take it all on himself. Not the credit for victory—just the blame for failure."

"Win or lose, the kid I pick is going to have a brutal time of it."

Bean got his summons during lunch. He reported at once to Dimak's quarters.

He found his teacher sitting at his desk, reading something. The light was set so that Bean couldn't read it through the dazzle.

"Have a seat," said Dimak.

Bean jumped up and sat on Dimak's bed, his legs dangling.

"Let me read you something," said Dimak. " 'There are no fortifications, no magazines, no strong points. . . . In the enemy solar system, there can be no living off the land, since access to habitable planets will be possible only after complete victory. . . . Supply lines are not a problem, since there are none to protect, but the cost of that is that all supplies and ordnance must be carried with the invading fleet. . . . In effect, all interstellar invasion fleets are suicide attacks, because time dilation means that even if a fleet returns intact, almost no one they knew will still be alive. They can never return, and so must be sure that their force is sufficient to be decisive and therefore is worth the sacrifice. . . . Mixed-sex forces allow the possibility of the army becoming a permanent colony and/or occupying force on the captured enemy planet.''

Bean listened complacently. He had left it in his desk for them to find it, and they had done so.

''You wrote this, Bean, but you never submitted it to anybody.''

''There was never an assignment that it fit.''

''You don't seem surprised that we found it.''

''I assume that you routinely scan our desks.''

''Just as you routinely scan ours?''

Bean felt his stomach twist with fear. They knew.

''Cute, naming your false log-in 'Graff' with a caret in front of it.''

Bean said nothing.

''You've been scanning all the other students' records. Why?''

''I wanted to know them. I've only made friends with a few.''

''Close friends with none.''

''I'm little and I'm smarter than they are. Nobody's standing in line.''

''So you use their records to tell you more about them. Why do you feel the need to understand them?''

''Someday I'll be in command of one of these armies.''

''Plenty of time to get to know your soldiers then.''

''No sir,'' said Bean. ''No time at all.''

''Why do you say that?''

''Because of the way I've been promoted. And Wiggin. We're the two best students in this school, and we're being raced through. I'm not going to have much time when I get an army.''

''Bean, be realistic. It's going to be a long time before anybody's going to be willing to follow you into battle.''

Bean said nothing. He knew that this was false, even if Dimak didn't.

''Let's see just how good your analysis is. Let me give you an assignment.''

''For which class?''

''No class, Bean. I want you to create a hypothetical army. Working only with launchies, construct an entire roster, the full complement of forty-one soldiers.''

''*No* veterans?''

Bean meant the question neutrally, just checking to make sure he understood the rules. But Dimak seemed to take it as criticism of the unfairness of it. ''No, tell you what, you can include veterans who are posted for transfer at their commanders' request. That'll give you some experienced ones.''

The ones the commander couldn't work with. Some really were losers, but some were the opposite. "Fine," said Bean.

"How long do you think it will take you?"

Bean already had a dozen picked out. "I can tell the list to you right now."

"I want you to think about it seriously."

"I already have. But you need to answer a couple of questions first. You said forty-one soldiers, but that would include the commander."

"All right, forty, and leave the commander blank."

"I have another question. Am I to command the army?"

"You can write it up that way, if you want."

But Dimak's very unconcern told Bean that the army was not for him. "This army's for Wiggin, isn't it?"

Dimak glowered. "It's hypothetical."

"Definitely Wiggin," said Bean. "You can't boot somebody else out of command to make room for him, so you're giving Wiggin a whole new army. I bet it's Dragon."

Dimak looked stricken, though he tried to cover it.

"Don't worry," said Bean. "I'll give him the best army you can form, following those rules."

"I *said* this was hypothetical!"

"You think I wouldn't figure it out when I found myself in Wiggin's army and everybody else in it was also on my roster?"

"Nobody's said we're actually going to follow your roster!"

"You will. Because I'll be right and you'll know it," said Bean. "And I can promise you, it'll be a hell of an army. With Wiggin to train us, we'll kick ass."

"Just do the hypothetical assignment, and talk to no one about it. Ever."

That was dismissal, but Bean didn't want to be dismissed yet. They came to *him*. They were having *him* do their work. He wanted to have his say while they were still listening. "The reason this army can be so good is that your system's been promoting a lot of the wrong kids. About half the best kids in this school are launchies or on the transfer lists, because they're the ones who haven't already been beaten into submission by the kiss-ass idiots you put in command of armies or toons. These misfits and little kids are the ones who can win. Wiggin will figure that out. He'll know how to use us."

"Bean, you're not as smart about everything as you think you are!"

"Yes I am, sir," said Bean. "Or you wouldn't have given this assignment to me. May I be dismissed? Or do you want me to tell you the roster now?"

"Dismissed," said Dimak.

I probably shouldn't have provoked him, thought Bean. Now it's possible that he'll fiddle with my roster just to prove he can. But that's not the kind of man he is. If I'm not right about that, then I'm not right about anybody else, either.

Besides, it felt good to speak the truth to someone in power.

After working with the list a little while, Bean was just as glad that Dimak hadn't taken him up on his foolish offer to make up the roster on the spot. Because it wasn't just a matter of naming the forty best soldiers among the launchies and the transfer lists.

Wiggin was way early for command, and that would make it harder for older kids to take it—getting put into a kid's army. So he struck off the list all who were older than Wiggin.

That left him with nearly sixty kids who were good enough to be in the army. Bean was ranking them in order of value when he realized that he was about to make another mistake. Quite a few of these kids were in the group of launchies and soldiers that practiced with Wiggin during free time. Wiggin would know these kids best, and naturally he'd look to them to be his toon leaders. The core of his army.

The trouble was, while a couple of them would do fine as toon leaders, relying on that group would mean passing over several who weren't part of that group. Including Bean.

So he doesn't choose me to lead a toon. He isn't going to choose me anyway, right? I'm too little. He won't look at me and see a leader.

Is this just about me, then? Am I corrupting this process just to get myself a chance to show what I can do?

And if I am, what's wrong with that? I know what I can do, and no one else really gets it. The teachers think I'm a scholar, they know I'm smart, they trust my judgment, but they aren't making this army for me, they're making it for him. I still have to prove to them what I can do. And if I really am one of the best, it would be to the benefit of the program to have it revealed as quickly as possible.

And then he thought: Is this how idiots rationalize their stupidity to themselves?

"Ho, Bean," said Nikolai.

"Ho," said Bean. He passed a hand across his desk, blanking the display. "Tell me."

"Nothing to tell. *You* looked grim."

"Just doing an assignment."

Nikolai laughed. "You never look that serious doing classwork. You just read for a while and then you type for a while. Like it was nothing. This is something."

"An extra assignment."

"A hard one, neh?"

"Not very."

"Sorry to break in. Just thought maybe something was wrong. Maybe a letter from home."

They both laughed at that. Letters weren't that common here. Every few months at the most. And the letters were pretty empty when they came. Some never got mail at all. Bean was one of them, and Nikolai knew why. It wasn't a secret, he was just the only one who noticed and the only one who asked about it. "No family at *all?*" he had said. "Some kids' families, maybe I'm the lucky one," Bean answered him, and Nikolai agreed. "But not mine. I wish you had parents like mine." And then he went on about how he was an only child, but his parents really worked hard to get him. "They did it with surgery, fertilized five or six eggs, then twinned the healthiest ones a few more times, and finally they picked me. I grew up like I was going to be king or the Dalai Lama or something. And then one day the I.F. says, we need him. Hardest thing my parents ever did, saying yes. But I said, What if I'm the next Mazer Rackham? And they let me go."

That was months ago, but it was still between them, that conversation. Kids didn't talk much about home. Nikolai didn't discuss his family with anybody else, either. Just with Bean. And in return, Bean told him a little about life on the street. Not a lot of details, because it would sound like he was asking for pity or trying to look cool. But he mentioned how they were organized into a family. Talked about how it was Poke's crew, and then it became Achilles' family, and how they got into a charity kitchen. Then Bean waited to see how much of this story started circulating.

None of it did. Nikolai never said a word about it to anyone else. That was when Bean was sure that Nikolai was worth having as a friend. He could keep things to himself without even having to be asked to do it.

And now here Bean was, making up the roster for this great army, and here sat Nikolai, asking him what he was doing. Dimak had said to tell no one, but Nikolai could keep a secret. What harm could it do?

Then Bean recovered his senses. Knowing about this wouldn't help Nikolai in any way. Either he'd be in Dragon Army or he wouldn't. If he wasn't, he'd know Bean hadn't put him there. If he was, it would be worse, because he'd wonder if Bean had included him in the roster out of friendship instead of excellence.

Besides, Nikolai shouldn't be in Dragon Army. Bean liked him and trusted him, but Nikolai was not among the best of the launchies. He was smart, he was quick, he was good—but he was nothing special.

Except to me, thought Bean.

"It was a letter from *your* parents," said Bean. "They've stopped writing to you, they like me better."

"Yeah, and the Vatican is moving to Mecca."

"And I'm going to be made Polemarch."

"No jeito," said Nikolai. "You too tall, bicho." Nikolai picked up his desk. "I can't help you with your classwork tonight, Bean, so please don't beg me." He lay back on his bed, started into the fantasy game.

Bean lay back, too. He woke up his display and began wrestling with the names again. If he eliminated every one of the kids who'd been practicing with Wiggin, how many of the good ones would it leave? Fifteen veterans from the transfer lists. Twenty-two launchies, including Bean.

Why *hadn't* these launchies taken part in Wiggin's freetime practices? The veterans, they were already in trouble with their commanders, they weren't about to antagonize them any more, so it made sense for them not to have taken part. But these launchies, weren't they ambitious? Or were they bookish, trying to do it all through classwork instead of catching on that the battleroom was everything? Bean couldn't fault them for that—it had taken him a while to catch on, too. Were they so confident of their own abilities they didn't think they needed the extra prep? Or so arrogant they didn't want anybody to think they owed their success to Ender Wiggin? Or so shy they . . .

No. He couldn't possibly guess their motives. They were all too complex anyway. They were smart, with good evaluations—good by Bean's standards, not necessarily by the teachers'. That was all he needed to know. If he gave Wiggin an army without a single kid he'd worked with in practices, then all the army would start out equal in his eyes. Which meant Bean would have the same chance as any other kid to earn Wiggin's eye and maybe get command of a toon. If they couldn't compete with Bean for that position, then too damn bad for them.

But that left him with thirty-seven names on the roster. Three more slots to fill.

He went back and forth on a couple. Finally decided to include Crazy Tom, a veteran who held the unenviable record of being the most-transferred soldier in the history of the game who wasn't actually iced and sent home. So far. The thing was, Crazy Tom really was good. Sharp mind. But he couldn't stand it when somebody above him was stupid and unfair. And when he got pissed, he really went off. Ranting, throwing things, tearing bedding off every bed in his barracks once, another time writing a message about what an idiot his commander was and mailing it to every other student in the school. A few actually got it before the teachers intercepted it, and they said it was the hottest thing they ever read. Crazy Tom. Could be disruptive. But maybe he was just waiting for the right commander. He was in.

And a girl, Wu, which of course had become Woo and even Woo-*hoo*. Brilliant at her studies, absolutely a killer in the arcade games, but she refused to be a toon leader and as soon as her commanders asked her, she put in for a transfer and refused to fight until they gave it to her. Weird. Bean had no idea why she did that—the teachers were baffled, too. Nothing in her tests to show why. What the hell, thought Bean. She's in.

Last slot.

He typed in Nikolai's name.

Am I doing him a favor? He's not bad, he's just a little slower than these kids, just a little gentler. It'll be hard for him. And if he's left out of it, he won't mind. He'll just do his best with whatever army he gets sent to eventually.

And yet . . . Dragon Army is going to be a legend. Not just here in Battle School, either. These kids are going to go on to be leaders in the I.F. Or somewhere, anyway. And they'll tell stories about when they were in Dragon Army with the great Ender Wiggin. And if I include Nikolai, then even if he isn't the best of the soldiers, even if he's in fact the slowest, he'll still be *in,* he'll still be able to tell those stories someday. And he's not bad. He won't embarrass himself. He won't bring down the army. He'll do OK. So why not?

And I want him with me. He's the only one I've ever talked to. About personal things. The only one who knows the name of Poke. I want him. And there's a slot on the roster.

Bean went down the list one more time. Then he alphabetized it and mailed it to Dimak.

The next morning, Bean, Nikolai, and three other kids in their launch group had their assignment to Dragon Army. Months before they should have been promoted to soldiers. The unchosen kids were envious, hurt, furious by turn. Especially when they realized Bean was one of the chosen. "Do they *make* uniform flash suits that size?"

It was a good question. And the answer was no, they didn't. The colors of Dragon Army were grey, orange, grey. Because soldiers were usually a lot older than Bean when they came in, they had to cut a flash suit down for Bean, and they didn't do it all that well. Flash suits weren't manufactured in space, and nobody had the tools to do a first-rate job of alteration.

When they finally got it to fit him, Bean wore his flash suit to the Dragon Army barracks. Because it had taken him so long to be fitted, he was the last to arrive. Wiggin arrived at the door just as Bean was entering. "Go ahead," said Wiggin.

It was the first time Wiggin had ever spoken to him—for all Bean knew, the first time Wiggin had even noticed him. So thoroughly had Bean concealed his fascination with Wiggin that he had made himself effectively invisible.

Wiggin followed him into the room. Bean started down the corridor between the bunks, heading for the back of the room where the younger soldiers always had to sleep. He glanced at the other kids, who were all looking at him as he passed with a mixture of horror and amusement. They were in an army so lame that *this* little tiny kid was part of it?

Behind him, Wiggin was starting his first speech. Voice confident, loud enough but not shouting, not nervous. "I'm Ender Wiggin. I'm your commander. Bunking will be arranged by seniority."

Some of the launchies groaned.

"Veterans to the back of the room, newest soldiers to the front."

The groaning stopped. That was the opposite of the way things were usually arranged. Wiggin was already shaking things up. Whenever he came into the barracks, the kids closest to him would be the new ones. Instead of getting lost in the shuffle, they'd always have his attention.

Bean turned around and headed back to the front of the room. He was still the youngest kid in Battle School, but five of the soldiers were from more recently arrived launch groups, so they got the positions nearest the door. Bean got an upper bunk directly across from Nikolai, who had the same seniority, being from the same launch group.

Bean clambered up onto his bed, hampered by his flash suit, and put his palm beside the locker. Nothing happened.

"Those of you who are in an army for the first time," said Wiggin, "just pull the locker open by hand. No locks. Nothing private here."

Laboriously Bean pulled off his flash suit to stow it in his locker.

Wiggin walked along between the bunks, making sure that seniority was respected. Then he jogged to the front of the room. "All right, everybody. Put on your flash suits and come to practice."

Bean looked at him in complete exasperation. Wiggin had been looking right at him when he started taking off his flash suit. Why didn't he suggest that Bean not take the damn thing off?

"We're on the morning schedule," Wiggin continued. "Straight to practice after breakfast. Officially you have a free hour between breakfast and practice. We'll see what happens after I find out how good you are."

Truth was, Bean felt like an idiot. Of course Wiggin would head for practice immediately. He shouldn't have needed a warning not to take the suit off. He should have *known*.

He tossed his suit pieces onto the floor and slid down the frame of the bunk. A lot of the other kids were talking, flipping clothes at each other, playing with their weapons. Bean tried to put on the cut-down suit, but couldn't figure out some of the jury-rigged fastenings. He had to take off several pieces and examine them to see how they fit, and finally gave up, took it all off, and started assembling it on the floor.

Wiggin, unconcerned, glanced at his watch. Apparently three minutes was his deadline. "All right, everybody out, now! On your way!"

"But I'm naked!" said one boy—Anwar, from Ecuador, child of Egyptian immigrants. His dossier ran through Bean's mind.

"Dress faster next time," said Wiggin.

Bean was naked, too. Furthermore, Wiggin was standing right there, watching him struggle with his suit. He could have helped. He could have waited. What am I getting myself in for?

"Three minutes from first call to running out the door—that's the rule this week," said Wiggin. "Next week the rule is two minutes. Move!"

Out in the corridor, kids who were in the midst of free time or were heading for class stopped to watch the parade of the unfamiliar uniforms of Dragon Army. And to mock the ones that were even more unusual.

One thing for sure. Bean was going to have to practice getting dressed in his cut-down suit if he was going to avoid running naked through the corridors. And if Wiggin didn't make any exceptions for him the first day, when he'd only just got his nonregulation flash suit, Bean certainly was *not* going to ask for special favors.

I chose to put myself in this army, Bean reminded himself as he jogged along, trying to keep pieces of his flash suit from spilling out of his arms.

Part Four

SOLDIER

13

DRAGON ARMY

"I need access to Bean's genetic information," said Sister Carlotta.

"That's not for you," said Graff.

"And here I thought my clearance level would open *any* door."

"We invented a special new category of security, called 'Not
for Sister Carlotta.' We don't want you sharing Bean's genetic information with anyone else. And you were already planning on
putting it in other hands, weren't you?"

"Only to perform a test. So . . . you'll have to perform it for
me. I want a comparison between Bean's DNA and Volescu's."

"I thought you told me Volescu was the source of the cloned
DNA."

"I've been thinking about it since I told you that, Colonel Graff,
and you know what? Bean doesn't look anything like Volescu. I
couldn't see how he could possibly grow up to be like him, either."

"Maybe the difference in growth patterns makes him look different, too."

"Maybe. But it's also possible Volescu is lying. He's a vain
man."

"Lying about everything?"

"Lying about anything. About paternity, quite possibly. And if
he's lying about that—"

"Then maybe Bean's prognosis isn't so bleak? Don't you think
we've already checked with our genetics people? Volescu wasn't

lying about that, anyway. Anton's key will probably behave just the way he described."

"Please. Run the test and tell me the results."

"Because you don't want Bean to be Volescu's son."

"I don't want Bean to be Volescu's twin. And neither, I think, do you."

"Good point. Though I must tell you, the boy does have a vain streak."

"When you're as gifted as Bean, accurate self-assessment looks like vanity to other people."

"Yeah, but he doesn't have to rub it in, does he?"

"Uh-oh. Has someone's ego been hurt?"

"Not mine. Yet. But one of his teachers is feeling a little bruised."

"I notice you aren't telling me I faked his scores anymore."

"Yes, Sister Carlotta, you were right all along. He deserves to be here. And so does . . . Well, let's just say you hit the jackpot after all those years of searching."

"It's humanity's jackpot."

"I said he was worth bringing up here, not that he was the one who'll lead us to victory. The wheel's still spinning on that one. And my money's on another number."

Going up the ladderways while holding a flash suit wasn't practical, so Wiggin made the ones who were dressed run up and down the corridor, working up a sweat, while Bean and the other naked or partially-dressed kids got their suits on. Nikolai helped Bean get his suit fastened; it humiliated Bean to need help, but it would have been worse to be the last one finished—the pesky little teeny brat who slows everyone down. With Nikolai's help, he was not the last one done.

"Thanks."

"No ojjikay."

Moments later, they were streaming up the ladders to the battleroom level. Wiggin took them all the way to the upper door, the one that opened out into the middle of the battleroom wall. The one used for entering when it was an actual battle. There were handholds on the sides, the ceiling, and the floor, so students could swing out and hurl themselves into the null-G environment. The story was that gravity was lower in the battleroom because it was closer to the center of the station, but Bean had already realized that was bogus. There would still be some centrifugal force at the doors and a pronounced Coriolis effect. Instead, the battlerooms were completely null. To Bean, that meant that the I.F. had a device that would either block gravitation or, more likely, produce false gravity that was perfectly balanced to counter Coriolis and centrifugal forces in the battleroom, starting exactly at the door. It was a stunning technology—and it was never discussed inside the I.F., at least not in the literature available to students in Battle School, and completely unknown outside.

Wiggin assembled them in four files along the corridor and ordered them to jump up and use the ceiling handholds to fling their bodies into the room. "Assemble on the far wall, as if you were going for the enemy's gate." To the veterans that meant something. To the launchies, who had never been in a battle and had never, for that matter, entered through the upper door, it meant nothing at all. "Run up and go four at a time when I open the gate, one group per second." Wiggin walked to the back of the group and, using his hook, a controller strapped to the inside of his wrist and curved to conform to his left hand, he made the door, which had seemed quite solid, disappear.

"Go!" The first four kids started running for the gate. "Go!" The next group began to run before the first had even reached it. There would be no hesitation or somebody would crash into you from behind. "Go!" The first group grabbed and swung with varying degrees of clumsiness and heading out in various directions. "Go!" Later groups learned, or tried to, from the awkwardness of the earlier ones. "Go!"

Bean was at the end of the line, in the last group. Wiggin laid a hand on his shoulder. "You can use a side handhold if you want."

Right, thought Bean. *Now* you decide to baby me. Not because my meshugga flash suit didn't fit together right, but just because I'm short. "Go suck on it," said Bean.

"Go!"

Bean kept pace with the other three, though it meant pumping his legs half again as fast, and when he got near the gate he took a flying leap, tapped the ceiling handhold with his fingers as he passed, and sailed out into the room with no control at all, spinning in three nauseating directions at once.

But he didn't expect himself to do any better, and instead of fighting the spin, he calmed himself and did his anti-nausea routine, relaxing himself until he neared a wall and had to prepare for impact. He didn't land near one of the recessed handholds and wasn't facing the right way to grab anything even if he had. So he rebounded, but this time was a little more stable as he flew, and he ended up on the ceiling very near the back wall. It took him less time than some to make his way down to where the others were assembling, lined up along the floor under the middle gate on the back wall—the enemy gate.

Wiggin sailed calmly through the air. Because he had a hook, during practice he could maneuver in midair in ways that soldiers couldn't; during battle, though, the hook would be useless, so commanders had to make sure they didn't become dependent on the hook's added control. Bean noted approvingly that Wiggin seemed not to use the hook at all. He sailed in sideways, snagged a handhold on the floor about ten paces out from the back wall, and hung in the air. Upside down.

Fixing his gaze on one of them, Wiggin demanded, "Why are you upside down, soldier?"

Immediately some of the other soldiers started to turn themselves upside down like Wiggin.

"Attention!" Wiggin barked. All movement stopped. "I said why are you upside down!"

Bean was surprised that the soldier didn't answer. Had he forgotten what the teacher did in the shuttle on the way here? The deliberate disorientation? Or was that something that only Dimak did?

"I said why does every one of you have his feet in the air and his head toward the ground!"

Wiggin didn't look at Bean in particular, and this was one question Bean didn't want to answer. There was no assurance of which particular correct answer Wiggin was looking for, so why open his mouth just to get shut down?

It was a kid named Shame—short for Seamus—who finally spoke up. "Sir, this is the direction we were in coming out of the door." Good job, thought Bean. Better than some lame argument that there was no up or down in null-G.

"Well what difference is that supposed to make! What difference does it make what the gravity was back in the corridor! Are we going to fight in the corridor? Is there any gravity here?"

No sir, they all murmured.

"From now on, you forget about gravity before you go through that door. The old gravity is gone, erased. Understand me? Whatever your gravity is when you get to the door, remember—the enemy's gate is *down*. Your feet are toward the enemy gate. Up is toward your own gate. North is that way"—he pointed toward what had been the ceiling—"south is that way, east is that way, west is—what way?"

They pointed.

"That's what I expected," said Wiggin. "The only process you've mastered is the process of elimination, and the only reason you've mastered that is because you can do it in the toilet."

Bean watched, amused. So Wiggin subscribed to the you're-so-stupid-you-need-me-to-wipe-your-butts school of basic training. Well, maybe that was necessary. One of the rituals of training. Boring till it was over, but . . . commander's choice.

Wiggin glanced at Bean, but his eyes kept moving.

"What was the circus I saw out here! Did you call that forming up? Did you call that flying? Now everybody, launch and form up on the ceiling! Right now! Move!"

Bean knew what the trap was and launched for the wall they had just entered through before Wiggin had even finished talking. Most of the others also got what the test was, but a fair number of them launched the wrong way—toward the direction Wiggin had called *north* instead of the direction he had identified as *up*. This time Bean happened to arrive near a handhold, and he caught it with surprising ease. He had done it before in his launch group's battleroom practices, but he was small enough that, unlike the others, it was quite possible for him to land in a place that had no handhold within reach. Short arms were a definite drawback in the battleroom. On short bounds he could aim at a handhold and get there with some accuracy. On a cross-room jump there was little hope of that. So it felt good that this time, at least, he didn't look like an oaf. In fact, having launched first, he arrived first.

Bean turned around and watched as the ones who had blown it made the long, embarrassing second leap to join the rest of the army. He was a little surprised at who some of the bozos were. Inattention can make clowns of us all, he thought.

Wiggin was watching him again, and this time it was no passing glance. "You!" Wiggin pointed at him. "Which way is down?"

Didn't we just cover this? "Toward the enemy door."

"Name, kid?"

Come on, Wiggin really didn't know who the short kid with the highest scores in the whole damn school was? Well, if we're playing mean sergeant and hapless recruit, I better follow the script. "This soldier's name is Bean, sir."

"Get that for size or for brains?"

Some of the other soldiers laughed. But not many of them. *They* knew Bean's reputation. To them it was no longer funny that he was so small—it was just embarrassing that a kid that small could make perfect scores on tests that had questions they didn't even understand.

"Well, Bean, you're right onto things." Wiggin now included the whole group as he launched into a lecture on how coming through the door feet first made you a much smaller target for the enemy to shoot at. Harder for him to hit you and freeze you. "Now, what happens when you're frozen?"

"Can't move," somebody said.

"That's what frozen *means*," said Wiggin. "But what *happens* to you?"

Wiggin wasn't phrasing his question very clearly, in Bean's opinion, and there was no use in prolonging the agony while the others figured it out. So Bean spoke up. "You keep going in the direction you started in. At the speed you were going when you were flashed."

"That's true," said Wiggin. "You five, there on the end, move!" He pointed at five soldiers, who spent long enough looking at each other to make sure which five he meant that Wiggin had time to flash them all, freezing them in place. During practice, it took a few minutes for a freeze to wear off, unless the commander used his hook to unfreeze them earlier.

"The next five, move!"

Seven kids moved at once—no time to count. Wiggin flashed them as quickly as he flashed the others, but because they had already launched, they kept moving at a good clip toward the walls they had headed for.

The first five were hovering in the air near where they had been frozen.

"Look at these so-called soldiers. Their commander ordered them to move, and now look at them. Not only are they frozen, they're frozen right here, where they can get in the way. While the others, because they moved when they were ordered, are frozen down there, plugging up the enemy's lanes, blocking the enemy's vision. I imagine that about five of you have understood the point of this."

We all understand it, Wiggin. It's not like they bring stupid people up here to Battle School. It's not like I didn't pick you the best available army.

"And no doubt Bean is one of them. Right, Bean?"

Bean could hardly believe that Wiggin was singling him out *again*.

Just because I'm little, he's using me to embarrass the others. The little guy knows the answers, so why don't you big boys.

But then, Wiggin doesn't realize yet. He thinks he has an army of incompetent launchies and rejects. He hasn't had a chance to see that he actually has a select group. So he thinks of me as the most ludicrous of a sad lot. He's found out I'm not an idiot, but he still assumes the others are.

Wiggin was still looking at him. Oh, yeah, he had asked a question. "Right, sir," said Bean.

"Then what is the point?"

Spit back to him exactly what he just said to us. "When you are ordered to move, move fast, so if you get iced you'll bounce around instead of getting in the way of your own army's operations."

"Excellent. At least I have one soldier who can figure things out."

Bean was disgusted. This was the commander who was supposed to turn Dragon into a legendary army? Wiggin was supposed to be the alpha and omega of the Battle School, and he's playing the game of singling me out to be the goat. Wiggin didn't even find out our scores, didn't discuss his soldiers with the teachers. If he did, he'd already know that I'm the smartest kid in the school. The others all know it. That's why they're looking at each other in embarrassment. Wiggin is revealing his own ignorance.

Bean saw how Wiggin seemed to be registering the distaste of his own soldiers. It was just an eyeblink, but maybe Wiggin finally got it that his make-fun-of-the-shrimp ploy was backfiring. Because he finally got on with the business of training. He taught them how to kneel in midair—even flashing their own legs to lock them in place—and then fire between their knees as they moved downward toward the enemy, so that their legs became a shield, absorbing fire and allowing them to shoot for longer periods of time out in the open. A good tactic, and Bean finally began to get some idea of why Wiggin might not be a disastrous commander after all. He could sense the others giving respect to their new commander at last.

When they'd got the point, Wiggin thawed himself and all the soldiers he had frozen in the demonstration. "Now," he said, "which way is the enemy's gate?"

"Down!" they all answered.

"And what is our attack position?"

Oh, right, thought Bean, like we can all give an explanation in unison. The only way to answer was to demonstrate—so Bean flipped himself away from the wall, heading for the other side, firing between his knees as he went. He didn't do it perfectly—there was a little rotation as he went—but all in all, he did OK for his first actual attempt at the maneuver.

Above him, he heard Wiggin shout at the others. "Is Bean the only one who knows how?"

By the time Bean had caught himself on the far wall, the whole rest of the army was coming after him, shouting as if they were on the attack. Only Wiggin remained at the ceiling. Bean noticed, with amusement, that Wiggin was standing there oriented the same way he had been in the corridor—his head "north," the old "up." He might have the theory down pat, but in practice, it's hard to shake off the old gravity-based thinking. Bean had made it a point to orient himself sideways, his head to the west. And the soldiers near him did the same, taking their orientation from him. If Wiggin noticed, he gave no sign.

"Now come back at me, all of you, attack *me!*"

Immediately his flash suit lit up with forty weapons firing at him as his entire army converged on him, firing all the way. "Ouch," said Wiggin when they arrived. "You got me."

Most of them laughed.

"Now, what are your legs good for, in combat?"

Nothing, said some boys.

"Bean doesn't think so," said Wiggin.

So he isn't going to let up on me even now. Well, what does he want to hear? Somebody else muttered "shields," but Wiggin didn't key in on that, so he must have something else in mind. "They're the best way to push off walls," Bean guessed.

"Right," said Wiggin.

"Come on, pushing off is movement, not combat," said Crazy Tom. A few others murmured their agreement.

Oh good, now it starts, thought Bean. Crazy Tom picks a meaningless quarrel with his commander, who gets pissed off at him and . . .

But Wiggin didn't take umbrage at Crazy Tom's correction. He just corrected him back, mildly. "There *is* no combat without movement. Now, with your legs frozen like this, can you push off walls?"

Bean had no idea. Neither did anyone else.

"Bean?" asked Wiggin. Of course.

"I've never tried it," said Bean, "but maybe if you faced the wall and doubled over at the waist—"

"Right but wrong. Watch me. My back's to the wall, legs are frozen. Since I'm kneeling, my feet are against the wall. Usually, when you push off you have to push downward, so you string out your body behind you like a string *bean,* right?"

The group laughed. For the first time, Bean realized that maybe Wiggin wasn't being stupid to get the whole group laughing at the little guy. Maybe Wiggin knew perfectly well that Bean was the smartest kid, and had singled him out like this because he could tap into all the resentment the others felt for him. This whole session was guaranteeing that the other kids would all think it was OK to laugh at Bean, to despise him even though he was smart.

Great system, Wiggin. Destroy the effectiveness of your best soldier, make sure he gets no respect.

However, it was more important to learn what Wiggin was teaching than to feel sullen about the way he was teaching it. So Bean watched intently as Wiggin demonstrated a frozen-leg takeoff from the wall. He noticed that Wiggin gave himself a deliberate spin. It would make it harder for him to shoot as he flew, but it would also make it very hard for a distant enemy to focus enough light on any part of him for long enough to get a kill.

I may be pissed off, but that doesn't mean I can't learn.

It was a long and grueling practice, drilling over and over again on new skills. Bean saw that Wiggin wasn't willing to let them learn each technique separately. They had to do them all at once, integrating them into smooth, continuous movements. Like dancing, Bean thought. You don't learn to shoot and then learn to launch and then learn to do a controlled spin—you learn to launch-shoot-spin.

At the end, all of them dripping with sweat, exhausted, and flushed with the excitement of having learned stuff that they'd never heard of other soldiers doing, Wiggin assembled them at the lower door and announced that they'd have another practice during free time. "And don't tell me that free time is supposed to be free. I know that, and you're perfectly free to do what you want. I'm *inviting* you to come to an extra, *voluntary* practice."

They laughed. This group consisted entirely of kids who had *not* chosen to do extra battleroom practice with Wiggin before, and he was making sure they understood that he expected them to change their priorities now. But they didn't mind. After this morning they knew that when Wiggin ran a practice, every second was effective. They couldn't afford to miss a practice or they'd fall significantly behind. Wiggin would get their free time. Even Crazy Tom wasn't arguing about it.

But Bean knew that he had to change his relationship with Wiggin right now, or there was no chance that he would get a chance for leadership. What Wiggin had done to him in today's practice, feeding on the resentment of the other kids for this little pipsqueak, would make it even less plausible for Bean to be made a leader within the army—if the other kids despised him, who would follow him?

So Bean waited for Wiggin in the corridor after the others had gone on ahead.

"Ho, Bean," said Wiggin.

"Ho, Ender," said Bean. Did Wiggin catch the sarcasm in the way Bean said his name? Was that why he paused a moment before answering?

"*Sir*," said Wiggin softly.

Oh, cut out the merda, I've seen those vids, we all *laugh* at those vids. "I know what you're doing, *Ender,* sir, and I'm warning you."

"Warning me?"

"I can be the best man you've got, but don't play games with me."

"Or what?"

"Or I'll be the worst man you've got. One or the other." Not that Bean expected Wiggin to understand what he meant by that. How Bean could only be effective if he had Wiggin's trust and respect, how otherwise he'd just be the little kid, useful for nothing. Wiggin would probably take it to mean that Bean meant to cause trouble if Wiggin didn't use him. And maybe he did mean that, a little.

"And what do you want?" asked Wiggin. "Love and kisses?"

Say it flat out, put it in his mind so plainly he can't pretend not to understand. "I want a toon."

Wiggin walked close to Bean, looked down at him. To Bean, though, it was a good sign that Wiggin hadn't just laughed. "Why should you get a toon?"

"Because I'd know what to do with it."

"Knowing what to do with a toon is easy. It's getting them to do it that's hard. Why should any soldier want to follow a little pinprick like you?"

Wiggin had got straight to the crux of the problem. But Bean didn't like the malicious way he said it. "They used to call *you* that, I hear. I hear Bonzo Madrid still does."

Wiggin wasn't taking the bait. "I asked you a question, soldier."

"I'll earn their respect, sir, if you don't stop me."

To his surprise, Wiggin grinned. "I'm helping you."

"Like hell."

"Nobody would notice you, except to feel sorry for the little kid. But I made sure they *all* noticed you today."

You should have done your research, Wiggin. You're the only one who didn't know already who I was.

"They'll be watching every move you make," said Wiggin. "All you have to do to earn their respect now is be perfect."

"So I don't even get a chance to learn before I'm being judged." That's not how you bring along talent.

"Poor kid. Nobody's treatin' him fair."

Wiggin's deliberate obtuseness infuriated Bean. You're smarter than this, Wiggin!

Seeing Bean's rage, Wiggin brought a hand forward and pushed him until his back rested firmly against the wall. "I'll tell you how to get a toon. Prove to me you know what you're doing as a soldier. Prove to me you know how to use other soldiers. And then prove to me that somebody's willing to follow you into battle. Then you'll get your toon. But not bloody well until."

Bean ignored the hand pressing against him. It would take a lot more than that to intimidate him physically. "That's fair," he said. "*If* you actually work that way, I'll be a toon leader in a month."

Now it was Wiggin's turn to be angry. He reached down, grabbed Bean by the front of his flash suit, and slid him up the wall so they stood there eye to eye. "When I say I work a certain way, Bean, then that's the way I work."

Bean just grinned at him. In this low gravity, so high in the station, picking up little kids wasn't any big test of strength. And Wiggin was no bully. There was no serious threat here.

Wiggin let go of him. Bean slid down the wall and landed gently on his feet, rebounded slightly, settled again. Wiggin walked to the pole and slid down. Bean had won this encounter by getting under Wiggin's skin. Besides, Wiggin knew he hadn't handled this situation very well. He wouldn't forget. In fact, it was Wiggin who had lost a little respect, and he knew it, and he'd be trying to earn it back.

Unlike you, Wiggin, I *do* give the other guy a chance to learn what he's doing before I insist on perfection. You screwed up with me today, but I'll give you a chance to do better tomorrow and the next day.

But when Bean got to the pole and reached out to take hold, he realized his hands were trembling and his grip was too weak. He had to pause a moment, leaning on the pole, till he had calmed enough.

That face-to-face encounter with Wiggin, he hadn't won that. It might even have been a stupid thing to do. Wiggin *had* hurt him with those snide comments, that ridicule. Bean had been studying Wiggin as the subject of his private theology, and today he had found out that all this time Wiggin didn't even know Bean existed. Everybody compared Bean to Wiggin— but apparently Wiggin hadn't heard or didn't care. He had treated Bean like nothing. And after having worked so hard this past year to earn respect, Bean didn't find it easy to be nothing again. It brought back feelings he thought he left behind in Rotterdam. The sick fear of imminent death. Even though he knew that no one here would raise a hand against him, he still remembered being on the edge of dying when he first went up to Poke and put his life in her hands.

Is that what I've done, once again? By putting myself on this roster, I gave my future into this boy's hands. I counted on him seeing in me what I see. But of course he couldn't. I have to give him time.

If there *was* time. For the teachers were moving quickly now, and Bean might not *have* a year in this army to prove himself to Wiggin.

14

BROTHERS

"You have results for me?"

"Interesting ones. Volescu *was* lying. Somewhat."

"I hope you're going to be more precise than that."

"Bean's genetic alteration was not based on a clone of Volescu. But they *are* related. Volescu is definitely not Bean's father. But he is almost certainly Volescu's half-uncle or a double cousin. I hope Volescu has a half-brother or double first cousin, because such a man is the only possible father of the fertilized egg that Volescu altered."

"You have a list of Volescu's relatives, I assume?"

"We didn't need any family at the trial. And Volescu's mother was not married. He uses her name."

"So Volescu's father had another child somewhere only you don't even know his name. I thought you knew everything."

"We know everything that we knew was worth knowing. That's a crucial distinction. We simply haven't looked for Volescu's father. He's not guilty of anything important. We can't investigate everybody."

"Another matter. Since you know everything that you know is worth knowing, perhaps you can tell me why a certain crippled boy has been removed from the school where I placed him?"

"Oh. Him. When you suddenly stopped touting him, we got suspicious. So we checked him out. Tested him. He's no Bean, but he definitely belongs here."

"And it never crossed your mind that I had good reason for keeping him out of Battle School?"

"We assumed that you thought that we might choose Achilles over Bean, who was, after all, far too young, so you offered only your favorite."

"You assumed. I've been dealing with you as if you were intelligent, and you've been dealing with me as if I were an idiot. Now I see it should have been the exact reverse."

"I didn't know Christians got so angry."

"Is Achilles already in Battle School?"

"He's still recovering from his fourth surgery. We had to fix the leg on Earth."

"Let me give you a word of advice. Do *not* put him in Battle School while Bean is still there."

"Bean is only six. He's still too young to *enter* Battle School, let alone graduate."

"If you put Achilles in, take Bean out. Period."

"Why?"

"If you're too stupid to believe me after all my other judgments turned out to be correct, why should I give you the ammunition to let you second-guess me? Let me just say that putting them in school together is a probable death sentence for one of them."

"Which one?"

"That rather depends on which one sees the other first."

"Achilles says he owes everything to Bean. He loves Bean."

"Then by all means, believe him and not me. But don't send the body of the loser back to me to deal with. You bury your own mistakes."

"That sounds pretty heartless."

"I'm not going to weep over the grave of either boy. I tried to save both their lives. You apparently seem determined to let them find out which is fittest in the best Darwinian fashion."

"Calm down, Sister Carlotta. We'll consider what you've told us. We won't be foolish."

"You've already been foolish. I have no high expectations for you now."

As days became weeks, the shape of Wiggin's army began to unfold, and Bean was filled with both hope and despair. Hope, because Wiggin was setting up an army that was almost infinitely adaptable. Despair, because he was doing it without any reliance on Bean.

After only a few practices, Wiggin had chosen his toon leaders—every one of them a veteran from the transfer lists. In fact, every veteran was either a toon leader or a second. Not only that, instead of the normal organization—four toons of ten soldiers each—he had created five toons of eight, and then made them practice a lot in half-toons of four men each, one commanded by the toon leader, the other by the second.

No one had ever fragmented an army like that before. And it wasn't just an illusion. Wiggin worked hard to make sure the toon leaders and seconds had plenty of leeway. He'd tell them their objective and let the leader decide how to achieve it. Or he'd group three toons together under the operational command of one of the toon leaders to handle one operation, while Wiggin himself commanded the smaller remaining force. It was an extraordinary amount of delegation.

Some of the soldiers were critical at first. As they were milling around near the entrance to the barracks, the veterans talked about how they'd practiced that day—in ten groups of four. "Everybody knows it's loser strategy to divide your army," said Fly Molo, who commanded A toon.

Bean was a little disgusted that the soldier with the highest rank after Wiggin would say something disparaging about his commander's strategy. Sure, Fly was learning, too. But there's such a thing as insubordination.

"He hasn't divided the army," said Bean. "He's just organized it. And there's no such thing as a rule of strategy that you can't break. The idea is to have your army concentrated at the decisive point. Not to keep it huddled together all the time."

Fly glared at Bean. "Just cause you little guys can hear us doesn't mean you understand what we're talking about."

"If you don't want to believe me, think what you want. My talking isn't going to make you stupider than you already are."

Fly came at him, grabbing him by the arm and dragging him to the edge of his bunk.

At once, Nikolai launched himself from the bunk opposite and landed on Fly's back, bumping his head into the front of Bean's bunk. In moments, the other toon leaders had pulled Fly and Nikolai apart—a ludicrous fight anyway, since Nikolai wasn't that much bigger than Bean.

"Forget it, Fly," said Hot Soup—Han Tzu, leader of D toon. "Nikolai thinks he's Bean's big brother."

"What's the kid doing mouthing off to a toon leader?" demanded Fly.

"You were being insubordinate toward our commander," said Bean.

"And you were also completely wrong. By your view, Lee and Jackson were idiots at Chancellorsville."

"He keeps doing it!"

"Are you so stupid you can't recognize the truth just because the person telling it to you is short?" All of Bean's frustration at not being one of the officers was spilling out. He knew it, but he didn't feel like controlling it. They needed to hear the truth. And Wiggin needed to have the support when he was being taken down behind his back.

Nikolai was standing on the lower bunk, so he was as close to Bean as possible, affirming the bond between them. "Come on, Fly," said Nikolai. "This is *Bean,* remember?"

And, to Bean's surprise, that silenced Fly. Until this moment, Bean had not realized the power that his reputation had. He might be just a regular soldier in Dragon Army, but he was still the finest student of strategy and military history in the school, and apparently everybody—or at least everybody but Wiggin—knew it.

"I should have spoken with more respect," said Bean.

"Damn right," said Fly.

"But so should you."

Fly lunged against the grip of the boys holding him.

"Talking about Wiggin," said Bean. "You spoke without respect. 'Everybody knows it's loser strategy to divide your army.' " He got Fly's intonation almost exactly right. Several kids laughed. And, grudgingly, so did Fly.

"OK, right," said Fly. "I was out of line." He turned to Nikolai. "But I'm still an officer."

"Not when you're dragging a little kid off his bunk you're not," said Nikolai. "You're a bully when you do that."

Fly blinked. Wisely, no one else said a thing until Fly had decided how he was going to respond. "You're right, Nikolai. To defend your friend against a bully." He looked from Nikolai to Bean and back again. "Pusha, you guys even look like brothers." He walked past them, heading for his bunk. The other toon leaders followed him. Crisis over.

Nikolai looked at Bean then. "I was never as squished up and ugly as you," he said.

"And if I'm going to grow up to look like you, I'm going to kill myself now," said Bean.

"Do you have to talk to really *big* guys like that?"

"I didn't expect you to attack him like a one-man swarm of bee."

"I guess I wanted to jump on somebody," said Nikolai.

"You? Mr. Nice Guy?"

"I don't feel so nice lately." He climbed up on the bunk beside Bean, so they could talk more softly. "I'm out of my depth here, Bean. I don't belong in this army."

"What do you mean?"

"I wasn't ready to get promoted. I'm just average. Maybe not that good. And even though this army wasn't a bunch of heroes in the standings, these guys are good. Everybody learns faster than me. Everybody *gets* it and I'm still standing there thinking about it."

"So you work harder."

"I *am* working harder. You—you just get it, right away, everything, you see it all. And it's not that I'm stupid. I always get it, too. Just . . . a step behind."

"Sorry," said Bean.

"What are *you* sorry about? It's not *your* fault."

Yes it is, Nikolai. "Come on, you telling me you wish you weren't part of Ender Wiggin's army?"

Nikolai laughed a little. "He's really something, isn't he?"

"You'll do your part. You're a good soldier. You'll see. When we get into the battles, you'll do as well as anybody."

"Eh, probably. They can always freeze me and throw me around. A big lumpy projectile weapon."

"You're not so lumpy."

"Everybody's lumpy compared to you. I've watched you—you give away half your food."

"They feed me too much."

"I've got to study." Nikolai jumped across to his bunk.

Bean felt bad sometimes about having put Nikolai in this situation. But when they started winning, a lot of kids outside of Dragon Army would be wishing they could trade places with him. In fact, it was kind of surprising Nikolai realized he wasn't as qualified as the others. After all, the differences weren't that pronounced. Probably there were a lot of kids who felt just like Nikolai. But Bean hadn't really reassured him. In fact, he had probably reaffirmed Nikolai's feelings of inferiority.

What a sensitive friend I am.

There was no point in interviewing Volescu again, not after getting such lies from him the first time. All that talk of copies, and him the original— there was no mitigation now. He was a murderer, a servant of the Father of Lies. He would do nothing to help Sister Carlotta. And the need to find out what might be expected of the one child who evaded Volescu's little holocaust was too great to rely again on the word of such a man.

Besides, Volescu had made contact with his half-brother or double cousin—how else could he have obtained a fertilized egg containing his DNA? So Sister Carlotta should be able either to follow Volescu's trail or duplicate his research.

She learned quickly that Volescu was the illegitimate child of a Romanian woman in Budapest, Hungary. A little checking—and the judicious use of her security clearance—got her the name of the father, a Greek-born official in the League who had recently been promoted to service on the Hegemon's staff. That might have been a roadblock, but Sister Carlotta did not need to speak to the grandfather. She only needed to know who he was in order to find out the names of his three legitimate children. The daughter was eliminated because the shared parent was a male. And in checking the two sons, she decided to go first to visit the married one.

They lived on the island of Crete, where Julian ran a software company whose only client was the International Defense League. Obviously this was not a coincidence, but nepotism was almost honorable compared to some of the outright graft and favor-trading that was endemic in the League. In the long run such corruption was basically harmless, since the International Fleet had seized control of its own budget early on and never let the League touch it again. Thus the Polemarch and the Strategos had far more money at their disposal than the Hegemon, which made him, though first in title, weakest in actual power and independence of movement.

And just because Julian Delphiki owed his career to his father's political connections did not necessarily mean that his company's product was not adequate and that he himself was not an honest man. By the standards of honesty that prevailed in the world of business, anyway.

Sister Carlotta found that she did not need her security clearance to get a meeting with Julian and his wife, Elena. She called and said she would like to see them on a matter concerning the I.F., and they immediately opened their calendar to her. She arrived in Knossos and was immediately driven to their home on a bluff overlooking the Aegean. They looked nervous—indeed, Elena was almost frantic, wringing a handkerchief.

"Please," she said, after accepting their offer of fruit and cheese. "Please tell me why you are so upset. There's nothing about my business that should alarm you."

The two of them glanced at each other, and Elena became flustered. "Then there's nothing wrong with our boy?"

For a moment, Sister Carlotta wondered if they already knew about Bean—but how could they?

"Your son?"

"Then he's all right!" Elena burst into tears of relief and when her husband knelt beside her, she clung to him and sobbed.

"You see, it was very hard for us to let him go into service," said Julian. "So when a religious person calls to tell us she needs to see us on business pertaining to the I.F., we thought—we leapt to the conclusion—"

"Oh, I'm so sorry. I didn't know you had a son in the military, or I would have been careful to assure you from the start that . . . but now I fear I am here under false pretenses. The matter I need to speak to you about is personal, so personal you may be reluctant to answer. Yet it *is* about a matter that is of some importance to the I.F. Truthful answers cannot possibly expose you to any personal risk, I promise."

Elena got control of herself. Julian seated himself again, and now they looked at Sister Carlotta almost with cheerfulness. "Oh, ask whatever you want," said Julian. "We're just happy that—whatever you want to ask."

"We'll answer if we can," said Elena.

"You say you have a son. This raises the possibility that—there is reason to wonder if you might not at some point have . . . was your son conceived under circumstances that would have allowed a clone of his fertilized egg to be made?"

"Oh yes," said Elena. "That is no secret. A defect in one fallopian tube and an ectopic pregnancy in the other made it impossible for me to conceive in utero. We wanted a child, so they drew out several of my eggs, fertilized them with my husband's sperm, and then cloned the ones we chose. There were four that we cloned, six copies of each. Two girls and two boys. So far, we have implanted only the one. He was such a—such a special boy, we did not want to dilute our attention. Now that his education is out of our hands, however, we have been thinking of bearing one of the girls. It's time." She reached over and took Julian's hand and smiled. He smiled back.

Such a contrast to Volescu. Hard to believe there was any genetic material in common.

"You said six copies of each of the four fertilized eggs," said Sister Carlotta.

"Six including the original," said Julian. "That way we have the best chance of implanting each of the four and carrying them through a full pregnancy."

"A total of twenty-four fertilized eggs. And only one of them was implanted?"

"Yes, we were very fortunate, the first one worked perfectly."

"Leaving twenty-three."

"Yes. Exactly."

"Mr. Delphiki, all twenty-three of those fertilized eggs remain in storage, waiting for implantation?"

"Of course."

Sister Carlotta thought for a moment. "How recently have you checked?"

"Just last week," said Julian. "As we began talking about having another child. The doctor assured us that nothing has happened to the eggs and they can be implanted with only a few hours' notice."

"But did the doctor actually check?"

"I don't know," said Julian.

Elena was starting to tense up a little. "What have you heard?" she asked.

"Nothing," said Sister Carlotta. "What I am looking for is the source of a particular child's genetic material. I simply need to make sure that your fertilized eggs were not the source."

"But of course they were not. Except for our son."

"Please don't be alarmed. But I would like to know the name of your doctor and the facility where the eggs are stored. And then I would be glad if you would call your doctor and have him go, in person, to the facility and insist upon seeing the eggs himself."

"They can't be seen without a microscope," said Julian.

"See that they have not been disturbed," said Sister Carlotta.

They had both become hyperalert again, especially since they had no idea what this was all about—nor could they be told. As soon as Julian gave her the name of doctor and hospital, Sister Carlotta stepped onto the porch and, as she gazed at the sail-specked Aegean, she used her global and got herself put through to the I.F. headquarters in Athens.

It would take several hours, perhaps, for either her call or Julian's to bring in the answer, so she and Julian and Elena made a heroic effort to appear unconcerned. They took her on a walking tour of their neighborhood, which offered views both ancient and modern, and of nature verdant, desert, and marine. The dry air was refreshing as long as the breeze from the sea did not lag, and Sister Carlotta enjoyed hearing Julian talk about his company and Elena talk about her work as a teacher. All thought of their having risen in the world through government corruption faded as she realized that however he got his contract, Julian was a serious, dedicated creator of software, while Elena was a fervent teacher who treated her profession as a crusade. "I knew as soon as I started teaching our son how remarkable he was," Elena told her. "But it wasn't until his pre-tests for school placement that we first learned that his gifts were particularly suited for the I.F."

Alarm bells went off. Sister Carlotta had assumed that their son was an adult. After all, they were not a young couple. "How old is your son?"

"Eight years old now," said Julian. "They sent us a picture. Quite a little man in his uniform. They don't let many letters come through."

Their son was in Battle School. They appeared to be in their forties, but they might not have started to have a family until late, and then tried in vain for a while, going through a tubal pregnancy before finding out that Elena could no longer conceive. Their son was only a couple of years older than Bean.

Which meant that Graff could compare Bean's genetic code with that of the Delphiki boy and find out if they were from the same cloned egg. There would be a control, to compare what Bean was like with Anton's key turned, as opposed to the other, whose genes were unaltered.

Now that she thought about it, of *course* any true sibling of Bean's would have exactly the abilities that would bring the attention of the I.F. Anton's key made a child into a savant in general; the particular mix of skills that the I.F. looked for were not affected. Bean would have had those skills no matter what; the alteration merely allowed him to bring a far sharper intelligence to bear on abilities he already had.

If Bean was in fact their child. Yet the coincidence of twenty-three fertilized eggs and the twenty-three children that Volescu had produced in the "clean room"—what other conclusion could she reach?

And soon the answer came, first to Sister Carlotta, but immediately thereafter to the Delphikis. The I.F. investigators had gone to the clinic with the doctor and together they had discovered that the eggs were missing.

It was hard news for the Delphikis to bear, and Sister Carlotta discreetly waited outside while Elena and Julian took some time alone together. But soon they invited her in. "How much can you tell us?" Julian asked. "You came here because you suspected our babies might have been taken. Tell me, were they born?"

Sister Carlotta wanted to hide behind the veil of military secrecy, but in truth there was no military secret involved—Volescu's crime was a matter of public record. And yet . . . weren't they better off not knowing?

"Julian, Elena, accidents happen in the laboratory. They might have died anyway. Nothing is certain. Isn't it better just to think of this as a terrible accident? Why add to the burden of the loss you already have?"

Elena looked at her fiercely. "You *will* tell me, Sister Carlotta, if you love the God of truth!"

"The eggs were stolen by a criminal who . . . illegally caused them to be brought through gestation. When his crime was about to be discovered, he gave them a painless death by sedative. They did not suffer."

"And this man will be put on trial?"

"He has already been tried and sentenced to life in prison," said Sister Carlotta.

"Already?" asked Julian. "How long ago were our babies stolen?"

"More than seven years ago."

"Oh!" cried Elena. "Then our babies . . . when they died . . ."

"They were infants. Not a year old yet."

"But why *our* babies? Why would he steal them? Was he going to sell them for adoption? Was he . . ."

"Does it matter? None of his plans came to fruition," said Sister Carlotta. The nature of Volescu's experiments *was* a secret.

"What was the murderer's name?" asked Julian. Seeing her hesitation, he insisted. "His name is a matter of public record, is it not?"

"In the criminal courts of Rotterdam," said Sister Carlotta. "Volescu."

Julian reacted as if slapped—but immediately controlled himself. Elena did not see it.

He knows about his father's mistress, thought Sister Carlotta. He understands now what part of the motive had to be. The legitimate son's children were kidnapped by the bastard, experimented on, and eventually killed—and the legitimate son didn't find out about it for seven years. Whatever privations Volescu fancied that his fatherlessness had caused him, he had taken his vengeance. And for Julian, it also meant that his father's lusts had come back to cause this loss, this pain to Julian and his wife. The sins of the fathers are visited upon the children unto the third and fourth generation. . . .

But didn't the scripture say the third and fourth generation of them that hate me? Julian and Elena did not hate God. Nor did their innocent babies.

It makes no more sense than Herod's slaughter of the babes of Bethlehem. The only comfort was the trust that a merciful God caught up the spirits of the slain infants into his bosom, and that he brought comfort, eventually, to the parents' hearts.

"Please," said Sister Carlotta. "I cannot say you should not grieve for the children that you will never hold. But you can still rejoice in the child that you have.''

''A million miles away!'' cried Elena.

''I don't suppose . . . you don't happen to know if the Battle School ever lets a child come home for a visit,'' said Julian. ''His name is Nikolai Delphiki. Surely under the circumstances . . .''

''I'm so sorry,'' said Sister Carlotta. Reminding them of the child they had was not such a good idea after all, when they did not, in fact, have him. ''I'm sorry that my coming led to such terrible news for you.''

''But you learned what you came to learn,'' said Julian.

''Yes,'' said Sister Carlotta.

Then Julian realized something, though he said not a word in front of his wife. ''Will you want to return to the airport now?''

''Yes, the car is still waiting. Soldiers are much more patient than cab drivers.''

''I'll walk you to the car,'' said Julian.

''No, Julian,'' said Elena, ''don't leave me.''

''Just for a few moments, my love. Even now, we don't forget courtesy.'' He held his wife for a long moment, then led Sister Carlotta to the door and opened it for her.

As they walked to the car, Julian spoke of what he had come to understand. ''Since my father's bastard is already in prison, you did not come here because of his crime.''

''No,'' she said.

''One of our children is still alive,'' he said.

''What I tell you now I should not tell, because it is not within my authority,'' said Sister Carlotta. ''But my first allegiance is to God, not the I.F. If the twenty-two children who died at Volescu's hand were yours, then a twenty-third may be alive. It remains for genetic testing to be done.''

''But we will not be told,'' said Julian.

''Not yet,'' said Sister Carlotta. ''And not soon. Perhaps not ever. But if it is within my power, then a day will come when you will meet your second son.''

''Is he . . . do you know him?''

''If it is your son,'' she said, ''then yes, I know him. His life has been hard, but his heart is good, and he is such a boy as to make any father or mother proud. Please don't ask me more. I've already said too much.''

''Do I tell this to my wife?'' asked Julian. ''What will be harder for her, to know or not know?''

''Women are not so different from men. *You* preferred to know.''

Julian nodded. "I know that you were only the bearer of news, not the cause of our loss. But your visit here will not be remembered with happiness. Yet I want you to know that I understand how kindly you have done this miserable job."

She nodded. "And you have been unfailingly gracious in a difficult hour."

Julian opened the door of her car. She stooped to the seat, swung her legs inside. But before he could close the door for her, she thought of one last question, a very important one.

"Julian, I know you were planning to have a daughter next. But if you had gone on to bring another son into the world, what would you have named him?"

"Our firstborn was named for my father, Nikolai," he said. "But Elena wanted to name a second son for me."

"Julian Delphiki," said Sister Carlotta. "If this truly is your son, I think he would be proud someday to bear his father's name."

"What name does he use now?" asked Julian.

"Of course I cannot say."

"But . . . not Volescu, surely."

"No. As far as I'm concerned, he'll never hear that name. God bless you, Julian Delphiki. I will pray for you and your wife."

"Pray for our children's souls, too, Sister."

"I already have, and do, and will."

Major Anderson looked at the boy sitting across the table from him. "Really, it's not that important a matter, Nikolai."

"I thought maybe I was in trouble."

"No, no. We just noticed that you seemed to be a particular friend of Bean. He doesn't have a lot of friends."

"It didn't help that Dimak painted a target on him in the shuttle. And now Ender's gone and done the same thing. I suppose Bean can take it, but smart as he is, he kind of pisses off a lot of the other kids."

"But not you?"

"Oh, he pisses me off, too."

"And yet you became his friend."

"Well, I didn't mean to. I just had the bunk across from him in launchy barracks."

"You traded for that bunk."

"Did I? Oh. Eh."

"And you did that before you knew how smart Bean was."

"Dimak told us in the shuttle that Bean had the highest scores of any of us."

"Was that why you wanted to be near him?"

Nikolai shrugged.

"It was an act of kindness," said Major Anderson. "Perhaps I'm just an old cynic, but when I see such an inexplicable act I become curious."

"He really does kind of look like my baby pictures. Isn't that dumb? I saw him and I thought, he looks just like cute little baby Nikolai. Which is what my mother always called me in my baby pictures. I never thought of them as *me*. I was big Nikolai. That was cute little baby Nikolai. I used to pretend that he was my little brother and we just happened to have the same name. Big Nikolai and Cute Little Baby Nikolai."

"I see that you're ashamed, but you shouldn't be. It's a natural thing for an only child to do."

"I wanted a brother."

"Many who have a brother wish they didn't."

"But the brother I made up for myself, he and I got along fine." Nikolai laughed at the absurdity of it.

"And you saw Bean and thought of him as the brother you once imagined."

"At first. Now I know who he really is, and it's better. It's like . . . sometimes he's the little brother and I'm looking out for him, and sometimes he's the big brother and he's looking out for me."

"For instance?"

"What?"

"A boy that small—how does he look out for you?"

"He gives me advice. Helps me with classwork. We do some practice together. He's better at almost everything than I am. Only I'm bigger, and I think I like him more than he likes me."

"That may be true, Nikolai. But as far as we can tell, he likes you more than he likes anybody else. He just . . . so far, he may not have the same capacity for friendship that you have. I hope that my asking you these questions won't change your feelings and actions toward Bean. We don't assign people to be friends, but I hope you'll remain Bean's."

"I'm not his friend," said Nikolai.

"Oh?"

"I told you. I'm his brother." Nikolai grinned. "Once you get a brother, you don't give him up easy."

15

COURAGE

"Genetically, they're identical twins. The only difference is Anton's key."

"So the Delphiki have two sons."

"The Delphiki have one son, Nikolai, and he's with us for the duration. Bean was an orphan found on the streets of Rotterdam."

"Because he was kidnapped."

"The law is clear. Fertilized eggs are property. I know that this is a matter of religious sensitivity for you, but the I.F. is bound by law, not—"

"The I.F. uses law where possible to achieve its own ends. I know you're fighting a war. I know that some things are outside your power. But the war will not go on forever. All I ask is this: Make this information part of a record—part of many records. So that when the war ends, the proof of these things can and will survive. So the truth won't stay hidden."

"Of course."

"No, not of course. You know that the moment the Formics are defeated, the I.F. will have no reason to exist. It will try to continue to exist in order to maintain international peace. But the League is not politically strong enough to survive in the nationalist winds that will blow. The I.F. will break into fragments, each following its own leader, and God help us if any part of the fleet ever should use its weapons against the surface of the Earth."

"You've been spending too much time reading the Apocalypse."

"I may not be one of the genius children in your school, but I see how the tides of opinion are flowing here on Earth. On the nets a demagogue named Demosthenes is inflaming the West about illegal and secret maneuvers by the Polemarch to give an advantage to the New Warsaw Pact, and the propaganda is even more virulent from Moscow, Baghdad, Buenos Aires, Beijing. There are a few rational voices, like Locke, but they're given lip service and then ignored. You and I can't do anything about the fact that world war will certainly come. But we *can* do our best to make sure these children don't become pawns in that game."

"The only way they won't be pawns is if they're players."

"You've been raising them. Surely you don't *fear* them. Give them their chance to play."

"Sister Carlotta, all my work is aimed at preparing for the showdown with the Formics. At turning these children into brilliant, reliable commanders. I can't look beyond that mark."

"Don't *look*. Just leave the door open for their families, their nations to claim them."

"I can't think about that right now."

"Right now is the only time you'll have the power to do it."

"You overestimate me."

"You underestimate yourself."

Dragon Army had only been practicing for a month when Wiggin came into the barracks only a few seconds after lights-on, brandishing a slip of paper. Battle orders. They would face Rabbit Army at 0700. And they'd do it without breakfast.

"I don't want anybody throwing up in the battleroom."

"Can we at least take a leak first?" asked Nikolai.

"No more than a decaliter," said Wiggin.

Everybody laughed, but they were also nervous. As a new army, with only a handful of veterans, they didn't actually expect to win, but they didn't want to be humiliated, either. They all had different ways of dealing with nerves—some became silent, others talkative. Some joked and bantered, others turned surly. Some just lay back down on their bunks and closed their eyes.

Bean watched them. He tried to remember if the kids in Poke's crew ever did these things. And then realized: They were *hungry*, not afraid of being shamed. You don't get this kind of fear until you have enough to eat. So it was the bullies who felt like these kids, afraid of humiliation but not of going hungry. And sure enough, the bullies standing around in line showed all these attitudes. They were always performing, always aware of others watching them. Fearful they would have to fight; eager for it, too.

What do I feel?

What's wrong with me that I have to think about it to know?

Oh . . . I'm just sitting here, watching. I'm one of *those*.

Bean pulled out his flash suit, but then realized he had to use the toilet before putting it on. He dropped down onto the deck and pulled his towel from its hook, wrapped it around himself. For a moment he flashed back to that night he had tossed his towel under a bunk and climbed into the ventilation system. He'd never fit now. Too thickly muscled, too tall. He was still the shortest kid in Battle School, and he doubted if anyone else would notice how he'd grown, but he was aware of how his arms and legs were longer. He could reach things more easily. Didn't have to jump so often just to do normal things like palming his way into the gym.

I've changed, thought Bean. My body, of course. But also the way I think.

Nikolai was still lying in bed with his pillow over his head. Everybody had his own way of coping.

The other kids were all using the toilets and getting drinks of water, but Bean was the only one who thought it was a good idea to shower. They used to tease him by asking if the water was still warm when it got all the way down there, but the joke was old now. What Bean wanted was the steam. The blindness of the fog around him, of the fogged mirrors, everything hidden, so he could be anyone, anywhere, any size.

Someday they'll all see me as I see myself. Larger than any of them. Head and shoulders above the rest, seeing farther, reaching farther, carrying burdens they could only dream of. In Rotterdam all I cared about was staying alive. But here, well fed, I've found out who I am. What I might be. *They* might think I'm an alien or a robot or something, just because I'm not genetically ordinary. But when I've done the great deeds of my life, they'll be proud to claim me as a human, furious at anyone who questions whether I'm truly one of them.

Greater than Wiggin.

He put the thought out of his mind, or tried to. This wasn't a competition. There was room for two great men in the world at the same time. Lee and Grant were contemporaries, fought against each other. Bismarck and Disraeli. Napoleon and Wellington.

No, that's not the comparison. It's *Lincoln* and Grant. Two great men working together.

It was disconcerting, though, to realize how rare that was. Napoleon could never bear to let any of his lieutenants have real authority. All victories had to be his alone. Who was the great man beside Augustus? Alexander? They had friends, they had rivals, but they never had partners.

That's why Wiggin has kept me down, even though he knows by now from the reports they give to army commanders that I've got a mind better than anybody else in Dragon. Because I'm too obviously a rival. Because I made it clear that first day that I intended to rise, and he's letting me know that it won't happen while I'm with his army.

Someone came into the bathroom. Bean couldn't see who it was because of the fog. Nobody greeted him. Everybody else must have finished here and gone back to get ready.

The newcomer walked through the fog past the opening in Bean's shower stall. It was Wiggin.

Bean just stood there, covered with soap. He felt like an idiot. He was in such a daze he had forgotten to rinse, was just standing in the fog, lost in his thoughts. Hurriedly he moved under the water again.

"Bean?"

"Sir?" Bean turned to face him. Wiggin was standing in the shower entrance.

"I thought I ordered everybody to get down to the gym."

Bean thought back. The scene unfolded in his mind. Yes, Wiggin *had* ordered everybody to bring their flash suits to the gym.

"I'm sorry. I . . . was thinking of something else . . ."

"Everybody's nervous before their first battle."

Bean hated that. To have Wiggin see him doing something stupid. Not remembering an order—Bean remembered *everything*. It just hadn't registered. And now he was patronizing him. Everybody's nervous!

"*You* weren't," said Bean.

Wiggin had already stepped away. He came back. "Wasn't I?"

"Bonzo Madrid gave you orders not to take your weapon out. You were supposed to just stay there like a dummy. You weren't nervous about doing *that*."

"No," said Wiggin. "I was pissed."

"Better than nervous."

Wiggin started to leave. Then returned again. "Are *you* pissed?"

"I did that before I showered," said Bean.

Wiggin laughed. Then his smile disappeared. "You're late, Bean, and you're still busy rinsing. I've already got your flash suit down in the gym. All we need now is your ass in it." Wiggin took Bean's towel off its hook. "I'll have this waiting for you down there, too. Now move."

Wiggin left.

Bean turned the water off, furious. That was completely unnecessary, and Wiggin knew it. Making him go through the corridor wet and naked during the time when other armies would be coming back from breakfast. That was low, and it was stupid.

Anything to put me down. Every chance he gets.

Bean, you idiot, you're still standing here. You could have run down to the gym and beaten him there. Instead, you're shooting your stupid self in the stupid foot. And why? None of this makes sense. None of this is going to help you. You want him to make you a toon leader, not think of you with contempt. So why are you doing things to make yourself look stupid and young and scared and unreliable?

And still you're standing here, frozen.

I'm a coward.

The thought ran through Bean's mind and filled him with terror. But it wouldn't go away.

I'm one of those guys who freezes up or does completely irrational things when he's afraid. Who loses control and goes slack-minded and stupid.

But I didn't do that in Rotterdam. If I had, I'd be dead.

Or maybe I *did* do it. Maybe that's why I didn't call out to Poke and Achilles when I saw them there alone on the dock. He wouldn't have killed her if I'd been there to witness what happened. Instead I ran off until I realized the danger she was in. But why didn't I realize it before? Because I *did* realize it, just as I heard Wiggin tell us to meet in the gym. Realized it, understood it completely, but was too cowardly to act. Too afraid that something would go wrong.

And maybe that's what happened when Achilles lay on the ground and I told Poke to kill him. I was wrong and she was right. Because *any* bully she caught that way would probably have held a grudge—and might easily have acted on it immediately, killing her as soon as they let him up. Achilles was the likeliest one, maybe the only one that would agree to the arrangement Bean had thought up. There was no choice. But I got scared. Kill him, I said, because I wanted it to go away.

And still I'm standing here. The water is off. I'm dripping wet and cold. But I can't move.

Nikolai was standing in the bathroom doorway. "Too bad about your diarrhea," he said.

"What?"

"I told Ender about how you were up with diarrhea in the night. That's why you had to go to the bathroom. You were sick, but you didn't want to tell him because you didn't want to miss the first battle."

"I'm so scared I couldn't take a dump if I wanted to," said Bean.

"He gave me your towel. He said it was stupid of him to take it." Nikolai walked in and gave it to him. "He said he needs you in the battle, so he's glad you're toughing it out."

"He doesn't need me. He doesn't even want me."

"Come on, Bean," said Nikolai. "You can do this."

Bean toweled off. It felt good to be moving. Doing something.

"I think you're dry enough," said Nikolai.

Again, Bean realized he was simply drying and drying himself, over and over.

"Nikolai, what's wrong with me?"

"You're afraid that you'll turn out to be just a little kid. Well, here's a clue: You *are* a little kid."

"So are you."

"So it's OK to be really bad. Isn't that what you keep telling me?" Nikolai laughed. "Come on, if I can do it, bad as I am, so can you."

"Nikolai," said Bean.

"What now?"

"I really *do* have to crap."

"I sure hope you don't expect me to wipe your butt."

"If I don't come out in three minutes, come in after me."

Cold and sweating—a combination he wouldn't have thought possible— Bean went into the toilet stall and closed the door. The pain in his abdomen was fierce. But he couldn't get his bowel to loosen up and let go.

What am I so *afraid* of?

Finally, his alimentary system triumphed over his nervous system. It felt like everything he'd ever eaten flooded out of him at once.

"Time's up," said Nikolai. "I'm coming in."

"At peril of your life," said Bean. "I'm done, I'm coming out."

Empty now, clean, and humiliated in front of his only real friend, Bean came out of the stall and wrapped his towel around him.

"Thanks for keeping me from being a liar," said Nikolai.

"What?"

"About your having diarrhea."

"For you I'd get dysentery."

"Now that's friendship."

By the time they got to the gym, everybody was already in their flash suits, ready to go. While Nikolai helped Bean get into his suit, Wiggin had the rest of them lie down on the mats and do relaxation exercises. Bean even had time to lie down for a couple of minutes before Wiggin had them get up. 0656. Four minutes to get to the battleroom. He was cutting it pretty fine.

As they ran along the corridor, Wiggin occasionally jumped up to touch the ceiling. Behind him, the rest of the army would jump up and touch the same spot when they reached it. Except the smaller ones. Bean, his heart still burning with humiliation and resentment and fear, did not try. You do that kind of thing when you belong with the group. And he didn't belong. After all his brilliance in class, the truth was out now. He was a coward. He didn't belong in the military at all. If he couldn't even risk playing a game, what would he be worth in combat? The real generals exposed themselves to enemy fire. Fearless, they had to be, an example of courage to their men.

Me, I freeze up, take long showers, and dump a week's rations into the head. Let's see them follow *that* example.

At the gate, Wiggin had time to line them up in toons, then remind them. "Which way is the enemy's gate?"

"Down!" they all answered.

Bean only mouthed the word. Down. Down down down.

What's the best way to get down off a goose?

What are you doing up on a goose in the first place, you fool!

The grey wall in front of them disappeared, and they could see into the battleroom. It was dim—not dark, but so faintly lighted that the only way they could see the enemy gate was the light of Rabbit Army's flash suits pouring out of it.

Wiggin was in no hurry to get out of the gate. He stood there surveying the room, which was arranged in an open grid, with eight "stars"—large cubes that served as obstacles, cover, and staging platforms—distributed fairly evenly if randomly through the space.

Wiggin's first assignment was to C toon. Crazy Tom's toon. The toon Bean belonged to. Word was whispered down the file. "Ender says slide the wall." And then, "Tom says flash your legs and go in on your knees. South wall."

Silently they swung into the room, using the handholds to propel themselves along the ceiling to the east wall. "They're setting up their battle formation. All we want to do is cut them up a little, make them nervous, confused, because they don't know what to do with us. We're raiders. So we shoot them up, then get behind that star. *Don't* get stuck out in the middle. And *aim*. Make every shot count."

Bean did everything mechanically. It was habit now to get in position, freeze his own legs, and then launch with his body oriented the right way. They'd done it hundreds of times. He did it exactly right; so did the other seven soldiers in the toon. Nobody was looking for anyone to fail. He was right where they expected him to be, doing his job.

They coasted along the wall, always within reach of a handhold. Their frozen legs were dark, blocking the lights of the rest of their flash suits until they were fairly close. Wiggin was doing something up near the gate to distract Rabbit Army's attention, so the surprise was pretty good.

As they got closer, Crazy Tom said, "Split and rebound to the star— me north, you south."

It was a maneuver that Crazy Tom had practiced with his toon. It was the right time for it, too. It would confuse the enemy more to have two groups to shoot at, heading different directions.

They pulled up on handholds. Their bodies, of course, swung against the wall, and suddenly the lights of their flash suits were quite visible. Somebody in Rabbit saw them and gave the alarm.

But C was already moving, half the toon diagonally south, the other half north, and all angling downward toward the floor. Bean began firing; the enemy was also firing at him. He heard the low whine that said somebody's beam was on his suit, but he was twisting slowly, and far enough from the enemy that none of the beams was in one place long enough to do damage. In the meantime, he found that his arm tracked perfectly, not trembling at all. He had practiced this a lot, and he was good at it. A clean kill, not just an arm or leg.

He had time for a second before he hit the wall and had to rebound up to the rendezvous star. One more enemy hit before he got there, and then he snagged a handhold on the star and said, "Bean here."

"Lost three," said Crazy Tom. "But their formation's all gone to hell."

"What now?" said Dag.

They could tell from the shouting that the main battle was in progress.

Bean was thinking back over what he had seen as he approached the star.

"They sent a dozen guys to this star to wipe us out," said Bean. "They'll come around the east and west sides."

They all looked at him like he was insane. How could he know this?

"We've got about one more second," said Bean.

"All south," said Crazy Tom.

They swung up to the south side of the star. There were no Rabbits on that face, but Crazy Tom immediately led them in an attack around to the west face. Sure enough, there were Rabbits there, caught in the act of attacking what they clearly thought of as the "back" of the star—or, as Dragon Army was trained to think of it, the bottom. So to the Rabbits, the attack seemed to come from below, the direction they were least aware of. In moments, the six Rabbits on that face were frozen and drifting along below the star.

The other half of the attack force would see that and know what had happened.

"Top," said Crazy Tom.

To the enemy, that would be the front of the star—the position most exposed to fire from the main formation. The last place they'd expect Tom's toon to go.

And once they were there, instead of continuing to attempt to engage the strike force coming against them, Crazy Tom had them shoot at the main Rabbit formation, or what was left of it—mostly disorganized groups hiding behind stars and firing at Dragons coming down at them from several directions. The five of them in C toon had time to hit a couple of Rabbits each before the strike force found them again.

Without waiting for orders, Bean immediately launched away from the surface of the star so he could shoot downward at the strike force. This close, he was able to do four quick kills before the whining abruptly stopped and his suit went completely stiff and dark. The Rabbit who got him wasn't one of the strike force—it was somebody from the main force above him. And to his satisfaction, Bean could see that because of his firing, only one soldier from C toon was hit by the strike force sent against them. Then he rotated out of view.

It didn't matter now. He was out. But he had done well. Seven kills that he was sure of, maybe more. And it was more than his personal score. He had come up with the information Crazy Tom needed in order to make a good tactical decision, and then he had taken the bold action that kept the strike force from causing too many casualties. As a result, C toon remained in position to strike at the enemy from behind. Without any place to hide, Rabbit would be wiped out in moments. And Bean was part of it.

I didn't freeze once we got into action. I did what I was trained to do, and I stayed alert, and I thought of things. I can probably do better, move faster, see more. But for a first battle, I did fine. I can do this.

Because C toon was crucial to the victory, Wiggin used the other four toon leaders to press their helmets to the corners of the enemy gate, and gave Crazy Tom the honor of passing through the gate, which is what formally ended the game, bringing the lights on bright.

Major Anderson himself came in to congratulate the winning commander and supervise cleanup. Wiggin quickly unfroze the casualties. Bean was relieved when his suit could move again. Using his hook, Wiggin drew them all together and formed his soldiers into their five toons before he began unfreezing Rabbit Army. They stood at attention in the air, their feet pointed down, their heads up—and as Rabbit unfroze, they gradually oriented themselves in the same direction. They had no way of knowing it, but to Dragon, that was when victory became complete—for the enemy was now oriented as if their *own* gate was down.

Bean and Nikolai were already eating breakfast when Crazy Tom came to their table. "Ender says instead of fifteen minutes for breakfast, we have till 0745. And he'll let us out of practice in time to shower."

That was good news. They could slow down their eating.

Not that it mattered to Bean. His tray had little food on it, and he finished it immediately. Once he was in Dragon Army, Crazy Tom had caught him giving away food. Bean told him that he was always given too much, and Tom took the matter to Ender, and Ender got the nutritionists to stop overfeeding Bean. Today was the first time Bean ever wished for more. And that was only because he was so up from the battle.

"Smart," said Nikolai.

"What?"

"Ender tells us we've got fifteen minutes to eat, which feels rushed and we don't like it. Then right away he sends around the toon leaders, telling us we have till 0745. That's only ten minutes longer, but now it feels like forever. And a shower—we're supposed to be able to shower right after the game, but now we're grateful."

"*And* he gave the toon leaders the chance to bring good news," said Bean.

"Is that important?" asked Nikolai. "We know it was Ender's choice."

"Most commanders make sure all good news comes from them," said Bean, "and bad news from the toon leaders. But Wiggin's whole technique is building up his toon leaders. Crazy Tom went in there with nothing more than his training and his brains and a single objective—strike first from the wall and get behind them. All the rest was up to him."

"Yeah, but if his toon leaders screw up, it looks bad on Ender's record," said Nikolai.

Bean shook his head. "The point is that in his very first battle, Wiggin divided his force for tactical effect, and C toon was able to continue attacking even after we ran out of plans, because Crazy Tom was really, truly in charge of us. We didn't sit around wondering what Wiggin wanted us to do."

Nikolai got it, and nodded. "Bacana. That's right."

"Completely right," said Bean. By now everybody at the table was listening. "And that's because Wiggin isn't just thinking about Battle School and standings and merda like that. He keeps watching vids of the Second Invasion, did you know that? He's thinking about how to beat the *Buggers.* And he knows that the way you do that is to have as many commanders ready to fight them as you can get. Wiggin doesn't want to come out of this with Wiggin as the only commander ready to fight the Buggers. He wants to come out of this with him *and* the toon leaders *and* the seconds *and* if he can do it every single one of his soldiers ready to command a fleet against the Buggers if we have to."

Bean knew his enthusiasm was probably giving Wiggin credit for more than he had actually planned, but he was still full of the glow of victory. And besides, what he was saying was true—Wiggin was no Napoleon, holding on to the reins of control so tightly that none of his commanders was capable of brilliant independent command. Crazy Tom had performed well under pressure. He had made the right decisions—including the decision to listen to his smallest, most useless-looking soldier. And Crazy Tom had done that because Wiggin had set the example by listening to his toon leaders. You learn, you analyze, you choose, you act.

After breakfast, as they headed for practice, Nikolai asked him, "Why do you call him Wiggin?"

"Cause we're not friends," said Bean.

"Oh, so it's Mr. Wiggin and Mr. Bean, is that it?"

"No. *Bean* is my first name."

"Oh. So it's Mr. Wiggin and Who The Hell Are You."

"Got it."

Everybody expected to have at least a week to strut around and brag about their perfect won-lost record. Instead, the next morning at 0630, Wiggin appeared in the barracks, again brandishing battle orders. "Gentlemen, I hope you learned something yesterday, because today we're going to do it again."

All were surprised, and some were angry—it wasn't fair, they weren't ready. Wiggin just handed the orders to Fly Molo, who had just been heading out for breakfast. "Flash suits!" cried Fly, who clearly thought it was a cool thing to be the first army ever to fight two in a row like this.

But Hot Soup, the leader of D toon, had another attitude. "Why didn't you tell us earlier?"

"I thought you needed the shower," said Wiggin. "Yesterday Rabbit Army claimed we only won because the stink knocked them out."

Everybody within earshot laughed. But Bean was not amused. He knew that the paper hadn't been there first thing, when Wiggin woke up. The teachers planted it late. "Didn't find the paper till you got back from the showers, right?"

Wiggin gave him a blank look. "Of course. I'm not as close to the floor as you."

The contempt in his voice struck Bean like a blow. Only then did he realize that Wiggin had taken his question as a criticism—that Wiggin had been inattentive and hadn't *noticed* the orders. So now there was one more mark against Bean in Wiggin's mental dossier. But Bean couldn't let that upset him. It's not as if Wiggin didn't have him tagged as a coward. Maybe Crazy Tom told Wiggin about how Bean contributed to the victory yesterday, and maybe not. It wouldn't change what Wiggin had seen with his own eyes—Bean malingering in the shower. And now Bean apparently taunting him for making them all have to rush for their second battle. Maybe I'll be made toon leader on my thirtieth birthday. And then only if everybody else is drowned in a boat accident.

Wiggin was still talking, of course, explaining how they should expect battles any time, the old rules were coming apart. "I can't pretend I like the way they're screwing around with us, but I do like one thing—that I've got an army that can handle it."

As he put on his flash suit, Bean thought through the implications of what the teachers were doing. They were pushing Wiggin faster and also making it harder for him. And this was only the beginning. Just the first few sprinkles of a snotstorm.

Why? Not because Wiggin was so good he needed the testing. On the contrary—Wiggin was training his army well, and the Battle School would only benefit from giving him plenty of time to do it. So it had to be something outside Battle School.

Only one possibility, really. The Bugger invaders were getting close. Only a few years away. They had to get Wiggin through training.

Wiggin. Not all of us, just Wiggin. Because if it were everybody, then everybody's schedule would be stepped up like this. Not just ours.

So it's already too late for me. Wiggin's the one they've chosen to rest their hopes on. Whether I'm toon leader or not will never matter. All that matters is: Will Wiggin be ready?

If Wiggin succeeds, there'll still be room for me to achieve greatness in the aftermath. The League will come apart. There'll be war among humans. Either I'll be used by the I.F. to help keep the peace, or maybe I can get into some army on Earth. I've got plenty of life ahead of me. Unless Wiggin commands our fleet against the invading Buggers and loses. Then none of us has any life at all.

All I can do right now is my best to help Wiggin learn everything he can learn here. The trouble is, I'm not close enough to him for me to have any effect on him at all.

The battle was with Petra Arkanian, commander of Phoenix Army. Petra was sharper than Carn Carby had been; she also had the advantage of hearing how Wiggin worked entirely without formations and used little raiding parties to disrupt formations ahead of the main combat. Still, Dragon finished with only three soldiers flashed and nine partially disabled. A crushing defeat. Bean could see that Petra didn't like it, either. She probably felt like Wiggin had poured it on, deliberately setting her up for humiliation. But she'd get it, soon enough—Wiggin simply turned his toon leaders loose, and each of them pursued total victory, as he had trained them. Their system worked better, that's all, and the old way of doing battle was doomed.

Soon enough, all the other commanders would start adapting, learning from what Wiggin did. Soon enough, Dragon Army would be facing armies that were divided into five toons, not four, and that moved in a free-ranging style with a lot more discretion given to the toon leaders. The kids didn't get to Battle School because they were idiots. The only reason the techniques worked a second time was because there'd only been a day since the first battle, and nobody expected to have to face Wiggin again so soon. Now they'd know that changes would have to be made fast. Bean guessed that they'd probably never see another formation.

What then? Had Wiggin emptied his magazine, or would he have new tricks up his sleeve? The trouble was, innovation never resulted in victory over the long term. It was too easy for the enemy to imitate and improve on your innovations. The real test for Wiggin would be what he did when he was faced with slugfests between armies using similar tactics.

And the real test for me will be seeing if I can stand it when Wiggin makes some stupid mistake and I have to sit here as an ordinary soldier and watch him do it.

The third day, another battle. The fourth day, another. Victory. Victory. But each time, the score was closer. Each time, Bean gained more confidence as a soldier—and became more frustrated that the most he could contribute, beyond his own good aim, was occasionally making a suggestion to Crazy Tom, or reminding him of something Bean had noticed and remembered.

Bean wrote to Dimak about it, explaining how he was being underused and suggesting that he would be getting better trained by working with a worse commander, where he'd have a better chance of getting his own toon.

The answer was short. "Who else would want you? Learn from Ender."

Brutal but true. No doubt even Wiggin didn't really want him. Either he was forbidden to transfer any of his soldiers, or he had tried to trade Bean away and no one would take him.

It was free time of the evening after their fourth battle. Most of the others were trying to keep up with their classwork—the battles were really taking it out of them, especially because they could all see that they needed to practice hard to stay ahead. Bean, though, coasted through classwork like always, and when Nikolai told him he didn't need any more damned help with his assignments, Bean decided that he should take a walk.

Passing Wiggin's quarters—a space even smaller than the cramped quarters the teachers had, just space for a bunk, one chair, and a tiny table— Bean was tempted to knock on the door and sit down and have it out with Wiggin once and for all. Then common sense prevailed over frustration and vanity, and Bean wandered until he came to the arcade.

It wasn't as full as it used to be. Bean figured that was because everyone was holding extra practices now, trying to implement whatever they thought it was Wiggin was doing before they actually had to face him in battle. Still, a few were still willing to fiddle with the controllers and make things move on screens or in holodisplays.

Bean found a flat-screen game that had, as its hero, a mouse. No one was using it, so Bean started maneuvering it through a maze. Quickly the maze gave way to the wallspaces and crawlspaces of an old house, with traps set here and there, easy stuff. Cats chased him—ho hum. He jumped up onto a table and found himself face to face with a giant.

A giant who offered him a drink.

This was the fantasy game. This was the psychological game that everybody else played on their desks all the time. No wonder no one was playing it here. They all recognized it and that wasn't the game they came here to play.

Bean was well aware that he was the only kid in the school who had never played the fantasy game. They had tricked him into playing this once, but he doubted that anything important could be learned from what he had done so far. So screw 'em. They could trick him into playing up to a point, but he didn't have to go further.

Except that the giant's face had changed. It was Achilles.

Bean stood there in shock for a moment. Frozen, frightened. How did they know? Why did they do it? To put him face-to-face with Achilles, by surprise like that. Those bastards.

He walked away from the game.

Moments later, he turned around and came back. The giant was no longer on the screen. The mouse was running around again, trying to get out of the maze.

No, I won't play. Achilles is far away and he does not have the power to hurt me. Or Poke either, not anymore. I don't have to think about him and I sure as hell don't have to drink anything he offers me.

Bean walked away again, and this time did not come back.

He found himself down by the mess. It had just closed, but Bean had nothing better to do, so he sat down in the corridor beside the mess hall door and rested his forehead on his knees and thought about Rotterdam and sitting on top of a garbage can watching Poke working with her crew and how she was the most decent crew boss he'd seen, the way she listened to the little kids and gave them a fair share and kept them alive even if it meant not eating so much herself and that's why he chose her, because she had mercy—mercy enough that she just might listen to a child.

Her mercy killed her.

I killed her when I chose her.

There better be a God. So he can damn Achilles to hell forever.

Someone kicked at his foot.

"Go away," said Bean, "I'm not bothering you."

Whoever it was kicked again, knocking Bean's feet out from under him. With his hands he caught himself from falling over. He looked up. Bonzo Madrid loomed over him.

"I understand you're the littlest dingleberry clinging to the butt hairs of Dragon Army," said Bonzo.

He had three other guys with him. Big guys. They all had bully faces.

"Hi, Bonzo."

"We need to talk, pinprick."

"What is this, espionage?" asked Bean. "You're not supposed to talk to soldiers in other armies."

"I don't need espionage to find out how to beat Dragon Army," said Bonzo.

"So you're just looking for the littlest Dragon soldiers wherever you can find them, and then you'll push them around a little till they cry?"

Bonzo's face showed his anger. Not that it didn't always show anger.

"Are you begging to eat out of your own asshole, pinprick?"

Bean didn't like bullies right now. And since, at the moment, he felt guilty of murdering Poke, he didn't really care if Bonzo Madrid ended up being the one to administer the death penalty. It was time to speak his mind.

"You're at least three times my weight," said Bean, "except inside your skull. You're a second-rater who somehow got an army and never could figure out what to do with it. Wiggin is going to grind you into the ground and he isn't even going to have to try. So does it really matter what you do to me? I'm the smallest and weakest soldier in the whole school. Naturally *I'm* the one you choose to kick around."

"Yeah, the smallest and weakest," said one of the other kids.

Bonzo didn't say anything, though. Bean's words had stung. Bonzo had his pride, and he knew now that if he harmed Bean it would be a humiliation, not a pleasure.

"Ender Wiggin isn't going to beat me with that collection of launchies and rejects that he calls an army. He may have psyched out a bunch of dorks like Carn and . . . *Petra.*" He spat her name. "But whenever *we* find crap my army can pound it flat."

Bean affixed him with his most withering glare. "Don't you get it, Bonzo? The teachers have picked Wiggin. He's the best. The best ever. They didn't give him the worst army. They gave him the *best* army. Those veterans you call rejects—they were soldiers so good that the *stupid* commanders couldn't get along with them and tried to transfer them away. Wiggin knows how to use good soldiers, even if you don't. That's why Wiggin is winning. He's smarter than you. And his soldiers are all smarter than your soldiers. The deck is stacked against you, Bonzo. You might as well give up now. When your pathetic little Salamander Army faces us, you'll be so whipped you'll have to pee sitting down.''

Bean might have said more—it's not like he had a plan, and there was certainly a lot more he could have said—but he was interrupted. Two of Bonzo's friends scooped him up and held him high against the wall, higher than their own heads. Bonzo put one hand around his throat, just under his jaw, and pressed back. The others let go. Bean was hanging by his neck, and he couldn't breathe. Reflexively he kicked, struggling to get some purchase with his feet. But long-armed Bonzo was too far away for any of Bean's kicking to land on him.

"The game is one thing," Bonzo said quietly. "The teachers can rig that and give it to their little Wiggin catamite. But there'll come a time when it isn't a game. And when that time comes, it won't be a frozen flash suit that makes it so Wiggin can't move. Comprendes?''

What answer was he hoping for? It was a sure thing Bean couldn't nod or speak.

Bonzo just stood there, smiling maliciously, as Bean struggled.

Everything started turning black around the edges of Bean's vision before Bonzo finally let him drop to the floor. He lay there, coughing and gasping.

What have I done? I goaded Bonzo Madrid. A bully with none of Achilles' subtlety. When Wiggin beats him, Bonzo isn't going to take it. He won't stop with a demonstration, either. His hatred for Wiggin runs deep.

As soon as he could breathe again, Bean headed back to the barracks. Nikolai noticed the marks on his neck at once. "Who was choking you?"

"I don't know," said Bean.

"Don't give me that," said Nikolai. "He was facing you, look at the fingermarks."

"I don't remember."

"You remember the pattern of arteries on your own placenta."

"I'm not going to tell you," said Bean. To that, Nikolai had no answer, though he didn't like it.

Bean signed on as /\Graff and wrote a note to Dimak, even though he knew it would do no good.

"Bonzo is insane. He could kill somebody, and Wiggin's the one he hates the most."

The answer came back quickly, almost as if Dimak had been waiting for the message. "Clean up your own messes. Don't go crying to mama."

The words stung. It wasn't Bean's mess, it was Wiggin's. And, ultimately, the teachers', for having put Wiggin in Bonzo's army to begin with. And then to taunt him because he didn't have a mother—when did the teachers become the enemy here? They were supposed to protect us from crazy kids like Bonzo Madrid. How do they think I'm going to clean this mess up?

The only thing that will stop Bonzo Madrid is to kill him.

And then Bean remembered standing there looking down at Achilles, saying, "You got to kill him."

Why couldn't I have kept my mouth shut? Why did I have to goad Bonzo Madrid? Wiggin is going to end up like Poke. And it will be my fault again.

16

COMPANION

"So you see, Anton, the key you found has been turned, and it may be the salvation of the human race."

"But the poor boy. To live his life so small, and then die as a giant."

"Perhaps he'll be . . . amused at the irony."

"How strange to think that my little key might turn out to be the salvation of the human race. From the invading beasts, anyway. Who will save us when we become our own enemy again?"

"*We* are not enemies, you and I."

"Not many people are enemies to anyone. But the ones full of greed or hate, pride or fear—their passion is strong enough to lever all the world into war."

"If God can raise up a great soul to save us from one menace, might he not answer our prayers by raising up another when we need him?"

"But Sister Carlotta, you know the boy you speak of was not raised up by God. He was created by a kidnapper, a baby-killer, an outlaw scientist."

"Do you know why Satan is so angry all the time? Because whenever he works a particularly clever bit of mischief, God uses it to serve his own righteous purposes."

"So God uses wicked people as his tools."

"God gives us the freedom to do great evil, if we choose. Then he uses his own freedom to create goodness out of that evil, for that is what he chooses."

"So in the long run, God always wins."

"Yes."

"In the short run, though, it *can* be uncomfortable."

"And when, in the past, would you have preferred to die, instead of being alive here today?"

"There it is. We get used to everything. We find hope in anything."

"That's why I've never understood suicide. Even those suffering from great depression or guilt—don't they feel Christ the Comforter in their hearts, giving them hope?"

"You're asking me?"

"God not being convenient, I ask a fellow mortal."

"In my view, suicide is not really the wish for life to end."

"What is it, then?"

"It Is the only way a powerless person can find to make everybody else look away from his shame. The wish is not to die, but to hide."

"As Adam and Eve hid from the Lord."

"Because they were naked."

"If only such sad people could remember: Everyone is naked. Everyone wants to hide. But life is still sweet. Let it go on."

"You don't believe that the Formics are the beast of the Apocalypse, then, Sister?"

"No, Anton. I believe they are also children of God."

"And yet you found this boy specifically so he could grow up to destroy them."

"*Defeat* them. Besides, if God does not want them to die, they will not die."

"And if God wants *us* to die, we will. Why do you work so hard, then?"

"Because these hands of mine, I gave them to God, and I serve him as best I can. If he had not wanted me to find Bean, I would not have found him."

"And if God wants the Formics to prevail?"

"He'll find some other hands to do it. For that job, he can't have mine."

Lately, while the toon leaders drilled the soldiers, Wiggin had taken to disappearing. Bean used his ^Graff log-on to find what he was doing. He'd gone back to studying the vids of Mazer Rackham's victory, much more intensely and single-mindedly than ever before. And this time, because Wiggin's army was playing games daily and winning them all, the other commanders and many toon leaders and common soldiers as well began to go to the library and watch the same vids, trying to make sense of them, trying to see what Wiggin saw.

Stupid, thought Bean. Wiggin isn't looking for anything to use here in Battle School—he's created a powerful, versatile army and he'll figure out what to do with them on the spot. He's studying those vids in order to figure out how to beat the Buggers. Because he knows now: He will face them someday. The teachers would not be wrecking the whole system here in Battle School if they were not nearing the crisis, if they did not need Ender Wiggin to save us from the invading Buggers. So Wiggin studies the Buggers, desperate for some idea of what they want, how they fight, how they die.

Why don't the teachers see that Wiggin is done? He's not even thinking about Battle School anymore. They should take him out of here and move him into Tactical School, or whatever the next stage of his training will be. Instead, they're pushing him, making him tired.

Us too. We're tired.

Bean saw it especially in Nikolai, who was working harder than the others just to keep up. If we were an ordinary army, thought Bean, most of us would be like Nikolai. As it is, many of us are—Nikolai was not the first to show his weariness. Soldiers drop silverware or food trays at meal-times. At least one has wet his bed. We argue more at practice. Our class-work is suffering. Everyone has limits. Even me, even genetically-altered Bean the thinking machine, I need time to relubricate and refuel, and I'm not getting it.

Bean even wrote to Colonel Graff about it, a snippy little note saying only, "It is one thing to train soldiers and quite another to wear them out." He got no reply.

Late afternoon, with a half hour before mess call. They had already won a game that morning and then practiced after class, though the toon leaders, at Wiggin's suggestion, had let their soldiers go early. Most of Dragon Army was now dressing after showers, though some had already gone on to kill time in the game room or the video room . . . or the library. Nobody was paying attention to classwork now, but a few still went through the motions.

Wiggin appeared in the doorway, brandishing the new orders.

A second battle on the *same day*.

"This one's hot and there's no time," said Wiggin. "They gave Bonzo notice about twenty minutes ago, and by the time we get to the door they'll have been inside for a good five minutes at least."

He sent the four soldiers nearest the door—all young, but not launchies anymore, they were veterans now—to bring back the ones who had left. Bean dressed quickly—he had learned how to do it by himself now, but not without hearing plenty of jokes about how he was the only soldier who had to practice getting dressed, and it was still slow.

As they dressed, there was plenty of complaining about how this was getting stupid, Dragon Army should have a break now and then. Fly Molo was the loudest, but even Crazy Tom, who usually laughed at everything, was pissed about it. When Tom said, "Same day nobody ever do two battles!" Wiggin answered, "Nobody ever beat Dragon Army, either. This be your big chance to lose?"

Of course not. Nobody intended to lose. They just wanted to complain about it.

It took a while, but finally they were gathered in the corridor to the battleroom. The gate was already open. A few of the last arrivals were still putting on their flash suits. Bean was right behind Crazy Tom, so he could see down into the room. Bright light. No stars, no grid, no hiding place of any kind. The enemy gate was open, and yet there was not a Salamander soldier to be seen.

"My heart," said Crazy Tom. "They haven't come out yet, either."

Bean rolled his eyes. Of course they were out. But in a room without cover, they had simply formed themselves up on the ceiling, gathered around Dragon Army's gate, ready to destroy everybody as they came out.

Wiggin caught Bean's facial expression and smiled as he covered his own mouth to signal them all to be silent. He pointed all around the gate, to let them know where Salamander was gathered, then motioned for them to move back.

The strategy was simple and obvious. Since Bonzo Madrid had kindly pinned his army against a wall, ready to be slaughtered, it only remained to find the right way to enter the battleroom and carry out the massacre.

Wiggin's solution—which Bean liked—was to transform the larger soldiers into armored vehicles by having them kneel upright and freeze their legs. Then a smaller soldier knelt on each big kid's calves, wrapped one arm around the bigger soldier's waist, and prepared to fire. The largest soldiers were used as launchers, throwing each pair into the battleroom.

For once being small had its advantages. Bean and Crazy Tom were the pair Wiggin used to demonstrate what he wanted them all to do. As a result, when the first two pairs were thrown into the room, Bean got to begin the slaughter. He had three kills almost at once—at such close range, the beam was tight and the kills came fast. And as they began to go out of range, Bean climbed around Crazy Tom and launched off of him, heading east and somewhat up while Tom went even faster toward the far side of the room. When other Dragons saw how Bean had managed to stay within firing range, while moving sideways and therefore remaining hard to hit, many of them did the same. Eventually Bean was disabled, but it hardly mattered—Salamander was wiped out to the last man, and without a single one of them getting off the wall. Even when it was obvious they were easy, stationary targets, Bonzo didn't catch on that he was doomed until he himself was already frozen, and nobody else had the initiative to countermand his original order and start moving so they wouldn't be so easy to hit. Just one more example of why a commander who ruled by fear and made all the decisions himself would always be beaten, sooner or later.

The whole battle had taken less than a full minute from the time Bean rode Crazy Tom through the door until the last Salamander was frozen.

What surprised Bean was that Wiggin, usually so calm, was pissed off and showing it. Major Anderson didn't even have a chance to give the official congratulations to the victor before Wiggin shouted at him, ''I thought you were going to put us against an army that could match us in a fair fight.''

Why would he think that? Wiggin must have had some kind of conversation with Anderson, must have been promised something that hadn't been delivered.

But Anderson explained nothing. ''Congratulations on the victory, commander.''

Wiggin wasn't going to have it. It wasn't going to be business as usual. He turned to his army and called out to Bean by name. ''If you had commanded Salamander Army, what would you have done?''

Since another Dragon had used him to shove off in midair, Bean was now drifting down near the enemy gate, but he heard the question—Wiggin wasn't being subtle about this. Bean didn't want to answer, because he knew what a serious mistake this was, to speak slightingly of Salamander and call on the smallest Dragon soldier to correct Bonzo's stupid tactics. Wiggin hadn't had Bonzo's hand around his throat the way Bean had. Still, Wiggin was commander, and Bonzo's tactics had been stupid, and it was fun to say so.

"Keep a shifting pattern of movement going in front of the door," Bean answered, loudly, so every soldier could hear him—even the Salamanders, still clinging to the ceiling. "You never hold still when the enemy knows exactly where you are."

Wiggin turned to Anderson again. "As long as you're cheating, why don't you train the other army to cheat intelligently!"

Anderson was still calm, ignoring Wiggin's outburst. "I suggest that you remobilize your army."

Wiggin wasn't wasting time with rituals today. He pressed the buttons to thaw both armies at once. And instead of forming up to receive formal surrender, he shouted at once, "Dragon Army dismissed!"

Bean was one of those nearest the gate, but he waited till nearly last, so that he and Wiggin left together. "Sir," said Bean. "You just humiliated Bonzo and he's—"

"I know," said Wiggin. He jogged away from Bean, not wanting to hear about it.

"He's dangerous!" Bean called after him. Wasted effort. Either Wiggin already knew he'd provoked the wrong bully, or he didn't care.

Did he do it deliberately? Wiggin was always in control of himself, always carrying out a plan. But Bean couldn't think of any plan that required yelling at Major Anderson and shaming Bonzo Madrid in front of his whole army.

Why would Wiggin do such a stupid thing?

It was almost impossible to think of geometry, even though there was a test tomorrow. Classwork was utterly unimportant now, and yet they went on taking the tests and turning in or failing to turn in their assignments. The last few days, Bean had begun to get less-than-perfect scores. Not that he didn't know the answers, or at least how to figure them out. It's that his mind kept wandering to things that mattered more—new tactics that might surprise an enemy; new tricks that the teachers might pull in the way they set things up; what might be, must be going on in the larger war, to cause the system to start breaking apart like this; what would happen on Earth and in the I.F. once the Buggers were defeated. If they were defeated. Hard to care about volumes, areas, faces, and dimensions of solids. On a test yesterday, working out problems of gravity near planetary and stellar masses, Bean finally gave up and wrote:

$$2 + 2 = \pi \sqrt{2 + n}$$

WHEN YOU KNOW THE VALUE OF N, I'll FINISH THIS TEST.

He knew that the teachers all knew what was going on, and if they wanted to pretend that classwork still mattered, fine, let them, but *he* didn't have to play.

At the same time, he knew that the problems of gravity mattered to someone whose only likely future was in the International Fleet. He also needed a thorough grounding in geometry, since he had a pretty good idea of what math was yet to come. He wasn't going to be an engineer or artillerist or rocket scientist or even, in all likelihood, a pilot. But he had to know what they knew better than they knew it, or they'd never respect him enough to follow him.

Not tonight, that's all, thought Bean. Tonight I can rest. Tomorrow I'll learn what I need to learn. When I'm not so tired.

He closed his eyes.

He opened them again. He opened his locker and took out his desk.

Back on the streets of Rotterdam he had been tired, worn out by hunger and malnutrition and despair. But he kept watching. Kept thinking. And therefore he was able to stay alive. In this army everyone was getting tired, which meant that there would be more and more stupid mistakes. Bean, of all of them, could least afford to become stupid. Not being stupid was the only asset he had.

He signed on. A message appeared in his display.

    See me at once—Ender

It was only ten minutes before lights out. Maybe Wiggin sent the message three hours ago. But better late than never. He slid off his bunk, not bothering with shoes, and padded out into the corridor in his stocking feet. He knocked at the door marked

COMMANDER
DRAGON ARMY

"Come in," said Wiggin.

Bean opened the door and came inside. Wiggin looked tired in the way that Colonel Graff usually looked tired. Heavy skin around the eyes, face slack, hunched in the shoulders, but eyes still bright and fierce, watching, thinking. "Just saw your message," said Bean.

"Fine."

"It's near lights-out."

"I'll help you find your way in the dark."

The sarcasm surprised Bean. As usual, Wiggin had completely misunderstood the purpose of Bean's comment. "I just didn't know if you knew what time it was—"

"I always know what time it is."

Bean sighed inwardly. It never failed. Whenever he had any conversation with Wiggin, it turned into some kind of pissing contest, which Bean always lost even when it was Wiggin whose deliberate misunderstanding caused the whole thing. Bean hated it. He recognized Wiggin's genius and honored him for it. Why couldn't he see anything good in Bean?

But Bean said nothing. There was nothing he could say that would improve the situation. Wiggin had called him in. Let Wiggin move the meeting forward.

"Remember four weeks ago, Bean? When you told me to make you a toon leader?"

"Eh."

"I've made five toon leaders and five assistants since then. And none of them was you." Wiggin raised his eyebrows. "Was I right?"

"Yes, sir." But only because you didn't bother to give me a chance to prove myself before you made the assignments.

"So tell me how you've done in these eight battles."

Bean wanted to point out how time after time, his suggestions to Crazy Tom had made C toon the most effective in the army. How his tactical innovations and creative responses to flowing situations had been imitated by the other soldiers. But that would be brag and borderline insubordination. It wasn't what a soldier who wanted to be an officer would say. Either Crazy Tom had reported Bean's contribution or he hadn't. It wasn't Bean's place to report on anything about himself that wasn't public record. "Today was the first time they disabled me so early, but the computer listed me as getting eleven hits before I had to stop. I've never had less than five hits in a battle. I've also completed every assignment I've been given."

"Why did they make you a soldier so young, Bean?"

"No younger than you were." Technically not true, but close enough.

"But why?"

What was he getting at? It was the teachers' decision. Had he found out that Bean was the one who composed the roster? Did he know that Bean had chosen himself? "I don't know."

"Yes you do, and so do I."

No, Wiggin wasn't asking specifically about why *Bean* was made a soldier. He was asking why launchies were suddenly getting promoted so young. "I've tried to guess, but they're just guesses." Not that Bean's guesses were ever just guesses—but then, neither were Wiggin's. "You're—very good. They knew that, they pushed you ahead—"

"Tell me *why,* Bean."

And now Bean understood the question he was really asking. "Because they need us, that's why." He sat on the floor and looked, not into Wiggin's face, but at his feet. Bean knew things that he wasn't supposed to know. That the teachers didn't know he knew. And in all likelihood, there were teachers monitoring this conversation. Bean couldn't let his face give away how much he really understood. "Because they need somebody to beat the Buggers. That's the only thing they care about."

"It's important that you know that, Bean."

Bean wanted to demand, Why is it important that *I* know it? Or are you just saying that people in general should know it? Have you finally seen and understood who I am? That I'm *you,* only smarter and less likable, the better strategist but the weaker commander? That if you fail, if you break, if you get sick and die, then I'm the one? Is that why I need to know this?

"Because," Wiggin went on, "most of the boys in this school think the game is important *for itself,* but it isn't. It's only important because it helps them find kids who might grow up to be real commanders, in the real war. But as for the game, screw that. That's what they're doing. Screwing up the game."

"Funny," said Bean. "I thought they were just doing it to us." No, if Wiggin thought Bean needed to have this explained to him, he did *not* understand who Bean really was. Still, it was Bean in Wiggin's quarters, having this conversation with him. That was something.

"A game nine weeks earlier than it should have come. A game every day. And now two games in the same day. Bean, I don't know what the teachers are doing, but my army is getting tired, and I'm getting tired, and they don't care at all about the rules of the game. I've pulled the old charts up from the computer. No one has ever destroyed so many enemies and kept so many of his own soldiers whole in the history of the game.''

What was this, brag? Bean answered as brag was meant to be answered. ''You're the best, Ender.''

Wiggin shook his head. If he heard the irony in Bean's voice, he didn't respond to it. ''Maybe. But it was no accident that I got the soldiers I got. Launchies, rejects from other armies, but put them together and my worst soldier could be a toon leader in another army. They've loaded things my way, but now they're loading it all against me. Bean, they want to break us down.''

So Wiggin did understand how his army had been selected, even if he didn't know who had done the selecting. Or maybe he knew everything, and this was all that he cared to show Bean at this time. It was hard to guess how much of what Wiggin did was calculated and how much merely intuitive. ''They can't break you.''

''You'd be surprised.'' Wiggin breathed sharply, suddenly, as if there were a stab of pain, or he had to catch a sudden breath in a wind; Bean looked at him and realized that the impossible was happening. Far from baiting him, Ender Wiggin was actually confiding in him. Not much. But a little. Ender was letting Bean see that he was human. Bringing him into the inner circle. Making him . . . what? A counselor? A confidant?

''Maybe you'll be surprised,'' said Bean.

''There's a limit to how many clever new ideas I can come up with every day. Somebody's going to come up with something to throw at me that I haven't thought of before, and I won't be ready.''

''What's the worst that could happen?'' asked Bean. ''You lose one game.''

''Yes. That's the worst that could happen. I can't lose *any* games. Because if I lose *any* . . .''

He didn't complete the thought. Bean wondered what Ender imagined the consequences would be. Merely that the legend of Ender Wiggin, perfect soldier, would be lost? Or that his army would lose confidence in him, or in their own invincibility? Or was this about the larger war, and losing a game here in Battle School might shake the confidence of the teachers that Ender was the commander of the future, the one to lead the fleet, if he could be made ready before the Bugger invasion arrived?

Again, Bean did not know how much the teachers knew about what Bean had guessed about the progress of the wider war. Better to keep silence.

''I need you to be clever, Bean,'' said Ender. ''I need you to think of solutions to problems we haven't seen yet. I want you to try things that no one has ever tried because they're absolutely stupid.''

So what is this about, Ender? What have you decided about me, that brings me into your quarters tonight? ''Why me?''

''Because even though there are some better soldiers than you in Dragon Army—not many, but some—there's nobody who can think better and faster than you.''

He *had* seen. And after a month of frustration, Bean realized that it was better this way. Ender had seen his work in battle, had judged him by what he did, not by his reputation in classes or the rumors about his having the highest scores in the history of the school. Bean had earned this evaluation, and it had been given him by the only person in this school whose high opinion Bean longed for.

Ender held out his desk for Bean to see. On it were twelve names. Two or three soldiers from each toon. Bean immediately knew how Ender had chosen them. They were all good soldiers, confident and reliable. But not the flashy ones, the stunters, the show-offs. They were, in fact, the ones that Bean valued most highly among those who were not toon leaders. ''Choose five of these,'' said Ender. ''One from each toon. They're a special squad, and you'll train them. Only during the extra practice sessions. Talk to me about what you're training them to do. Don't spend too long on any one thing. Most of the time you and your squad will be part of the whole army, part of your regular toons. But when I need you. When there's something to be done that only you can do.''

There was something else about these twelve. ''These are all new. No veterans.''

''After last week, Bean, all our soldiers are veterans. Don't you realize that on the individual soldier standings, all forty of our soldiers are in the top fifty? That you have to go down seventeen places to find a soldier who *isn't* a Dragon?''

''What if I can't think of anything?'' asked Bean.

''Then I was wrong about you.''

Bean grinned. ''You weren't wrong.''

The lights went out.

''Can you find your way back, Bean?''

''Probably not.''

''Then stay here. If you listen very carefully, you can hear the good fairy come in the night and leave our assignment for tomorrow.''

''They won't give us another battle tomorrow, will they?'' Bean meant it as a joke, but Ender didn't answer.

Bean heard him climb into bed.

Ender was still small for a commander. His feet didn't come near the end of the bunk. There was plenty of room for Bean to curl up at the foot of the bed. So he climbed up and then lay still, so as not to disturb Ender's sleep. If he was sleeping. If he was not lying awake in the silence, trying to make sense of . . . what?

For Bean, the assignment was merely to think of the unthinkable—stupid ploys that might be used against them, and ways to counter them; equally stupid innovations they might introduce in order to sow confusion among the other armies and, Bean suspected, get them sidetracked into imitating completely nonessential strategies. Since few of the other commanders understood why Dragon Army was winning, they kept imitating the nonce tactics used in a particular battle instead of seeing the underlying method Ender used in training and organizing his army. As Napoleon said, the only thing a commander ever truly controls is his own army—training, morale, trust, initiative, command and, to a lesser degree, supply, placement, movement, loyalty, and courage in battle. What the enemy will do and what chance will bring, those defy all planning. The commander must be able to change his plans abruptly when obstacles or opportunities appear. If his army isn't ready and willing to respond to his will, his cleverness comes to nothing.

The less effective commanders didn't understand this. Failing to recognize that Ender won because he and his army responded fluidly and instantly to change, they could only think to imitate the specific tactics they saw him use. Even if Bean's creative gambits were irrelevant to the outcome of the battle, they would lead other commanders to waste time imitating irrelevancies. Now and then something he came up with might actually be useful. But by and large, he was a sideshow.

That was fine with Bean. If Ender wanted a sideshow, what mattered was that he had chosen Bean to create that show, and Bean would do it as well as it could be done.

But if Ender was lying awake tonight, it was not because he was concerned about Dragon Army's battles tomorrow and the next day and the next. Ender was thinking about the Buggers and how he would fight them when he got through his training and was thrown into war, with the real lives of real men depending on his decisions, with the survival of humanity depending on the outcome.

In *that* scheme, what is my place? thought Bean. I'm glad enough that the burden is on Ender, not because I could not bear it—maybe I could—but because I have more confidence that Ender can bring it off than that I could. Whatever it is that makes men love the commander who decides when they will die, Ender has that, and if I have it no one has yet seen evidence of it. Besides, even without genetic alteration, Ender has abilities that the tests didn't measure for, that run deeper than mere intellect.

But he shouldn't have to bear all this alone. I can help him. I can forget geometry and astronomy and all the other nonsense and concentrate on the problems he faces most directly. I'll do research into the way other animals wage war, especially swarming hive insects, since the Formics resemble ants the way we resemble primates.

And I can watch his back.

Bean thought again of Bonzo Madrid. Of the deadly rage of bullies in Rotterdam.

Why have the teachers put Ender in this position? He's an obvious target for the hatred of the other boys. Kids in Battle School had war in their hearts. They hungered for triumph. They loathed defeat. If they lacked these attributes, they would never have been brought here. Yet from the start, Ender had been set apart from the others—younger but smarter, the leading soldier and now the commander who makes all other commanders look like babies. Some commanders responded to defeat by becoming submissive—Carn Carby, for instance, now praised Ender behind his back and studied his battles to try to learn how to win, never realizing that you had to study Ender's training, not his battles, to understand his victories. But most of the other commanders were resentful, frightened, ashamed, angry, jealous, and it was in their character to translate such feelings into violent action . . . if they were sure of victory.

Just like the streets of Rotterdam. Just like the bullies, struggling for supremacy, for rank, for respect. Ender has stripped Bonzo naked. It cannot be borne. He'll have his revenge, as surely as Achilles avenged his humiliation.

And the teachers understand this. They intend it. Ender has clearly mastered every test they set for him—whatever Battle School usually taught, he was done with. So why didn't they move him on to the next level? Because there was a lesson they were trying to teach, or a test they were trying to get him to pass, which was not within the usual curriculum. Only this particular test could end in death. Bean had felt Bonzo's fingers around his throat. This was a boy who, once he let himself go, would relish the absolute power that the murderer achieves at his victim's moment of death.

They're putting Ender into a street situation. They're testing him to see if he can survive.

They don't know what they're doing, the fools. The street is not a test. The street is a lottery.

I came out a winner—I was alive. But Ender's survival won't depend on his ability. Luck plays too large a role. Plus the skill and resolve and power of the opponent.

Bonzo may be unable to control the emotions that weaken him, but his presence in Battle School means that he is not without skill. He was made a commander because a certain type of soldier will follow him into death and horror. Ender is in mortal danger. And the teachers, who think of us as children, have no idea how quickly death can come. Look away for only a few minutes, step away far enough that you can't get back in time, and your precious Ender Wiggin, on whom all your hopes are pinned, will be quite, quite dead. I saw it on the streets of Rotterdam. It can happen just as easily in your nice clean rooms here in space.

So Bean set aside classwork for good that night, lying at Ender's feet. Instead, he had two new courses of study. He would help Ender prepare for the war he cared about, with the Buggers. But he would also help him in the street fight that was being set up for him.

It wasn't that Ender was oblivious, either. After some kind of fracas in the battleroom during one of Ender's early freetime practices, Ender had taken a course in self-defense, and knew something about fighting man to man. But Bonzo would not come at him man to man. He was too keenly aware of having been beaten. Bonzo's purpose would not be a rematch, it would not be vindication. It would be punishment. It would be elimination. He would bring a gang.

And the teachers would not realize the danger until it was too late. They still didn't think of anything the children did as "real."

So after Bean thought of clever, stupid things to do with his new squad, he also tried to think of ways to set Bonzo up so that, in the crunch, he would have to take on Ender Wiggin alone or not at all. Strip away Bonzo's support. Destroy the morale, the reputation of any bully who might go along with him.

This is one job Ender *can't* do. But it can be done.

Part Five

LEADER

17

DEADLINE

"I don't even know how to interpret this. The mind game had only one shot at Bean, and it puts up this one kid's face, and he goes off the charts with—what, fear? Rage? Isn't there anybody who knows how this so-called game works? It ran Ender through a wringer, brought in those pictures of his brother that it couldn't possibly have had, only it got them. And this one—was it some deeply insightful gambit that leads to powerful new conclusions about Bean's psyche? Or was it simply the only person Bean knew whose picture was already in the Battle School files?"

"Was that a rant, or is there any particular one of those questions you want answered?"

"What I want you to answer is this question: How the hell can you tell me that something was 'very significant' if you have no idea what it signifies!"

"If someone runs after your car, screaming and waving his arms, you know that something significant is intended, even if you can't hear a word he's saying."

"So that's what this was? Screaming?"

"That was an analogy. The image of Achilles was extraordinarily important to Bean."

"Important positive, or important negative?"

"That's too cut-and-dried. If it was negative, are his negative feelings because Achilles caused some terrible trauma in Bean? Or negative because having been torn away from Achilles was traumatic, and Bean longs to be restored to him?"

"So if we have an independent source of information that tells us to keep them apart . . ."

"Then either that independent source is really really right. . . ."

"Or really really wrong."

"I'd be more specific if I could. We only had a minute with him."

"That's disingenuous. You've had the mind game linked to all his work with his teacher-identity."

"And we've reported to you about that. It's partly his hunger to have control—that's how it began—but it has since become a way of taking responsibility. He has, in a way, *become* a teacher. He has also used his inside information to give himself the illusion of belonging to the community."

"He does belong."

"He has only one close friend, and that's more of a big brother, little brother thing."

"I have to decide whether I can put Achilles into Battle School while Bean is there, or give up one of them in order to keep the other. Now, from Bean's response to Achilles' face, what counsel can you give me."

"You won't like it."

"Try me."

"From that incident, we can tell you that putting them together will be either a really really bad thing, or—"

"I'm going to have to take a long, hard look at your budget."

"Sir, the whole purpose of the program, the way it works, is that the computer makes connections we would never think of, and gets responses we weren't looking for. It's not actually under our control."

"Just because a program isn't out of control doesn't mean intelligence is present, either in the program or the programmer."

"We don't use the word 'intelligence' with software. We regard that as a naive idea. We say that it's 'complex.' Which means that we don't always understand what it's doing. We don't always get conclusive information."

"Have you *ever* gotten conclusive information about anything?"

"*I* chose the wrong word this time. 'Conclusive' isn't ever the goal when we are studying the human mind."

"Try 'useful.' Anything useful?"

"Sir, I've told you what we know. The decision was yours before we reported to you, and it's still your decision now. Use our information or not, but is it sensible to shoot the messenger?"

"When the messenger won't tell you what the hell the message *is*, my trigger finger gets twitchy. Dismissed."

Nikolai's name was on the list that Ender gave him, but Bean ran into problems immediately.

"I don't want to," said Nikolai.

It had not occurred to Bean that anyone would refuse.

"I'm having a hard enough time keeping up as it is."

"You're a good soldier."

"By the skin of my teeth. With a big helping of luck."

"That's how *all* good soldiers do it."

"Bean, if I lose one practice a day from my regular toon, then I'll fall behind. How can I make it up? And one practice a day with you won't be enough. I'm a smart kid, Bean, but I'm not Ender. I'm not you. That's the thing that I don't think you really get. How it feels *not* to be you. Things just aren't as easy and clear."

"It's not easy for me, either."

"Look, I know that, Bean. And there are some things I can do for you. This isn't one of them. Please."

It was Bean's first experience with command, and it wasn't working. He found himself getting angry, wanting to say Screw you and go on to someone else. Only he couldn't be angry at the only true friend he had. And he also couldn't easily take no for an answer. "Nikolai, what we're doing won't be hard. Stunts and tricks."

Nikolai closed his eyes. "Bean, you're making me feel bad."

"I don't want you to feel bad, Sinterklaas, but this is the assignment I was given, because Ender thinks Dragon Army needs this. You were on the list, his choice not mine."

"But you don't have to choose me."

"So I ask the next kid, and he says, 'Nikolai's on this squad, right?' and I say, No, he didn't want to. That makes them all feel like they can say no. And they'll *want* to say no, because nobody wants to be taking orders from me."

"A month ago, sure, that would have been true. But they know you're a solid soldier. I've heard people talk about you. They respect you."

Again, it would have been so easy to do what Nikolai wanted and let him off the hook on this. And, as a friend, that would be the *right* thing to do. But Bean couldn't think as a friend. He had to deal with the fact that he had been given a command and he had to make it work.

Did he really need Nikolai?

"I'm just thinking out loud, Nikolai, because you're the only one I can say this to, but see, I'm scared. I wanted to lead a toon, but that's because I didn't know anything about what leaders do. I've had a week of battles to see how Crazy Tom holds the group of us together, the voice he uses for command. To see how Ender trains us and trusts us, and it's a dance, tiptoe, leap, spin, and I'm afraid that I'll fail, and there isn't *time* to fail, I have to make this work, and when you're with me, I know there's at least one person who isn't halfway hoping for this smart little kid to fail."

"Don't kid yourself," said Nikolai. "As long as we're being honest."

That stung. But a leader had to take that, didn't he? "No matter what you feel, Nikolai, you'll give me a chance," said Bean. "And because you're giving me a chance, the others will, too. I need . . . loyalty."

"So do I, Bean."

"You need my loyalty as a friend, in order to let you, personally, be happy," said Bean. "I need loyalty as a leader, in order to fulfil the assignment given to us by our commander."

"That's mean," said Nikolai.

"Eh," said Bean. "Also true."

"You're mean, Bean."

"Help me, Nikolai."

"Looks like our friendship goes only one way."

Bean had never felt like this before—this knife in his heart, just because of the words he was hearing, just because somebody *else* was angry with him. It wasn't just because he wanted Nikolai to think well of him. It was because he knew that Nikolai was at least partly right. Bean was using his friendship against him.

It wasn't because of that pain, however, that Bean decided to back off. It was because a soldier who was with him against his will would not serve him well. Even if he was a friend. "Look, if you won't, you won't. I'm sorry I made you mad. I'll do it without you. And you're right, I'll do fine. Still friends, Nikolai?"

Nikolai took his offered hand, held it. "Thank you," he whispered.

Bean went immediately to Shovel, the only one on Ender's list who was also from C toon. Shovel wasn't Bean's first choice—he had just the slightest tendency to delay, to do things halfheartedly. But because he was in C toon, Shovel had been there when Bean advised Crazy Tom. He had observed Bean in action.

Shovel set aside his desk when Bean asked if they could talk for a minute. As with Nikolai, Bean clambered up onto the bunk to sit beside the larger boy. Shovel was from Cagnes-sur-Mer, a little town on the French Riviera, and he still had that open-faced friendliness of Provence. Bean liked him. Everybody liked him.

Quickly Bean explained what Ender had asked him to do—though he didn't mention that it was just a sideshow. Nobody would give up a daily practice for a something that wouldn't be crucial to victory. "You were on the list Ender gave me, and I'd like you to—"

"Bean, what are you doing?"

Crazy Tom stood in front of Shovel's bunk.

At once Bean realized his mistake. "Sir," said Bean, "I should have talked to you first. I'm new at this and I just didn't think."

"New at what?"

Again Bean laid out what he had been asked to do by Ender.

"And Shovel's on the list?"

"Right."

"So I'm going to lose you *and* Shovel from my practices?"

"Just one practice per day."

"I'm the only toon leader who loses two."

"Ender said one from each toon. Five, plus me. Not my choice."

"Merda," said Crazy Tom. "You and Ender just didn't think of the fact that this is going to hit me harder than any of the other toon leaders. Whatever you're doing, why can't you do it with five instead of six? You and four others—one from each of the other toons?"

Bean wanted to argue, but realized that going head to head wasn't going to get him anywhere. "You're right, I didn't think of that, and you're right that Ender might very well change his mind when he realizes what he's doing to your practices. So when he comes in this morning, why don't you talk to him and let me know what the two of you decide? In the meantime, though, Shovel might tell me no, and then the question doesn't matter anymore, right?"

Crazy Tom thought about it. Bean could see the anger ticking away in him. But leadership had changed Crazy Tom. He no longer blew up the way he used to. He caught himself. He held it in. He waited it out.

"OK, I'll talk to Ender. If Shovel wants to do it."

They both looked at Shovel.

"I think it'd be OK," said Shovel. "To do something weird like this."

"I won't let up on either of you," said Crazy Tom. "And you don't talk about your wacko toon during my practices. You keep it outside."

They both agreed to that. Bean could see that Crazy Tom was wise to insist on that. This special assignment would set the two of them apart from the others in C toon. If they rubbed their noses in it, the others could feel shut out of an elite. That problem wouldn't show up as much in any of the other toons, because there'd only be one kid from each toon in Bean's squad. No chat. Therefore no nose-rubbing.

"Look, I don't have to talk to Ender about this," said Crazy Tom. "Unless it becomes a problem. OK?"

"Thanks," said Bean.

Crazy Tom went back to his own bunk.

I did that OK, thought Bean. I didn't screw up.

"Bean?" said Shovel.

"Eh?"

"One thing."

"Eh."

"Don't call me Shovel."

Bean thought back. Shovel's real name was Ducheval. "You prefer 'Two Horses'? Sounds kind of like a Sioux warrior."

Shovel grinned. "That's better than sounding like the tool you use to clean the stable."

"Ducheval," said Bean. "From now on."

"Thanks. When do we start?"

"Freetime practice today."

"Bacana."

Bean almost danced away from Ducheval's bunk. He had done it. He had handled it. Once, anyway.

And by the time breakfast was over, he had all five on his toon. With the other four, he checked with their toon leaders first. No one turned him down. And he got his squad to promise to call Ducheval by his right name from then on.

Graff had Dimak and Dap in his makeshift office in the battleroom bridge when Bean came. It was the usual argument between Dimak and Dap—that is, it was about nothing, some trivial question of one violating some minor protocol or other, which escalated quickly into a flurry of formal complaints. Just another skirmish in their rivalry, as Dap and Dimak tried to gain some advantage for their proteges, Ender and Bean, while at the same time trying to keep Graff from putting them in the physical danger that both saw looming. When the knock came at the door, voices had been raised for some time, and because the knock was not loud, it occurred to Graff to wonder what might have been overheard.

Had names been mentioned? Yes. Both Bean and Ender. And also Bonzo. Had Achilles' name come up? No. He had just been referred to as "another irresponsible decision endangering the future of the human race, all because of some insane theory about games being one thing and genuine life-and-death struggles being another, completely unproven and unprovable except in the blood of some child!" That was Dap, who had a tendency to wax eloquent.

Graff, of course, was already sick at heart, because he agreed with both teachers, not only in their arguments against each other, but also in their arguments against his own policy. Bean was demonstrably the better candidate on all tests; Ender was just as demonstrably the better candidate based on his performance in actual leadership situations. And Graff *was* being irresponsible to expose both boys to physical danger.

But in both cases, the child had serious doubts about his own courage. Ender had his long history of submission to his older brother, Peter, and the mind game had shown that in Ender's unconscious, Peter was linked to the Buggers. Graff knew that Ender had the courage to strike, without restraint, when the time came for it. That he could stand alone against an enemy, without anyone to help him, and destroy the one who would destroy him. But Ender didn't know it, and he had to know.

Bean, for his part, had shown physical symptoms of panic before his first battle, and while he ended up performing well, Graff didn't need any psychological tests to tell him that the doubt was there. The only difference was, in Bean's case Graff shared his doubt. There *was* no proof that Bean would strike.

Self-doubt was the one thing that neither candidate could afford to have. Against an enemy that did not hesitate—that *could* not hesitate—there could be no pause for reflection. The boys had to face their worst fears, knowing that no one would intervene to help. They had to know that when failure would be fatal, they would not fail. They had to pass the test and know that they had passed it. And both boys were so perceptive that the danger could not be faked. It had to *be* real.

Exposing them to that risk was utterly irresponsible of Graff. Yet he knew that it would be just as irresponsible not to. If Graff played it safe, no one would blame him if, in the actual war, Ender or Bean failed. That would be small consolation, though, given the consequences of failure. Whichever way he guessed, if he was wrong, everybody on Earth might pay the ultimate price. The only thing that made it possible was that if either of them was killed, or damaged physically or mentally, the other was still there to carry on as the sole remaining candidate.

If both failed, what then? There were many bright children, but none who were that much better than commanders already in place, who had graduated from Battle School many years ago.

Somebody has to roll the dice. Mine are the hands that hold those dice. I'm not a bureaucrat, placing my career above the larger purpose I was put here to serve. I will not put the dice in someone else's hands, or pretend that I don't have the choice I have.

For now, all Graff could do was listen to both Dap and Dimak, ignore their bureaucratic attacks and maneuvers against him, and try to keep them from each other's throats in their vicarious rivalry.

That small knock at the door—Graff knew before the door opened who it would be.

If he had heard the argument, Bean gave no sign. But then, that was Bean's specialty, giving no sign. Only Ender managed to be more secretive—and he, at least, had played the mind game long enough to give the teachers a map of his psyche.

"Sir," said Bean.

"Come in, Bean." Come in, Julian Delphiki, longed-for child of good and loving parents. Come in, kidnapped child, hostage of fate. Come and talk to the Fates, who are playing such clever little games with your life.

"I can wait," said Bean.

"Captain Dap and Captain Dimak can hear what you have to say, can't they?" asked Graff.

"If you say so, sir. It's not a secret. I would like to have access to station supplies."

"Denied."

"That's not acceptable, sir."

Graff saw how both Dap and Dimak glanced at him. Amused at the audacity of the boy? "Why do you think so?"

"Short notice, games every day, soldiers exhausted and yet still being pressured to perform in class—fine, Ender's dealing with it and so are we. But the only possible reason you could be doing this is to test our resourcefulness. So I want some resources."

"I don't remember your being commander of Dragon Army," said Graff. "I'll listen to a requisition for specific equipment from your commander."

"Not possible," said Bean. "He doesn't have time to waste on foolish bureaucratic procedures."

Foolish bureaucratic procedures. Graff had used that exact phrase in the argument just a few minutes ago. But Graff's voice had *not* been raised. How long *had* Bean been listening outside the door? Graff cursed himself silently. He had moved his office up here specifically because he knew Bean was a sneak and a spy, gathering intelligence however he could. And then he didn't even post a guard to stop the boy from simply walking up and listening at the door.

"And you do?" asked Graff.

"I'm the one he assigned to think of stupid things you might do to rig the game against us, and think of ways to deal with them."

"What do you think you're going to find?"

"I don't know," said Bean. "I just know that the only things *we* ever see are our uniforms and flash suits, our weapons and our desks. There are other supplies here. For instance, there's paper. We never get any except during written tests, when our desks are closed to us."

"What would you do with paper in the battleroom?"

"I don't know," said Bean. "Wad it up and throw it around. Shred it and make a cloud of dust out of it."

"And who would clean this up?"

"Not my problem," said Bean.

"Permission denied."

"That's not acceptable, sir," said Bean.

"I don't mean to hurt your feelings, Bean, but it matters less than a cockroach's fart whether you accept my decision or not."

"I don't mean to hurt *your* feelings, sir, but you clearly have no idea what you're doing. You're improvising. Screwing with the system. The damage you're doing is going to take years to undo, and you don't care. That means that it doesn't matter what condition this school is in a year from now. That means that everybody who matters is going to be graduated soon. Training is being accelerated because the Buggers are getting too close for delays. So you're pushing. And you're especially pushing Ender Wiggin."

Graff felt sick. He knew that Bean's powers of analysis were extraordinary. So, also, were his powers of deception. Some of Bean's guesses weren't right—but was that because he didn't know the truth, or because he simply didn't want them to know how much he knew, or how much he guessed? I never wanted you here, Bean, because you're too dangerous.

Bean was still making his case. "When the day comes that Ender Wiggin is looking for ways to stop the Buggers from getting to Earth and scouring the whole planet the way they started to back in the First Invasion, are you going to give him some bullshit answer about what resources he can or cannot use?''

''As far as you're concerned, the ship's supplies don't exist.''

''As far as I'm concerned,'' said Bean, ''Ender is *this* close to telling you to fry up your game and eat it. He's sick of it—if you can't see that, you're not much of a teacher. He doesn't care about the standings. He doesn't care about beating other kids. All he cares about is preparing to fight the Buggers. So how hard do you think it will be for me to persuade him that your program here is crocked, and it's time to quit playing?''

''All right,'' said Graff. ''Dimak, prepare the brig. Bean is to be confined until the shuttle is ready to take him back to Earth. This boy is out of Battle School.''

Bean smiled slightly. ''Go for it, Colonel Graff. I'm done here anyway. I've got everything *I* wanted here—a first-rate education. I'll never have to live on the street again. I'm home free. Let me out of your game, right now, I'm ready.''

''You won't be free on Earth, either. Can't risk having you tell these wild stories about Battle School,'' said Graff.

''Right. Take the best student you ever had here and put him in jail because he asked for access to the supply closet and you didn't like it. Come on, Colonel Graff. Swallow hard and back down. You need my cooperation more than I need yours.''

Dimak could barely conceal his smile.

If only confronting Graff like this were sufficient proof of Bean's courage. And for all that Graff had doubts about Bean, he didn't deny that he was good at maneuver. Graff would have given almost anything not to have Dimak and Dap in the room at this moment.

''It was your decision to have this conversation in front of witnesses,'' said Bean.

What, was the kid a mind reader?

No, Graff had glanced at the two teachers. Bean simply knew how to read his body language. The kid missed nothing. That's why he was so valuable to the program.

Isn't this why we pin our hopes on these kids? Because they're good at maneuver?

And if I know anything about command, don't I know this—that there are times when you cut your losses and leave the field?

''All right, Bean. One scan through supply inventory.''

"With somebody to explain to me what it all is."

"I thought you already knew everything."

Bean was polite in victory; he did not respond to taunting. The sarcasm gave Graff a little compensation for having to back down. He knew that's all it was, but this job didn't have many perks.

"Captain Dimak and Captain Dap will accompany you," said Graff. "One scan, and either one of them can veto anything you request. They will be responsible for the consequences of any injuries resulting from your use of any item they let you have."

"Thank you, sir," said Bean. "In all likelihood I won't find anything useful. But I appreciate your fair-mindedness in letting us search the station's resources to further the educational objectives of the Battle School."

The kid had the jargon down cold. All those months of access to the student data, with all the notations in the files, Bean had clearly learned more than just the factual contents of the dossiers. And now Bean was giving him the spin that he should use in writing up a report about his decision. As if Graff were not perfectly capable of creating his own spin.

The kid is patronizing me. Little bastard thinks that he's in control.

Well, I have some surprises for him, too.

"Dismissed," said Graff. "All of you."

They got up, saluted, left.

Now, thought Graff, I have to second-guess all my future decisions, wondering how much my choices are influenced by the fact that this kid really pisses me off.

———

As Bean scanned the inventory list, he was really searching primarily for something, anything, that might be made into a weapon that Ender or some of his army could carry to protect him from physical attack by Bonzo. But there was nothing that would be both concealable from the teachers and powerful enough to give smaller kids sufficient leverage over larger ones.

It was a disappointment, but he'd find other ways to neutralize the threat. And now, as long as he was scanning the inventory, *was* there anything that he might be able to use in the battleroom? Cleaning supplies weren't very promising. Nor would the hardware stocks make much sense in the battleroom. What, throw a handful of screws?

The safety equipment, though . . .

"What's a deadline?" asked Bean.

Dimak answered. "Very fine, strong cord that's used to secure maintenance and construction workers when they're working outside the station."

"How long?"

"With links, we can assemble several kilometers of secure deadline," said Dimak. "But each coil unspools to a hundred meters."

"I want to see it."

They took him into parts of the station that children never went to. The decor was far more utilitarian here. Screws and rivets were visible in the plates on the walls. The intake ducts were visible instead of being hidden inside the ceiling. There were no friendly lightstripes for a child to touch and get directions to his barracks. All the palm pads were too high for a child to comfortably use. And the staff they passed saw Bean and then looked at Dap and Dimak as if they were crazy.

The coil was amazingly small. Bean hefted it. Light, too. He unspooled a few decameters of it. It was almost invisible. "This will hold?"

"The weight of two adults," said Dimak.

"It's so fine. Will it cut?"

"Rounded so smoothly it can't cut anything. Wouldn't do us any good if it went slicing through things. Like spacesuits."

"Can I cut it into short lengths?"

"With a blowtorch," said Dimak.

"This is what I want."

"Just one?" asked Dap, rather sarcastically.

"And a blowtorch," said Bean.

"Denied," said Dimak.

"I was joking," said Bean. He walked out of the supply room and started jogging down the corridor, retracing the route they had just taken.

They jogged after him. "Slow down!" Dimak called out.

"Keep up!" Bean answered. "I've got a toon waiting for me to train them with this."

"Train them to do what!"

"I don't know!" He got to the pole and slid down. It passed him right through to the student levels. Going this direction, there was no security clearance at all.

His toon was waiting for him in the battleroom. They'd been working hard for him the past few days, trying all kinds of lame things. Formations that could explode in midair. Screens. Attacks without guns, disarming enemies with their feet. Getting into and out of spins, which made them almost impossible to hit but also kept them from shooting at anybody else.

The most encouraging thing was the fact that Ender spent almost the entire practice time watching Bean's squad whenever he wasn't actually responding to questions from leaders and soldiers in the other toons. Whatever they came up with, Ender would know about it and have his own ideas about when to use it. And, knowing that Ender's eyes were on them, Bean's soldiers worked all the harder. It gave Bean more stature in their eyes, that Ender really did care about what they did.

Ender's good at this, Bean realized again for the hundredth time. He knows how to form a group into the shape he wants it to have. He knows how to get people to work together. And he does it by the most minimal means possible.

If Graff were as good at this as Ender, I wouldn't have had to act like such a bully in there today.

The first thing Bean tried with the deadline was to stretch it across the battleroom. It reached, with barely enough slack to allow knots to be tied at both ends. But a few minutes of experimentation showed that it would be completely ineffective as a tripwire. Most enemies would simply miss it; those that did run into it might be disoriented or flipped around, but once it was known that it was there, it could be used like part of a grid, which meant it would work to the advantage of a creative enemy.

The deadline was designed to keep a man from drifting off into space. What happens when you get to the end of the line?

Bean left one end fastened to a handhold in the wall, but coiled the other end around his waist several times. The line was now shorter than the width of the battleroom's cube. Bean tied a knot in the line, then launched himself toward the opposite wall.

As he sailed through the air, the deadline tautening behind him, he couldn't help thinking: I hope they were right about this wire not being capable of cutting. What a way to end—sliced in half in the battleroom. *That* would be an interesting mess for them to clean up.

When he was a meter from the wall, the line went taut. Bean's forward progress was immediately halted at his waist. His body jacknifed and he felt like he'd been kicked in the gut. But the most surprising thing was the way his inertia was translated from forward movement into a sideways arc that whipped him across the battleroom toward where D toon was practicing. He hit the wall so hard he had what was left of his breath knocked out of him.

"Did you see that!" Bean screamed, as soon as he could breathe. His stomach hurt—he might not have been sliced in half, but he would have a vicious bruise, he knew that at once, and if he hadn't had his flash suit on, he could well believe there would have been internal injuries. But he'd be OK, and the deadline had let him change directions abruptly in midair. "Did you see it! Did you see it!"

"Are you all right!" Ender shouted.

He realized that Ender thought he was injured. Slowing down his speech, Bean called out again, "Did you see how fast I went! Did you see how I changed direction!"

The whole army stopped practice to watch as Bean played more with the deadline. Tying two soldiers together got interesting results when one of them stopped, but it was hard to hold on. More effective was when Bean had Ender use his hook to pull a star out of the wall and put it into the middle of the battleroom. Bean tied himself and launched from the star; when the line went taut, the edge of the star acted as a fulcrum, shortening the length of the line as he changed direction. And as the line wrapped around the star, it shortened even more upon reaching each edge. At the end, Bean was moving so fast that he blacked out for a moment upon hitting the star. But the whole of Dragon Army was stunned at what they had seen. The deadline was completely invisible, so it looked as though this little kid had launched himself and then suddenly started changing direction and speeding up in midflight. It was seriously disturbing to see it.

"Let's do it again, and see if I can shoot while I'm doing it," said Bean.

Evening practice didn't end till 2140, leaving little time before bed. But having seen the stunts Bean's squad was preparing, the army was excited instead of weary, fairly scampering through the corridors. Most of them probably understood that what Bean had come up with were stunts, nothing that would be decisive in battle. It was fun anyway. It was new. And it was Dragon.

Bean started out leading the way, having been given that honor by Ender. A time of triumph, and even though he knew he was being manipulated by the system—behavior modification through public honors—it still felt good.

Not so good, though, that he let up his alertness. He hadn't gone far along the corridor until he realized that there were too many Salamander uniforms among the other boys wandering around in this section. By

2140, most armies were in their barracks, with only a few stragglers coming back from the library or the vids or the game room. Too many Salamanders, and the other soldiers were often big kids from armies whose commanders bore no special love toward Ender. It didn't take a genius to recognize a trap.

Bean jogged back and tagged Crazy Tom, Vlad, and Hot Soup, who were walking together. "Too many Salamanders," Bean said. "Stay back with Ender." They got it at once—it was public knowledge that Bonzo was breathing out threats about what "somebody" ought to do to Ender Wiggin, just to put him in his place. Bean continued his shambling, easy-going run toward the back of the army, ignoring the smaller kids but tagging the other two toon leaders and all the seconds—the older kids, the ones who might have some chance of standing up to Bonzo's crew in a fight. Not *much* of a chance, but all that was needed was to keep them from getting at Ender until the teachers intervened. No way could the teachers stand aloof if an out-and-out riot erupted. Or could they?

Bean passed right by Ender, got behind him. He saw, coming up quickly, Petra Arkanian in her Phoenix Army uniform. She called out. "Ho, Ender!"

To Bean's disgust, Ender stopped and turned around. The boy was too trusting.

Behind Petra, a few Salamanders fell into step. Bean looked the other way, and saw a few more Salamanders and a couple of set-faced boys from other armies, drifting down the corridor past the last of the Dragons. Hot Soup and Crazy Tom were coming quickly, with more toon leaders and the rest of the larger Dragons coming behind them, but they weren't moving fast enough. Bean beckoned, and he saw Crazy Tom pick up his pace. The others followed suit.

"Ender, can I talk to you," said Petra.

Bean was bitterly disappointed. Petra was the Judas. Setting Ender up for Bonzo—who would have guessed? She *hated* Bonzo when she was in his army.

"Walk with me," said Ender.

"It's just for a moment," said Petra.

Either she was a perfect actress or she was oblivious, Bean realized. She only seemed aware of the other Dragon uniforms, never as much as glancing at anybody else. She isn't in on it after all, thought Bean. She's just an idiot.

At last, Ender seemed to be aware of his exposed position. Except for Bean, all the other Dragons were past him now, and that was apparently enough—at last—to make him uncomfortable. He turned his back on Petra and walked away, briskly, quickly closing the gap between him and the older Dragons.

Petra was angry for a moment, then jogged quickly to catch up with him. Bean stood his ground, looking at the oncoming Salamanders. They didn't even glance at him. They just picked up their pace, continuing to gain on Ender almost as fast as Petra was.

Bean took three steps and slapped the door of Rabbit Army barracks. Somebody opened it. Bean had only to say, "Salamander's making a move against Ender," and at once Rabbits started to pour out the door into the corridor. They emerged just as the Salamanders reached them, and started following along.

Witnesses, thought Bean. And helpers, too, if the fight seemed unfair.

Ahead of him, Ender and Petra were talking, and the larger Dragons fell in step around them. The Salamanders continued to follow closely, and the other thugs joined them as they passed. But the danger was dissipating. Rabbit Army and the older Dragons had done the job. Bean breathed a little easier. For the moment, at least, the danger was over.

Bean caught up with Ender in time to hear Petra angrily say, "How can you think I did? Don't you know who your friends are?" She ran off, ducked into a ladderway, scrambled upward.

Carn Carby of Rabbit caught up with Bean. "Everything OK?"

"I hope you don't mind my calling out your army."

"They came and got me. We seeing Ender safely to bed?"

"Eh."

Carn dropped back and walked along with the bulk of his soldiers. The Salamander thugs were now outnumbered about three to one. They backed off even more, and some of them peeled away and disappeared up ladderways or down poles.

When Bean caught up with Ender again, he was surrounded by his toon leaders. There was nothing subtle about it now—they were clearly his bodyguards, and some of the younger Dragons had realized what was happening and were filling out the formation. They got Ender to the door of his quarters and Crazy Tom pointedly entered before him, then allowed him to go in when he certified that no one was lying in wait. As if one of them could palm open a commander's door. But then, the teachers had been changing a lot of the rules lately. Anything could happen.

Bean lay awake for a while, trying to think what he could do. There was no way they could be with Ender every moment. There was class-work—armies were deliberately broken up then. Ender was the only one who could eat in the commanders' mess, so if Bonzo jumped him there . . . but he wouldn't, not with so many other commanders around him. Showers. Toilet stalls. And if Bonzo assembled the right group of thugs, they'd slap Ender's toon leaders aside like balloons.

What Bean had to do was try to peel away Bonzo's support. Before he slept, he had a half-assed little plan that might help a little, or might make things work, but at least it was something, and it would be public, so the teachers couldn't claim after the fact, in their typical bureaucrat cover-my-butt way that they hadn't known anything was going on.

He thought he could do something at breakfast, but of course there was a battle first thing in the morning. Pol Slattery, Badger Army. The teachers had found a new way to mess with the rules, too. When Badgers were flashed, instead of staying frozen till the end of the game they thawed after five minutes, the way it worked in practice. But Dragons, once hit, stayed rigid. Since the battleroom was packed with stars—plenty of hiding places—it took a while to realize that they were having to shoot the same soldiers more than once as they maneuvered through the stars, and Dragon Army came closer to losing than it ever had. It was all hand to hand, with a dozen of the remaining Dragons having to watch batches of frozen Badgers, reshooting them periodically and meanwhile frantically looking around for some other Badger sneaking up from behind.

The battle took so long that by the time they got out of the battleroom, breakfast was over. Dragon Army was pissed off—the ones who had been frozen early on, before they knew the trick, had spent more than an hour, some of them, floating in their rigid suits, growing more and more frustrated as the time wore on. The others, who had been forced to fight outnumbered and with little visibility against enemies who kept reviving, they were exhausted. Including Ender.

Ender gathered his army in the corridor and said, "Today you know everything. No practice. Get some rest. Have some fun. Pass a test."

They were all grateful for the reprieve, but still, they weren't getting any breakfast today and nobody felt like cheering. As they walked back to the barracks, some of them grumbled, "Bet they're serving breakfast to Badger Army right now."

"No, they got them up and served them breakfast before."

"No, they ate breakfast and then five minutes later they get to eat another."

Bean, however, was frustrated because he hadn't had a chance to carry out his plan at breakfast. It would have to wait till lunch.

The good thing was that because Dragon wasn't practicing, Bonzo's guys wouldn't know where to lie in wait for him. The bad thing was that if Ender went off by himself, there'd be nobody to protect him.

So Bean was relieved when he saw Ender go into his quarters. In consultation with the other toon leaders, Bean set up a watch on Ender's door. One Dragon sat outside the barracks for a half-hour shift, then knocked on the door and his replacement came out. No way was Ender going to go wandering off without Dragon Army knowing it.

But Ender never came out and finally it was lunchtime. All the toon leaders sent the soldiers on ahead and then detoured past Ender's door. Fly Molo knocked loudly—actually, he slapped the door hard five times. "Lunch, Ender."

"I'm not hungry." His voice was muffled by the door. "Go on and eat."

"We can wait," said Fly. "Don't want you walking to the commanders' mess alone."

"I'm not going to eat any lunch at all," said Ender. "Go on and I'll see you after."

"You heard him," said Fly to the others. "He'll be safe in here while we eat."

Bean had noticed that Ender did not promise to stay in his room throughout lunch. But at least Bonzo's people wouldn't know where he was. Unpredictability was helpful. And Bean wanted to get the chance to make his speech at lunch.

So he ran to the messroom and did not get in line, but instead bounded up onto a table and clapped his hands loudly to get attention. "Hey, everybody!"

He waited until the group went about as close to silent as it was going to get.

"There's some of you here who need a reminder of a couple of points of I.F. law. If a soldier is ordered to do something illegal or improper by his commanding officer, he has a responsibility to refuse the order and report it. A soldier who obeys an illegal or improper order is fully responsible for the consequences of his actions. Just in case any of you here are too dim to know what that means, the law says that if some commander orders you to commit a crime, that's no excuse. You are forbidden to obey."

Nobody from Salamander would meet Bean's gaze, but a thug in Rat uniform answered in a surly tone. "You got something in mind, here, pinprick?"

"I've got *you* in mind, Lighter. Your scores are pretty much in the bottom ten percent in the school, so I thought you might need a little extra help."

"You can shut your facehole right now, that's the help I need!"

"Whatever Bonzo had you set to do last night, Lighter, you and about twenty others, what I'm telling you is *if* you'd actually tried something, every single one of you would have been out of Battle School on his ass. Iced. A complete failure, because you listened to Bonehead Madrid. Can I be any more clear than that?"

Lighter laughed—it sounded forced, but then, he wasn't the only one laughing. "You don't even know what's going on, pinprick," one of them said.

"I know Bonehead's trying to turn you into a street crew, you pathetic losers. He can't beat Ender in the battleroom, so he's going to get a dozen tough guys to beat up one little kid. You all hear that? You know what Ender is—the best damn commander ever to come through here. He might be the only one able to do what Mazer Rackham did and beat the Buggers when they come back, did you think of that? And these guys are so *smart* they want to beat his brains out. So when the Buggers come, and we've only got pus-brains like Bonzo Madrid to lead our fleets to defeat, then as the Buggers scour the Earth and kill every last man, woman, and child, the survivors will all know that *these* fools are the ones who got rid of the one guy who could have led us to victory!"

The whole place was dead silent now, and Bean could see, looking at the ones he recognized as having been with Bonzo's group last night, that he was getting through to them.

"Oh, you *forgot* the Buggers, is that it? You *forgot* that this Battle School wasn't put here so you could write home to Mommy about your high standings on the scoreboard. So you go ahead and help Bonzo out, and while you're at it, why not just slit your own throats, too, cause that's what you're doing if you hurt Ender Wiggin. But for the rest of us—well, how many here think that Ender Wiggin is the one commander we would all want to follow into battle? Come on, how many of you!"

Bean began to clap his hands slowly, rhythmically. Immediately, all the Dragons joined in. And very quickly, most of the rest of the soldiers were also clapping. The ones who weren't were conspicuous and could see how the others looked at them with scorn or hate.

Pretty soon, the whole room was clapping. Even the food servers.

Bean thrust both his hands straight up in the air. "The butt-faced Buggers are the only enemy! Humans are all on the same side! Anybody who raises a hand against Ender Wiggin is a Bugger-lover!''

They responded with cheers and applause, leaping to their feet.

It was Bean's first attempt at rabble-rousing. He was pleased to see that, as long as the cause was right, he was pretty damn good at it.

Only later, when he had his food and was sitting with C toon, eating it, did Lighter himself come up to Bean. He came up from behind, and the rest of C toon was on their feet, ready to take him on, before Bean even knew he was there. But Lighter motioned them to sit down, then leaned over and spoke right into Bean's ear. "Listen to this, Queen Stupid. The soldiers who are planning to take Wiggin apart aren't even *here*. So much for your stupid speech.''

Then he was gone.

And, a moment later, so was Bean, with C toon gathering the rest of Dragon Army to follow behind him.

Ender wasn't in his quarters, or at least he didn't answer. Fly Molo, as A toon commander, took charge and divided them into groups to search the barracks, the game room, the vid room, the library, the gym.

But Bean called out for his squad to follow him. To the bathroom. That's the one place that Bonzo and his boys could plan on Ender having to go, eventually.

By the time Bean got there, it was all over. Teachers and medical staff were clattering down the halls. Dink Meeker was walking with Ender, his arm across Ender's shoulder, away from the bathroom. Ender was wearing only his towel. He was wet, and there was blood all over the back of his head and dripping down his back. It took Bean only a moment to realize that it was not his blood. The others from Bean's squad watched as Dink led Ender back to his quarters and helped him inside. But Bean was already on his way to the bathroom.

The teachers ordered him out of the way, out of the corridor. But Bean saw enough. Bonzo lying on the floor, medical staff doing CPR. Bean knew that you don't do that to somebody whose heart is beating. And from the inattentive way the others were standing around, Bean knew it was only a formality. Nobody expected Bonzo's heart to start again. No surprise. His nose had been jammed up inside his head. His face was a mass of blood. Which explained the bloody back of Ender's head.

All our efforts didn't amount to squat. But Ender won anyway. He knew this was coming. He learned self-defense. He used it, and he didn't do a half-assed job of it, either.

If Ender had been Poke's friend, Poke wouldn't have died.

And if Ender had depended on Bean to save him, he'd be just as dead as Poke.

Rough hands dragged Bean off his feet, pushed him against a wall. "What did you see!" demanded Major Anderson.

"Nothing," said Bean. "Is that Bonzo in there? Is he hurt?"

"This is none of your business. Didn't you hear us order you away?"

Colonel Graff arrived then, and Bean could see that the teachers around him were furious at him—yet couldn't say anything, either because of military protocol or because one of the children was present.

"I think Bean has stuck his nose into things once too often," said Anderson.

"Are you going to send Bonzo home?" asked Bean. "Cause he's just going to try it again."

Graff gave him a withering glance. "I heard about your speech in the mess hall," said Graff. "I didn't know we brought you up here to be a politician."

"If you don't ice Bonzo and get him *out* of here, Ender's never going to be safe, and we won't stand for it!"

"Mind your own business, little boy," said Graff. "This is men's work here."

Bean let himself be dragged away by Dimak. Just in case they still wondered whether Bean saw that Bonzo was dead, he kept the act going just a little longer. "He's going to come after me, too," he said. "I don't want Bonzo coming after me."

"He's not coming after you," said Dimak. "He's going home. Count on it. But don't talk about this to anyone else. Let them find out when the official word is given out. Got it?"

"Yes, sir," said Bean.

"And where did you get all that nonsense about not obeying a commander who gives illegal orders?"

"From the Uniform Code of Military Conduct," said Bean.

"Well, here's a little fact for you—nobody has ever been prosecuted for obeying orders."

"That," said Bean, "is because nobody's done anything so outrageous that the general public got involved."

"The Uniform Code doesn't apply to students, at least not that part of it."

"But it applies to teachers," said Bean. "It applies to *you*. Just in case you obeyed any illegal or improper orders today. By . . . what, I don't know . . . standing by while a fight broke out in a bathroom? Just because your commanding officer told you to let a big kid beat up on a little kid.''

If that information bothered Dimak, he gave no sign. He stood in the corridor and watched as Bean went into the Dragon Army barracks.

It was crazy inside. Dragon Army felt completely helpless and stupid, furious and ashamed. Bonzo Madrid had outsmarted them! Bonzo had gotten Ender alone! Where were Ender's soldiers when he needed them?

It took a long time for things to calm down. Through it all, Bean just sat on his bunk, thinking his own thoughts. Ender didn't just win his fight. Didn't just protect himself and walk away. Ender killed him. Struck a blow so devastating that his enemy will never, never come after him again.

Ender Wiggin, you're the one who was born to be commander of the fleet that defends Earth from the Third Invasion. Because that's what we need—someone who'll strike the most brutal blow possible, with perfect aim and with no regard for consequences. Total war.

Me, I'm no Ender Wiggin. I'm just a street kid whose only skill was staying alive. Somehow. The only time I was in real danger, I ran like a squirrel and took refuge with Sister Carlotta. Ender went alone into battle. I go alone into my hidey-hole. I'm the guy who makes big brave speeches standing on tables in the mess hall. Ender's the guy who meets the enemy naked and overpowers him against all odds.

Whatever genes they altered to make me, they weren't the ones that mattered.

Ender almost died because of me. Because I goaded Bonzo. Because I failed to keep watch at the crucial time. Because I didn't stop and think like Bonzo and figure out that he'd wait for Ender to be alone in the shower.

If Ender had died today, it would have been my fault all over again.

He wanted to kill somebody.

Couldn't be Bonzo. Bonzo was already dead.

Achilles. That's the one he needed to kill. And if Achilles had been there at that moment, Bean would have tried. Might have succeeded, too, if violent rage and desperate shame were enough to beat down any advantage of size and experience Achilles might have had. And if Achilles killed Bean anyway, it was no worse than Bean deserved, for having failed Ender Wiggin so completely.

He felt his bed bounce. Nikolai had jumped the gap between the upper bunks.

"It's OK," murmured Nikolai, touching Bean's shoulder. Bean rolled onto his back, to face Nikolai.

"Oh," said Nikolai. "I thought you were crying."

"Ender won," said Bean. "What's to cry about?"

18

FRIEND

"This boy's death was not necessary."

"This boy's death was not foreseen."

"But it was foreseeable."

"You can always foresee things that already happened. These are children, after all. We did *not* anticipate this level of violence."

"I don't believe you. I believe that this is precisely the level of violence you anticipated. This is what you set up. You think that the experiment succeeded."

"I can't control your opinions. I can merely disagree with them."

"Ender Wiggin is ready to move on to Command School. That is my report."

"I have a separate report from Dap, the teacher assigned to watch him most closely. And that report—for which there are to be *no* sanctions against Captain Dap—tells me that Andrew Wiggin is 'psychologically unfit for duty.' "

"*If* he is, which I doubt, it is only temporary."

"How much time do you think we have? No, Colonel Graff, for the time being we have to regard your course of action regarding Wiggin as a failure, and the boy as ruined not only for our purposes but quite possibly for any other as well. So, if it can be done without further killings, I want the other one pushed forward. I want him here in Command School as close to immediately as possible."

"Very well, sir. Though I must tell you that I regard Bean as unreliable."

"Why, because you haven't turned him into a killer yet?"

"Because he is not human, sir."

"The genetic difference is well within the range of ordinary variation."

"He was manufactured, and the manufacturer was a criminal, not to mention a certified loon."

"I could see some danger if his *father* were a criminal. Or his mother. But his *doctor?* The boy is exactly what we need, as quickly as we can get him."

"He is unpredictable."

"And the Wiggin boy is not?"

"Less unpredictable, sir."

"Very carefully answered, considering that you just insisted that the murder today was 'not foreseeable.' "

"*Not* murder, sir!"

"Killing, then."

"The mettle of the Wiggin boy is proved, sir, while Bean's is not."

"I have Dimak's report—for which, again, he is not to be—"

"Punished, I know, sir."

"Bean's behavior throughout this set of events has been exemplary."

"Then Captain Dimak's report was incomplete. Didn't he inform you that it was Bean who may have pushed Bonzo over the edge to violence by breaking security and informing him that Ender's army was composed of exceptional students?"

"That *was* an act with unforeseeable consequences."

"Bean was acting to save his own life, and in so doing he shunted the danger onto Ender Wiggin's shoulders. That he later tried to ameliorate the danger does not change the fact that when Bean is under pressure, he turns traitor."

"Harsh language!"

"This from the man who just called an obvious act of self-defense 'murder'?"

"Enough of this! You are on leave of absence from your position as commander of Battle School for the duration of Ender Wiggin's so-called rest and recuperation. If Wiggin recovers enough to come to Command School, you may come with him and continue to have influence over the education of the children we bring here. If he does not, you may await your court-martial on Earth."

"I am relieved effective when?"

"When you get on the shuttle with Wiggin. Major Anderson will stand in as acting commander."

"Very well, sir. Wiggin *will* return to training, sir."

"*If* we still want him."

"When you are over the dismay we all feel at the unfortunate death of the Madrid boy, you will realize that I am right, and Ender is the only viable candidate, all the more now than before."

"I allow you that Parthian shot. And, if you are right, I wish you Godspeed on your work with the Wiggin boy. Dismissed."

Ender was still wearing only his towel when he stepped into the barracks. Bean saw him standing there, his face a rictus of death, and thought: He knows that Bonzo is dead, and it's killing him.

"Ho, Ender," said Hot Soup, who was standing near the door with the other toon leaders.

"There gonna be a practice tonight?" asked one of the younger soldiers.

Ender handed a slip of paper to Hot Soup.

"I guess that means not," said Nikolai softly.

Hot Soup read it. "Those sons of bitches! Two at once?"

Crazy Tom looked over his shoulder. "Two armies!"

"They'll just trip over each other," said Bean. What appalled him most about the teachers was not the stupidity of trying to combine armies, a ploy whose ineffectiveness had been proved time after time throughout history, but rather the get-back-on-the-horse mentality that led them to put *more* pressure on Ender at this of all times. Couldn't they see the damage they were doing to him? Was their goal to train him or break him? Because he was trained long since. He should have been promoted out of Battle School the week before. And now they give him one more battle, a completely meaningless one, when he's already over the edge of despair?

"I've got to clean up," said Ender. "Get them ready, get everybody together, I'll meet you there, at the gate." In his voice, Bean heard a complete lack of interest. No, something deeper than that. Ender doesn't *want* to win this battle.

Ender turned to leave. Everyone saw the blood on his head, his shoulders, down his back. He left.

They all ignored the blood. They had to. "Two fart-eating armies!" cried Crazy Tom. "We'll whip their butts!"

That seemed to be the general consensus as they got into their flash suits.

Bean tucked the coil of deadline into the waist of his flash suit. If Ender ever needed a stunt, it would be for this battle, when he was no longer interested in winning.

As promised, Ender joined them at the gate before it opened—just barely before. He walked down the corridor lined with his soldiers, who looked at him with love, with awe, with trust. Except Bean, who looked at him with anguish. Ender Wiggin was not larger than life, Bean knew. He was exactly life-sized, and so his larger-than-life burden was too much for him. And yet he was bearing it. So far.

The gate went transparent.

Four stars had been combined directly in front of the gate, completely blocking their view of the battleroom. Ender would have to deploy his forces blind. For all he knew, the enemy had already been let into the room fifteen minutes ago. For all he could possibly know, they were deployed just as Bonzo had deployed *his* army, only this time it would be completely effective, to have the gate ringed with enemy soldiers.

But Ender said nothing. Just stood there looking at the barrier.

Bean had halfway expected this. He was ready. What he did wasn't all that obvious—he only walked forward to stand directly beside Ender at the gate. But he knew that was all it would take. A reminder.

"Bean," said Ender. "Take your boys and tell me what's on the other side of this star."

"Yes *sir*," said Bean. He pulled the coil of deadline from his waist, and with his five soldiers he made the short hop from the gate to the star. Immediately the gate he had just come through became the ceiling, the star their temporary floor. Bean tied the deadline around his waist while the other boys unspooled the line, arranging it in loose coils on the star. When it was about one-third played out, Bean declared it to be sufficient. He was guessing that the four stars were really eight—that they made a perfect cube. If he was wrong, then he had way too much deadline and he'd crash into the ceiling instead of making it back behind the star. Worse things could happen.

He slipped out beyond the edge of the star. He was right, it was a cube.

It was too dim in the room to see well what the other armies were doing, but they seemed to be deploying. There had been no head start this time, apparently. He quickly reported this to Ducheval, who would repeat it to Ender while Bean did his stunt. Ender would no doubt start bringing out the rest of the army at once, before the time clicked down to zero.

Bean launched straight down from the ceiling. Above him, his toon was holding the other end of the deadline secure, making sure it fed out properly and stopped abruptly.

Bean did not enjoy the wrenching of his gut when the deadline went taut, but there was kind of a thrill to the increase of speed as he suddenly moved south. He could see the distant flashing of the enemy firing up at him. Only soldiers from one half of the enemy's area were firing.

When the deadline reached the next edge of the cube, his speed increased again, and now he was headed upward in an arc that, for a moment, looked like it was going to scrape him against the ceiling. Then the last edge bit, and he scooted in behind the star and was caught deftly by his toon. Bean wiggled his arms and legs to show that he was none the worse for his ride. What the enemy was thinking about his magical maneuvers in midair he could only guess. What mattered was that Ender had *not* come through the gate. The timer must be nearly out.

Ender came alone through the gate. Bean made his report as quickly as possible. "It's really dim, but light enough you can't follow people easily by the lights on their suits. Worst possible for seeing. It's all open space from this star to the enemy side of the room. They've got eight stars making a square around their door. I didn't see anybody except the ones peeking around the boxes. They're just sitting there waiting for us."

In the distance, they heard the enemy begin catcalls. "Hey! We be hungry, come and feed us! Your ass is draggin'! Your ass is Dragon!"

Bean continued his report, but had no idea if Ender was even listening. "They fired at me from only one half their space. Which means that the two commanders are *not* agreeing and neither one has been put in supreme command."

"In a real war," said Ender, "any commander with brains at all would retreat and save this army."

"What the hell," said Bean. "It's only a game."

"It stopped being a game when they threw away the rules."

This wasn't good, thought Bean. How much time did they have to get their army through the gate? "So, you throw 'em away, too." He looked Ender in the eye, demanding that he wake up, pay attention, *act.*

The blank look left Ender's face. He grinned. It felt damn good to see that. "OK. Why not. Let's see how they react to a formation."

Ender began calling the rest of the army through the gate. It was going to get crowded on the top of that star, but there was no choice.

As it turned out, Ender's plan was to use another of Bean's stupid ideas, which he had watched Bean practice with his toon. A screen formation of frozen soldiers, controlled by Bean's toon, who remained unfrozen behind them. Having once told Bean what he wanted him to do, Ender joined the formation as a common soldier and left everything up to Bean to organize. "It's your show," he said.

Bean had never expected Ender to do any such thing, but it made a kind of sense. What Ender wanted was not to have this battle; allowing himself to be part of a screen of frozen soldiers, pushed through the battle by someone else, was as close to sleeping through it as he could get.

Bean set to work at once, constructing the screen in four parts consisting of one toon each. Each of toons A through C lined up four and three, arms interlocked with the men beside them, the upper row of three with toes hooked under the arms of the four soldiers below. When everybody was clamped down tight, Bean and his toon froze them. Then each of Bean's men took hold of one section of the screen and, careful to move very slowly so that inertia would not carry the screen out of their control, they maneuvered them out from above the star and slowly moved them down until they were just under it. Then they joined them back together into a single screen, with Bean's squad forming the interlock.

"When did you guys practice this?" asked Dumper, the leader of E toon.

"We've never done this before," Bean answered truthfully. "We've done bursting and linking with one-man screens, but seven men each? It's all new to us."

Dumper laughed. "And there's Ender, plugged into the screen like anybody. That's trust, Bean old boy."

That's despair, thought Bean. But he didn't feel the need to say *that* aloud.

When all was ready, E toon got into place behind the screen and, on Bean's command, pushed off as hard as they could.

The screen drifted down toward the enemy's gate at a pretty good clip. Enemy fire, though it was intense, hit only the already-frozen soldiers in front. E toon and Bean's squad kept moving, very slightly, but enough that no stray shot could freeze them. And they managed to do some return fire, taking out a few of the enemy soldiers and forcing them to stay behind cover.

When Bean figured they were as far as they could get before Griffin or Tiger launched an attack, he gave the word and his squad burst apart, causing the four sections of the screen also to separate and angle slightly so they were drifting now toward the corners of the stars where Griffin and Tiger were gathered. E toon went with the screens, firing like crazy, trying to make up for their tiny numbers.

After a count of three, the four members of Bean's squad who had gone with each screen pushed off again, this time angling to the middle and downward, so that they rejoined Bean and Ducheval, with momentum carrying them straight toward the enemy gate.

They held their bodies rigid, *not* firing a shot, and it worked. They were all small; they were clearly drifting, not moving with any particular purpose; the enemy took them for frozen soldiers if they were noticed at all. A few were partially disabled with stray shots, but even when under fire they never moved, and the enemy soon ignored them.

When they got to the enemy gate, Bean slowly, wordlessly, got four of them with their helmets in place at the corners of the gate. They pressed, just as in the end-of-game ritual, and Bean gave Ducheval a push, sending him through the gate as Bean drifted upward again.

The lights in the battleroom went on. The weapons all went dead. The battle was over.

It took a few moments before Griffin and Tiger realized what had happened. Dragon only had a few soldiers who weren't frozen or disabled, while Griffin and Tiger were mostly unscathed, having played conservative strategies. Bean knew that if either of them had been aggressive, Ender's strategy wouldn't have worked. But having seen Bean fly around the star, doing the impossible, and then watching this weird screen approach so slowly, they were intimidated into inaction. Ender's legend was such that they dared not commit their forces for fear of falling into a trap. Only . . . that *was* the trap.

Major Anderson came into the room through the teachergate. "Ender," he called.

Ender was frozen; he could only answer by grunting loudly through clenched jaws. That was a sound that victorious commanders rarely had to make.

Anderson, using the hook, drifted over to Ender and thawed him. Bean was half the battleroom away, but he heard Ender's words, so clear was his speech, so silent was the room. "I beat you again, sir."

Bean's squad members glanced at him, obviously wondering if he was resentful at Ender for claiming credit for a victory that was engineered and executed entirely by Bean. But Bean understood what Ender was saying. He wasn't talking about the victory over Griffin and Tiger armies. He was talking about a victory over the teachers. And *that* victory *was* the decision to turn the army over to Bean and sit it out himself. If they thought they were putting Ender to the ultimate test, making him fight two armies right after a personal fight for survival in the bathroom, he beat them—he side-stepped the test.

Anderson knew what Ender was saying, too. "Nonsense, Ender," said Anderson. He spoke softly, but the room was so silent that his words, too, could be heard. "Your battle was with Griffin and Tiger."

"How stupid do you think I am?" said Ender.

Damn right, said Bean silently.

Anderson spoke to the group at large. "After that little maneuver, the rules are being revised to require that all of the enemy's soldiers must be frozen or disabled before the gate can be reversed."

"Rules?" murmured Ducheval as he came back through the gate. Bean grinned at him.

"It could only work once anyway," said Ender.

Anderson handed the hook to Ender. Instead of thawing his soldiers one at a time, and only then thawing the enemy, Ender entered the command to thaw everyone at once, then handed the hook back to Anderson, who took it and drifted away toward the center, where the end-of-game rituals usually took place.

"Hey!" Ender shouted. "What is it next time? My army in a cage without guns, with the rest of the Battle School against them? How about a little equality?"

So many soldiers murmured their agreement that the sound of it was loud, and not all came from Dragon Army. But Anderson seemed to pay no attention.

It was William Bee of Griffin Army who said what almost everyone was thinking. "Ender, if you're on one side of the battle, it won't be equal no matter what the conditions are."

The armies vocally agreed, many of the soldiers laughing, and Talo Momoe, not to be outclassed by Bee, started clapping his hands rhythmically. "Ender Wiggin!" he shouted. Other boys took up the chant.

But Bean knew the truth—knew, in fact, what Ender knew. That no matter how good a commander was, no matter how resourceful, no matter how well-prepared his army, no matter how excellent his lieutenants, no matter how courageous and spirited the fight, victory almost always went to the side with the greater power to inflict damage. Sometimes David kills Goliath, and people never forget. But there were a lot of little guys Goliath had already mashed into the ground. Nobody sang songs about *those* fights, because they knew that was the likely outcome. No, that was the *inevitable* outcome, except for the miracles.

The Buggers wouldn't know or care how legendary a commander Ender might be to his own men. The human ships wouldn't have any magical tricks like Bean's deadline to dazzle the Buggers with, to put them off their stride. Ender knew that. Bean knew that. What if David hadn't had a sling, a handful of stones, and the time to throw? What good would the excellence of his aim have done him then?

So yes, it was good, it was right for the soldiers of all three armies to cheer Ender, to chant his name as he drifted toward the enemy gate, where Bean and his squad waited for him. But in the end it meant nothing, except that everyone would have too much hope in Ender's ability. It only made the burden on Ender heavier.

I would carry some of it if I could, Bean said silently. Like I did today, you can turn it over to me and I'll do it, if I can. You don't have to do this alone.

Only even as he thought this, Bean knew it wasn't true. If it could be done, Ender was the one who would have to do it. All those months when Bean refused to see Ender, hid from him, it was because he couldn't bear to face the fact that Ender was what Bean only wished to be—the kind of person on whom you could put all your hopes, who could carry all your fears, and he would not let you down, would not betray you.

I want to be the kind of boy you are, thought Bean. But I don't want to go through what you've been through to get there.

And then, as Ender passed through the gate and Bean followed behind him, Bean remembered falling into line behind Poke or Sergeant or Achilles on the streets of Rotterdam, and he almost laughed as he thought, I don't want to have to go through what *I've* gone through to get here, either.

Out in the corridor, Ender walked away instead of waiting for his soldiers. But not fast, and soon they caught up with him, surrounded him, brought him to a stop through their sheer ebullience. Only his silence, his impassivity, kept them from giving full vent to their excitement.

"Practice tonight?" asked Crazy Tom.

Ender shook his head.

"Tomorrow morning then?"

"No."

"Well, when?"

"Never again, as far as I'm concerned."

Not everyone had heard, but those who did began to murmur to each other.

"Hey, that's not fair," said a soldier from B toon. "It's not our fault the teachers are screwing up the game. You can't just stop teaching us stuff because—"

Ender slammed his hand against the wall and shouted at the kid. "I don't care about the game anymore!" He looked at other soldiers, met their gaze, refused to let them pretend they didn't hear. "Do you understand that?" Then he whispered. "The game is over."

He walked away.

Some of the boys wanted to follow him, took a few steps. But Hot Soup grabbed a couple of them by the neck of their flash suits and said, "Let him be alone. Can't you see he wants to be alone?"

Of course he wants to be alone, thought Bean. He killed a kid today, and even if he doesn't know the outcome, he knows what was at stake. These teachers were willing to let him face death without help. Why should he play along with them anymore? Good for you, Ender.

Not so good for the rest of us, but it's not like you're our father or something. More like a brother, and the thing with brothers is, you're supposed to take turns being the keeper. Sometimes you get to sit down and be the brother who is kept.

Fly Molo led them back to the barracks. Bean followed along, wishing he could go with Ender, talk to him, assure him that he agreed completely, that he understood. But that was pathetic, Bean realized. Why should Ender care whether *I* understand him or not? I'm just a kid, just one of his army. He knows me, he knows how to use me, but what does he care whether I know him?

Bean climbed to his bunk and saw a slip of paper on it.

Transfer

Bean

Rabbit Army

Commander

That was Carn Carby's army. Carn was being removed from command? He was a good guy—not a great commander, but why couldn't they wait till he graduated?

Because they're through with this school, that's why. They're advancing everybody they think needs some experience with command, and they're graduating other students to make room for them. I might have Rabbit Army, but not for long, I bet.

He pulled out his desk, meaning to sign on as ^Graff and check the rosters. Find out what was happening to everybody. But the ^Graff log-in didn't work. Apparently they no longer considered it useful to permit Bean to keep his inside access.

From the back of the room, the older boys were raising a hubbub. Bean heard Crazy Tom's voice rising above the rest. "You mean I'm supposed to figure out how to beat Dragon Army?" Word soon filtered to the front. The toon leaders and seconds had all received transfer orders. Every single one of them was being given command of an army. Dragon had been stripped.

After about a minute of chaos, Fly Molo led the other toon leaders along between the bunks, heading toward the door. Of course—they had to go tell Ender what the teachers had done to him now.

But to Bean's surprise, Fly stopped at his bunk and looked up at him, then glanced at the other toon leaders behind him.

"Bean, somebody's got to tell Ender."

Bean nodded.

"We thought . . . since you're his friend . . ."

Bean let nothing show on his face, but he was stunned. Me? Ender's friend? No more than anyone else in this room.

And then he realized. In this army, Ender had everyone's love and admiration. And they all knew they had Ender's trust. But only Bean had been taken inside Ender's confidence, when Ender assigned him his special squad. And when Ender wanted to stop playing the game, it was Bean to whom he had turned over his army. Bean was the closest thing to a friend they had seen Ender have since he got command of Dragon.

Bean looked across at Nikolai, who was grinning his ass off. Nikolai saluted him and mouthed the word *commander*.

Bean saluted Nikolai back, but could not smile, knowing what this would do to Ender. He nodded to Fly Molo, then slid off the bunk and went out the door.

He didn't go straight to Ender's quarters, though. Instead, he went to Carn Carby's room. No one answered. So he went on to Rabbit barracks and knocked. "Where's Carn?" he asked.

"Graduated," said Itú, the leader of Rabbit's A toon. "He found out about half an hour ago."

"We were in a battle."

"I know—two armies at once. You won, right?"

Bean nodded. "I bet Carn wasn't the only one graduated early."

"A lot of commanders," said Itú. "More than half."

"Including Bonzo Madrid? I mean, he graduated?"

"That's what the official notice said." Itú shrugged. "Everybody knows that if anything, Bonzo was probably iced. I mean, they didn't even list his assignment. Just 'Cartagena.' His hometown. Is that iced or what? But let the teachers call it what they want."

"I'll bet the total who graduated was nine," said Bean. "Neh?"

"Eh," said Itú. "Nine. So you know something?"

"Bad news, I think," said Bean. He showed Itú his transfer orders.

"Santa merda," said Itú. Then he saluted. Not sarcastically, but not enthusiastically, either.

"Would you mind breaking it to the others? Give them a chance to get used to the idea before I show up for real? I've got to go talk to Ender. Maybe he already knows they've just taken his entire leadership and given them armies. But if he doesn't, I've got to tell him."

"*Every* Dragon toon leader?"

"And every second." He thought of saying, Sorry Rabbit got stuck with me. But Ender would never have said anything self-belittling like that. And if Bean was going to be a commander, he couldn't start out with an apology. "I think Carn Carby had a good organization," said Bean, "so I don't expect to change any of the toon leadership for the first week, anyway, till I see how things go in practice and decide what shape we're in for the kind of battles we're going to start having now that most of the commanders are kids trained in Dragon."

Itú understood immediately. "Man, that's going to be strange, isn't it? Ender trained all you guys, and now you've got to fight each other."

"One thing's for sure," said Bean. "I have no intention of trying to turn Rabbit into a copy of Ender's Dragon. We're not the same kids and we won't be fighting the same opponents. Rabbit's a good army. We don't have to copy anybody."

Itú grinned. "Even if that's just bullshit, sir, it's first-rate bullshit. I'll pass it on." He saluted.

Bean saluted back. Then he jogged to Ender's quarters.

Ender's mattress and blankets and pillow had been thrown out into the corridor. For a moment Bean wondered why. Then he saw that the sheets and mattress were still damp and bloody. Water from Ender's shower. Blood from Bonzo's face. Apparently Ender didn't want them in his room.

Bean knocked on the door.

"Go away," said Ender softly.

Bean knocked again. Then again.

"Come in," said Ender.

Bean palmed the door open.

"Go away, Bean," said Ender.

Bean nodded. He understood the sentiment. But he had to deliver his message. So he just looked at his shoes and waited for Ender to ask him his business. Or yell at him. Whatever Ender wanted to do. Because the other toon leaders were wrong. Bean didn't have any special relationship with Ender. Not outside the game.

Ender said nothing. And continued to say nothing.

Bean looked up from the ground and saw Ender gazing at him. Not angry. Just . . . watching. What does he see in me, Bean wondered. How well does he know me? What does he think of me? What do I amount to in his eyes?

That was something Bean would probably never know. And he had come here for another purpose. Time to carry it out.

He took a step closer to Ender. He turned his hand so the transfer slip was visible. He didn't offer it to Ender, but he knew Ender would see it.

"You're transferred?" asked Ender. His voice sounded dead. As if he'd been expecting it.

"To Rabbit Army," said Bean.

Ender nodded. "Carn Carby's a good man. I hope he recognizes what you're worth."

The words came to Bean like a longed-for blessing. He swallowed the emotion that welled up inside him. He still had more of his message to deliver.

"Carn Carby was graduated today," said Bean. "He got his notice while we were fighting our battle."

"Well," said Ender. "Who's commanding Rabbit then?" He didn't sound all that interested. The question was expected, so he asked it.

"Me," said Bean. He was embarrassed; a smile came inadvertently to his lips.

Ender looked at the ceiling and nodded. "Of course. After all, you're only four years younger than the regular age."

"It isn't funny," said Bean. "I don't know what's going on here." Except that the system seems to be running on sheer panic. "All the changes in the game. And now this. I wasn't the only one transferred, you know. They graduated half the commanders, and transferred a lot of our guys to command their armies.''

"Which guys?'' Now Ender did sound interested.

"It looks like—every toon leader and every assistant.''

"Of course. If they decide to wreck my army, they'll cut it to the ground. Whatever they're doing, they're thorough.''

"You'll still win, Ender. We all know that. Crazy Tom, he said, 'You mean I'm supposed to figure out how to beat Dragon Army?' Everybody knows you're the best.'' His words sounded empty even to himself. He wanted to be encouraging, but he knew that Ender knew better. Still he babbled on. "They can't break you down, no matter what they—''

"They already have.''

They've broken trust, Bean wanted to say. That's not the same thing. *You* aren't broken. *They're* broken. But all that came out of his mouth were empty, limping words. "No, Ender, they can't—''

"I don't care about their game anymore, Bean,'' said Ender. "I'm not going to play it anymore. No more practices. No more battles. They can put their little slips of paper on the floor all they want, but I won't go. I decided that before I went through the door today. That's why I had you go for the gate. I didn't think it would work, but I didn't care. I just wanted to go out in style.''

I know that, thought Bean. You think I didn't know that? But if it comes down to style, you certainly got *that.* "You should've seen William Bee's face. He just stood there trying to figure out how he had lost when you only had seven boys who could wiggle their toes and he only had three who couldn't.''

"Why should I want to see William Bee's face?'' said Ender. "Why should I want to beat anybody?''

Bean felt the heat of embarrassment in his face. He'd said the wrong thing. Only . . . he didn't know what the right thing was. Something to make Ender feel better. Something to make him understand how much he was loved and honored.

Only that love and honor were part of the burden Ender bore. There was nothing Bean could say that would not make it all the heavier on Ender. So he said nothing.

Ender pressed his palms against his eyes. "I hurt Bonzo really bad today, Bean. I really hurt him bad.''

Of course. All this other stuff, that's nothing. What weighs on Ender is that terrible fight in the bathroom. The fight that your friends, your army, did nothing to prevent. And what hurts you is not the danger you were in, but the harm you did in protecting yourself.

"He had it coming," said Bean. He winced at his own words. Was that the best he could come up with? But what else could he say? No problem, Ender. Of course, he looked dead to *me,* and I'm probably the only kid in this school who actually knows what death looks like, but . . . no problem! Nothing to worry about! He had it coming!

"I knocked him out standing up," said Ender. "It was like he was dead, standing there. And I kept hurting him."

So he did know. And yet . . . he didn't actually *know.* And Bean wasn't about to tell him. There were times for absolute honesty between friends, but this wasn't one of them.

"I just wanted to make sure he never hurt me again."

"He won't," said Bean. "They sent him home."

"Already?"

Bean told him what Itú had said. All the while, he felt like Ender could see that he was concealing something. Surely it was impossible to deceive Ender Wiggin.

"I'm glad they graduated him," said Ender.

Some graduation. They're going to bury him, or cremate him, or whatever they're doing with corpses in Spain this year.

Spain. Pablo de Noches, who saved his life, came from Spain. And now a body was going back there, a boy who turned killer in his heart, and died for it.

I must be losing it, thought Bean. What does it matter that Bonzo was Spanish and Pablo de Noches was Spanish? What does it matter that anybody is anything?

And while these thoughts ran through Bean's mind, he babbled, trying to talk like someone who didn't know anything, trying to reassure Ender but knowing that if Ender believed that he knew nothing, then his words were meaningless, and if Ender realized that Bean was only faking ignorance, then his words were all lies. "Was it true he had a whole bunch of guys gang up on you?" Bean wanted to run from the room, he sounded so lame, even to himself.

"No," said Ender. "It was just him and me. He fought with honor."

Bean was relieved. Ender was turned so deeply inward right now that he didn't even register what Bean was saying, how false it was.

"I didn't fight with honor," said Ender. "I fought to win."

Yes, that's right, thought Bean. Fought the only way that's worth fighting, the only way that has any point. "And you did. Kicked him right out of orbit.'' It was as close as Bean could come to telling him the truth.

There was a knock on the door. Then it opened, immediately, without waiting for an answer. Before Bean could turn to see who it was, he knew it was a teacher—Ender looked up too high for it to be a kid.

Major Anderson and Colonel Graff.

"Ender Wiggin,'' said Graff.

Ender rose to his feet. "Yes sir.'' The deadness had returned to his voice.

"Your display of temper in the battleroom today was insubordinate and is not to be repeated.''

Bean couldn't believe the stupidity of it. After what Ender had been through—what the teachers had *put* him through—and they have to keep playing this oppressive game with him? Making him feel utterly alone even *now?* These guys were relentless.

Ender's only answer was another lifeless "Yes sir.'' But Bean was fed up. "I think it was about time somebody told a teacher how we felt about what you've been doing.''

Anderson and Graff didn't show a sign they'd even heard him. Instead, Anderson handed Ender a full sheet of paper. Not a transfer slip. A full-fledged set of orders. Ender was being transferred out of the school.

"Graduated?'' Bean asked.

Ender nodded.

"What took them so long?'' asked Bean. "You're only two or three years early. You've already learned how to walk and talk and dress yourself. What will they have left to teach you?'' The whole thing was such a joke. Did they really think anybody was fooled? You reprimand Ender for insubordination, but then you graduate him because you've got a war coming and you don't have a lot of time to get him ready. He's your hope of victory, and you treat him like something you scrape off your shoe.

"All I know is, the game's over,'' said Ender. He folded the paper. "None too soon. Can I tell my army?''

"There isn't time,'' said Graff. "Your shuttle leaves in twenty minutes. Besides, it's better not to talk to them after you get your orders. It makes it easier.''

"For them or for you?'' Ender asked.

He turned to Bean, took his hand. To Bean, it was like the touch of the finger of God. It sent light all through him. Maybe I am his friend. Maybe he feels toward me some small part of the . . . feeling I have for him.

And then it was over. Ender let go of his hand. He turned toward the door.

"Wait," said Bean. "Where are you going? Tactical? Navigational? Support?"

"Command School," said Ender.

"*Pre*-command?"

"Command." Ender was out the door.

Straight to Command School. The elite school whose location was even a secret. Adults went to Command School. The battle must be coming very soon, to skip right past all the things they were supposed to learn in Tactical and Pre-Command.

He caught Graff by the sleeve. "Nobody goes to Command School until they're sixteen!" he said.

Graff shook off Bean's hand and left. If he caught Bean's sarcasm, he gave no sign of it.

The door closed. Bean was alone in Ender's quarters.

He looked around. Without Ender in it, the room was nothing. Being here meant nothing. Yet it was only a few days ago, not even a week, when Bean had stood here and Ender told him he was getting a toon after all.

For some reason what came into Bean's mind was the moment when Poke handed him six peanuts. It was life that she handed to him then.

Was it life that Ender gave to Bean? Was it the same thing?

No. Poke gave him life. Ender gave it meaning.

When Ender was here, this was the most important room in Battle School. Now it was no more than a broom closet.

Bean walked back down the corridor to the room that had been Carn Carby's until today. Until an hour ago. He palmed it—it opened. Already programmed in.

The room was empty. Nothing in it.

This room is mine, thought Bean.

Mine, and yet still empty.

He felt powerful emotions welling up inside him. He should be excited, proud to have his own command. But he didn't really care about it. As Ender said, the game was nothing. Bean would do a decent job, but the reason he'd have the respect of his soldiers was because he would carry some of Ender's reflected glory with him, a shrimpy little Napoleon flumping around wearing a man's shoes while he barked commands in a little tiny child's voice. Cute little Caligula, "Little Boot," the pride of Germanicus's army. But when he was wearing his father's boots, those boots were empty, and Caligula knew it, and nothing he ever did could change that. Was that his madness?

It won't drive *me* mad, thought Bean. Because I don't covet what Ender has or what he is. It's enough that *he* is Ender Wiggin. I don't have to be.

He understood what this feeling was, welling up in him, filling his throat, making tears stand out in his eyes, making his face burn, forcing a gasp, a silent sob. He bit on his lip, trying to let pain force the emotion away. It didn't help. Ender was gone.

Now that he knew what the feeling was, he could control it. He lay down on the bunk and went into the relaxing routine until the need to cry had passed. Ender had taken his hand to say good-bye. Ender had said, "I hope he recognizes what you're worth." Bean didn't really have anything left to prove. He'd do his best with Rabbit Army because maybe at some point in the future, when Ender was at the bridge of the flagship of the human fleet, Bean might have some role to play, some way to help. Some stunt that Ender might need him to pull to dazzle the Buggers. So he'd please the teachers, impress the hell out of them, so that they would keep opening doors for him, until one day a door would open and his friend Ender would be on the other side of it, and he could be in Ender's army once again.

19

REBEL

"Putting in Achilles was Graff's last act, and we know there were grave concerns. Why not play it safe and at least change Achilles to another army?"

"This is not necessarily a Bonzo Madrid situation for Bean."

"But we have no assurance that it's not, sir. Colonel Graff kept a lot of information to himself. A lot of conversations with Sister Carlotta, for instance, with no memo of what was said. Graff knows things about Bean and, I can promise you, about Achilles as well. I think he's laid a trap for us."

"Wrong, Captain Dimak. If Graff laid a trap, it was not for us."

"You're sure of that?"

"Graff doesn't play bureaucratic games. He doesn't give a damn about you and me. If he laid a trap, it's for Bean."

"Well that's my point!"

"I understand your point. But Achilles stays."

"Why?"

"Achilles' tests show him to be of a remarkably even temperament. He is no Bonzo Madrid. Therefore Bean is in no physical danger. The stress seems to be psychological. A test of character. And that is precisely the area where we have the very least data about Bean, given his refusal to play the mind game and the ambiguity of the information we got from his playing with his teacher log-in. Therefore I think this forced relationship with his bugbear is worth pursuing."

"Bugbear or nemesis, sir?"

"We will monitor closely. I will *not* be keeping adults so far removed that we can't get there to intervene in time, the way Graff arranged it with Ender and Bonzo. Every precaution will be taken. I am not playing Russian roulette the way Graff was."

"Yes you are, sir. The only difference is that he knew he had only one empty chamber, and you don't know how many chambers are empty because he loaded the gun."

On his first morning as commander of Rabbit Army, Bean woke to see a paper lying on his floor. For a moment he was stunned at the thought that he would be given a battle before he even met his army, but to his relief the note was about something much more mundane.

Because of the number of new commanders, the tradition of not joining the commanders' mess until after the first victory is abolished. You are to dine in the commanders' mess starting immediately.

It made sense. Since they were going to accelerate the battle schedule for everyone, they wanted to have the commanders in a position to share information right from the start. And to be under social pressure from their peers, as well.

Holding the paper in his hand, Bean remembered how Ender had held his orders, each impossible new permutation of the game. Just because this order made sense did not make it a good thing. There was nothing sacred about the game itself that made Bean resent changes in the rules and customs, but the way the teachers were manipulating them *did* bother him.

Cutting off his access to student information, for instance. The question wasn't why they cut it off, or even why they let him have it for so long. The question was why the other commanders didn't have that much information all along. If they were supposed to be learning to lead, then they should have the tools of leadership.

And as long as they were changing the system, why not get rid of the really pernicious, destructive things they did? For instance, the scoreboards in the mess halls. Standings and scores! Instead of fighting the battle at hand, those scores made soldiers and commanders alike more cautious, less willing to experiment. That's why the ludicrous custom of fighting in formations had lasted so long—Ender can't have been the first commander to see a better way. But nobody wanted to rock the boat, to be the one who innovated and paid the price by dropping in the rankings. Far better to treat each battle as a completely separate problem, and to feel free to engage in battles as if they were *play* rather than work. Creativity and challenge would increase drastically. And commanders wouldn't have to worry when they gave an order to a toon or an individual whether they were causing a particular soldier to sacrifice his standing for the good of the army.

Most important, though, was the challenge inherent in Ender's decision to reject the game. The fact that he graduated before he could really go on strike didn't change the fact that if he had done so, Bean would have supported him in it.

Now that Ender was gone, a boycott of the game didn't make sense. Especially if Bean and the others were to advance to a point where they might be part of Ender's fleet when the real battles came. But they could take charge of the game, use it for their own purposes.

So, dressed in his new—and ill-fitting—Rabbit Army uniform, Bean soon found himself once again standing on a table, this time in the much smaller officers' mess. Since Bean's speech the day before was already the stuff of legend, there was laughter and some catcalling when he got up.

"Do people where you come from eat with their feet, Bean?"

"Instead of getting up on tables, why don't you just *grow*, Bean?"

"Put some stilts on so we can keep the tables clean!"

But the other new commanders who had, until yesterday, been toon leaders in Dragon Army, made no catcalls and did not laugh. Their respectful attention to Bean soon prevailed, and silence fell over the room.

Bean flung up an arm to point to the scoreboard that showed the standings. "Where's Dragon Army?" he asked.

"They dissolved it," said Petra Arkanian. "The soldiers have been folded into the other armies. Except for you guys who used to be Dragon."

Bean listened, keeping his opinion of her to himself. All he could think of, though, was two nights before, when she was, wittingly or not, the judas who was supposed to lure Ender into a trap.

"Without Dragon up there," said Bean, "that board means nothing. Whatever standing any of us gets would not be the same if Dragon were still there."

"There's not a hell of a lot we can do about it," said Dink Meeker.

"The problem isn't that Dragon is missing," said Bean. "The problem is that we shouldn't have that board at all. *We're* not each other's enemies. The *Buggers* are the only enemy. *We're* supposed to be allies. We should be learning from each other, sharing information and ideas. We should feel free to experiment, trying new things without being afraid of how it will affect our standings. That board up there, that's the *teachers'* game, getting us to turn against each other. Like Bonzo. Nobody here is as crazy with jealousy as he was, but come on, he was what those standings were bound to create. He was all set to beat in the brains of our best commander, our best hope against the next Bugger invasion, and why? Because Ender humiliated him in the *standings.* Think about that! The standings were more important to him than the war against the Formics!"

"Bonzo was crazy," said William Bee.

"So let's *not* be crazy," said Bean. "Let's get those standings out of the game. Let's take each battle one at a time, a clean slate. Try anything you can think of to win. And when the battle is over, both commanders sit down and explain what they were thinking, why they did what they did, so we can learn from each other. No secrets! Everybody try everything! And screw the standings!"

There were murmurs of assent, and not just from the former Dragons.

"That's easy for you to say," said Shen. "*Your* standing right now is tied for last."

"And there's the problem, right there," said Bean. "You're suspicious of my motives, and why? Because of the standings. But aren't we all supposed to be commanders in the same fleet someday? Working together? Trusting each other? How sick would the I.F. be, if all the ship captains and strike force commanders and fleet admirals spent all their time worrying about their standings instead of working together to try to beat the Formics! I want to learn from you, Shen. I don't want to *compete* with you for some empty rank that the teachers put up on that wall in order to manipulate us."

"I'm sure you guys from Dragon are all concerned about learning from us losers," said Petra.

There it was, out in the open.

"Yes! Yes, I *am* concerned. Precisely because I've been in Dragon Army. There are nine of us here who know pretty much only what we learned from Ender. Well, brilliant as he was, he's not the only one in the fleet or even in the school who knows anything. I need to learn how *you* think. I don't need you keeping secrets from me, and you don't need me keeping secrets from you. Maybe part of what made Ender so good was that he kept all his toon leaders talking to each other, free to try things but only as long as we shared what we were doing.''

There was more assent this time. Even the doubters were nodding thoughtfully.

''So what I propose is this. A unanimous rejection of that board up there, not only the one in here but the one in the soldiers' mess, too. We all agree not to pay attention to it, period. We ask the teachers to disconnect the things or leave them blank. If they refuse, we bring in sheets to cover it, or we throw chairs until we break it. We don't have to play *their* game. We can take charge of our own education and get ready to fight the *real* enemy. We have to remember, always, who the real enemy is.''

''Yeah, the teachers,'' said Dink Meeker.

Everybody laughed. But then Dink Meeker stood up on the table beside Bean. ''I'm the senior commander here, now they've graduated all the oldest guys. I'm probably the oldest soldier left in Battle School. So I propose that we adopt Bean's proposal right now, and I'll go to the teachers to demand that the boards be shut off. Is there anyone opposed?''

Not a sound.

''That makes it unanimous. If the boards are still on at lunch, let's bring sheets to cover them up. If they're still on at dinner, then forget using chairs to vandalize, let's just refuse to take our armies to any battles until the boards are off.''

Alai spoke up from where he stood in the serving line. ''*That'll* shoot our standings all to . . .''

Then Alai realized what he was saying, and laughed at himself. ''Damn, but they've got us brainwashed, haven't they!''

Bean was still flushed with victory when, after breakfast, he made his way to Rabbit barracks in order to meet his soldiers officially for the first time. Rabbit was on a midday practice schedule, so he only had about half an hour between breakfast and the first classes of the morning. Yesterday, when he talked to Itú, his mind had been on other things, with only the most cursory attention to what was going on inside Rabbit barracks. But now he realized that, unlike Dragon Army, the soldiers in Rabbit were all of the regular age. Not one was even close to Bean's height. He looked like somebody's doll, and worse, he felt like that too, walking down the corridor between the bunks, seeing all these huge boys—and a couple of girls—looking down at him.

Halfway down the bunks, he turned to face those he had already passed. Might as well address the problem immediately.

"The first problem I see," said Bean loudly, "is that you're all way too tall."

Nobody laughed. Bean died a little. But he had to go on.

"I'm growing as fast as I can. Beyond that, I don't know what I can do about it."

Only now did he get a chuckle or two. But that was a relief, that even a few were willing to meet him partway.

"Our first practice together is at 1030. As to our first battle together, I can't predict that, but I can promise you this—the teachers are *not* going to give me the traditional three months after my assignment to a new army. Same with all the other new commanders just appointed. They gave Ender Wiggin only a few weeks with Dragon before they went into battle—and Dragon was a new army, constructed out of nothing. Rabbit is a good army with a solid record. The only new person here is me. I expect the battles to begin in a matter of days, a week at most, and I expect battles to come frequently. So for the first couple of practices, you'll really be training me in your existing system. I need to see how you work with your toon leaders, how the toons work with each other, how you respond to orders, what commands you use. I'll have a couple of things to say that are more about attitude than tactics, but by and large, I want to see you doing things as you've always done them under Carn. It would help me, though, if you practiced with intensity, so I can see you at your sharpest. Are there any questions?"

None. Silence.

"One other thing. Day before yesterday, Bonzo and some of his friends were stalking Ender Wiggin in the halls. I saw the danger, but the soldiers in Dragon Army were mostly too small to stand up against the crew Bonzo had assembled. It wasn't an accident that when I needed help for my commander, I came to the door of Rabbit Army. This wasn't the closest barracks. I came to you because I knew that you had a fair-minded commander in Carn Carby, and I believed that his army would have the same attitude. Even if you didn't have any particular love for Ender Wiggin or Dragon Army, I knew that you would not stand by and let a bunch of thugs pound on a smaller kid that they couldn't beat fair and square in battle. And I was

right about you. When you poured out of this barracks and stood as witnesses in the corridor, I was proud of what you stood for. I'm proud now
to be one of you.''

That did it. Flattery rarely fails, and never does if it's sincere. By letting
them know they had already earned his respect, he dissipated much of the
tension, for of course they were worried that as a former Dragon he would
have contempt for the first army that Ender Wiggin beat. Now they knew
better, and so he'd have a chance to win their respect as well.

Itú started clapping, and the other boys joined in. It wasn't a long
ovation, but it was enough to let him know the door was open, at least a
crack.

He raised his hands to silence the applause—just in time, since it was
already dying down. ''I'd like to speak to the toon leaders for a few minutes
in my quarters. The rest of you are dismissed till practice.''

Almost at once, Itú was beside him. ''Good job,'' he said. ''Only one
mistake.''

''What was that?''

''You aren't the only new person here.''

''They assigned one of the Dragon soldiers to Rabbit?'' For a moment,
Bean allowed himself to hope that it would be Nikolai. He could use a
reliable friend.

No such luck.

''No, a Dragon soldier would be a veteran! I mean this guy is *new*. He
just got to Battle School yesterday afternoon and he was assigned here last
night, after you came by.''

''A launchy? Assigned straight to an army?''

''Oh, we asked him about that, and he's had a lot of the same classwork. He went through a bunch of surgeries down on Earth, and he studied
through it all, but—''

''You mean he's recovering from surgery, too?''

''No, he walks fine, he's—look, why don't you just meet him? All I
need to know is, do you want to assign him to a toon or what?''

''Eh, let's see him.''

Itú led him to the back of the barracks. There he was, standing beside
his bunk, several inches taller than Bean remembered, with legs of even
length now, both of them straight. The boy he had last seen fondling Poke,
minutes before her dead body went into the river.

''Ho, Achilles,'' said Bean.

''Ho, Bean,'' said Achilles. He grinned winningly. ''Looks like you're
the big guy here.''

"So to speak," said Bean.

"You two know each other?" said Itú.

"We knew each other in Rotterdam," said Achilles.

They can't have assigned him to me by accident. I never told anybody but Sister Carlotta about what he did, but how can I guess what she told the I.F.? Maybe they put him here because they thought both of us being from the Rotterdam streets, from the same crew—the same family—I might be able to help him get into the mainstream of the school faster. Or maybe they knew that he was a murderer who was able to hold a grudge for a long, long time, and strike when least expected. Maybe they knew that he planned for my death as surely as he planned for Poke's. Maybe he's here to be my Bonzo Madrid.

Except that I haven't taken any personal defense classes. And I'm half his size—I couldn't jump high enough to hit him in the nose. Whatever they were trying to accomplish by putting Ender's life at risk, Ender always had a better chance of surviving than I will.

The only thing in my favor is that Achilles wants to survive and prosper more than he wants vengeance. Since he can hold a grudge forever, he's in no hurry to act on it. And, unlike Bonzo, he'll never allow himself to be goaded into striking under circumstances where he'd be identifiable as the killer. As long as he thinks he needs me and as long as I'm never alone, I'm probably safe.

Safe. He shuddered. Poke felt safe, too.

"Achilles was *my* commander there," said Bean. "He kept a group of us kids alive. Got us into the charity kitchens."

"Bean is too modest," said Achilles. "The whole thing was his idea. He basically taught us the whole idea of working together. I've studied a lot since then, Bean. I've had a year of nothing but books and classes—when they weren't cutting into my legs and pulverizing and regrowing my bones. And I finally know enough to understand just what a leap you helped us make. From barbarism into civilization. Bean here is like a replay of human evolution."

Bean was not so stupid as to fail to recognize when flattery was being used on him. At the same time, it was more than a little useful to have this new boy, straight from Earth, already know who Bean was and show respect for him.

"The evolution of the pygmies, anyway," said Bean.

"Bean was the toughest little bastard you ever saw on the street, I got to tell you."

No, this was not what Bean needed right now. Achilles had just crossed the line from flattery into possession. Stories about Bean as a "tough little bastard" would, of necessity, set Achilles up as Bean's superior, able to evaluate him. The stories might even be to Bean's credit—but they would serve more to validate Achilles, make him an insider far faster than he would otherwise have been. And Bean did not want Achilles to be inside yet.

Achilles was already going on, as more soldiers gathered closer to hear. "The way I got recruited into Bean's crew was—"

"It wasn't my crew," said Bean, cutting him off. "And here in Battle School, we don't tell stories about home and we don't listen to them either. So I'd appreciate it if you never spoke again of anything that happened Rotterdam, not while you're in my army."

He'd done the nice bit during his opening speech. But now was the time for authority.

Achilles didn't show any sign of embarrassment at the reprimand. "I get it. No problem."

"It's time for you to get ready to go to class," said Bean to the soldiers. "I need to confer with my toon leaders only." Bean pointed to Ambul, a Thai soldier who, according to what Bean read in the student reports, would have been a toon leader long ago, except for his tendency to disobey stupid orders. "You, Ambul. I assign you to get Achilles to and from his correct classes and acquaint him with how to wear a flash suit, how it works, and the basics of movement in the battleroom. Achilles, you are to obey Ambul like God until I assign you to a regular toon."

Achilles grinned. "But I don't obey God."

You think I don't know that? "The correct answer to an order from me is 'Yes sir.' "

Achilles' grin faded. "Yes sir."

"I'm glad to have you here," Bean lied.

"Glad to be here, sir," said Achilles. And Bean was reasonably sure that while Achilles was *not* lying, his reason for being glad was very complicated, and certainly included, by now, a renewed desire to see Bean die.

For the first time, Bean understood the reason Ender had almost always acted as if he was oblivious to the danger from Bonzo. It was a simple choice, really. Either he could act to save himself, or he could act to maintain control over his army. In order to hold real authority, Bean had to insist on complete obedience and respect from his soldiers, even if it meant putting Achilles down, even if it meant increasing his personal danger.

And yet another part of him thought: Achilles wouldn't be here if he didn't have the ability to be a leader. He performed extraordinarily well as our papa in Rotterdam. It's my responsibility now to get him up to speed as quickly as possible, for the sake of his potential usefulness to the I.F. I can't let my personal fear interfere with that, or my hatred of him for what he did to Poke. So even if Achilles is evil incarnate, my job is to turn him into a highly effective soldier with a good shot at becoming a commander.

And in the meantime, I'll watch my back.

20

TRIAL AND ERROR

"You brought him up to Battle School, didn't you?"

"Sister Carlotta, I'm on a leave of absence right now. That means I've been sacked, in case you don't understand how the I.F. handles these things."

"Sacked! A miscarriage of justice. You ought to be shot."

"If the Sisters of St. Nicholas had convents, your abbess would make you do serious penance for that un-Christian thought."

"You took him out of the hospital in Cairo and directly into space. Even though I warned you."

"Didn't you notice that you telephoned me on a regular exchange? I'm on Earth. Someone else is running Battle School."

"He's a serial murderer now, you know. Not just the girl in Rotterdam. There was a boy there, too, the one Helga called Ulysses. They found his body a few weeks ago."

"Achilles has been in medical care for the past year."

"The coroner estimates that the killing took place at least that long ago. The body was hidden behind some long-term storage near the fish market. It covered the smell, you see. And it goes on. A teacher at the school I put him in."

"Ah. That's right. *You* put him in a school long before I did."

"The teacher fell to his death from an upper story."

"No witnesses. No evidence."

"Exactly."

"You see a trend here?"

"But that's *my* point. Achilles does not kill carelessly. Nor does

he choose his victims at random. Anyone who has seen him helpless, crippled, beaten—he can't bear the shame. He has to ex-
punge it by getting absolute power over the person who dared to
humiliate him."

"You're a psychologist now?"

"I laid the facts before an expert."

"The supposed facts."

"I'm not in court, Colonel. I'm talking to the man who put this
killer in school with the child who came up with the original plan
to humiliate him. Who called for his death. My expert assured me
that the chance of Achilles *not* striking against Bean is zero."

"It's not as easy as you think, in space. No dock, you see."

"Do you know how I knew you had taken him into space?"

"I'm sure you have your sources, both mortal and heavenly."

"My dear friend, Dr. Vivian Delamar, was the surgeon who
reconstructed Achilles' leg."

"As I recall, you recommended her."

"Before I knew what Achilles really was. When I found out, I
called her. Warned her to be careful. Because my expert also said
that *she* was in danger."

"The one who restored his leg? Why?"

"No one has seen him more helpless than the surgeon who
cuts into him as he lies there drugged to the gills. Rationally, I'm
sure he knew it was wrong to harm this woman who did him so
much good. But then, the same would apply to Poke, the first time
he killed. *If* it was the first time."

"So . . . Dr. Vivian Delamar. You alerted her. What did she
see? Did he murmur a confession under anaesthetic?"

"We'll never know. He killed her."

"You're joking."

"I'm in Cairo. Her funeral is tomorrow. They were calling it a
heart attack until I urged them to look for a hypodermic insertion
mark. Indeed they found one, and now it's on the books as a
murder. Achilles *does* know how to read. He learned which
drugs would do the job. How he got her to sit still for it, I don't
know."

"How can I believe this, Sister Carlotta? The boy is generous,
gracious, people are drawn to him, he's a born leader. People like
that don't kill."

"Who are the dead? The teacher who mocked him for his

ignorance when he first arrived in the school, showed him up in front of the class. The doctor who saw him laid out under anaesthetic. The street girl whose crew took him down. The street boy who vowed to kill him and made him go into hiding. Maybe the coincidence argument would sway a jury, but it shouldn't sway you."

"Yes, you've convinced me that the danger might well be real. But I already alerted the teachers at Battle School that there might be some danger. And now I really am not in charge of Battle School."

"You're still in *touch*. If you give them a more urgent warning, they'll take steps."

"I'll give the appropriate warning."

"You're lying to me."

"You can tell that over the phone?"

"You *want* Bean exposed to danger!"

"Sister . . . yes, I do. But not this much of it. Whatever I can do, I'll do."

"If you let Bean come to harm, God will have an accounting from you."

"He'll have to get in line, Sister Carlotta. The I.F. court-martial takes precedence."

Bean looked down into the air vent in his quarters and marveled that he had ever been small enough to fit in there. What was he then, the size of a rat?

Fortunately, with a room of his own now he wasn't limited to the outflow vents. He put his chair on top of his table and climbed up to the long, thin intake vents along the wall on the corridor side of his room. The vent trim pried out as several long sections. The paneling above it was separate from the riveted wall below. And it, too, came off fairly easily. Now there was room enough for almost any kid in Battle School to shinny in to the crawl space over the corridor ceiling.

Bean stripped off his clothes and once again crawled into the air system. It was more cramped this time—it was surprising how much he'd grown. He made his way quickly to the maintenance area near the furnaces. He found how the lighting systems worked, and carefully went around removing lightbulbs and wall glow units in the areas he'd be needing. Soon there was a wide vertical shaft that was utterly dark when the door was closed, with deep shadows even when it was open. Carefully he laid his trap.

Achilles never ceased to be astonished at how the universe bent to his will. Whatever he wished seemed to come to him. Poke and her crew, raising him above the other bullies. Sister Carlotta, bringing him to the priests' school in Bruxelles. Dr. Delamar, straightening his leg so he could *run*, so he looked no different from any other boy his age. And now here he was in Battle School, and who should be his first commander but little Bean, ready to take him under his wing, help him rise within this school. As if the universe were created to serve him, with all the people in it tuned to resonate with his desires.

The battleroom was cool beyond belief. War in a box. Point the gun, the other kid's suit freezes. Of course, Ambul had made the mistake of demonstrating this by freezing Achilles and then laughing at his consternation at floating in the air, unable to move, unable to change the direction of his drift. People shouldn't do that. It was wrong, and it always gnawed at Achilles until he was able to set things right. There should be more kindness and respect in the world.

Like Bean. It looked so promising at first, but then Bean started putting him down. Making sure the others saw that Achilles *used* to be Bean's papa, but now he was just a soldier in Bean's army. There was no need for that. You don't go putting people down. Bean had changed. Back when Poke first put Achilles on his back, shaming him in front of all those little children, it was Bean who showed him respect. "Kill him," Bean had said. He knew, then, that tiny boy, he knew that even on his back, Achilles was dangerous. But he seemed to have forgotten that now. In fact, Achilles was pretty sure that Bean must have told Ambul to freeze his flash suit and humiliate him in the practice room, setting him up for the others to laugh at him.

I was your friend and protector, Bean, because you showed respect for me. But now I have to weigh that in the balance with your behavior here in Battle School. No respect for me at all.

The trouble was, the students in Battle School were given nothing that could be used as a weapon, and everything was made completely safe. No one was ever alone, either. Except the commanders. Alone in their quarters. That was promising. But Achilles suspected that the teachers had a way of tracking where every student was at any given time. He'd have to learn the system, learn how to evade it, before he could start setting things to rights.

But he knew this: He'd learn what he needed to learn. Opportunities would appear. And he, being Achilles, would see those opportunities and seize them. Nothing could interrupt his rise until he held all the power there was to hold within his hands. Then there would be perfect justice in the world, not this miserable system that left so many children starving and ignorant and crippled on the streets while others lived in privilege and safety and health. All those adults who had run things for thousands of years were fools or failures. But the universe obeyed Achilles. He and he alone could correct the abuses.

On his third day in Battle School, Rabbit Army had its first battle with Bean as commander. They lost. They would not have lost if Achilles had been commander. Bean was doing some stupid touchy-feely thing, leaving things up to the toon leaders. But it was obvious that the toon leaders had been badly chosen by Bean's predecessor. If Bean was to win, he needed to take tighter control. When he tried to suggest this to Bean, the child only smiled knowingly—a maddeningly superior smile—and told him that the key to victory was for each toon leader and, eventually, each soldier to see the whole situation and act independently to bring about victory. It made Achilles want to slap him, it was so stupid, so wrongheaded. The one who knew how to order things did not leave it up to others to create their little messes in the corners of the world. He took the reins and pulled, sharp and hard. He whipped his men into obedience. As Frederick the Great said: The soldier must fear his officers more than he fears the bullets of the enemy. You could not rule without the naked exercise of power. The followers must bow their heads to the leader. They must *surrender* their heads, using only the mind and will of the leader to rule them. No one but Achilles seemed to understand that this was the great strength of the Buggers. They had no individual minds, only the mind of the hive. They submitted perfectly to the queen. We cannot defeat the Buggers until we learn from them, become like them.

But there was no point in explaining this to Bean. He would not listen. Therefore he would never make Rabbit Army into a hive. He was working to create chaos. It was unbearable.

Unbearable—yet, just when Achilles thought he couldn't bear the stupidity and waste any longer, Bean called him to his quarters.

Achilles was startled, when he entered, to find that Bean had removed the vent cover and part of the wall panel, giving him access to the air-duct system. This was not at all what Achilles had expected.

"Take your clothes off," said Bean.

Achilles smelled an attempt at humiliation.

Bean was taking off his own uniform. "They track us through the uniforms," said Bean. "If you aren't wearing one, they don't know where you are, except in the gym and the battleroom, where they have really expensive equipment to track each warm body. We aren't going to either of those places, so strip."

Bean was naked. As long as Bean went first, Achilles could not be shamed by doing the same.

"Ender and I used to do this," said Bean. "Everybody thought Ender was such a brilliant commander, but the truth is he knew all the plans of the other commanders because we'd go spying through the air ducts. And not just the commanders, either. We found out what the teachers were planning. We always knew it in advance. Not hard to win that way."

Achilles laughed. This was too cool. Bean might be a fool, but this Ender that Achilles had heard so much about, *he* knew what he was doing.

"It takes two people, is that it?"

"To get where I can spy on the teachers, there's a wide shaft, pitch black. I can't climb down. I need somebody to lower me down and haul me back up. I didn't know who in Rabbit Army I could trust, and then . . . there you were. A friend from the old days."

It was happening again. The universe, bending to his will. He and Bean would be alone. No one would be tracking where they were. No one would know what had happened.

"I'm in," said Achilles.

"Boost me up," said Bean. "You're tall enough to climb up alone."

Clearly, Bean had come this way many times before. He scampered through the crawl space, his feet and butt flashing in the spill from the corridor lights. Achilles noted where he put his hands and feet, and soon was as adept at Bean at picking his way through. Every time he used his leg, he marveled at the use of it. It went where he wanted it to go, and had the strength to hold him. Dr. Delamar might be a skilled surgeon, but even she said that she had never seen a body respond to the surgery as Achilles' did. His body knew how to be whole, expected to be strong. All the time before, those crippled years, had been the universe's way of teaching Achilles the unbearability of disorder. And now Achilles was perfect of body, ready to move ahead in setting things to rights.

Achilles very carefully noted the route they took. If the opportunity presented itself, he would be coming back alone. He could not afford to get lost, or give himself away. No one could know that he had ever been in the air system. As long as he gave them no reason, the teachers would never suspect him. All they knew was that he and Bean were friends. And when Achilles grieved for the child, his tears would be real. They always were, for there was a nobility to these tragic deaths. A grandeur as the great universe worked its will through Achilles' adept hands.

The furnaces roared as they came into a room where the framing of the station was visible. Fire was good. It left so little residue. People died when they accidentally fell into fire. It happened all the time. Bean, crawling around alone . . . it would be good if they went near the furnace.

Instead, Bean opened a door into a dark space. The light from the opening showed a black gap not far inside. "Don't step over the edge of that," Bean said cheerfully. He picked up a loop of very fine cord from the ground. "It's a deadline. Safety equipment. Keeps workmen from drifting off into space when they're working on the outside of the station. Ender and I set it up—it goes over a beam up there and keeps me centered in the shaft. You can't grip it in your hands, it cuts too easily if it slides across your skin. So you loop it tight around your body—no sliding, see?—and brace yourself. The gravity's not that intense, so I just jump off. We measured it out, so I stop right at the level of the vents leading to the teachers' quarters."

"Doesn't it hurt when you stop?"

"Like a bitch," said Bean. "No pain no gain, right? I take off the deadline, I snag it on a flap of metal and it stays there till I get back. I'll tug on it three times when I get it back on. Then you pull me back up. But *not* with your hands. You go out the door and walk out there. When you get to place where we came in, go around the beam there and go till you touch the wall. Just wait there until I can get myself swinging and land back here on this ledge. Then I unloop myself and you come back in and we leave the deadline for next time. Simple, see?"

"Got it," said Achilles.

Instead of walking to the wall, it would be simple enough to just keep walking. Get Bean floating in the air where he couldn't get hold of anything. Plenty of time, then, to find a way to tie it off inside that dark room. With the roar of the furnaces and fans, nobody would hear Bean calling for help. Then Achilles would have time to explore. Figure out how to get into the furnaces. Swing Bean back, strangle him, carry the body to the fire. Drop the deadline down the shaft. Nobody would find it. Quite possibly no one would ever find Bean, or if they did, his soft tissues would be consumed. All evidence of strangulation would be gone. Very neat. There'd be some improvisation, but there always was. Achilles could handle little problems as they came up.

Achilles looped the deadline over his head, then drew it tight under his arms as Bean climbed into the loop at the other end.

"Set," said Achilles.

"Make sure it's tight, so it doesn't have any slack to cut you when I hit bottom."

"Yes, it's tight."

But Bean had to check. He got a finger under the line. "Tighter," said Bean.

Achilles tightened it more.

"Good," said Bean. "That's it. Do it."

Do it? Bean was the one who was supposed to do it.

Then the deadline went taut and Achilles was lifted off his feet. With a few more yanks, he hung in the air in the dark shaft. The deadline dug harshly into his skin.

When Bean said "do it" he was talking to someone else. Someone who was already here, lying in wait. The traitorous little bastard.

Achilles said nothing, however. He reached up to see if he could touch the beam above him, but it was out of reach. Nor could he climb the line, not with bare hands, not with the line drawn taut by his own body weight.

He wriggled on the line, starting himself swinging. But no matter how far he went in any direction, he touched nothing. No wall, no place where he might find purchase.

Time to talk.

"What's this about, Bean?"

"It's about Poke," said Bean.

"She's dead, Bean."

"You kissed her. You killed her. You put her in the river."

Achilles felt the blood run hot into his face. No one saw that. He was guessing. But then . . . how did he know that Achilles had kissed her first, unless he saw?

"You're wrong," said Achilles.

"How sad if I am. Then the wrong man will die for the crime."

"Die? Be serious, Bean. You aren't a killer."

"But the hot dry air of the shaft will do it for me. You'll dehydrate in a day. Your mouth's already a little dry, isn't it? And then you'll just keep hanging here, mummifying. This is the intake system, so the air gets filtered and purified. Even if your body stinks for a while, nobody will smell it. Nobody will see you—you're above where the light shines from the door. And nobody comes in here anyway. No, the disappearance of Achilles will be the mystery of Battle School. They'll tell ghost stories about you to frighten the launchies."

"Bean, I didn't do it."

"I saw you, Achilles, you poor fool. I don't care what you say, I *saw* you. I never thought I'd have the chance to make you pay for what you did to her. Poke did nothing but good to you. I told her to kill you, but she had mercy. She made you king of the streets. And for that you killed her?"

"I didn't kill her."

"Let me lay it out for you, Achilles, since you're clearly too stupid to see where you are. First thing is, you forgot where you were. Back on Earth, you were used to being a lot smarter than everybody around you. But here in Battle School, *everybody* is as smart as you, and most of us are smarter. You think Ambul didn't see the way you looked at him? You think he didn't know he was marked for death after he laughed at you? You think the other soldiers in Rabbit doubted me when I told them about you? They'd already seen that there was something wrong with you. The adults might have missed it, they might buy into the way you suck up to them, but *we* didn't. And since we just had a case of one kid trying to kill another, nobody was going to put up with it again. Nobody was going to wait for you to strike. Because here's the thing—we don't give a shit about fairness here. We're soldiers. Soldiers do not give the other guy a sporting chance. Soldiers shoot in the back, lay traps and ambushes, lie to the enemy and outnumber the other bastard every chance they get. Your kind of murder only works among civilians. And you were too cocky, too stupid, too insane to realize that."

Achilles knew that Bean was right. He had miscalculated grossly. He had forgotten that when Bean said for Poke to kill him, he had not just been showing respect for Achilles. He had also been trying to get Achilles killed.

This just wasn't working out very well.

"So you have only two ways for this to end. One way, you just hang there, we take turns watching to make sure you don't figure some way out of this, until you're dead and then we leave you and go about our lives. The other way, you confess to everything—and I mean everything, not just what you think I already know—and you keep confessing. Confess to the teachers. Confess to the psychiatrists they send you to. Confess your way into a mental hospital back on Earth. We don't care which you choose. All that matters is that you never again walk freely through the corridors of

Battle School. Or anywhere else. So . . . what will it be? Dry out on the line, or let the teachers know just how crazy you are?''

"Bring me a teacher, I'll confess.''

"Didn't you hear me explain how stupid we're not? You confess now. Before witnesses. With a recorder. We don't bring some teacher up here to see you hanging there and feel all squishy sorry for you. Any teacher who comes here will know exactly what you are, and there'll be about six marines to keep you subdued and sedated because, Achilles, they don't play around here. They don't give people chances to escape. You've got no rights here. You don't get rights again until you're back on Earth. Here's your last chance. Confession time.''

Achilles almost laughed out loud. But it was important for Bean to think that he had won. As, for the moment, he had. Achilles could see now that there was no way for him to remain in Battle School. But Bean wasn't smart enough just to kill him and have done. No, Bean was, completely unnecessarily, allowing him to live. And as long as Achilles was alive, then time would move things his way. The universe would bend until the door was opened and Achilles went free. And it would happen sooner rather than later.

You shouldn't have left a door open for me, Bean. Because I *will* kill you someday. You and everyone else who has seen me helpless here.

"All right,'' said Achilles. "I killed Poke. I strangled her and put her in the river.''

"Go on.''

"What more? You want to know how she wet herself and took a shit while she was dying? You want to know how her eyes bugged out?''

"One murder doesn't get you psychiatric confinement, Achilles. You know you've killed before.''

"What makes you think so?''

"Because it didn't bother you.''

It never bothered, not even the first time. You just don't understand power. If it *bothers* you, you aren't fit to *have* power. "I killed Ulysses, of course, but just because he was a nuisance.''

"And?''

"I'm not a mass murderer, Bean.''

"You live to kill, Achilles. Spill it all. And then convince me that it really *was* all.''

But Achilles had just been playing. He had already decided to tell it all.

"The most recent was Dr. Vivian Delamar," he said. "I told her not to do the operations under total anaesthetic. I told her to leave me alert, I could take it even if there was pain. But she had to be in control. Well, if she really loved control so much, why did she turn her back on me? And why was she so stupid as to think I really had a gun? By pressing hard in her back, I made it so she didn't even feel the needle go in right next to where the tongue depressors were poking her. Died of a heart attack right there in her own office. Nobody even knew I'd been in there. You want more?"

"I want it all, Achilles."

It took twenty minutes, but Achilles gave them the whole chronicle, all seven times he had set things right. He liked it, actually, telling them like this. Nobody had ever had a chance to understand how powerful he was till now. He wanted to see their faces, that's the only thing that was missing. He wanted to see the disgust that would reveal their weakness, their inability to look power in the face. Machiavelli understood. If you intend to rule, you don't shrink from killing. Saddam Hussein knew it—you have to be willing to kill with your own hand. You can't stand back and let others do it for you all the time. And Stalin understood it, too—you can never be loyal to anybody, because that only weakens you. Lenin was good to Stalin, gave him his chance, raised him out of nothing to be the keeper of the gate to power. But that didn't stop Stalin from imprisoning Lenin and then killing him. That's what these fools would never understand. All those military writers were just armchair philosophers. All that military history— most of it was useless. War was just one of the tools that the great men used to get and keep their power. And the only way to stop a great man was the way Brutus did it.

Bean, you're no Brutus.

Turn on the light. Let me see the faces.

But the light did not go on. When he was finished, when they left, there was only the light through the door, silhouetting them as they left. Five of them. All naked, but carrying the recording equipment. They even tested it, to make sure it had picked up Achilles' confession. He heard his own voice, strong and unwavering. Proud of what he'd done. That would prove to the weaklings that he was "insane." They would keep him alive. Until the universe bent things to his will yet again, and set him free to reign with blood and horror on Earth. Since they hadn't let him see their faces, he'd have no choice. When all the power was in his hands, he'd have to kill everyone who was in Battle School at this time. That would be a good idea, anyway. Since all the brilliant military minds of the age had been assembled here at one time or another, it was obvious that in order to rule safely, Achilles would have to get rid of everyone whose name had ever been on a Battle School roster. Then there'd be no rivals. And he'd keep testing children as long as he lived, finding any with the slightest spark of military talent. Herod understood how you stay in power.

Part Six

VICTOR

21

GUESSWORK

"We're not waiting any longer for Colonel Graff to repair the damage done to Ender Wiggin. Wiggin doesn't need Tactical School for the job he'll be doing. And we need the others to move on at once. *They* have to get the feel of what the old ships can do before we bring them here and put them on the simulators, and that takes time."

"They've only had a few games."

"I shouldn't have allowed them as much time as I have. ISL is two months away from you, and by the time they're done with Tactical, the voyage from there to FleetCom will be four months. That gives them only three months in Tactical before we have to bring them to Command School. Three months in which to compress three years of training."

"I should tell you that Bean seems to have passed Colonel Graff's last test."

"Test? When I relieved Colonel Graff, I thought his sick little testing program ended as well."

"We didn't know how dangerous this Achilles was. We had been warned of *some* danger, but . . . he seemed so likable . . . I'm not faulting Colonel Graff, you understand, *he* had no way of knowing."

"Knowing what?'

"That Achilles is a serial killer."

"That should make Graff happy. Ender's count is up to two."

"I'm not joking, sir. Achilles has seven murders on his tally."

"And he passed the screening?"

"He knew how to answer the psychological tests."

"Please tell me that none of the seven took place at Battle School."

"Number eight would have. But Bean got him to confess."

"Bean's a priest now?"

"Actually, sir, it was deft strategy. He outmaneuvered Achilles—led him into an ambush, and confession was the only escape."

"So Ender, the nice middle-class American boy, kills the kid who wants to beat him up in the bathroom. And Bean, the hoodlum street kid, turns a serial killer over to law enforcement."

"The more significant thing for our purposes is that Ender was good at building teams, but he beat Bonzo hand to hand, one on one. And then Bean, a loner who had almost no friends after a year in the school, he beats Achilles by assembling a team to be his defense and his witnesses. I have no idea if Graff predicted these outcomes, but the result was that his tests got each boy to act not only against our expectations, but also against his own predilections."

"Predilections. Major Anderson."

"It will all be in my report."

"Try to write the entire thing without using the word *predilection* once."

"Yes, sir."

"I've assigned the destroyer *Condor* to take the group."

"How many do you want, sir?"

"We have need of a maximum of eleven at any one time. We have Carby, Bee, and Momoe on their way to Tactical already, but Graff tells me that of those three, only Carby is likely to work well with Wiggin. We do need to hold a slot for Ender, but it wouldn't hurt to have a spare. So send ten."

"*Which* ten?"

"How the hell should I know? Well . . . Bean, him for sure. And the nine others that you think would work best with either Bean or Ender in command, whichever one it turns out to be."

"One list for both possible commanders?"

"With Ender as the first choice. We want them all to train together. Become a team."

The orders came at 1700. Bean was supposed to board the *Condor* at 1800. It's not as if he had anything to pack. An hour was more time than they gave Ender. So Bean went and told his army what was happening, where he was going.

"We've only had five games," said Itú.

"Got to catch the bus when it comes to the stop, neh?" said Bean.

"Eh," said Itú.

"Who else?" asked Ambul.

"They didn't tell me. Just . . . Tactical School."

"We don't even know where it is."

"Somewhere in space," said Itú.

"No, really?" It was lame, but they laughed. It wasn't all that hard a good-bye. He'd only been with Rabbit for eight days.

"Sorry we didn't win any for you," said Itú.

"We would have won, if I'd wanted to," said Bean.

They looked at him like he was crazy.

"I was the one who proposed that we get rid of the standings, stop caring who wins. How would it look if we do that and I win every time?"

"It would look like you really did care about the standings," said Itú.

"That's not what bothers me," said another toon leader. "Are you telling me you set us up to *lose?*"

"No, I'm telling you I had a different priority. What do we learn from beating each other? Nothing. We're never going to have to fight human children. We're going to have to fight Buggers. So what do we need to learn? How to coordinate our attacks. How to respond to each other. How to feel the course of the battle, and take responsibility for the whole thing even if you don't have command. *That's* what I was working on with you guys. And if we *won,* if we went in and mopped up the walls with them, using *my* strategy, what does that teach *you?* You already worked with a good commander. What you needed to do was work with each other. So I put you in tough situations and by the end you were finding ways to bail each other out. To make it work."

"We never made it work well enough to win."

"That's not how I measured it. You made it work. When the Buggers come again, they're going to make things go wrong. Besides the normal friction of war, they're going to be doing stuff we couldn't think of because they're not human, they don't think like us. So plans of attack, what good are they then? We try, we do what we can, but what really counts is what you do when command breaks down. When it's just you with your squadron, and you with your transport, and you with your beat-up strike force that's got only five weapons among eight ships. How do you help each other? How do you make do? That's what I was working on. And then I went back to the officers' mess and told them what I learned. What you guys showed me. I learned stuff from them, too. I told you all the stuff I learned from them, right?''

"Well, you *could* have told us what you were learning from *us,*'' said Itú. They were all still a bit resentful.

"I didn't have to *tell* you. You learned it.''

"At least you could have told us it was OK not to win.''

"But you were supposed to *try* to win. I didn't tell you because it only works if you think it counts. Like when the Buggers come. It'll count then, for real. That's when you get really smart, when losing means that you and everybody you ever cared about, the whole human race, will die. Look, I didn't think we'd have long together. So I made the best use of the time, for you and for me. You guys are all ready to take command of armies.''

"What about you, Bean?'' asked Ambul. He was smiling, but there was an edge to it. "You ready to command a fleet?''

"I don't know. It depends on whether they want to win.'' Bean grinned.

"Here's the thing, Bean,'' said Ambul. "Soldiers don't like to lose.''

"And *that,*'' said Bean, "is why losing is a much more powerful teacher than winning.''

They heard him. They thought about it. Some of them nodded.

"*If* you live,'' Bean added. And grinned at them.

They smiled back.

"I gave you the best thing I could think of to give you during this week,'' said Bean. "And learned from you as much as I was smart enough to learn. Thank you.'' He stood and saluted them.

They saluted back.

He left.

And went to Rat Army barracks.

"Nikolai just got his orders,'' a toon leader told him.

For a moment Bean wondered if Nikolai would be going to Tactical School with him. His first thought was, No way is he ready. His second thought was, I wish he could come. His third thought was, I'm not much of a friend, to think first how he doesn't deserve to be promoted.

"What orders?'' Bean asked.

"He's got him an army. Hell, he wasn't even a toon leader here. Just *got* here last week.''

"Which army?"

"Rabbit." The toon leader looked at Bean's uniform again. "Oh. I guess he's replacing *you.*"

Bean laughed and headed for the quarters he had just left.

Nikolai was sitting inside with the door open, looking lost.

"Can I come in?"

Nikolai looked up and grinned. "Tell me you're here to take your army back."

"I've got a hint for you. Try to win. They think that's important."

"I couldn't believe you lost all five."

"You know, for a school that doesn't list standings anymore, everybody sure keeps track."

"I keep track of *you.*"

"Nikolai, I wish you were coming with me."

"What's happening, Bean? Is this it? Are the Buggers here?"

"I don't know."

"Come on, you figure these things out."

"If the Buggers were really coming, would they leave all you guys here in the station? Or send you back to Earth? Or evacuate you to some obscure asteroid? I don't know. Some things point to the end being really close. Other things seem like nothing important's going to happen anywhere around here."

"So maybe they're about to launch this huge fleet against the Bugger world and you guys are supposed to grow up on the voyage."

"Maybe," said Bean. "But the time to launch *that* fleet was right after the Second Invasion."

"Well, what if they didn't find out where the Bugger home world *was* until now?"

That stopped Bean cold. "Never crossed my mind," said Bean. "I mean, they must have been sending signals home. All we had to do was track that direction. Follow the light, you know. That's what it says in the manuals."

"What if they don't communicate by light?"

"Light may take a year to go a lightyear, but it's still faster than anything else."

"Anything else that we know about," said Nikolai.

Bean just looked at him.

"Oh, I know, that's stupid. The laws of physics and all that. I just— you know, I keep thinking, that's all. I don't like to rule things out just because they're impossible."

Bean laughed. "Merda, Nikolai, I should have let you talk more and me talk less back when we slept across from each other."

"Bean, you know I'm not a genius."

"All geniuses here, Nikolai."

"I was scraping by."

"So maybe you're not a Napoleon, Nikolai. Maybe you're just an Eisenhower. Don't expect me to cry for you."

It was Nikolai's turn to laugh.

"I'll miss you, Bean."

"Thanks for coming with me to face Achilles, Nikolai."

"Guy gave me nightmares."

"Me too."

"And I'm glad you brought the others along too. Itú, Ambul, Crazy Tom, I felt like we could've used six more, and Achilles was hanging from a wire. Guys like him, you can understand why they invented hanging."

"Someday," said Bean, "you're going to need me the way I needed you. And I'll be there."

"I'm sorry I didn't join your squad, Bean."

"You were right," said Bean. "I asked you because you were my friend, and I thought I needed a friend, but I should have *been* a friend, too, and seen what *you* needed."

"I'll never let you down again."

Bean threw his arms around Nikolai. Nikolai hugged him back.

Bean remembered when he left Earth. Hugging Sister Carlotta. Analyzing. This is what she needs. It costs me nothing. Therefore I'll give her the hug.

I'm not that kid anymore.

Maybe because I was able to come through for Poke after all. Too late to help her, but I still got her killer to admit it. I still got him to pay something, even if it can never be enough.

"Go meet your army, Nikolai," said Bean. "I've got a spaceship to catch."

He watched Nikolai go out the door and knew, with a sharp pang of regret, that he would never see his friend again.

Dimak stood in Major Anderson's quarters.

"Captain Dimak, I watched Colonel Graff indulge your constant complaints, your resistance to his orders, and I kept thinking, Dimak might be right, but I would never tolerate such lack of respect if *I* were in command.

I'd throw him out on his ass and write 'insubordinate' in about forty places in his dossier. I thought I should tell you that before you make your complaint.''

Dimak blinked.

"Go ahead, I'm waiting.''

"It isn't so much a complaint as a question.''

"Then ask your question.''

"I thought you were supposed to choose a team that was equally compatible with Ender *and* with Bean.''

"The word *equally* was never used, as far as I can recall. But even if it was, did it occur to you that it might be impossible? I could have chosen forty brilliant children who would all have been proud and eager to serve under Andrew Wiggin. How many would be *equally* proud and eager to serve under Bean?''

Dimak had no answer for that.

"The way I analyze it, the soldiers I chose to send on this destroyer are the students who are emotionally closest and most responsive to Ender Wiggin, while also being among the dozen or so best commanders in the school. These soldiers also have no particular animosity toward Bean. So if they find him placed over them, they'll probably do their best for him.''

"They'll never forgive him for not being Ender.''

"I guess that will be Bean's challenge. Who else should I have sent? Nikolai is Bean's friend, but he'd be out of his depth. Someday he'll be ready for Tactical School, and then Command, but not yet. And what other friends does Bean have?''

"He's won a lot of respect.''

"And lost it again when he lost all five of his games.''

"I've explained to you why he—''

"Humanity doesn't need explanations, Captain Dimak! It needs winners! Ender Wiggin had the fire to win. Bean is capable of losing five in a row as if they didn't even matter.''

"They didn't matter. He learned what he needed to learn from them.''

"Captain Dimak, I can see that I'm falling into the same trap that Colonel Graff fell into. You have crossed the line from teaching into advocacy. I would dismiss you as Bean's teacher, were it not for the fact that the question is already moot. I'm sending the soldiers I decided on already. If Bean is really so brilliant, he'll figure out a way to work with them.''

"Yes sir,'' said Dimak.

"If it's any consolation, do remember that Crazy Tom was one of the ones Bean brought along to hear Achilles' confession. Crazy Tom *went.*

That suggests that the better they know Bean, the more seriously they take him.''

"Thank you, sir.''

"Bean is no longer your responsibility, Captain Dimak. You did well with him. I salute you for it. Now . . . get back to work.''

Dimak saluted.

Anderson saluted.

Dimak left.

On the destroyer *Condor,* the crew had no idea what to do with these children. They all knew about the Battle School, and both the captain and the pilot were Battle School graduates. But after perfunctory conversation— What army were you in? Oh, in my day Rat was the best, Dragon was a complete loser, how things change, how things stay the same—there was nothing more to say.

Without the shared concerns of being army commanders, the children drifted into their natural friendship groups. Dink and Petra had been friends almost from their first beginnings in Battle School, and they were so senior to the others that no one tried to penetrate that closed circle. Alai and Shen had been in Ender Wiggin's original launch group, and Vlad and Dumper, who had commanded B and E toons and were probably the most worshipful of Ender, hung around with them. Crazy Tom, Fly Molo, and Hot Soup had already been a trio back in Dragon Army. On a personal level, Bean did not expect to be included in any of these groups, and he wasn't particularly excluded, either; Crazy Tom, at least, showed real respect for Bean, and often included him in conversation. If Bean belonged to any of these groups, it was Crazy Tom's.

The only reason the division into cliques bothered him was that this group was clearly being assembled, not just randomly chosen. Trust needed to grow between them all, strongly if not equally. But they had been chosen for Ender—any idiot could see that—and it was not Bean's place to suggest that they play the onboard games together, learn together, do anything together. If Bean tried to assert any kind of leadership, it would only build more walls between him and the others than already existed.

There was only one of the group that Bean didn't think belonged there. And he couldn't do anything about that. Apparently the adults did not hold Petra responsible for her near-betrayal of Ender in the corridor the evening before Ender's life-or-death struggle with Bonzo. But Bean was not so sure. Petra was one of the best of the commanders, smart, able to see the big picture. How could she possibly have been fooled by Bonzo? Of course she couldn't have been hoping for Ender's destruction. But she had been careless, at best, and at worst might have been playing some kind of game that Bean did not yet understand. So he remained suspicious of her. Which wasn't good, to have such mistrust, but there it was.

Bean passed the four months of the voyage in the ship's library, mostly. Now that they were out of Battle School, he was reasonably sure that they weren't being spied on so intensely. The destroyer simply wasn't equipped for it. So he no longer had to choose his reading material with an eye to what the teachers would make of his selections.

He read no military history or theory whatsoever. He had already read all the major writers and many of the minor ones and knew the important campaigns backward and forward, from both sides. Those were in his memory to be called upon whenever he needed them. What was missing from his memory was the big picture. How the world worked. Political, social, economic history. What happened in nations when they weren't at war. How they got into and out of wars. How victory and defeat affected them. How alliances were formed and broken.

And, most important of all, but hardest to find: What was going on in the world today. The destroyer library had only the information that had been current when last it docked at Interstellar Launch—ISL—which is where the authorized list of documents was made available for download. Bean could make requests for more information, but that would require the library computer to make requisitions and use communications bandwidth that would have to be justified. It would be noticed, and then they'd wonder why this child was studying matters that could have no possible concern for him.

From what he could find on board, however, it was still possible to piece together the basic situation on Earth, and to reach some conclusions. During the years before the First Invasion, various power blocs had jockeyed for position, using some combination of terrorism, "surgical" strikes, limited military operations, and economic sanctions, boycotts, and embargos to gain the upper hand or give firm warnings or simply express national or ideological rage. When the Buggers showed up, China had just emerged as the dominant world power, economically and militarily, having finally reunited itself as a democracy. The North Americans and Europeans played at being China's "big brothers," but the economic balance had finally shifted.

What Bean saw as the driving force of history, however, was the resurgent Russian Empire. Where the Chinese simply took it for granted that they were and should be the center of the universe, the Russians, led by a series of ambitious demagogues and authoritarian generals, felt that history had cheated them out of their rightful place, century after century, and it was time for that to end. So it was Russia that forced the creation of the New Warsaw Pact, bringing its effective borders back to the peak of Soviet power—and beyond, for this time Greece was its ally, and an intimidated Turkey was neutralized. Europe was on the verge of being neutralized, the Russian dream of hegemony from the Pacific to the Atlantic at last within reach.

And then the Formics came and cut a swath of destruction through China that left a hundred million dead. Suddenly land-based armies seemed trivial, and questions of international competition were put on hold.

But that was only superficial. In fact, the Russians used their domination of the office of the Polemarch to build up a network of officers in key places throughout the fleet. Everything was in place for a vast power play the moment the Buggers were defeated—or before, if they thought it was to their advantage. Oddly, the Russians were rather open about their intentions—they always had been. They had no talent for subtlety, but they made up for it with amazing stubbornness. Negotiations for anything could take decades. And meanwhile, their penetration of the fleet was nearly total. Infantry forces loyal to the Strategos would be isolated, unable to get to the places where they were needed because there would be no ships to carry them.

When the war with the Buggers ended, the Russians clearly planned that within hours they would rule the fleet and therefore the world. It was their destiny. The North Americans were as complacent as ever, sure that destiny would work everything out in their favor. Only a few demagogues saw the danger. The Chinese and the Muslim world were alert to the danger, and even they were unable to make any kind of stand for fear of breaking up the alliance that made resistance to the Buggers possible.

The more he studied, the more Bean wished that he did not have to go to Tactical School. This war would belong to Ender and his friends. And while Bean loved Ender as much as any of them, and would gladly serve with them against the Buggers, the fact was that they didn't need him. It was the next war, the struggle for world domination, that fascinated him. The Russians *could* be stopped, if the right preparations were made.

But then he had to ask himself: *Should* they be stopped? A quick, bloody, but effective coup which would bring the world under a single government—it would mean the end of war among humans, wouldn't it? And in such a climate of peace, wouldn't all nations be better off?

So, even as Bean developed his plan for stopping the Russians, he tried to evaluate what a worldwide Russian Empire would be like.

And what he concluded was that it would not last. For along with their national vigor, the Russians had also nurtured their astonishing talent for misgovernment, that sense of personal entitlement that made corruption a way of life. The institutional tradition of competence that would be essential for a successful world government was nonexistent. It was in China that those institutions and values were most vigorous. But even China would be a poor substitute for a genuine world government that transcended any national interest. The wrong world government would eventually collapse under its own weight.

Bean longed to be able to talk these things over with someone—with Nikolai, or even with one of the teachers. It slowed him down to have his own thoughts move around in circles—without outside stimulation it was hard to break free of his own assumptions. One mind can think only of its own questions; it rarely surprises itself. But he made progress, slowly, during that voyage, and then during the months of Tactical School.

Tactical was a blur of short voyages and detailed tours of various ships. Bean was disgusted that they seemed to concentrate entirely on older designs, which seemed pointless to him—why train your commanders in ships they won't actually be using in battle? But the teachers treated his objection with contempt, pointing out that ships were ships, in the long run, and the newest vessels had to be put into service patrolling the perimeters of the solar system. There were none to spare for training children.

They were taught very little about the art of pilotry, for they were not being trained to fly the ships, only to command them in battle. They had to get a sense of how the weapons worked, how the ships moved, what could be expected of them, what their limitations were. Much of it was rote learning . . . but that was precisely the kind of learning Bean could do almost in his sleep, being able to recall anything that he had read or heard with any degree of attention.

So throughout Tactical School, while he performed as well as anyone, his real concentration was still on the problems of the current political situation on Earth. For Tactical School was at ISL, and so the library there was constantly being updated, and not just with the material authorized for inclusion in finite ships' libraries. For the first time, Bean began to read the writings of current political thinkers on Earth. He read what was coming out of Russia, and once again was astonished at how nakedly they pursued their ambitions. The Chinese writers saw the danger, but being Chinese, made no effort to rally support in other nations for any kind of resistance.

To the Chinese, once something was known in China, it was known everywhere that mattered. And the Euro-American nations seemed dominated by a studied ignorance that to Bean appeared to be a death wish. Yet there were some who were awake, struggling to create coalitions.

Two popular commentators in particular came to Bean's attention. Demosthenes at first glance seemed to be a rabble-rouser, playing on prejudice and xenophobia. But he was also having considerable success in leading a popular movement. Bean didn't know if life under a government headed by Demosthenes would be any better than living under the Russians, but Demosthenes would at least make a contest out of it. The other commentator that Bean took note of was Locke, a lofty, high-minded fellow who nattered about world peace and forging alliances—yet amid his apparent complacency, Locke actually seemed to be working from the same set of facts as Demosthenes, taking it for granted that the Russians were vigorous enough to "lead" the world, but unprepared to do so in a "beneficial" way. In a way, it was as if Demosthenes and Locke were doing their research together, reading all the same sources, learning from all the same correspondents, but then appealing to completely different audiences.

For a while, Bean even toyed with the possibility that Locke and Demosthenes were the same person. But no, the writing styles were different, and more importantly, they thought and analyzed differently. Bean didn't think anyone was smart enough to fake that.

Whoever they were, these two commentators were the people that seemed to see the situation most accurately, and so Bean began to conceive of his essay on strategy in the post-Formic world as a letter to both Locke and Demosthenes. A private letter. An anonymous letter. Because his observations should be known, and these two seemed to be in the best position to bring Bean's ideas to fruition.

Resorting to old habits, Bean spent some time in the library watching several officers log on to the net, and soon had six log-ins that he could use. He then wrote his letter in six parts, using a different log-in for each part, and then sent the parts to Locke and Demosthenes within minutes of each other. He did it during an hour when the library was crowded, and made sure that he himself was logged on to the net on his own desk in his barracks, ostensibly playing a game. He doubted they'd be counting his keystrokes and realize that he wasn't actually doing anything with his desk during that time. And if they did trace the letter back to him, well, too bad. In all likelihood, Locke and Demosthenes would not try to trace him—in his letter he asked them not to. They would either believe him or not; they would agree with him or not; beyond that he could not go. He had spelled out for them exactly what the dangers were, what the Russian strategy obviously was, and what steps must be taken to ensure that the Russians did not succeed in their preemptive strike.

One of the most important points he made was that the children from Battle, Tactical, and Command School had to be brought back to Earth as quickly as possible, once the Buggers were defeated. If they remained in space, they would either be taken by the Russians or kept in ineffectual isolation by the I.F. But these children were the finest military minds that humanity had produced in this generation. If the power of one great nation was to be subdued, it would require brilliant commanders in opposition to them.

Within a day, Demosthenes had an essay on the nets calling for the Battle School to be dissolved at once and all those children brought home. "They have kidnapped our most promising children. Our Alexanders and Napoleons, our Rommels and Pattons, our Caesars and Fredericks and Washingtons and Saladins are being kept in a tower where we can't reach them, where they can't help their own people remain free from the threat of Russian domination. And who can doubt that the Russians intend to seize those children and use them? Or, if they can't, they will certainly try, with a single well-placed missile, to blast them all to bits, depriving us of our natural military leadership." Delicious demagoguery, designed to spark fear and outrage. Bean could imagine the consternation in the military as their precious school became a political issue. It was an emotional issue that Demosthenes would not let go of and other nationalists all over the world would fervently echo. And because it was about children, no politician could dare oppose the principle that all the children in Battle School would come home the *moment* the war ended. Not only that, but on this issue, Locke lent his prestigious, moderate voice to the cause, openly supporting the principle of the return of the children. "By all means, pay the piper, rid us of the invading rats—and then bring our children home."

I saw, I wrote, and the world changed a little. It was a heady feeling. It made all the work at Tactical School seem almost meaningless by comparison. He wanted to bound into the classroom and tell the others about his triumph. But they would look at him like he was crazy. They knew nothing about the world at large, and took no responsibility for it. They were closed into the military world.

Three days after Bean sent his letters to Locke and Demosthenes, the children came to class and found that they were to depart immediately for Command School, this time joined by Carn Carby, who had been a class ahead of them in Tactical School. They had spent only three months at

ISL, and Bean couldn't help wondering if his letters had not had some influence over the timing. If there was some danger that the children might be sent home prematurely, the I.F. had to make sure their prize specimens were out of reach.

22

REUNION

"I suppose I should congratulate you for undoing the damage you did to Ender Wiggin."

"Sir, I respectfully disagree that I did any damage."

"Ah, good then, I *don't* have to congratulate you. You do realize that your status here will be as observer."

"I hope that I will also have opportunities to offer advice based on my years of experience with these children."

"Command School has worked with children for years."

"Respectfully, sir, Command School has worked with adolescents. Ambitious, testosterone-charged, competitive teenagers. And quite aside from that, we have a lot riding on these particular children, and I know things about them that must be taken into account."

"All those things should be in your reports."

"They are. But with all respect, is there anyone there who has memorized my reports so thoroughly that the appropriate details will come to mind the instant they're needed?"

"I'll listen to you, Colonel Graff. And please stop assuring me of how respectful you are whenever you're about to tell me I'm an idiot."

"I thought that my leave of absence was designed to chasten me. I'm trying to show that I've been chastened."

"Are there any of these details about the children that come to mind right now?"

"An important one, sir. Because so much depends on what

Ender does or does not know, it is vital that you isolate him from the other children. During actual practices he can be there, but under no circumstances can you allow free conversation or sharing of information."

"And why is that?"

"Because if Bean ever comes to know about the ansible, he'll leap straight to the core situation. He may figure it out on his own as it is—you have no idea how difficult it is to conceal information from him. Ender is more trusting—but Ender can't do his job *unless* he knows about the ansible. You see? He and Bean cannot be allowed to have any free time together. Any conversation that is not on point."

"But if this is so, then Bean is not capable of being Ender's backup, because then he would *have* to be told about the ansible."

"It won't matter then."

"But you yourself were the author of the proposition that only a child—"

"Sir, none of that applies to Bean."

"Because?"

"Because he's not human."

"Colonel Graff, you make me tired."

The voyage to Command School was four long months, and this time they were being trained continuously, as thorough an education in the mathematics of targeting, explosives, and other weapons-related subjects as could be managed on board a fast-moving cruiser. Finally, too, they were being forged again into a team, and it quickly became clear to everyone that the leading student was Bean. He mastered everything immediately, and was soon the one whom the others turned to for explanations of concepts they didn't grasp at once. From being the lowest in status on the first voyage, a complete outsider, Bean now became an outcast for the opposite reason— he was alone in the position of highest status.

He struggled with the situation, because he knew that he needed to be able to function as part of the team, not just as a mentor or expert. Now it became vital that he take part in their downtime, relaxing with them, joking, joining in with reminiscences about Battle School. And about even earlier times.

For now, at last, the Battle School tabu against talking about home was gone. They all spoke freely of mothers and fathers who by now were distant memories, but who still played a vital role in their lives.

The fact that Bean had no parents at first made the others a little shy with him, but he seized the opportunity and began to speak openly about his entire experience. Hiding in the toilet tank in the clean room. Going home with the Spanish custodian. Starving on the streets as he scouted for his opportunity. Telling Poke how to beat the bullies at their own game. Watching Achilles, admiring him, fearing him as he created their little street family, marginalized Poke, and finally killed her. When he told them of finding Poke's body, several of them wept. Petra in particular broke down and sobbed.

It was an opportunity, and Bean seized it. Naturally, she soon fled the company of others, taking her emotions into the privacy of her quarters. As soon afterward as he could, Bean followed her.

"Bean, I don't want to talk."

"I do," said Bean. "It's something we have to talk about. For the good of the team."

"Is that what we are?" she asked.

"Petra, you know the worst thing I've ever done. Achilles was dangerous, I knew it, and I still went away and left Poke alone with him. She died for it. That burns in me every day of my life. Every time I start to feel happy, I remember Poke, how I owe my life to her, how I could have saved her. Every time I love somebody, I have that fear that I'll betray them the same way I did her."

"Why are you telling me this, Bean?"

"Because you betrayed Ender and I think it's eating at you."

Her eyes flashed with rage. "I did not! And it's eating at *you,* not me!"

"Petra, whether you admit it to yourself or not, when you tried to slow Ender down in the corridor that day, there's no way you didn't know what you were doing. I've seen you in action, you're sharp, you see everything. In some ways you're the best tactical commander in the whole group. It's absolutely impossible that you didn't see how Bonzo's thugs were all there in the corridor, waiting to beat the crap out of Ender, and what did you do? You tried to slow him down, peel him off from the group."

"And you stopped me," said Petra. "So it's moot, isn't it?"

"I have to know why."

"You don't have to know squat."

"Petra, we have to fight shoulder to shoulder someday. We have to be able to trust each other. I don't trust you because I don't know why you did that. And now you won't trust me because you know I don't trust *you.*"

"Oh what a tangled web we weave."

"What the hell does that mean?"

"My father said it. Oh what a tangled web we weave when first we practice to deceive."

"Exactly. Untangle this for me."

"You're the one who's weaving a web for me, Bean. You know things you don't tell the rest of us. You think I don't see that? So you want me to restore your trust in me, but you don't tell me anything useful."

"I opened my soul to you," said Bean.

"You told me about your *feelings.*" She said it with utter contempt. "So good, it's a relief to know you have them, or at least to know that you think it's worth pretending to have them, nobody's quite sure about that. But what you don't ever tell us is what the hell is actually going on here. We think you know."

"All I have are guesses."

"The teachers told you things back in Battle School that none of the rest of us knew. You knew the name of every kid in the school, you knew things about us, all of us. You knew things you had no business knowing."

Bean was stunned to realize that his special access had been so noticeable to her. Had he been careless? Or was she even more observant than he had thought? "I broke into the student data," said Bean.

"And they didn't catch you?"

"I think they did. Right from the start. Certainly they knew about it later." And he told her about choosing the roster for Dragon Army.

She flopped down on her bunk and addressed the ceiling. "You chose them! All those rejects and those little launchy bastards, *you* chose them!"

"Somebody had to. The teachers weren't competent to do it."

"So Ender had the best. He didn't *make* them the best, they already *were* the best."

"The best that weren't already in armies. I'm the only one who was a launchy when Dragon was formed who's with this team now. You and Shen and Alai and Dink and Carn, you weren't in Dragon, and you're obviously among the best. Dragon won because they were good, yes, but also because Ender knew what to do with them."

"It still turns one little corner of my universe upside down."

"Petra, this was a trade."

"Was it?"

"Explain why you weren't a judas back in Battle School."

"I was a judas," said Petra. "How's that for an explanation?"

Bean was sickened. "You can say it like that? Without shame?"

"Are you stupid?" asked Petra. "I was doing the same thing you were doing, trying to save Ender's life. I knew Ender had trained for combat, and those thugs hadn't. I was also trained. Bonzo had been working these guys up into a frenzy, but the fact is, they didn't like Bonzo very much, he had just pissed them off at Ender. So if they got in a few licks against Ender, right there in the corridor where Dragon Army and other soldiers would get into it right away, where Ender would have me beside him in a limited space so only a few of them could come at us at once—I figured that Ender would get bruised, get a bloody nose, but he'd come out of it OK. And all those walking scabies would be satisfied. Bonzo's ranting would be old news. Bonzo would be alone again. Ender would be safe from anything worse."

"You were gambling a lot on your fighting ability."

"And Ender's. We were both damn good then, and in excellent shape. And you know what? I think Ender understood what I was doing, and the only reason he didn't go along with it was you."

"Me?"

"He saw you plunging right into the middle of everything. You'd get your head beaten in, that was obvious. So he had to avoid the violence then. Which means that because of you, he got set up the next day when it really *was* dangerous, when Ender was completely alone with no one for backup."

"So why didn't you explain this before?"

"Because you were the only one besides Ender who knew I was setting him up, and I didn't really care what you thought then, and I'm not that concerned about it now."

"It was a stupid plan," said Bean.

"It was better than yours," said Petra.

"Well, I guess when you look at how it all turned out, we'll never know how stupid your plan was. But we sure know that mine was shot to hell."

Petra flashed him a brief, insincere grin. "Now, do you trust me again? Can we go back to the intimate friendship we've shared for so long?"

"You know something, Petra? All that hostility is wasted on me. In fact, it's bad aim on your part to even try it. Because I'm the best friend you've got here."

"Oh really?"

"Yes, really. Because I'm the only one of these boys who ever chose to have a girl as his commander."

She paused a moment, staring at him blankly before saying, "I got over the fact that I'm a girl a long time ago."

"But they didn't. And you know they didn't. You know that it bothers them all the time, that you're not really one of the guys. They're your friends, sure, at least Dink is, but they all like you. At the same time, there were what, a dozen girls in the whole school? And except for you, none of them were really topflight soldiers. They didn't take you seriously."

"Ender did," said Petra.

"And I do," said Bean. "The others all know what happened in the corridor, you know. It's not like it was a secret. But you know why they haven't had this conversation with you?"

"Why?"

"Because *they* all figured you were an idiot and didn't realize how close you came to getting Ender pounded into the deck. I'm the only one who had enough respect for you to realize that you would never make such a stupid mistake by accident."

"I'm supposed to be flattered?"

"You're supposed to stop treating me like the enemy. You're almost as much of an outsider in this group as I am. And when it comes down to actual combat, you need someone who'll take you as seriously as you take yourself."

"Do me no favors."

"I'm leaving now."

"About time."

"And when you think about this more and you realize I'm right, you don't have to apologize. You cried for Poke, and that makes us friends. You can trust me, and I can trust you, and that's all."

She was starting some retort as he left, but he didn't stick around long enough to hear what it was. Petra was just that way—she had to act tough. Bean didn't mind. He knew they'd said the things they needed to say.

Command School was at FleetCom, and the location of FleetCom was a closely guarded secret. The only way you ever found out where it was was to be assigned there, and very few people who had been there ever came back to Earth.

Just before arrival, the kids were briefed. FleetCom was in the wandering asteroid Eros. And as they approached, they realized that it really was *in* the asteroid. Almost nothing showed on the surface except the dock-ing station. They boarded the shuttlebug, which reminded them of school-buses, and took the five-minute ride down to the surface. There the shuttlebug slid inside what looked like a cave. A snakelike tube reached out to the bug and enclosed it completely. They got out of the shuttlebug into near-zero gravity, and a strong air current sucked them like a vacuum cleaner up into the bowels of Eros.

Bean knew at once that this place was not shaped by human hands. The tunnels were all too low—and even then, the ceilings had obviously been raised after the initial construction, since the lower walls were smooth and only the top half-meter showed tool marks. The Buggers made this, probably when they were mounting the Second Invasion. What was once their forward base was now the center of the International Fleet. Bean tried to imagine the battle required to take this place. The Buggers scuttering along the tunnels, the infantry coming in with low-power explosives to burn them out. Flashes of light. And then cleanup, dragging the Formic bodies out of the tunnels and bit by bit converting it into a human space.

This is how we got our secret technologies, thought Bean. The Buggers had gravity-generating machines. We learned how they worked and built our own, installing them in the Battle School and wherever else they were needed. But the I.F. never announced the fact, because it would have frightened people to realize how advanced their technology was.

What else did we learn from them?

Bean noticed how even the children hunched a little to walk through the tunnels. The headroom was at least two meters, and not one of the kids was nearly that tall, but the proportions were all wrong for human comfort, so the roof of the tunnels seemed oppressively low, ready to collapse. It must have been even worse when we first arrived, before the roofs were raised.

Ender would thrive here. He'd hate it, of course, because he was human. But he'd also use the place to help him get inside the minds of the Buggers who built it. Not that you could ever really understand an alien mind. But this place gave you a decent chance to try.

The boys were bunked up in two rooms; Petra had a smaller room to herself. It was even more bare here than Battle School, and they could never escape the coldness of the stone around them. On Earth, stone had always seemed solid. But in space, it seemed downright porous. There were bubble holes all through the stone, and Bean couldn't help feeling that air was leaking out all the time. Air leaking out, and cold leaking in, and perhaps something else, the larvae of the Buggers chewing like earthworms through the solid stone, crawling out of the bubble holes at night when the room was dark, crawling over their foreheads and reading their minds and . . .

He woke up, breathing heavily, his hand clutching his forehead. He hardly dared to move his hand. Had something been crawling on him?

His hand was empty.

He wanted to go back to sleep, but it was too close to reveille for him to hope for that. He lay there thinking. The nightmare was absurd—there could not possibly be any Buggers alive here. But something made him afraid. Something was bothering him, and he wasn't sure what.

He thought back to a conversation with one of the technicians who serviced the simulators. Bean's had malfunctioned during practice, so that suddenly the little points of light that represented his ships moving through three-dimensional space were no longer under his control. To his surprise, they didn't just drift on in the direction of the last orders he gave. Instead, they began to swarm, to gather, and then changed color as they shifted to be under someone else's control.

When the technician arrived to replace the chip that had blown, Bean asked him why the ships didn't just stop or keep drifting. "It's part of the simulation," the technician said. "What's being simulated here is not that you're the pilot or even the captain of these ships. You're the admiral, and so inside each ship there's a simulated captain and a simulated pilot, and so when your contact got cut off, they acted the way the real guys would act if they lost contact. See?"

"That seems like a lot of trouble to go to."

"Look, we've had a lot of time to work on these simulators," said the technician. "They're *exactly* like combat."

"Except," said Bean, "the time-lag."

The technician looked blank for a moment. "Oh, right. The time-lag. Well, that just wasn't worth programming in." And then he was gone.

It was that moment of blankness that was bothering Bean. These simulators were as perfect as they could make them, *exactly* like combat, and yet they didn't include the time-lag that came from lightspeed communications. The distances being simulated were large enough that most of the time there should be at least a slight delay between a command and its execution, and sometimes it should be several seconds. But no such delay was programmed in. All communications were being treated as instantaneous. And when Bean asked about it, his question was blown off by the teacher who first trained them on the simulators. "It's a simulation. Plenty of time to get used to the lightspeed delay when you train with the real thing."

That sounded like typically stupid military thinking even at the time, but now Bean realized it was simply a lie. If they programmed in the behavior of pilots and captains when communications were cut off, they could very easily have included the time-lag. The reason these ships were simulated with instantaneous response was because that *was* an accurate simulation of conditions they would meet in combat.

Lying awake in the darkness, Bean finally made the connection. It was so obvious, once he thought of it. It wasn't just gravity control they got from the Buggers. It was faster-than-light communication. It's a big secret from people on Earth, but our ships can talk to each other instantaneously.

And if the ships can, why not FleetCom here on Eros? What was the range of communication? Was it truly instantaneous regardless of distance, or was it merely faster than light, so that at truly great distances it began to have its own time-lag?

His mind raced through the possibilities, and the implications of those possibilities. Our patrol ships will be able to warn us of the approaching enemy fleet long before it reaches us. They've probably known for years that it was coming, and how fast. That's why we've been rushed through our training like this—they've known for years when the Third Invasion would begin.

And then another thought. If this instantaneous communication works regardless of distance, then we could even be talking to the invasion fleet we sent against the Formic home planet right after the Second Invasion. If our starships were going near lightspeed, the relative time differential would complicate communication, but as long as we're imagining miracles, that would be easy enough to solve. We'll know whether our invasion of their world succeeded or not, moments afterward. Why, if the communication is really powerful, with plenty of bandwidth, FleetCom could even watch the battle unfold, or at least watch a simulation of the battle, and . . .

A simulation of the battle. Each ship in the expeditionary force sending back its position at all times. The communications device receives that data and feeds it into a computer and what comes out is . . . the simulation we've been practicing with.

We are training to command ships in combat, not here in the solar system, but lightyears away. They sent the pilots and the captains, but the admirals who will command them are still back here. At FleetCom. They had generations to find the right commanders, and we're the ones.

It left him gasping, this realization. He hardly dared to believe it, and yet it made far better sense than any of the other more plausible scenarios. For one thing, it explained perfectly why the kids had been trained on older ships. The fleet they would be commanding had launched decades ago, when those older designs were the newest and the best.

They didn't rip us through Battle School and Tactical School because the Bugger fleet is about to reach our solar system. They're in a hurry because *our* fleet is about to reach the Buggers' world.

It was like Nikolai said. You can't rule out the impossible, because you never know which of your assumptions about what was possible might turn out, in the real universe, to be false. Bean hadn't been able to think of this simple, rational explanation because he had been locked in the box of thinking that lightspeed limited both travel *and* communication. But the technician let down just the tiniest part of the veil they had covering the truth, and because Bean finally found a way to open his mind to the possibility, he now knew the secret.

Sometime during their training, anytime at all, without the slightest warning, without ever even telling us they're doing it, they can switch over and we'll be commanding real ships in a real battle. We'll think it's a game, but we'll be fighting a war.

And they don't tell us because we're children. They think we can't handle it. Knowing that our decisions will cause death and destruction. That when we lose a ship, real men die. They're keeping it a secret to protect us from our own compassion.

Except me. Because now I know.

The weight of it suddenly came upon him and he could hardly breathe, except shallowly. Now I know. How will it change the way I play? I can't let it, that's all. I was already doing my best—knowing this won't make me work harder or play better. It might make me do worse. Might make me hesitate, might make me lose concentration. Through their training, they had all learned that winning depended on being able to forget everything but what you were doing at that moment. You could hold all your ships in your mind at once—but only if any ship that no longer matters could be blocked out completely. Thinking about dead men, about torn bodies having the air sucked out of their lungs by the cold vacuum of space, who could still play the game knowing that this was what it really meant?

The teachers were right to keep this secret from us. That technician should be court-martialed for letting me see behind the curtain.

I can't tell anyone. The other kids shouldn't know this. And if the teachers know that I know it, they'll take me out of the game.

So I have to fake it.

No. I have to disbelieve it. I have to forget that it's true. It *isn't* true.

The truth is what they've been telling us. The simulation is simply ignoring lightspeed. They trained us on old ships because the new ones are all deployed and can't be wasted. The fight we're preparing for is to repel invading Formics, not to invade their solar system. This was just a crazy dream, pure self-delusion. Nothing goes faster than light, and therefore information can't be transmitted faster than light.

Besides, if we really did send an invasion fleet that long ago, they don't need little kids to command them. Mazer Rackham must be with that fleet, no way would it have launched without him. Mazer Rackham is still alive, preserved by the relativistic changes of near-lightspeed travel. Maybe it's only been a few years to him. And he's ready. We aren't needed.

Bean calmed his breathing. His heartrate slowed. I can't let myself get carried away with fantasies like that. I would be so embarrassed if anyone knew the stupid theory I came up with in my sleep. I can't even tell this as a dream. The game is as it always was.

Reveille sounded over the intercom. Bean got out of bed—a bottom bunk, this time—and joined in as normally as possible with the banter of Crazy Tom and Hot Soup, while Fly Molo kept his morning surliness to himself and Alai did his prayers. Bean went to mess and ate as he normally ate. Everything was normal. It didn't mean a thing that he couldn't get his bowels to unclench at the normal time. That his belly gnawed at him all day, and at mealtime he was faintly nauseated. That was just lack of sleep.

Near the end of three months on Eros, their work on the simulators changed. There would be ships directly under their control, but they also had others under them to whom they had to give commands out loud, besides using the controls to enter them manually. "Like combat," said their supervisor.

"In combat," said Alai, "we'd know who the officers serving under us were."

"That would matter if you depended on them to give you information. But you do not. All the information you need is conveyed to your simulator and appears in the display. So you give your orders orally as well as manually. Just assume that you will be obeyed. Your teachers will be monitoring the orders you give to help you learn to be explicit and immediate. You will also have to master the technique of switching back and forth between crosstalk among yourselves and giving orders to individual ships. It's quite simple, you see. Turn your heads to the left or right to speak to each other, whichever is more comfortable for you. But when your face is pointing straight at the display, your voice will be carried to whatever ship or squadron you have selected with your controls. And to address all the ships under your control at once, head straight forward and duck your chin, like this.''

''What happens if we raise our heads?'' asked Shen.

Alai answered before the teacher could. ''Then you're talking to God.''

After the laughter died down, the teacher said, ''Almost right, Alai. When you raise your chin to speak, you'll be talking to *your* commander.''

Several spoke at once. ''*Our* commander?''

''You did not think we were training all of you to be supreme commander at once, did you? No no. For the moment, we will assign one of you at random to be that commander, just for practice. Let's say . . . the little one. You. Bean.''

''I'm supposed to be commander?''

''Just for the practices. Or is he not competent? You others will not obey him in battle?''

The others answered the teacher with scorn. Of course Bean was competent. Of course they'd follow him.

''But then, he never did win a battle when he commanded Rabbit Army,'' said Fly Molo.

''Excellent. That means that you will all have the challenge of making this little one a winner in spite of himself. If you do not think *that* is a realistic military situation, you have not been reading history carefully enough.''

So it was that Bean found himself in command of the ten other kids from Battle School. It was exhilarating, of course, for neither he nor the others believed for one moment that the teacher's choice had been random. They knew that Bean was better at the simulator than anybody. Petra was the one who said it after practice one day. ''Hell, Bean, I think you have this all in your head so clear you could close your eyes and still play.'' It was almost true. He did not have to keep checking to see where everyone was. It was all in his head at once.

It took a couple of days for them to handle it smoothly, taking orders from Bean and giving their own orders orally along with the physical controls. There were constant mistakes at first, heads in the wrong position so that comments and questions and orders went to the wrong destination. But soon enough it became instinctive.

Bean then insisted that others take turns being in the command position. ''I need practice taking orders just like they do,'' he said. ''And learning how to change my head position to speak up and sideways.'' The teacher agreed, and after another day, Bean had mastered the technique as well as any of the others.

Having other kids in the master seat had another good effect as well. Even though no one did so badly as to embarrass himself, it was clear that Bean was sharper and faster than anyone else, with a keener grasp of developing situations and a better ability to sort out what he was hearing and remember what everybody had said.

"You're not *human*," said Petra. "*Nobody* can do what you do!"

"Am so human," said Bean mildly. "And I know somebody who can do it better than me."

"Who's that?" she demanded.

"Ender."

They all fell silent for a moment.

"Yeah, well, he ain't here," said Vlad.

"How do *you* know?" said Bean. "For all we know, he's been here all along."

"That's stupid," said Dink. "Why wouldn't they have him practice with us? Why would they keep it a secret?"

"Because they like secrets," said Bean. "And maybe because they're giving him different training. And maybe because it's like Sinterklaas. They're going to bring him to us as a present."

"And maybe you're full of merda," said Dumper.

Bean just laughed. Of course it would be Ender. This group was assembled for Ender. Ender was the one all their hopes were resting on. The reason they put Bean in that master position was because Bean was the substitute. If Ender got appendicitis in the middle of the war, it was Bean they'd switch the controls to. Bean who'd start giving commands, deciding which ships would be sacrificed, which men would die. But until then, it would be Ender's choice, and for Ender, it would only be a game. No deaths, no suffering, no fear, no guilt. Just . . . a game.

Definitely it's Ender. And the sooner the better.

The next day, their supervisor told them that Ender Wiggin was going to be their commander starting that afternoon. When they didn't act surprised, he asked why. "Because Bean already told us."

"They want me to find out how you've been getting your inside information, Bean." Graff looked across the table at the painfully small child who sat there looking at him without expression.

"I don't have any inside information," said Bean.

"You knew that Ender was going to be the commander."

"I *guessed,*" said Bean. "Not that it was hard. Look at who we are. Ender's closest friends. Ender's toon leaders. He's the common thread. There were plenty of other kids you could have brought here, probably about as good as us. But these are the ones who'd follow Ender straight into space without a suit, if he told us he needed us to do it."

"Nice speech, but you have a history of sneaking."

"Right. *When* would I be doing this sneaking? When are any of us alone? Our desks are just dumb terminals and we never get to see anybody else log on so it's not like I can capture another identity. I just do what I'm told all day every day. You guys keep assuming that we kids are stupid, even though you chose us because we're really, really smart. And now you sit there and accuse me of having to *steal* information that any idiot could guess."

"Not *any* idiot."

"That was just an expression."

"Bean," said Graff, "I think you're feeding me a line of complete bullshit."

"Colonel Graff, even if that were true, which it isn't, so what? So I found out Ender was coming. I'm secretly monitoring your dreams. So *what?* He'll still come, he'll be in command, he'll be brilliant, and then we'll all graduate and I'll sit in a booster seat in a ship somewhere and give commands to grownups in my little-boy voice until they get sick of hearing me and throw me out into space."

"I don't care about the fact that you knew about Ender. I don't care that it was a guess."

"I know you don't care about those things."

"I need to know what else you've figured out."

"Colonel," said Bean, sounding very tired, "doesn't it occur to you that the very fact that you're asking me this question *tells* me there's something else for me to figure out, and therefore greatly increases the chance that I *will* figure it out?"

Graff's smile grew even broader. "That's just what I told the . . . officer who assigned me to talk to you and ask these questions. I told him that we would end up telling you more, just by having the interview, than you would ever tell us, but he said, 'The kid is *six,* Colonel Graff.' "

"I think I'm seven."

"He was working from an old report and hadn't done the math."

"Just tell me what secret you want to make sure I don't know, and I'll tell you if I already knew it."

"Very helpful."

"Colonel Graff, am I doing a good job?"

"Absurd question. Of course you are."

"If I do know anything that you don't want us kids to know, have I talked about it? Have I told any of the other kids? Has it affected my performance in any way?"

"No."

"To me that sounds like a tree falling in the forest where no one can hear. If I *do* know something, because I figured it out, but I'm not telling anybody else, and it's not affecting my work, then why would you waste time finding out whether I know it? Because after this conversation, you may be sure that I'll be looking very hard for any secret that might be lying around where a seven-year-old might find it. Even if I do find such a secret, though, I *still* won't tell the other kids, so it *still* won't make a difference. So why don't we just drop it?"

Graff reached under the table and pressed something.

"All right," said Graff. "They've got the recording of our conversation and if that doesn't reassure them, nothing will."

"Reassure them of what? And who is 'them'?"

"Bean, this part is not being recorded."

"Yes it is," said Bean.

"I turned it off."

"Puh-leeze."

In fact, Graff was not altogether sure that the recording *was* off. Even if the machine he controlled was off, that didn't mean there wasn't another.

"Let's walk," said Graff.

"I hope not outside."

Graff got up from the table—laboriously, because he'd put on a lot of weight and they kept Eros at full gravity—and led the way out into the tunnels.

As they walked, Graff talked softly. "Let's at least make them work for it," he said.

"Fine," said Bean.

"I thought you'd want to know that the I.F. is going crazy because of an apparent security leak. It seems that someone with access to the most secret archives wrote letters to a couple of net pundits who then started agitating for the children of Battle School to be sent home to their native countries."

"What's a pundit?" asked Bean.

"My turn to say puh-leeze, I think. Look, I'm not accusing you. I just happen to have seen a text of the letters sent to Locke and Demosthenes—they're both being closely watched, as I'm sure you would expect—and when I read those letters—interesting the differences between them, by the way, very cleverly done—I realized that there was not really any top secret information in there, beyond what any child in Battle School knows. No, the thing that's really making them crazy is that the political analysis is dead on, even though it's based on insufficient information. From what is publicly known, in other words, the writer of those letters couldn't have figured out what he figured out. The Russians are claiming that somebody's been spying on them—and lying about what they found, of course. But I accessed the library on the destroyer *Condor* and found out what you were reading. And then I checked your library use on the ISL while you were in Tactical School. You've been a busy boy."

"I try to keep my mind occupied."

"You'll be happy to know that the first group of children has already been sent home."

"But the war's not over."

"You think that when you start a political snowball rolling, it will always go where you wanted it to go? You're smart but you're naive, Bean. Give the universe a push, and you don't know which dominoes will fall. There are always a few you never thought were connected. Someone will always push back a little harder than you expected. But still, I'm happy that you remembered the other children and set the wheels in motion to free them."

"But not us."

"The I.F. has no obligation to remind the agitators on Earth that Tactical School and Command School are still full of children."

"I'm not going to remind them."

"I know you won't. No, Bean, I got a chance to talk to you because you panicked some of the higher-ups with your educated guess about who would command your team. But I was hoping for a chance to talk to you because there are a couple of things I wanted to tell you. Besides the fact that your letter had pretty much the desired effect."

"I'm listening, though I admit to no letter."

"First, you'll be fascinated to know the identity of Locke and Demosthenes."

"Identity? Just one?"

"One mind, two voices. You see, Bean, Ender Wiggin was born third in his family. A special waiver, not an illegal birth. His older brother and sister are just as gifted as he is, but for various reasons were deemed inappropriate for Battle School. But the brother, Peter Wiggin, is a very ambitious young man. With the military closed off to him, he's gone into politics. Twice.''

"He's Locke *and* Demosthenes," said Bean.

"He plans the strategy for both of them, but he only writes Locke. His sister Valentine writes Demosthenes."

Bean laughed. "Now it makes sense."

"So both your letters went to the same people."

"If I wrote them."

"And it's driving poor Peter Wiggin crazy. He's really tapping into all his sources inside the fleet to find out who sent those letters. But nobody in the Fleet knows, either. The six officers whose log-ins you used have been ruled out. And as you can guess, *nobody* is checking to see if the only seven-year-old ever to go to Tactical School might have dabbled in political epistolary in his spare time."

"Except you."

"Because, by God, I'm the only person who understands exactly how brilliant you children actually are."

"How brilliant are we?" Bean grinned.

"Our walk won't last forever, and I won't waste time on flattery. The other thing I wanted to tell you is that Sister Carlotta, being unemployed after you left, devoted a lot of effort to tracking down your parentage. I can see two officers approaching us right now who will put an end to this unrecorded conversation, and so I'll be brief. You have a name, Bean. You are Julian Delphiki."

"That's Nikolai's last name."

"Julian is the name of Nikolai's father. And of your father. Your mother's name is Elena. You are identical twins. Your fertilized eggs were implanted at different times, and your genes were altered in one very small but significant way. So when you look at Nikolai, you see yourself as you would have been, had you not been genetically altered, and had you grown up with parents who loved you and cared for you."

"Julian Delphiki," said Bean.

"Nikolai is among those already heading for Earth. Sister Carlotta will see to it that, when he is repatriated to Greece, he is informed that you are indeed his brother. His parents already know that you exist—Sister Carlotta told them. Your home is a lovely place, a house on the hills of Crete overlooking the Aegean. Sister Carlotta tells me that they are good people, your parents. They wept with joy when they learned that you exist. And now our interview is coming to an end. We were discussing your low opinion of the quality of teaching here at Command School.''

"How did you guess."

"You're not the only one who can do that."

The two officers—an admiral and a general, both wearing big false smiles—greeted them and asked how the interview had gone.

"You have the recording," said Graff. "Including the part where Bean insisted that it was still being recorded."

"And yet the interview continued."

"I was telling him," said Bean, "about the incompetence of the teachers here at Command School."

"Incompetence?"

"Our battles are always against exceptionally stupid computer opponents. And then the teachers insist on going through long, tedious analyses of these mock combats, even though no enemy could possibly behave as stupidly and predictably as these simulations do. I was suggesting that the only way for us to get decent competition here is if you divide us into two groups and have us fight each other."

The two officers looked at each other. "Interesting point," said the general.

"Moot," said the admiral. "Ender Wiggin is about to be introduced into your game. We thought you'd want to be there to greet him."

"Yes," said Bean. "I do."

"I'll take you," said the admiral.

"Let's talk," the general said to Graff.

On the way, the admiral said little, and Bean could answer his chat without thought. It was a good thing. For he was in turmoil over the things that Graff had told him. It was almost not a surprise that Locke and Demosthenes were Ender's siblings. If they were as intelligent as Ender, it was inevitable that they would rise into prominence, and the nets allowed them to conceal their identity enough to accomplish it while they were still young. But part of the reason Bean was drawn to them had to be the sheer familiarity of their voices. They must have sounded like Ender, in that subtle way in which people who have lived long together pick up nuances of speech from each other. Bean didn't realize it consciously, but unconsciously it would have made him more alert to those essays. He should have known, and at some level he did know.

But the other, that Nikolai was really his brother—how could he believe that? It was as if Graff had read his heart and found the lie that would penetrate most deeply into his soul and told it to him. I'm Greek? My brother happened to be in my launch group, the boy who became my dearest friend? Twins? Parents who love me?

Julian Delphiki?

No, I can't believe this. Graff has never dealt honestly with us. Graff was the one who did not lift a finger to protect Ender from Bonzo. Graff does nothing except to accomplish some manipulative purpose.

My name is Bean. Poke gave me that name, and I won't give it up in exchange for a lie.

They heard his voice, first, talking to a technician in another room. "How can I work with squadron leaders I never see?"

"And why would you need to see them?" asked the technician.

"To know who they are, how they think—"

"You'll learn who they are and how they think from the way they work with the simulator. But even so, I think you won't be concerned. They're listening to you right now. Put on the headset so you can hear them."

They all trembled with excitement, knowing that he would soon hear their voices as they now heard his.

"Somebody say something," said Petra.

"Wait till he gets the headset on," said Dink.

"How will we know?" asked Vlad.

"Me first," said Alai.

A pause. A new faint hiss in their earphones.

"Salaam," Alai whispered.

"Alai," said Ender.

"And me," said Bean. "The dwarf."

"Bean," said Ender.

Yes, thought Bean, as the others talked to him. That's who I am. That's the name that is spoken by the people who know me.

23

ENDER'S GAME

"General, you are the Strategos. You have the authority to do this, and you have the obligation."

"I don't need disgraced former Battle School commandants to tell me my obligations."

"If you do not arrest the Polemarch and his conspirators—"

"Colonel Graff, if I *do* strike first, then I will bear the blame for the war that ensues."

"Yes, you would, sir. Now tell me, which would be the better outcome—everybody blames you, but we win the war, or nobody blames you, because you've been stood up against a wall and shot after the Polemarch's coup results in worldwide Russian hegemony?"

"I will not fire the first shot."

"A military commander not willing to strike preemptively when he has firm intelligence—"

"The politics of the thing—"

"If you let them win it's the end of politics!"

"The Russians stopped being the bad guys back in the twentieth century!"

"Whoever is doing the bad things, that's the bad guy. You're the sheriff, sir, whether people approve of you or not. Do your job."

With Ender there, Bean immediately stepped back into his place among the toon leaders. No one mentioned it to him. He had been the leading commander, he had trained them well, but Ender had always been the natural commander of this group, and now that he was here, Bean was small again.

And rightly so, Bean knew. He had led them well, but Ender made him look like a novice. It wasn't that Ender's strategies were better than Bean's—they weren't, really. Different sometimes, but more often Bean watched Ender do exactly what he would have done.

The important difference was in the way he led the others. He had their fierce devotion instead of the ever-so-slightly-resentful obedience Bean got from them, which helped from the start. But he also earned that devotion by noticing, not just what was going on in the battle, but what was going on in his commanders' minds. He was stern, sometimes even snappish, making it clear that he expected better than their best. And yet he had a way of giving an intonation to innocuous words, showing appreciation, admiration, closeness. They felt known by the one whose honor they needed. Bean simply did not know how to do that. His encouragement was always more obvious, a bit heavy-handed. It meant less to them because it felt more calculated. It *was* more calculated. Ender was just . . . himself. Authority came from him like breath.

They flipped a genetic switch in me and made me an intellectual athlete. I can get the ball into the goal from anywhere on the field. But knowing *when* to kick. Knowing how to forge a team out of a bunch of players. What switch was it that was flipped in Ender Wiggin's genes? Or is that something deeper than the mechanical genius of the body? Is there a spirit, and is what Ender has a gift from God? We follow him like disciples. We look to him to draw water from the rock.

Can I learn to do what he does? Or am I to be like so many of the military writers I've studied, condemned to be second-raters in the field, remembered only because of their chronicles and explanations of other commanders' genius? Will I write a book after this, telling all about how Ender did it?

Let Ender write that book. Or Graff. I have work to do here, and when it's done, I'll choose my own work and do it as well as I can. If I'm remembered only because I was one of Ender's companions, so be it. Serving with Ender is its own reward.

But ah, how it stung to see how happy the others were, and how they paid no attention to him at all, except to tease him like a little brother, like a mascot. How they must have hated it when he was their leader.

And the worst thing was, that's how Ender treated him, too. Not that any of them were ever allowed to see Ender. But during their long separation, Ender had apparently forgotten how he once relied on Bean. It was

Petra that he leaned on most, and Alai, and Dink, and Shen. The ones who had never been in an army with him. Bean and the other toon leaders from Dragon Army were still used, still trusted, but when there was something hard to do, something that required creative flair, Ender never thought of Bean.

Didn't matter. Couldn't think about that. Because Bean knew that along with his primary assignment as one of the squadron chiefs, he had another, deeper work to do. He had to watch the whole flow of each battle, ready to step in at any moment, should Ender falter. Ender seemed not to guess that Bean had that kind of trust from the teachers, but Bean knew it, and if sometimes it made him a little distracted in fulfilling his official assignments, if sometimes Ender grew impatient with him for being a little late, a little inattentive, that was to be expected. For what Ender did not know was that at any moment, if the supervisor signaled him, Bean could take over and continue Ender's plan, watching over all of the squadron leaders, saving the game.

At first, that assignment seemed empty—Ender was healthy, alert. But then came the change.

It was the day after Ender mentioned to them, casually, that he had a different teacher from theirs. He referred to him as "Mazer" once too often, and Crazy Tom said, "He must have gone through hell, growing up with that name."

"When he was growing up," said Ender, "the name wasn't famous."

"Anybody that old is dead," said Shen.

"Not if he was put on a lightspeed ship for a lot of years and then brought back."

That's when it dawned on them. "Your teacher is *the* Mazer Rackham?"

"You know how they say he's a brilliant hero?" said Ender.

Of course they knew.

"What they don't mention is, he's a complete hard-ass."

And then the new simulation began and they got back to work.

Next day, Ender told them that things were changing. "So far we've been playing against the computer or against each other. But starting now, every few days Mazer himself and a team of experienced pilots will control the opposing fleet. Anything goes."

A series of tests, with Mazer Rackham himself as the opponent. It smelled fishy to Bean.

These aren't tests, these are setups, preparations for the conditions that might come when they face the actual Bugger fleet near their home planet.

The I.F. is getting preliminary information back from the expeditionary fleet, and they're preparing us for what the Buggers are actually going to throw at us when battle is joined.

The trouble was, no matter how bright Mazer Rackham and the other officers might be, they were still human. When the real battle came, the Buggers were bound to show them things that humans simply couldn't think of.

Then came the first of these "tests"—and it was embarrassing how juvenile the strategy was. A big globe formation, surrounding a single ship.

In this battle it became clear that Ender knew things that he wasn't telling them. For one thing, he told them to ignore the ship in the center of the globe. It was a decoy. But how could Ender know that? Because he knew that the Buggers would *show* a single ship like that, and it was a lie. Which means that the Buggers expect us to go for that one ship.

Except, of course, that this was not really the Buggers, this was Mazer Rackham. So why would Rackham expect the Buggers to expect humans to strike for a single ship?

Bean thought back to those vids that Ender had watched over and over in Battle School—all the propaganda film of the Second Invasion.

They never showed the battle because there wasn't one. Nor did Mazer Rackham command a strike force with a brilliant strategy. Mazer Rackham hit a single ship and the war was over. That's why there's no video of hand-to-hand combat. Mazer Rackham killed the queen. And now he expects the Buggers to show a central ship as a decoy, because that's how we won last time.

Kill the queen, and all the Buggers are defenseless. Mindless. That's what the vids meant. Ender knows that, but he also knows that the Buggers know that we know it, so he doesn't fall for their sucker bait.

The second thing that Ender knew and they didn't was the use of a weapon that hadn't been in any of their simulations till this first test. Ender called it "Dr. Device" and then said nothing more about it—until he ordered Alai to use it where the enemy fleet was most concentrated. To their surprise, the thing set off a chain reaction that leapt from ship to ship, until all but the most outlying Formic ships were destroyed. And it was an easy matter to mop up those stragglers. The playing field was clear when they finished.

"Why was their strategy so stupid?" asked Bean.

"That's what I was wondering," said Ender. "But we didn't lose a ship, so that's OK."

Later, Ender told them what Mazer said—they were simulating a whole invasion sequence, and so he was taking the simulated enemy through a learning curve. "Next time they'll have learned. It won't be so easy."

Bean heard that and it filled him with alarm. An invasion sequence? Why a scenario like that? Why not warmups before a single battle?

Because the Buggers have more than one world, thought Bean. Of course they do. They found Earth and expected to turn it into yet another colony, just as they've done before.

We have more than one fleet. One for each Formic world.

And the reason they can learn from battle to battle is because they, too, have faster-than-light communication across interstellar space.

All of Bean's guesses were confirmed. He also knew the secret behind these tests. Mazer Rackham wasn't commanding a simulated Bugger fleet. It was a real battle, and Rackham's only function was to watch how it flowed and then coach Ender afterward on what the enemy strategies meant and how to counter them in future.

That was why they were giving most of their commands orally. They were being transmitted to real crews of real ships who followed their orders and fought real battles. Any ship we lose, thought Bean, means that grown men and women have died. Any carelessness on our part takes lives. Yet they don't tell us this precisely because we can't afford to be burdened with that knowledge. In wartime, commanders have always had to learn the concept of "acceptable losses." But those who keep their humanity never really accept the idea of acceptability, Bean understood that. It gnaws at them. So they protect us child-soldiers by keeping us convinced that it's only games and tests.

Therefore I can't let on to anyone that I do know. Therefore I must accept the losses without a word, without a visible qualm. I must try to block out of my mind the people who will die from our boldness, whose sacrifice is not of a mere counter in a game, but of their lives.

The "tests" came every few days, and each battle lasted longer. Alai joked that they ought to be fitted with diapers so they didn't have to be distracted when their bladder got full during a battle. Next day, they were fitted out with catheters. It was Crazy Tom who put a stop to that. "Come on, just get us a jar to pee in. We can't play this game with something hanging off our dicks." Jars it was, after that. Bean never heard of anyone using one, though. And though he wondered what they provided for Petra, no one ever had the courage to brave her wrath by asking.

Bean began to notice some of Ender's mistakes pretty early on. For one thing, Ender was relying too much on Petra. She always got command of the core force, watching a hundred different things at once, so that Ender could concentrate on the feints, the ploys, the tricks. Couldn't Ender see that Petra, a perfectionist, was getting eaten alive by guilt and shame over every mistake she made? He was so good with people, and yet he seemed to think she was really tough, instead of realizing that toughness was an act she put on to hide her intense anxiety. Every mistake weighed on her. She wasn't sleeping well, and it showed up as she got more and more fatigued during battles.

But then, maybe the reason Ender didn't realize what he was doing to her was that he, too, was tired. So were all of them. Fading a little under the pressure, and sometimes a lot. Getting more fatigued, more error-prone as the tests got harder, as the odds got longer.

Because the battles were harder with each new "test," Ender was forced to leave more and more decisions up to others. Instead of smoothly carrying out Ender's detailed commands, the squadron leaders had more and more of the battle to carry on their own shoulders. For long sequences, Ender was too busy in one part of the battle to give new orders in another. The squadron leaders who were affected began to use crosstalk to determine their tactics until Ender noticed them again. And Bean was grateful to find that, while Ender never gave him the interesting assignments, some of the others talked to him when Ender's attention was elsewhere. Crazy Tom and Hot Soup came up with their own plans, but they routinely ran them past Bean. And since, in each battle, he was spending half his attention observing and analyzing Ender's plan, Bean was able to tell them, with pretty good accuracy, what they should do to help make the overall plan work out. Now and then Ender praised Tom or Soup for decisions that came from Bean's advice. It was the closest thing to praise that Bean heard.

The other toon leaders and the older kids simply didn't turn to Bean at all. He understood why; they must have resented it greatly when the teachers placed Bean above them during the time before Ender was brought in. Now that they had their true commander, they were never again going to do anything that smacked of subservience to Bean. He understood—but that didn't keep it from stinging.

Whether or not they wanted him to oversee their work, whether or not his feelings were hurt, that was still his assignment and he was determined never to be caught unprepared. As the pressure became more and more intense, as they became wearier and wearier, more irritable with each other, less generous in their assessment of each other's work, Bean became all the more attentive because the chances of error were all the greater.

One day Petra fell asleep during battle. She had let her force drift too far into a vulnerable position, and the enemy took advantage, tearing her squadron to bits. Why didn't she give the order to fall back? Worse yet, Ender didn't notice soon enough, either. It was Bean who told him: Something's wrong with Petra.

Ender called out to her. She didn't answer. Ender flipped control of her two remaining ships to Crazy Tom and then tried to salvage the overall battle. Petra had, as usual, occupied the core position, and the loss of most of her large squadron was a devastating blow. Only because the enemy was overconfident during mop-up was Ender able to lay a couple of traps and regain the initiative. He won, but with heavy losses.

Petra apparently woke up near the end of the battle and found her controls cut off, with no voice until it was all over. Then her microphone came on again and they could hear her crying, "I'm sorry, I'm sorry. Tell Ender I'm sorry, he can't hear me, I'm so sorry . . ."

Bean got to her before she could return to her room. She was staggering along the tunnel, leaning against the wall and crying, using her hands to find her way because she couldn't see through her tears. Bean came up and touched her. She shrugged off his hand.

"Petra," said Bean. "Fatigue is fatigue. You can't stay awake when your brain shuts down."

"It was *my* brain that shut down! You don't know how that feels because you're always so smart you could do all our jobs and play chess while you're doing it!"

"Petra, he was relying on you too much, he never gave you a break—"

"He doesn't take breaks either, and I don't see him—"

"Yes you *do*. It was obvious there was something wrong with your squadron for several seconds before somebody called his attention to it. And even then, he tried to rouse you before assigning control to somebody else. If he'd acted faster you would have had six ships left, not just two."

"*You* pointed it out to him. You were watching me. Checking up on me."

"Petra, I watch everybody."

"You said you'd trust me, but you don't. And you shouldn't, nobody should trust me."

She broke into uncontrollable sobbing, leaning against the stone of the wall.

A couple of officers showed up then, led her away. Not to her room.

Graff called him in soon afterward. "You handled it just right," said Graff. "That's what you're there for."

"I wasn't quick either," said Bean.

"You were watching. You saw where the plan was breaking down, you called Ender's attention to it. You did your job. The other kids don't realize it and I know that has to gall you—"

"I don't care what they notice—"

"But you did the job. On that battle you get the save."

"Whatever the hell that means."

"It's baseball. Oh yeah. That wasn't big on the streets of Rotterdam."

"Can I please go sleep now?"

"In a minute. Bean, Ender's getting tired. He's making mistakes. It's all the more important that you watch everything. Be there for him. You saw how Petra was."

"We're all getting fatigued."

"Well, so is Ender. Worse than anyone. He cries in his sleep. He has strange dreams. He's talking about how Mazer seems to know what he's planning, spying on his dreams."

"You telling me he's going crazy?"

"I'm telling you that the only person he pushed harder than Petra is himself. Cover for him, Bean. Back him up."

"I already am."

"You're angry all the time, Bean."

Graff's words startled him. At first he thought, No I'm not! Then he thought, Am I?

"Ender isn't using you for anything important, and after having run the show that has to piss you off, Bean. But it's not Ender's fault. Mazer has been telling Ender that he has doubts about your ability to handle large numbers of ships. That's why you haven't been getting the complicated, interesting assignments. Not that Ender takes Mazer's word for it. But everything you do, Ender sees it through the lens of Mazer's lack of confidence."

"Mazer Rackham thinks I—"

"Mazer Rackham knows exactly what you are and what you can do. But we had to make sure Ender didn't assign you something so complicated you couldn't keep track of the overall flow of the game. And we had to do it without telling Ender you're his backup."

"So why are you telling me this?"

"When this test is over and you go on to real commands, we'll tell Ender the truth about what you were doing, and why Mazer said what he said. I know it means a lot to you to have Ender's confidence, and you don't feel like you have it, and so I wanted you to know why. We did it."

"Why this sudden bout of honesty?"

"Because I think you'll do better knowing it."

"I'll do better *believing* it whether it's true or not. You could be lying. So do I really know anything at all from this conversation?"

"Believe what you want, Bean."

Petra didn't come to practice for a couple of days. When she came back, of course Ender didn't give her the heavy assignments anymore. She did well at the assignments she had, but her ebullience was gone. Her heart was broken.

But dammit, she had *slept* for a couple of days. They were all just the tiniest bit jealous of her for that, even though they'd never willingly trade places with her. Whether they had any particular god in mind, they all prayed: Let it not happen to me. Yet at the same time they also prayed the opposite prayer: Oh, let me sleep, let me have a day in which I don't have to think about this game.

The tests went on. How many worlds did these bastards colonize before they got to Earth? Bean wondered. And are we sure we have them all? And what good does it do to destroy their fleets when we don't have the forces there to occupy the defeated colonies? Or do we just leave our ships there, shooting down anything that tries to boost from the surface of the planet?

Petra wasn't the only one to blow out. Vlad went catatonic and couldn't be roused from his bunk. It took three days for the doctors to get him awake again, and unlike Petra, he was out for the duration. He just couldn't concentrate.

Bean kept waiting for Crazy Tom to follow suit, but despite his nickname, he actually seemed to get saner as he got wearier. Instead it was Fly Molo who started laughing when he lost control of his squadron. Ender cut him off immediately, and for once he put Bean in charge of Fly's ships. Fly was back the next day, no explanation, but everyone understood that he wouldn't be given crucial assignments now.

And Bean became more and more aware of Ender's decreasing alertness. His orders came after longer and longer pauses now, and a couple of times his orders weren't clearly stated. Bean immediately translated them into a more comprehensible form, and Ender never knew there had been confusion. But the others were finally becoming aware that Bean was following the whole battle, not just his part of it. Perhaps they even saw how Bean would ask a question during a battle, make some comment that alerted Ender to something that he needed to be aware of, but never in a way that sounded like Bean was criticizing anybody. After the battles one or two of the older kids would speak to Bean. Nothing major. Just a hand on his shoulder, on his back, and a couple of words. "Good game." "Good work." "Keep it up." "Thanks, Bean."

He hadn't realized how much he needed the honor of others until he finally got it.

"Bean, this next game, I think you should know something."

"What?"

Colonel Graff hesitated. "We couldn't get Ender awake this morning. He's been having nightmares. He doesn't eat unless we make him. He bites his hand in his sleep—bites it bloody. And today we couldn't get him to wake up. We were able to hold off on the . . . test . . . so he's going to be in command, as usual, but . . . not as usual."

"I'm ready. I always am."

"Yeah, but . . . look, advance word on this test is that it's . . . there's no . . ."

"It's hopeless."

"Anything you can do to help. Any suggestion."

"This Dr. Device thing, Ender hasn't let us use it in a long time."

"The enemy learned enough about how it works that they never let their ships get close enough together for a chain reaction to spread. It takes a certain amount of mass to be able to maintain the field. Basically, right now it's just ballast. Useless."

"It would have been nice if you'd told *me* how it works before now."

"There are people who don't want us to tell you anything, Bean. You have a way of using every scrap of information to guess ten times more than we want you to know. It makes them a little leery of giving you those scraps in the first place."

"Colonel Graff, you know that I know that these battles are real. Mazer Rackham isn't making them up. When we lose ships, real men die."

Graff looked away.

"And these are men that Mazer Rackham knows, neh?"

Graff nodded slightly.

"You don't think Ender can sense what Mazer is feeling? I don't know the guy, maybe he's like a rock, but *I* think that when he does his critiques with Ender, he's letting his . . . what, his anguish . . . Ender feels it. Because Ender is a lot more tired *after* a critique than before it. He may not know what's really going on, but he knows that something terrible is at stake. He knows that Mazer Rackham is really upset with every mistake Ender makes."

"Have you found some way to sneak into Ender's room?"

"I know how to listen to Ender. I'm not wrong about Mazer, am I?"

Graff shook his head.

"Colonel Graff, what you don't realize, what nobody seems to remember—that last game in Battle School, where Ender turned his army over to me. That wasn't a strategy. He was quitting. He was through. He was on strike. You didn't find that out because you graduated him. The thing with Bonzo finished him. I think Mazer Rackham's anguish is doing the same thing to him now. I think even when Ender doesn't *consciously* know that he's killed somebody, he knows it deep down, and it burns in his heart."

Graff looked at him sharply.

"I know Bonzo was dead. I saw him. I've seen death before, remember? You don't get your nose jammed into your brain and lose two gallons of blood and get up and walk away. You never told Ender that Bonzo was dead, but you're a fool if you think he doesn't know. And he knows, thanks to Mazer, that every ship we've lost means good men are dead. He can't stand it, Colonel Graff."

"You're more insightful than you get credit for, Bean," said Graff.

"I know, I'm the cold inhuman intellect, right?" Bean laughed bitterly. "Genetically altered, therefore I'm just as alien as the Buggers."

Graff blushed. "No one's ever said that."

"You mean you've never said it in front of me. Knowingly. What you don't seem to understand is, sometimes you have to just tell people the truth and ask them to do the thing you want, instead of trying to trick them into it."

"Are you saying we should tell Ender the game is real?"

"No! Are you insane? If he's this upset when the knowledge is unconscious, what do you think would happen if he *knew* that he knew? He'd freeze up."

"But you don't freeze up. Is that it? You should command this next battle?"

"You still don't get it, Colonel Graff. I don't freeze up because it isn't my battle. I'm helping. I'm watching. But I'm free. Because it's Ender's game."

Bean's simulator came to life.

"It's time," said Graff. "Good luck."

"Colonel Graff, Ender may go on strike again. He may walk out on it. He might give up. He might tell himself, It's only a game and I'm sick of it, I don't care what they do to me, I'm done. That's in him, to do that. When it seems completely unfair and utterly pointless.''

"What if I promised him it was the last one?"

Bean put on his headset as he asked, "Would it be true?"

Graff nodded.

"Yeah, well, I don't think it would make much difference. Besides, he's Mazer's student now, isn't he?"

"I guess. Mazer was talking about telling him that it was the final exam.''

"Mazer is Ender's teacher now," Bean mused. "And you're left with me. The kid you didn't want."

Graff blushed again. "That's right," he said. "Since you seem to know everything. I didn't want you."

Even though Bean already knew it, the words still hurt.

"But Bean," said Graff, "the thing is, I was wrong." He put a hand on Bean's shoulder and left the room.

Bean logged on. He was the last of the squadron leaders to do so.

"Are you there?" asked Ender over the headsets.

"All of us," said Bean. "Kind of late for practice this morning, aren't you?"

"Sorry," said Ender. "I overslept."

They laughed. Except Bean.

Ender took them through some maneuvers, warming up for the battle. And then it was time. The display cleared.

Bean waited, anxiety gnawing at his gut.

The enemy appeared in the display.

Their fleet was deployed around a planet that loomed in the center of the display. There had been battles near planets before, but every other time, the world was near the edge of the display—the enemy fleet always tried to lure them away from the planet.

This time there was no luring. Just the most incredible swarm of enemy ships imaginable. Always staying a certain distance away from each other, thousands and thousands of ships followed random, unpredictable, intertwining paths, together forming a cloud of death around the planet.

This is the home planet, thought Bean. He almost said it aloud, but caught himself in time. This is a *simulation* of the Bugger defense of their home planet.

They've had generations to prepare for us to come. All the previous battles were nothing. These Formics can lose any number of individual Buggers and they don't care. All that matters is the queen. Like the one

Mazer Rackham killed in the Second Invasion. And they haven't put a queen at risk in any of these battles. Until now.

That's why they're swarming. There's a queen here.

Where?

On the planet surface, thought Bean. The idea is to keep us from getting to the planet surface.

So that's precisely where we need to go. Dr. Device needs mass. Planets have mass. Pretty simple.

Except that there was no way to get this small force of human ships through that swarm and near enough to the planet to deploy Dr. Device. For if there was anything that history taught, it was this: Sometimes the other side is irresistibly strong, and then the only sensible course of action is to retreat in order to save your force to fight another day.

In this war, however, there would be no other day. There was no hope of retreat. The decisions that lost this battle, and therefore this war, were made two generations ago when these ships were launched, an inadequate force from the start. The commanders who set this fleet in motion may not even have known, then, that this was the Buggers' home world. It was no one's fault. They simply didn't have enough of a force even to make a dent in the enemy's defenses. It didn't matter how brilliant Ender was. When you have only one guy with a shovel, you can't build a dike to hold back the sea.

No retreat, no possibility of victory, no room for delay or maneuver, no reason for the enemy to do anything but continue to do what they were doing.

There were only twenty starships in the human fleet, each with four fighters. And they were the oldest design, sluggish compared to some of the fighters they'd had in earlier battles. It made sense—the Bugger home world was probably the farthest away, so the fleet that got there now had left before any of the other fleets. Before the better ships came on line.

Eighty fighters. Against five thousand, maybe ten thousand enemy ships. It was impossible to determine the number. Bean saw how the display kept losing track of individual enemy ships, how the total count kept fluctuating. There were so many it was overloading the system. They kept winking in and out like fireflies.

A long time passed—many seconds, perhaps a minute. By now Ender usually had them all deployed, ready to move. But still there was nothing from him but silence.

A light blinked on Bean's console. He knew what it meant. All he had to do was press a button, and control of the battle would be his. They were offering it to him, because they thought that Ender had frozen up.

He hasn't frozen up, thought Bean. He hasn't panicked. He has simply understood the situation, exactly as I understand it. There *is* no strategy. Only he doesn't see that this is simply the fortunes of war, a disaster that can't be helped. What he sees is a test set before him by his teachers, by Mazer Rackham, a test so absurdly unfair that the only reasonable course of action is to refuse to take it.

They were so clever, keeping the truth from him all this time. But now was it going to backfire on them. If Ender understood that it was not a game, that the real war had come down to this moment, then he might make some desperate effort, or with his genius he might even come up with an answer to a problem that, as far as Bean could see, had no solution. But Ender did not understand the reality, and so to him it was like that day in the battleroom, facing two armies, when Ender turned the whole thing over to Bean and, in effect, refused to play.

For a moment Bean was tempted to scream the truth. It's not a game, it's the real thing, this is the last battle, we've lost this war after all! But what would be gained by that, except to panic everyone?

Yet it was absurd to even contemplate pressing that button to take over control himself. Ender hadn't collapsed or failed. The battle was unwinnable; it should not even be fought. The lives of the men on those ships were not to be wasted on such a hopeless Charge of the Light Brigade. I'm not General Burnside at Fredericksburg. I don't send my men off to senseless, hopeless, meaningless death.

If I had a plan, I'd take control. I have no plan. So for good or ill, it's Ender's game, not mine.

And there was another reason for not taking over.

Bean remembered standing over the supine body of a bully who was too dangerous to ever be tamed, telling Poke, Kill him now, kill him.

I was right. And now, once again, the bully must be killed. Even though I don't know how to do it, we *can't* lose this war. I don't know how to win it, but I'm not God, I don't see everything. And maybe Ender doesn't *see* a solution either, but if anyone can find one, if anyone can make it happen, it's Ender.

Maybe it isn't hopeless. Maybe there's some way to get down to the planet's surface and wipe the Buggers out of the universe. Now is the time for miracles. For Ender, the others will do their best work. If I took over, they'd be so upset, so distracted that even if I came up with a plan that had some kind of chance, it would never work because their hearts wouldn't be in it.

Ender has to try. If he doesn't, we all die. Because even if they weren't going to send another fleet against us, after this they'll *have* to send one. Because we beat all their fleets in every battle till now. If we don't win this one, with finality, destroying their capability to make war against us, then they'll be back. And this time they'll have figured out how to make Dr. Device themselves.

We have only the one world. We have only the one hope.

Do it, Ender.

There flashed into Bean's mind the words Ender said in their first day of training as Dragon Army: Remember, the enemy's gate is down. In Dragon Army's last battle, when there was no hope, that was the strategy that Ender had used, sending Bean's squad to press their helmets against the floor around the gate and win. Too bad there was no such cheat available now.

Deploying Dr. Device against the planet's surface to blow the whole thing up, that might do the trick. You just couldn't get there from here.

It was time to give up. Time to get out of the game, to tell them not to send children to do grownups' work. It's hopeless. We're done.

"Remember," Bean said ironically, "the enemy's gate is down."

Fly Molo, Hot Soup, Vlad, Dumper, Crazy Tom—they grimly laughed. They had been in Dragon Army. They remembered how those words were used before.

But Ender didn't seem to get the joke.

Ender didn't seem to understand that there was no way to get Dr. Device to the planet's surface.

Instead, his voice came into their ears, giving them orders. He pulled them into a tight formation, cylinders within cylinders.

Bean wanted to shout, Don't do it! There are real men on those ships, and if you send them in, they'll die, a sacrifice with no hope of victory.

But he held his tongue, because, in the back of his mind, in the deepest corner of his heart, he still had hope that Ender might do what could not be done. And as long as there was such a hope, the lives of those men were, by their own choice when they set out on this expedition, expendable.

Ender set them in motion, having them dodge here and there through the ever-shifting formations of the enemy swarm.

Surely the enemy sees what we're doing, thought Bean. Surely they see how every third or fourth move takes us closer and closer to the planet.

At any moment the enemy could destroy them quickly by concentrating their forces. So why weren't they doing it?

One possibility occurred to Bean. The Buggers didn't dare concentrate their forces close to Ender's tight formation, because the moment they drew their ships that close together, Ender could use Dr. Device against them.

And then he thought of another explanation. Could it be that there were simply too many Bugger ships? Could it be that the queen or queens had to spend all their concentration, all their mental strength just keeping ten thousand ships swarming through space without getting too close to each other?

Unlike Ender, the Bugger queen couldn't turn control of her ships over to subordinates. She *had* no subordinates. The individual Buggers were like her hands and her feet. Now she had hundreds of hands and feet, or perhaps thousands of them, all wiggling at once.

That's why she wasn't responding intelligently. Her forces were too numerous. That's why she wasn't making the obvious moves, setting traps, blocking Ender from taking his cylinder ever closer to the planet with every swing and dodge and shift that he made.

In fact, the maneuvers the Buggers were making were ludicrously wrong. For as Ender penetrated deeper and deeper into the planet's gravity well, the Buggers were building up a thick wall of forces *behind* Ender's formation.

They're blocking our retreat!

At once Bean understood a third and most important reason for what was happening. The Buggers had learned the wrong lessons from the previous battles. Up to now, Ender's strategy had always been to ensure the survival of as many human ships as possible. He had always left himself a line of retreat. The Buggers, with their huge numerical advantage, were finally in a position to guarantee that the human forces would not get away.

There was no way, at the beginning of this battle, to predict that the Buggers would make such a mistake. Yet throughout history, great victories had come as much because of the losing army's errors as because of the winner's brilliance in battle. The Buggers have finally, finally learned that we humans value each and every individual human life. We don't throw our forces away because every soldier is the queen of a one-member hive. But they've learned this lesson just in time for it to be hopelessly wrong— for we humans *do,* when the cause is sufficient, spend our own lives. We throw ourselves onto the grenade to save our buddies in the foxhole. We rise out of the trenches and charge the entrenched enemy and die like

maggots under a blowtorch. We strap bombs on our bodies and blow ourselves up in the midst of our enemies. We are, when the cause is sufficient,
insane.

They don't believe we'll use Dr. Device because the only way to use
it is to destroy our own ships in the process. From the moment Ender started
giving orders, it was obvious to everyone that this was a suicide run. These
ships were not made to enter an atmosphere. And yet to get close enough
to the planet to set off Dr. Device, they had to do exactly that.

Get down into the gravity well and launch the weapon just before the
ship burns up. And if it works, if the planet is torn apart by whatever force
it is in that terrible weapon, the chain reaction will reach out into space
and take out any ships that might happen to survive.

Win or lose, there'd be no human survivors from this battle.

They've never seen us make a move like that. They don't understand
that, yes, humans will always act to preserve their own lives—except for
the times when they don't. In the Buggers' experience, autonomous beings
do not sacrifice themselves. Once they understood our autonomy, the seed
of their defeat was sown.

In all of Ender's study of the Buggers, in all his obsession with them
over the years of his training, did he somehow come to *know* that they
would make such deadly mistakes?

I did not know it. I would not have pursued this strategy. I *had* no
strategy. Ender was the only commander who could have known, or
guessed, or unconsciously hoped that when he flung out his forces the
enemy would falter, would trip, would fall, would fail.

Or *did* he know at all? Could it be that he reached the same conclusion
as I did, that this battle was unwinnable? That he decided not to play it
out, that he went on strike, that he quit? And then my bitter words, "the
enemy's gate is down," triggered his futile, useless gesture of despair,
sending his ships to certain doom because he did not know that there were
real ships out there, with real men aboard, that he was sending to their
deaths? Could it be that he was as surprised as I was by the mistakes of
the enemy? Could our victory be an accident?

No. For even if my words provoked Ender into action, he was still the
one who chose *this* formation, *these* feints and evasions, *this* meandering
route. It was Ender whose previous victories taught the enemy to think of
us as one kind of creature, when we are really something quite different.
He pretended all this time that humans were rational beings, when we are
really the most terrible monsters these poor aliens could ever have con-

ceived of in their nightmares. They had no way of knowing the story of blind Samson, who pulled down the temple on his own head to slay his enemies.

On those ships, thought Bean, there are individual men who gave up homes and families, the world of their birth, in order to cross a great swatch of the galaxy and make war on a terrible enemy. Somewhere along the way they're bound to understand that Ender's strategy requires them all to die. Perhaps they already have. And yet they obey and will continue to obey the orders that come to them. As in the famous Charge of the Light Brigade, these soldiers give up their lives, trusting that their commanders are using them well. While we sit safely here in these simulator rooms, playing an elaborate computer game, they are obeying, dying so that all of humankind can live.

And yet we who command them, we children in these elaborate game machines, have no idea of their courage, their sacrifice. We cannot give them the honor they deserve, because we don't even know they exist.

Except for me.

There sprang into Bean's mind a favorite scripture of Sister Carlotta's. Maybe it meant so much to her because she had no children. She told Bean the story of Absalom's rebellion against his own father, King David. In the course of a battle, Absalom was killed. When they brought the news to David, it meant victory, it meant that no more of his soldiers would die. His throne was safe. His *life* was safe. But all he could think about was his son, his beloved son, his dead boy.

Bean ducked his head, so his voice would be heard only by the men under his command. And then, for just long enough to speak, he pressed the override that put his voice into the ears of all the men of that distant fleet. Bean had no idea how his voice would sound to them; would they hear his childish voice, or were the sounds distorted, so they would hear him as an adult, or perhaps as some metallic, machinelike voice? No matter. In some form the men of that distant fleet would hear his voice, transmitted faster than light, God knows how.

"O my son Absalom," Bean said softly, knowing for the first time the kind of anguish that could tear such words from a man's mouth. "My son, my son Absalom. Would God I could die for thee, O Absalom, my son. My sons!"

He had paraphrased it a little, but God would understand. Or if he didn't, Sister Carlotta would.

Now, thought Bean. Do it now, Ender. You're as close as you can get without giving away the game. They're beginning to understand their danger. They're concentrating their forces. They'll blow us out of the sky before our weapons can be launched—

"All right, everybody except Petra's squadron," said Ender. "Straight down, as fast as you can. Launch Dr. Device against the planet. Wait till the last possible second. Petra, cover as you can."

The squadron leaders, Bean among them, echoed Ender's commands to their own fleets. And then there was nothing to do but watch. Each ship was on its own.

The enemy understood now, and rushed to destroy the plummeting humans. Fighter after fighter was picked off by the inrushing ships of the Formic fleet. Only a few human fighters survived long enough to enter the atmosphere.

Hold on, thought Bean. Hold on as long as you can.

The ships that launched too early watched their Dr. Device burn up in the atmosphere before it could go off. A few other ships burned up themselves without launching.

Two ships were left. One was in Bean's squadron.

"Don't launch it," said Bean into his microphone, head down. "Set it off inside your ship. God be with you."

Bean had no way of knowing whether it was his ship or the other that did it. He only knew that both ships disappeared from the display without launching. And then the surface of the planet started to bubble. Suddenly a vast eruption licked outward toward the last of the human fighters, Petra's ships, on which there might or might not still be men alive to see death coming at them. To see their victory approach.

The simulator put on a spectacular show as the exploding planet chewed up all the enemy ships, engulfing them in the chain reaction. But long before the last ship was swallowed up, all the maneuvering had stopped. They drifted, dead. Like the dead Bugger ships in the vids of the Second Invasion. The queens of the hive had died on the planet's surface. The destruction of the remaining ships was a mere formality. The Buggers were already dead.

Bean emerged into the tunnel to find that the other kids were already there, congratulating each other and commenting on how cool the explosion effect was, and wondering if something like that could really happen.

"Yes," said Bean. "It could."

"As if you know," said Fly Molo, laughing.

"Of course I know it could happen," said Bean. "It *did* happen."

They looked at him uncomprehendingly. When did it happen? I never heard of anything like that. Where could they have tested that weapon against a planet? I know, they took out Neptune!

"It happened just now," said Bean. "It happened at the home world of the Buggers. We just blew it up. They're all dead."

They finally began to realize that he was serious. They fired objections at him. He explained about the faster-than-light communications device. They didn't believe him.

Then another voice entered the conversation. "It's called the ansible."

They looked up to see Colonel Graff standing a ways off, down the tunnel.

Is Bean telling the truth? Was that a real battle?

"They were all real," said Bean. "All the so-called tests. Real battles. Real victories. Right, Colonel Graff? We were fighting the real war all along."

"It's over now," said Graff. "The human race will continue. The Buggers won't."

They finally believed it, and became giddy with the realization. It's over. We won. We weren't practicing, we were actually commanders.

And then, at last, a silence fell.

"They're *all* dead?" asked Petra.

Bean nodded.

Again they looked at Graff. "We have reports. All life activity has ceased on all the other planets. They must have gathered their queens back on their home planet. When the queens die, the Buggers die. There is no enemy now."

Petra began to cry, leaning against the wall. Bean wanted to reach out to her, but Dink was there. Dink was the friend who held her, comforted her.

Some soberly, some exultantly, they went back to their barracks. Petra wasn't the only one who cried. But whether the tears were shed in anguish or in relief, no one could say for sure.

Only Bean did not return to his room, perhaps because Bean was the only one not surprised. He stayed out in the tunnel with Graff.

"How's Ender taking it?"

"Badly," said Graff. "We should have broken it to him more carefully, but there was no holding back. In the moment of victory."

"All your gambles paid off," said Bean.

"I know what happened, Bean," said Graff. "Why did you leave control with him? How did you know he'd come up with a plan?"

"I didn't," said Bean. "I only knew that I had no plan at all."

"But what you said—'the enemy's gate is down.' That's the plan Ender used."

"It wasn't a plan," said Bean. "Maybe it made him think of a plan. But it was him. It was Ender. You put your money on the right kid."

Graff looked at Bean in silence, then reached out and put a hand on Bean's head, tousled his hair a little. "I think perhaps you pulled each other across the finish line."

"It doesn't matter, does it?" said Bean. "It's finished, anyway. And so is the temporary unity of the human race."

"Yes," said Graff. He pulled his hand away, ran it through his own hair. "I believed in your analysis. I tried to give warning. *If* the Strategos heeded my advice, the Polemarch's men are getting arrested here on Eros and all over the fleet."

"Will they go peacefully?" asked Bean.

"We'll see," said Graff.

The sound of gunfire echoed from some distant tunnel.

"Guess not," said Bean.

They heard the sound of men running in step. And soon they saw them, a contingent of a dozen armed marines.

Bean and Graff watched them approach. "Friend or foe?"

"They all wear the same uniform," said Graff. "You're the one who called it, Bean. Inside those doors"—he gestured toward the doors to the kids' quarters—"those children are the spoils of war. In command of armies back on Earth, they're the hope of victory. *You* are the hope."

The soldiers came to a stop in front of Graff. "We're here to protect the children, sir," said their leader.

"From what?"

"The Polemarch's men seem to be resisting arrest, sir," said the soldier. "The Strategos has ordered that these children be kept safe at all costs."

Graff was visibly relieved to know which side these troops were on. "The girl is in that room over there. I suggest you consolidate them all into those two barrack rooms for the duration."

"Is this the kid who did it?" asked the soldier, indicating Bean.

"He's one of them."

"It was Ender Wiggin who did it," said Bean. "Ender was our commander."

"Is he in one of those rooms?" asked the soldier.

"He's with Mazer Rackham," said Graff. "And this one stays with me."

The soldier saluted. He began positioning his men in more advanced positions down the tunnel, with only a single guard outside each door to prevent the kids from going out and getting lost somewhere in the fighting.

Bean trotted along beside Graff as he headed purposefully down the tunnel, beyond the farthest of the guards.

"If the Strategos did this right, the ansibles have already been secured. I don't know about you, but I want to be where the news is coming in. And going out."

"Is Russian a hard language to learn?" asked Bean.

"Is that what passes for humor with you?" asked Graff.

"It was a simple question."

"Bean, you're a great kid, but shut up, OK?"

Bean laughed. "OK."

"You don't mind if I still call you Bean?"

"It's my name."

"Your name should have been Julian Delphiki. If you'd had a birth certificate, that's the name that would have been on it."

"You mean that was true?"

"Would I lie about something like that?"

Then, realizing the absurdity of what he had just said, they laughed. Laughed long enough to still be smiling when they passed the detachment of marines protecting the entrance to the ansible complex.

"You think anybody will ask me for military advice?" asked Bean. "Because I'm going to get into this war, even if I have to lie about my age and enlist in the marines."

24

HOMECOMING

"I thought you'd want to know. Some bad news."

"There's no shortage of that, even in the midst of victory."

"When it became clear that the IDL had control of Battle School and was sending the kids home under I.F. protection, the New Warsaw Pact apparently did a little research and found that there was one student from Battle School who wasn't under our control. Achilles."

"But he was only there a couple of days."

"He passed our tests. He got in. He was the only one they could get."

"Did they? Get him?"

"All the security there was designed to keep inmates inside. Three guards dead, all the inmates released into the general population. They've all been recovered, except one."

"So he's loose."

"I wouldn't call it loose, exactly. They intend to use him."

"Do they know what he is?"

"No. His records were sealed. A juvenile, you see. They weren't coming for his dossier."

"They'll find out. They don't like serial killers in Moscow, either."

"He's hard to pin down. How many died before any of us suspected him?"

"The war is over for now."

"And the jockeying for advantage in the next war has begun."

"With any luck, Colonel Graff, I'll be dead by then."

"I'm not actually a colonel anymore, Sister Carlotta."

"They're really going to go ahead with that court-martial?"

"An investigation, that's all. An inquiry."

"I just don't understand why they have to find a scapegoat for victory."

"I'll be fine. The sun still shines on planet Earth."

"But never again on *their* tragic world."

"Is your God also their God, Sister Carlotta? Did he take them into heaven?"

"He's not *my* God, Mr. Graff. But I am his child, as are you. I don't know whether he looks at the Formics and sees them, too, as his children."

"Children. Sister Carlotta, the things I did to these children."

"You gave them a world to come home to."

"All but one of them."

It took days for the Polemarch's men to be subdued, but at last Fleetcom was entirely under the Strategos's command, and not one ship had been launched under rebel command. A triumph. The Hegemon resigned as part of the truce, but that only formalized what had already been the reality.

Bean stayed with Graff throughout the fighting, as they read every dispatch and listened to every report about what was happening elsewhere in the fleet and back on Earth. They talked through the unfolding situation, tried to read between the lines, interpreted what was happening as best they could. For Bean, the war with the Buggers was already behind him. All that mattered now was how things went on Earth. When a shaky truce was signed, temporarily ending the fighting, Bean knew that it would not last. He would be needed. Once he got to Earth, he could prepare himself to play his role. Ender's war is over, he thought. This next one will be mine.

While Bean was avidly following the news, the other kids were confined to their quarters under guard, and during the power failures in their part of Eros they did their cowering in darkness. Twice there were assaults on that section of the tunnels, but whether the Russians were trying to get at the kids or merely happened to probe in that area, looking for weaknesses, no one could guess.

Ender was under much heavier guard, but didn't know it. Utterly exhausted, and perhaps unwilling or unable to bear the enormity of what he had done, he remained unconscious for days.

Not till the fighting stopped did he come back to consciousness.

They let the kids get together then, their confinement over for now. Together they made the pilgrimage to the room where Ender had been under protection and medical care. They found him apparently cheerful, able to joke. But Bean could see a deep weariness, a sadness in Ender's eyes that it was impossible to ignore. The victory had cost him deeply, more than anybody.

More than me, thought Bean, even though I knew what I was doing, and he was innocent of any bad intent. He tortures himself, and I move on. Maybe because to me the death of Poke was more important than the death of an entire species that I never saw. I knew her—she has stayed with me in my heart. The Buggers I never knew. How can I grieve for them?

Ender can.

After they filled Ender in on the news about what happened while he slept, Petra touched his hair. "You OK?" she asked. "You scared us. They said you were crazy, and we said *they* were crazy."

"I'm crazy," said Ender. "But I think I'm OK."

There was more banter, but then Ender's emotions overflowed and for the first time any of them could remember, they saw Ender cry. Bean happened to be standing near him, and when Ender reached out, it was Bean and Petra that he embraced. The touch of his hand, the embrace of his arm, they were more than Bean could bear. He also cried.

"I missed you," said Ender. "I wanted to see you so bad."

"You saw us pretty bad," said Petra. She was not crying. She kissed his cheek.

"I saw you magnificent," said Ender. "The ones I needed most, I used up soonest. Bad planning on my part."

"Everybody's OK now," said Dink. "Nothing was wrong with any of us that five days of cowering in blacked-out rooms in the middle of a war couldn't cure."

"I don't have to be your commander anymore, do I?" asked Ender. "I don't want to command anybody again."

Bean believed him. And believed also that Ender never *would* command in battle again. He might still have the talents that brought him to this place. But the most important ones didn't have to be used for violence. If the universe had any kindness in it, or even simple justice, Ender would never have to take another life. He had surely filled his quota.

"You don't have to command anybody," said Dink, "but you're always our commander."

Bean felt the truth of that. There was not one of them who would not carry Ender with them in their hearts, wherever they went, whatever they did.

What Bean didn't have the heart to tell them was that on Earth, both sides had insisted that they be given custody of the hero of the war, young Ender Wiggin, whose great victory had captured the popular imagination. Whoever had him would not only have the use of his fine military mind—they thought—but would also have the benefit of all the publicity and public adulation that surrounded him, that filled every mention of his name.

So as the political leaders worked out the truce, they reached a simple and obvious compromise. All the children from Battle School would be repatriated. Except Ender Wiggin.

Ender Wiggin would not be coming home. Neither party on Earth would be able to use him. That was the compromise.

And it had been proposed by Locke. By Ender's own brother.

When he learned that it made Bean seethe inside, the way he had when he thought Petra had betrayed Ender. It was wrong. It couldn't be borne.

Perhaps Peter Wiggin did it to keep Ender from becoming a pawn. To keep him free. Or perhaps he did it so that Ender could not use his celebrity to make his own play for political power. Was Peter Wiggin saving his brother, or eliminating a rival for power?

Someday I'll meet him and find out, thought Bean. And if he betrayed his brother, I'll destroy him.

When Bean shed his tears there in Ender's room, he was weeping for a cause the others did not yet know about. He was weeping because, as surely as the soldiers who died in those fighting ships, Ender would not be coming home from the war.

"So," said Alai, breaking the silence. "What do we do now? The Bugger War's over, and so's the war down there on Earth, and even the war here. What do we do now?"

"We're kids," said Petra. "They'll probably make us go to school. It's a law. You have to go to school till you're seventeen."

They all laughed until they cried again.

They saw each other off and on again over the next few days. Then they boarded several different cruisers and destroyers for the voyage back to Earth. Bean knew well why they traveled in separate ships. That way no one would ask why Ender wasn't on board. If Ender knew, before they left, that he was not going back to Earth, he said nothing about it.

Elena could hardly contain her joy when Sister Carlotta called, asking if she and her husband would both be at home in an hour. "I'm bringing you your son," she said.

Nikolai, Nikolai, Nikolai. Elena sang the name over and over again in her mind, with her lips. Her husband Julian, too, was almost dancing as he hurried about the house, making things ready. Nikolai had been so little when he left. Now he would be so much older. They would hardly know him. They would not understand what he had been through. But it didn't matter. They loved him. They would learn who he was all over again. They would not let the lost years get in the way of the years to come.

"I see the car!" cried Julian.

Elena hurriedly pulled the covers from the dishes, so that Nikolai could come into a kitchen filled with the freshest, purest food of his childhood memories. Whatever they ate in space, it couldn't be as good as this.

Then she ran to the door and stood beside her husband as they watched Sister Carlotta get out of the front seat.

Why didn't she ride in back with Nikolai?

No matter. The back door opened, and Nikolai emerged, unfolding his lanky young body. So tall he was growing! Yet still a boy. There was a little bit of childhood left for him.

Run to me, my son!

But he didn't run to her. He turned his back on his parents.

Ah. He was reaching into the back seat. A present, perhaps?

No. Another boy.

A smaller boy, but with the same face as Nikolai. Perhaps too careworn for a child so small, but with the same open goodness that Nikolai had always had. Nikolai was smiling so broadly he could not contain it. But the small one was not smiling. He looked uncertain. Hesitant.

"Julian," said her husband.

Why would he say his own name?

"Our second son," he said. "They didn't all die, Elena. One lived."

All hope of those little ones had been buried in her heart. It almost hurt to open that hidden place. She gasped at the intensity of it.

"Nikolai met him in Battle School," he went on. "I told Sister Carlotta that if we had another son, you meant to name him Julian."

"You knew," said Elena.

"Forgive me, my love. But Sister Carlotta wasn't sure then that he was ours. Or that he would ever be able to come home. I couldn't bear it, to tell you of the hope, only to break your heart later."

"I have two sons," she said.

"If you want him," said Julian. "His life has been hard. But he's a stranger here. He doesn't speak Greek. He's been told that he's coming just for a visit. That legally he is not our child, but rather a ward of the state. We don't have to take him in, if you don't want to, Elena."

"Hush, you foolish man," she said. Then, loudly, she called out to the approaching boys. "Here are my two sons, home from the wars! Come to your mother! I have missed you both so much, and for so many years!"

They ran to her then, and she held them in her arms, and her tears fell on them both, and her husband's hands rested upon both boys' heads.

Her husband spoke. Elena recognized his words at once, from the gospel of St. Luke. But because he had only memorized the passage in Greek, the little one did not understand him. No matter. Nikolai began to translate into Common, the language of the fleet, and almost at once the little one recognized the words, and spoke them correctly, from memory, as Sister Carlotta had once read it to him years before.

"Let us eat, and be merry: for this my son was dead, and is alive again; he was lost, and is found." Then the little one burst into tears and clung to his mother, and kissed his father's hand.

"Welcome home, little brother," said Nikolai. "I told you they were nice."

ACKNOWLEDGMENTS

One book was particularly useful in preparing this novel: Peter Paret, ed., *Makers of Modern Strategy: From Machiavelli to the Nuclear Age* (Princeton University Press, 1986). The essays are not all of identical quality, but they gave me a good idea of the writings that might be in the library in Battle School.

I have nothing but fond memories of Rotterdam, a city of kind and generous people. The callousness toward the poor shown in this novel would be impossible today, but the business of science fiction is sometimes to show impossible nightmares.

I owe individual thanks to:

Erin and Phillip Absher, for, among other things, the lack of vomiting on the shuttle, the size of the toilet tank, and the weight of the lid;

Jane Brady, Laura Morefield, Oliver Withstandley, Matt Tolton, Kathryn H. Kidd, Kristine A. Card, and others who read the advance manuscript and made suggestions and corrections. Some annoying contradictions between *Ender's Game* and this book were thereby averted; any that remain are not errors at all, but merely subtle literary effects designed to show the difference in perception and memory between the two accounts of the same event. As my programmer friends would say, there are no bugs, only features;

Tom Doherty, my publisher; Beth Meacham, my editor; and Barbara Bova, my agent, for responding so positively to the idea of this book when I proposed it as a collaborative project and then realized I wanted to write it entirely myself. And if I still think *Urchin* was the better title for this book, it doesn't mean that I don't agree that my second title, *Ender's Shadow,* is the more marketable one;

My assistants, Scott Allen and Kathleen Bellamy, who at various times defy gravity and perform other useful miracles;

My son Geoff, who, though he is no longer the five-year-old he was when I wrote the novel *Ender's Game,* is still the model for Ender Wiggin;

My wife, Kristine, and the children who were home during the writing of this book: Emily, Charlie Ben, and Zina. Their patience with me when I was struggling to figure out the right approach to this novel was surpassed only by their patience when I finally found it and became possessed by the story. When I brought Bean home to a loving family I knew what it should look like, because I see it every day.